A Quiet Madness

***

A biographical novel of Edgar Allan Poe

John Isaac Jones

Table of Contents

1
Birth

In the city by the River Charles, the winter of 1808 proved to be one of the most brutal in its history. While October and November had been relatively mild, two savage nor'easters had blown through in late December and dumped more than nine feet of snow on hapless residents in less than a week. Daily temperatures hovered in the mid-teens; the river and vast stretches of Boston harbor were frozen solid and giant sailing ships were trapped firmly in their moorings, bringing shipping to a standstill. In suburban areas, city crews worked day and night to keep streets and sidewalks clear of snow so businesses could open and citizens could go about their daily activities. Workers with huge shovels would load wagon after wagon to the brim with fresh powder, then follow them to the harbor where it would be dumped. At Boston Common, the city's public park on Tremont Street where snow went untouched during such times, massive banks of snow lay ten to twelve feet deep.

Despite the harsh weather, wealthy Bostonians were not about to be deprived of their entertainment and, on the night of January 19, the 1000-seat Orpheum Theater on Cambridge Street was packed with attendees. On that particular evening, the Charleston Players theatrical troupe was winding up the final performance of a successful two-month run of Shakespeare's *King Lear*. Once the play ended, the audience brought the players out again and again for multiple celebratory curtain calls. Among the players taking bows was David Poe Jr., who played Edgar, the Earl of Gloucester's legitimate son, in the drama.

When the curtain rang down for a final time, all of the players, including Poe, rushed off the stage. As Poe, a tall, strikingly handsome twenty-five-year-old with a shock of black hair, started down the hallway to his dressing room, he heard someone call his name.

"David!"

He stopped and turned.

It was Oliver, a short, middle-aged, balding man who served as assistant to Luke Usher, the theatrical company's owner and manager.

"Yes, Oliver?"

Poe could see the older man was agitated.

"Oliver? What's wrong?"

"I have to tell you this…"

"Tell me what?"

"Constable Ross is waiting for you in the lobby."

"The constable? What does he want?"

"He said he had some papers to serve."

"Papers?"

For a moment, Poe peered thoughtfully at the older man. Then he had a realization.

"Bloody hell! Those damn creditors have gotten a judgment against me. He's going to take me to debtor's prison. Are you sure it's the constable?"

"Of course, I'm sure."

Poe stared again at Oliver, then went to the door between the lobby and the theater proper and peeked through the round glass.

He turned back to Oliver.

"That's him. Is there a back way?"

"Yes. I'll show you. But you'll need a greatcoat. It's cold out there."

"Go to my dressing room and get my greatcoat, scarf, and hat. I'll hide in the property room. Hurry!"

Instantly, Oliver shot off down the hallway toward the dressing room while Poe ducked inside the property room.

Five minutes later, Oliver reappeared with the greatcoat and scarf.

"I couldn't find your hat."

"That's all right. Where's the back exit?"

"Follow me!"

Five minutes later, Poe, wearing the greatcoat over his Edgar costume, was hurriedly following Oliver down the theater's backstairs to the basement. Once Oliver unlocked one door, they went back up another long flight of stairs to a barred back door, which opened to the alleyway behind the theater. Oliver removed the bar.

"Thanks!" Poe said. "Bye!"

"David!!"

Poe turned.

"Don't forget we leave Monday morning at 9 a.m. for New York to start *Richard the Third*."

"I know. Eliza and I will be there."

"What about the costume?"

"I'll have it for you when we get on the boat on Monday."

"Remember… promptly at 9 a.m. If you miss the boat, there will be hell to pay."

"We'll be there. Be sure to tell Mr. Usher."

"I will."

***

Five minutes later, David Poe was trudging along Cambridge Street in the bitter cold. Overhead, the gas-lit streetlamps cast ghostly shadows across the snowbanks along either side of the street and the huge incrustations of ice on the stone sidewalk made a crunching sound with his every footstep. As he walked east on Cambridge Street, the stinging wind bit into his face. After several minutes, his ears were numb with cold and he removed the scarf from around his neck and tied it around his head. At Chambers Street, he turned north and made his way to Poplar, then to the boarding house at the corner of Poplar and Brighton Streets where he lived with his wife and young son. Once he was inside the boarding house vestibule, the warmth was a welcome relief. Moments later, he was striding down the hallway to the family apartment.

When he opened the door, all was quiet. His wife Eliza, her midsection bulging with child, was dozing in a chair, a small candle burning on the table beside her. In her lap was a copy of Lord Byron's *Childe Harold's Pilgrimage*. At age twenty-two, Eliza Poe was a petite, bosomy woman with large eyes and a pert nose. Like her husband, she was a member of the Charleston Players, but she had left the production ten days earlier to prepare for the birth of their second child. Nearby, on a small cot, their two-year-old son Henry was sleeping.

Quietly, Poe closed the door then went to a dresser, took a seat, and began removing his makeup. Once his face was clean, he slipped out of his Edgar costume, a padded gray doublet over a white puff-sleeved shirt and knee trousers with a codpiece. Then, as quietly as possible, he hefted down a trunk from the closet, opened it, and neatly placed the costume inside. Next, he began gathering clothing, books, toilet items, and personal mementoes, and throwing them into the trunk. As he worked, Eliza opened her eyes.

"Dear?"

"Yes, darling," David said. "I'm here. I have bad news."

Suddenly, Eliza sprang wide awake.

"What is it?" she said in a strong British accent.

"The constable was at the theater tonight looking for me."

"Why?"

"He has court papers to arrest me and send me to debtor's prison. We've got to leave. Now! Tonight!"

"Leave? In this cold weather, and I'm about to have a child."

"The doctor said you wouldn't deliver until day after tomorrow."

"No. It's going to be sooner than that."

"How soon?"

"Maybe tonight."

"Oh, Lord! Do you want me to go to debtor's prison?"

"No. Of course not…"

"Then let's get moving. As soon as he discovers I'm not at the theater, he will come here looking for me."

Eliza shook her head in frustration.

"I don't know why I contend with this madness you call your life."

"Dear! We don't have time to argue. Get Henry ready and I'll finish packing."

Eliza, now wide awake, leapt out of the chair and began throwing their belongings into a small suitcase. Meanwhile, David continued to fill the trunk.

Fifteen minutes later, their belongings packed, Eliza went to the small cot in the corner of the room and awakened their son. Then, taking him into her arms, she wrapped him tightly in a wool blanket.

"I'll carry the trunk," David said. "Can you manage Henry and the small suitcase?"

She hesitated. She still wasn't convinced she wanted to do this.

"Dear, please!" David said. "Don't waste time. We must hurry!"

"Do I have a choice?"

"Please, dear. Let's not argue."

Suddenly, there was a sharp rap at the door.

"David Poe!" a voice shouted. "This is the constable. Open the door! Open up in the name of the law!"

David put his finger to his lips, indicating that she should remain silent. Then, with his index finger, he pointed to the back bedroom.

"Poe! David Poe! Open this door!"

In the back bedroom, Poe opened a window. A chill winter wind blew into the bedroom as David threw the small suitcase outside, then hefted the large trunk through the open window. While David held their son, Eliza pulled her bulging body through the open window, then David, carefully protecting Henry, squeezed the two of them through the window. Inside, they could still hear the constable's shouts.

Five minutes later, Eliza, carrying their son and the small suitcase, and Poe, struggling with the heavy trunk, were trudging down the alleyway behind the boarding house to Brighton Street.

"Where are we going?"

"Let's go to McCarthy's boarding house. It's up the street."

For several minutes, they walked silently. David struggled with the large trunk, and Eliza, her head into the wind and carrying the two-year-old, trudged along the snow-packed sidewalk. Finally, at the corner of Leverett and Dorset streets, they saw McCarthy's boarding house. The sign read: No rooms.

"Damn!" David said.

"What do we do now?"

"Let's go to Flannigan's."

"How far?"

"Two blocks!"

"Oh, Lord. In this cold, it will seem like two miles."

"Come on," David said. "It won't be long."

Over the next ten minutes, the Poe family made their way up Leverett Street past several shops to the corner of Franklin and Pearl streets. They stopped in front of Flannigan's boarding house.

"They don't have a sign out," David said. "Maybe they have a room."

"Come on, let's go inside."

Moments later, they were inside the boarding house vestibule and David was talking to the proprietor.

"We're full at the moment," the man said. "But I'll have some rooms in the morning."

"We're desperate for a room tonight," Poe said. "My wife is going have a baby."

"Sorry. We won't have anything until tomorrow."

Poe turned to Eliza. Henry was wide awake.

"Mommy, I'm cold," he said, pulling himself closer to his mother.

Eliza pulled the wool blanket closer around the child's face.

"Please be patient, baby. We're trying to find a room."

David turned back to the proprietor.

"Do you know of anyone who has rooms tonight?"

"You might try Harrow's Hotel. It's two blocks up the street."

David turned, shaking his head in frustration.

"Two more blocks?" Eliza said. "Give me just a few minutes to warm up."

Ten minutes later, they were back outside in the cold, trudging up Leverett Street past businesses, a bakery, a saddlery, a bank, and a hardware store. Suddenly, Eliza stopped.

"Oh, no!!"

"What is it?"

"Oh god, it's happening. My water is breaking. I'm about to have this child."

"Let's stop in here for a moment," David said, indicating the alcove in front of one of the shops. "It will get us out of the wind."

David dropped the trunk inside the alcove, then, after taking Henry in his arms, he guided Eliza to sit on the trunk. Resting on the trunk, she raised her head, her face contorted in pain, and she held her bulging stomach. The sign in the window read: "Simpson's Funeral Emporium." The front portion of the business was dark, but a dim light was shining somewhere in the rear.

"Oh, Lord," Eliza said. "I'm going to have this baby soon. Very soon."

As they waited, a transport carriage pulled up in front of the funeral parlor and stopped. The driver stepped down from the seat and started to the door. As he approached, he saw Eliza sitting on the trunk.

"Missy!" he said as he rapped on the door. "What are you doing here?"

"I'm going to have a baby."

"You can't have a baby here. You've got to clear the doorway. I've got three stiff ones to deliver."

The door to the funeral parlor opened. A dour, middle-aged man wearing glasses and dressed in black appeared. He held an oil lamp.

"What's going on out here?"

"I'm delivering three stiff ones," the carriage driver said. "And this woman is having a baby."

The man peered at Eliza.

"Having a baby? You can't have a baby at the door of my establishment. Get away from here!"

Suddenly, a somber-looking middle-aged woman with her hair in a bun and dressed in black appeared behind him.

"Silas!" the woman said. "What is it?"

"This woman is about to have a baby at our doorstep."

The woman brushed past the man and stared at Eliza.

"You're about to have a baby?"

"Yes. And very soon."

For a long moment, the woman peered into Eliza's face, then she turned to Silas.

"Hand me that oil lamp."

Silas passed the oil lamp to the woman, then she held it to Eliza's face.

"My Heavens! Aren't you Eliza Poe? The stage actress known as the Nightingale?"

"Yes," Eliza said. "Please help us."

"You people have got to leave!" Silas said. "I'm running a business here. Go away! Now!"

"And I've got three stiff ones to deliver," said the carriage driver.

"Silas!" the woman said, raising her voice. "We are not going to leave this poor woman out here in the cold to have this baby."

"Abigail, we're running a funeral parlor here, not a hospital."

"Do you know who this is?"

"I don't care who it is," Silas said. "Just get her away from my door."

"This is Eliza Poe!"

"Who in God's name is Eliza Poe?"

"Just the most famous stage actress in New England. We saw her three years ago in *Miss in Her Teens* at the Grandview. Don't you remember?"

"If she's so famous, why is she having a baby out here in the cold?"

Abigail looked at Eliza.

"We've had some financial problems."

"Your problems are no concern of mine," Silas said. "Get away from my door! Now!"

Abigail gave her husband a stern look, then turned back to Eliza.

"Come with me, dear," she said, reaching down to help Eliza to her feet. "You can have your baby in the embalming room. As a midwife, I know about these things."

Then she reached down, grasped Eliza's arms, and pulled the pregnant woman to her feet.

"Let's go inside."

"Abigail! What in God's name are you doing?" Silas said.

"I'm going to help this woman have her baby and her family is going to stay here for the night."

"Abigail! You can't do this!"

"Get out of my way!" Abigail said. "It's not every day you get to do something for a person as famous as this."

Silas glared angrily at her, then, without another word, stepped aside.

"Come on," Abigail said. "Let's go inside where it's warm."

***

Moments later, Eliza was lying on a wooden table in the funeral parlor's embalming room.

"Go ahead and remove your garments," Abigail said, handing Eliza a clean sheet. "You can cover yourself with this. I'm going to take your husband and your son to the spare bedroom. Then I'll put some water on to boil. I'll be back in a few minutes."

"Thank you!" Eliza said. "Please hurry! I feel myself opening up."

Moments later, Abigail, with David carrying Henry behind her, was strolling down the funeral home hallway. At the rear of the building, she stopped and opened the door to a bedroom.

"You'll be comfortable and warm here," Abigail said. "I'm going back to help your wife."

"Thanks!"

Five minutes later, Abigail was back in the embalming room. Eliza was naked under the sheet, the bulge in her midsection looming hugely. Abigail pulled back the sheet and examined her.

"You're ready," she said. "You're going to have this baby any minute."

Suddenly, Eliza's face grimaced in pain. She screamed and her body convulsed violently.

"Hold my arms!" Abigail said, standing behind her.

Eliza grabbed both of Abigail's arms tightly.

"Now take a deep breath and push!"

Eliza's body lurched forward.

"Ooooh! Ooooh!"

"Push! Push!"

Eliza took another deep breath.

"OHHHHHH!" she said as she strained with all her might.

"Push! Push harder!"

"Oh!" Eliza said, her back arching upward. "Oh, God! Here it comes!"

"Push! Push!"

Suddenly, the walls of the embalming room reverberated with the screams of a woman giving birth. It was a sound as old as humankind and a truly odd one in a funeral parlor.

"Push! Push as hard as you can!"

Eliza let out another series of loud screams, then, just as suddenly as the screams started, they stopped and the embalming room was filled with a new sound, the crying of a newborn baby.

"It's a boy," Abigail said. "And he's a fine one. Ten fingers and ten toes."

Eliza, still lying flat on her back on the corpse table, tried to raise herself, but she didn't have enough strength.

"Can I see him?"

"Let me clean him up first."

Abigail presented the newborn to its mother. Eliza took the infant into her arms and put it to her breast.

"Oh yes," Eliza said. "He is a beautiful baby."

"Now be quiet and rest," Abigail said.

Suddenly, Eliza's nose caught the scent of an unpleasant odor.

"What's that smell?"

"Embalming fluid. We have three burials tomorrow. There was a gunfight at Haymarket Square this morning. See the bodies."

Eliza turned and peered across the embalming room. On each of the three tables beside her were corpses.

"I must tell you I'm more accustomed to sending people to their graves than bringing new life into this world," Abigail said.

"I can see that," Eliza said.

"We need to get the embalmer in here. Do you have enough strength to walk back to the spare bedroom to be with your family?"

"I think I can make it."

An hour later, Eliza and the new baby were settled in with David and Henry in the spare bedroom. Abigail had brought three large bowls of vegetable soup and biscuits and provided extra covering for the bed. When the Poe family went to sleep that night, they had a new member.

***

The following morning, the Poe family was up early, got dressed, and had a breakfast of fried eggs and pig's knuckles with the Simpsons. Twenty minutes later, David hauled their luggage to the front of the funeral parlor, where a cab carriage was waiting. Then, he loaded the luggage into the carriage.

"Thanks for everything," Eliza said.

"Oh, it was my pleasure," Abigail replied. "It is not every day that I get to do something for a big stage star. Until the day I die, I will remember you singing 'Loving Thee' in *Miss in Her Teens*. Sometimes when I get lonely, I'll start singing it. It always lifts my spirits."

"It makes me happy that I can make you happy," Eliza said.

"Oh, one last thing," Abigail said.

"What's that?"

"Can you give me your signature so I will have a memento of our meeting?"

"Sure."

Abigail produced a sheet of paper and a graphite pencil.

Eliza signed the paper and handed it and the pencil back to Abigail.

Abigail looked at the signature, smiled, and clasped it to her breast.

"I'll always remember you," she said. "Who knows? The baby I helped deliver might be famous one day."

"I hope so," Eliza said. "Thanks again!"

"Where you going?" the carriage driver asked.

"Flannigan's boarding house."

Then, as the carriage pulled away from the front of the funeral parlor, Abigail waved, watching the carriage as it disappeared down the street.

***

An hour later, the Poe family was comfortably settled in at Flannigan's boarding house. David had a roaring fire going in the fireplace and was in the kitchenette making tea. Eliza, her legs wrapped in a heavy blanket, was seated in an armchair reading the poems of Lord Byron. At the window, Henry was watching the snow fall, while nearby, on a small cot, the newborn was sound asleep.

"Dear," David said, pouring hot tea into a cup on the table beside Eliza's armchair, "do you want one lump of sugar or two?"

"One will be fine."

Once Eliza's cup was filled, David dropped in a single lump of sugar, stirred it, then poured a cup for himself.

"It's so nice to be inside where it's safe and warm," Eliza said, taking a sip of tea.

Suddenly, the newborn awakened and started crying.

Quickly, Eliza set aside her tea cup, went to the infant, took him in her arms, and returned to the armchair. As she nursed, father and mother looked down happily.

"He's a beautiful child," David said.

"Yes. He's got a fine face and a strong jaw. What shall we call him?"

"Let's name him Edgar... after the Earl of Gloucester's noble son in King Lear."

For a long moment, Eliza peered at her husband thoughtfully then returned her gaze to the infant suckling at her breast.

"Yes. Edgar. That's a good name. It has a certain ring of nobleness to it. His name will be Edgar Poe. We'll call him Eddie."

2
Marital Discord

The following Tuesday morning, when the carriage with the Poe family arrived at Boston Harbor, David could see members of the Charleston Players boarding the Atlantic Lines Steamship, the USS *Calpurnia*. As his eyes scanned the area near the boarding platform, his eyes instantly caught sight of Constable Willard Ross.

"Bloody hell!"

"What is it?" Eliza asked.

"The constable is waiting at the boarding platform. He's going to arrest me the minute I try to board the ship."

"What are you going to do?"

"I'll get off here. You go ahead and board with the children. I'm going to talk to Luke."

Quickly, David paid the carriage driver, then, keeping a watchful eye on the constable, he skirted around the boarding platform past the line of waiting passengers to the rear of the ship where Oliver and Luke Usher, owner of the Charleston Players, were overseeing the loading of stage equipment.

"Luke!!!"

Usher turned at the sound of his name.

Luke Usher was a stocky, balding man in his late forties with long sideburns, a constant scowl, and the stub of a cigar clenched in his teeth.

"Poe!" he said upon seeing David. "Oliver told me you were in trouble with the law again. What is it this time?"

"I had some unpaid debts and…"

Usher shook his head and didn't let Poe finish.

"…And the court ruled in favor of the creditors and now they're sending you to debtor's prison?"

David nodded sheepishly.

"Holy Christ! We are staging *Richard III* in New York next week and you're the only Richard III I've got."

Usher shook his head in frustration.

"Where's Eliza? Did she have her baby?"

"Yes. She and the children are boarding."

Usher turned and looked toward the rear of the steamship, where he saw the ship's captain inspecting the mooring lines.

"Come on!" he said.

They approached the captain, a stout-looking, fiftyish man with a beard.

"Usher! How are you?" the captain greeted. "I see you're taking the show to New York."

"Yes, but I have a problem."

"What's that?"

"I have a passenger I want to board in a... shall we say, 'non-conventional manner.'"

"You want to slip a passenger on board?"

"Yes."

The captain laughed.

"I saw the constable at the boarding platform."

He looked to David.

"Is this the man the constable's looking for?"

"Yes."

The captain laughed again

"A paying stowaway, huh?"

"That's right."

The captain studied Usher.

"Well... that can be arranged," he said finally. "On one condition..."

"What's that?"

"I want two free passes to *Richard III* in New York. Box seats as close to the stage as possible."

Luke turned to Oliver.

"Give me a sheet of paper."

Oliver ripped a blank sheet of paper from the property checklist and handed it and a pencil to Usher. Usher scribbled a note for two free passes and handed them to the captain. He stroked his beard and examined the two scraps of paper.

Satisfied, he turned back to Oliver and pointed to one of the wooden crates waiting to be loaded.

"What's in this crate?"

"Costumes and props," Oliver replied.

The captain moved to the next crate.

"And this one?"

"More costumes, scripts, and background scenes."

"What about this one?"

"Empty wooden horses."

"Wooden horses?"

"Yes," Usher said. "They're props for *Richard III*."

The captain pointed to the crate.

"Open it."

Seconds later, Oliver, using a hammer, pried open the crate. Inside were four life-sized, empty wooden horses standing side-by-side.

The captain turned to David.

"Get inside and remain quiet," the captain said. "Lie on the crate floor between the horses' legs. Once we're underway, I'll get you out."

Poe ducked inside the crate and lay on the floor as instructed. Then Oliver started to nail the crate shut.

"Hold it!" Usher said.

"This is the last time, Poe," Usher said, angrily waving his finger. "I bailed you out of jail in Richmond. Your barroom brawl in Philadelphia last year cost me three performances. Next time you cause a problem, you'll no longer be a member of the Charleston Players. If the playbills for *Richard III* hadn't already been circulated, I would leave you here in Boston. Do you understand?"

Poe nodded.

Usher wasn't satisfied.

"Say it!" he shouted.

"Yes. I understand."

Satisfied, Usher stepped back, then nodded for Oliver to nail the cargo crate shut.

***

Twenty minutes later, Usher, Eliza, and the two Poe children were boarding the steamship under the watchful eye of the captain. As they started up the platform, Constable Ross eyed Eliza suspiciously.

"Hold up!" he called. "Aren't you David Poe's wife?"

"Yes," Eliza replied.

"Do you know where I can find him?"

"No, I haven't seen him in three weeks."

"Were you aware that he left behind $670 in debts when your company was here last year?"

"No. I didn't know."

"This year, he added another $870."

"I told you I haven't seen him."

A pause as the constable eyed Eliza suspiciously.

"Where were you last night?"

Instantly, Usher stepped forward.

"Constable, do you have grounds for suspecting this woman of a crime? She is one of my employees."

"No," the constable replied. "But she can provide information, which could lead me to her husband."

"She told you she hasn't seen her husband in three weeks."

"That's not good enough," the constable said.

He turned back to Eliza.

"I'll ask you again…. Where were you last night?"

Usher quickly interrupted again.

"I demand that you cease and desist from this harassment."

"I have a job to do and I'm going to do it."

"You're a bit too zealous for my taste. I demand that you end this questioning and permit us to board."

"No," the constable said. "She's going to have to go down to the station."

"She will do no such thing," Usher said.

"We'll see about that," the constable said.

Instantly, the captain, who had been listening, stepped forward.

"Constable," he said. "Can I have a word with you?"

Seconds later, the captain strode down the loading platform and pulled Constable Ross aside. The captain got up close to speak.

"Now you let these people board quietly," he whispered. "If you don't, I'll go downtown and report what happened down at Clancy's Tavern last week to your superiors."

Instantly, the constable, a look of irritation in his eyes, pulled back.

"You wouldn't do that...?"

"Oh, yes I would."

Constable Ross dropped his head and looked away for a long moment. Then, shaking his head in frustration, he turned back to Usher and Eliza.

"All right! All right!" he said. "The questioning is over. Go ahead and board."

With that, the hapless constable turned and walked away.

***

At the time of Edgar's birth, David Poe Jr. and Elizabeth Arnold Poe had been married three years. Eliza, born in London and an actress since the age of nine, was a celebrated star on the English stage long before she came to America and joined the Charleston Players. Her performances at London's Drury Lane and Convent Garden as Ophelia and Lady Macbeth had brought rave reviews from both the London press and theater goers alike. Although she was an accomplished Shakespearean actress, her fame in America grew out of her singing roles in romantic comedies such as *The Coquette* and *The Clandestine Marriage*. Her golden singing voice in these productions earned her the nickname "the Nightingale."

David, the son of a famous Boston patriot, began his acting career as a member of the Philadelphia Comedians in 1804 in the role of Puck in *A Midsummer Night's Dream* and Duke Frederick in *As You Like It*. The following year, he became an overnight star after his performances as Richard III at the outdoor summer theater in New York. "David Poe is a rising star of the American stage," gushed one New York reviewer. "His verve, interpretation, and fire as Richard III last night was a performance seldom seen on the New York stage."

The couple first met in the early summer of 1806 while playing David Garrick's farce *Miss in Her Teens* in

Philadelphia. Eliza played the lead role of Biddy Bellair and David was one of her suitors. From the first, David was smitten with her classic beauty and natural theatrical talents and, after a short courtship, he proposed. Their marriage, in the fall of 1806, was a *cause célèbre* for New Yorkers. In announcing the marriage, the *New York Advertiser* blared the front-page headline: "Stage Stars Plan Royal Wedding" while the *Philadelphia Bulletin* coined it "A Marriage Made in Heaven." On the day of the event, fans, newspaper reporters, political notables, and curiosity seekers packed into St. Paul's Chapel in lower Manhattan and, when the crowd spilled out on Broadway, quick-thinking entrepreneurs set up stands to sell hot coffee and sweet cakes. After a short honeymoon at Niagara Falls, the lovebirds returned to New York. Now, as "strolling" theatrical players, David and Eliza had been touring with the Charleston Players for more than three years.

***

Late that afternoon, just before nightfall, the USS *Calpurnia* arrived at New York harbor. Before disembarking, Usher gathered company members together for a parting word.

"Rehearsals start promptly at 9 a.m. tomorrow at the Strand," he said. "All of you know where the theater is located. Anybody that's late will answer to me. Is that understood?"

This brought a round of yeses from the members.

That night, the Poe family settled into an apartment near what is now Ninth Avenue and 44th Street. It was a spacious, second-floor affair with a large window overlooking a saddlery and a bake shop and was only two blocks from the Strand. Eliza said she wanted to buy a cradle and sit Eddie in front of the big window.

Over the following week, David left the boarding house each morning for rehearsals while Eliza remained at home to care for the children. Although David had performed the role of Richard III more than fifty times, Usher, an actor himself, was very particular that certain scenes had to be played exactly as he saw fit. This was especially true in Act 5, Scene three, Usher said, where King Richard keeps asking his lieutenants about his horse. Those lines had to be made perfectly clear to the audience, Usher said, because they were a forewarning of what was to come during the battle the following day. Luke Usher was a stern task maker.

***

When the play opened on Thursday of the following week, the house was packed. After the performance, David and the other players received four curtain calls and newspapers lauded the production as "the best performance of *Richard III* this city has seen in years."

Back at the apartment that night, Eliza was waiting for him.

"I heard you brought down the house tonight," she said. "I'm so proud of you."

"I'm the greatest Richard III that ever lived."

"You don't think you're a bit full of yourself?"

"I know when I'm doing good work."

***

The following Monday, which was an off day for the players, David went to the theater and collected his weekly pay of $55. Back on the street, he went shopping for a new top hat. After buying the hat, the proprietor explained that he was running a discount on pants and shoes, so David bought two new pairs of trousers and a pair of stylish pointed-toe shoes.

Back at the boarding house, he could not wait to try on the new hat.

"What have you bought?" Eliza asked when he threw the packages on the settee.

"A new top hat, two pairs of trousers, and a new pair of shoes. Also, I have a discount ticket you can use to buy some new dresses for yourself."

Eliza looked at him, aghast.

"Have you gone mad? I told you this morning we needed a cradle for Eddie and Henry needs to go to the doctor."

"The doctor? What's wrong with him?"

"He's got the croup."

"The croup? Give him a tablespoonful of honey and lemon and rub his chest with horse liniment. That's what my mother did for me."

Eliza shook her head slowly in frustration.

"Where is your pay?"

"Right here," he said, pulling a wad of cash out of his pocket.

"How did you pay for these clothes?"

"I bought them on credit."

She stared angrily at him.

"Oh, my God!" she said. "You're already running from debtor's prison in Boston, now you're working toward the same end in New York."

"Dear! I'll get another $55 dollars next week and I'll bring it to you. Until then, we've got a roof over our heads and plenty of food."

"You're so extravagant. You have no sense of managing money. The minute you get it, you spend it. Then, when the money runs out, you buy on credit. Open your eyes. We have two little children to care for. Their needs come before our own."

"Next week, when I get my pay, I will bring it all to you and you can spend it as you wish. I promise."

"Oh, Lord! I don't know why I stay with you."

David calmly went to her, put his hands on her shoulders, and looked into her eyes.

"You stay with me because you love me. And because we're a family."

He kissed her on the lips.

Unimpressed, she pulled away.

"Very well," she replied calmly. "You stay with the children. I'm going to buy a cradle for Eddie."

Eliza put on her coat and threw a scarf around her neck.

"Don't spend too much!" David said.

"What?" she said, turning angrily. "You say that to me after you went out and spent money on trousers and shoes you didn't need? And on credit?"

"Dear!" David said, trying to be conciliatory.

Eliza turned without answering, opened the door, and slammed it behind her.

***

The following Monday, after David collected his pay, he did not appear at the apartment until 9 p.m. When he entered, his speech was slurred and his gait was unsteady. Eliza was reading. Henry and Eddie were asleep.

"Where have you been?"

"I made a stop at Ryan's Tavern and had a few drinks."

"A few drinks? You're drunker than a vicar's daughter. Did you spend all of your pay?"

"I've got $11 left."

"Eleven dollars?"

"I got into a card game at the tavern and lost the rest of it."

"Oh, dear God," Eliza said, looking upward. "Why do I stay with this man? Why? Why? Why?"

"Hush up! Now don't start!"

"No! You hush up. I'm just about ready to divorce you."

"You can't divorce me!"

"Don't tell me what I can do!" she shouted back.

"Now you're going to listen to me!"

"Get away from me!" she shouted. "I can't bear the smell of whiskey!"

Suddenly, at the shouting, Henry awoke and started crying. Moments later, at Henry's crying, Eddie was wailing.

"Now look what you've done!" Eliza said.

"I didn't do it," he said. "You were shouting as loud as I!"

They were calm for a moment. Then he advanced and glowered down at her.

"Now you listen to me!" he said.

"Get away!" she said, pushing him roughly. "I've got to take care of these children."

Twenty minutes, the children were sound asleep and the apartment was quiet again. David slept on the settee that night.

***

The following week, problems began at the theater. For years, the Strand, located at Seventh Avenue and 44th Street, had been a problem child among New York's theaters. From 1799 until 1808, the theater had changed hands a total of five times, with managers claiming they couldn't make money due to poor attendance, unruly crowds, and claims by attendees that the theater was filled with large rats, which, once the performances began, scurried about the floor feeding on fallen peanuts and pieces of orange and banana peel. To make the situation worse, in the fall of 1808, a hurricane blew through and tore away the roof and part of the second story. The building was closed for almost a month while the rats were removed and the roof and upper structure were repaired. Total cost for the renovations was $5500.

When tickets went on sale for the second week, a notice at the theater entrance proclaimed that ticket prices had increased to pay for the repairs. Box seats went from $2.50 to $4. Common area seats were raised to $2 and tickets for the first twenty front-row seats went up to $3. Only hours after the announcement, angry protestors began gathering outside the entrance and shouting, "Lower prices! Lower prices!" When the theater owner appeared and tried to explain that the higher prices were necessary to pay for repairs of the previous fall, protestors jeered and booed him away. Then, when the theater opened that night and attendees began lining up for tickets, the protestors urged them to walk away rather than pay the higher prices. Some heeded the urging of the protestors while others ignored them, paid the higher prices, and went inside.

When the production opened, the box seats were filled, but the common area had only a smattering of attendees. Halfway through the performance, an angry crowd burst into the theater and began throwing tomatoes, eggs, old shoes, and bricks at the players. Pandemonium erupted, and in the ensuing mclee, David was hit in the head with a brick and knocked unconscious. Fights broke out among attendees and protestors. Wooden chairs and theatrical props were used as weapons. One attendee was beaten unconscious and one woman broke her leg trying to escape the melee. Police were summoned and, once peace was restored, the police chief announced that the theater was being closed for a week as a public nuisance.

***

Back at the Poe apartment that night, David was unable to believe what had happened.

"Bloody hell!" he said as Eliza rubbed liniment into his bruised head. "What's the world coming to? Here I am trying to entertain these fools and some son of a whore hits me in the head with a brick. As an entertainer, I am supposed to be loved and admired, not hated and despised. What kind of business am I in? Am I nothing more than a target for bricks and half-rotten tomatoes?"

"Oh, quit complaining," Eliza said. "My mother was once hit in the face with a pair of opera glasses while performing on London's Drury Lane. These things happen in theater."

"Not to me," Poe said. "No one has ever thrown a brick at me. Especially while I was performing. These people are nothing more than street ruffians. They have the culture and sensitivity of toads."

Eliza didn't want to hear any more.

"Go into the bedroom and lie down," Eliza said. "I'll prepare a hot towel for your head. It will ease the pain."

"All my life, I've tried to be a good performer. Now this! This is the thanks I get for devoting myself to my art."

"Go on to the bedroom," Eliza said. "I've got to nurse Eddie."

"I'm in the wrong business," he said. "I could have been killed tonight."

***

The following morning, a Friday, Usher gathered the troupe in front of the theater and announced that they would not be performing again until repairs were made to the theater.

"Now I want everybody to be patient," he said. "Repairs will be completed over the next two days and the theater will be ready again on Monday. That's two days away. That's when we'll begin rehearsals again and the production will open again on Thursday. Any questions?"

"What about our pay?" one member asked.

"Everybody will be paid half of their salary while we're idle."

"It's not our fault the protestors tore up the theater."

"It's not mine either," Usher said. "I can't afford to pay your full salary when I have no money coming in from the production. Any more questions?"

No additional questions.

"Then I'll see all of you here next Monday."

***

The following morning, Eliza announced that she had to go to the market and asked David to mind the children while she was gone.

"Don't open the window by the cradle," she said. "Eddie was coughing in his sleep last night. I'm afraid he'll catch the croup."

"I'll take care of it."

"And don't let Henry play in the cupboard. Yesterday, he spilled a full bag of flour and it took over an hour to clean it up."

"Go on!" he said, waving her away. "We'll be fine."

***

Two hours later, she returned to the apartment with both arms filled with sacks of groceries. Since both hands were occupied with the bags, she kicked on the door to notify David she had returned. No answer. She waited for a moment. She listened. Inside, she could hear Edgar coughing. She kicked on the door again, louder this time. No answer again. Then, shaking her head in frustration, she set down the bags and opened the door.

"Holy Christ!" she said as she surveyed the room. The table beside the armchair was turned over. The glass oil lamp, which normally sat on the table, lay in shattered pieces on the floor.

At the cradle, Edgar was bawling. She could smell his dirty diaper. At the table, Henry was making a sandwich with stale bread. At the window, which was wide open, David was dog drunk, gesturing and quoting Gloucester's opening line from *Richard III*.

"Now is the winter of our discontent, made summer by this sun of York; and all the clouds that lowered upon our house, in the deep bosom of the ocean buried…"

Seeing Eliza, he stopped, staggered forward, then squinted at her through drunken eyes.

"Drunk again!" she said, trying to stay calm. "Just can't keep your nose out of a bottle."

Once she brought in the groceries, she went to the window and slammed it shut. Then she turned to her husband.

"What happened to the oil lamp?"

David staggered and peered uncertainly at her.

"Now are our brows bound with victorious wreaths; our bruised arms hung up for monuments; our stern alarums changed to merry meetings…"

"Shut up!" Eliza shouted.

David laughed and collapsed on the settee.

At the table, Henry was eating his sandwich.

"Henry, what happened to the oil lamp?"

"Daddy knocked over the table and it broke."

Then she picked up the pieces of the broken lamp, mopped up the spilled oil, and disposed of the pieces. She changed Edgar's diaper and gave him a bottle. Finally, normalcy returned, she put on a pot of tea.

On the settee, David was sound asleep

"Mother," Henry said. "What's wrong with Father?"

"He's sick. Very sick!"

***

The following morning, when Eliza awoke, David was seated in the living room reading the *New York Gazette* and having coffee. Eliza poured coffee for herself and took a seat at the table.

"Are you sober enough to talk to me?"

Miffed at the question, he peered over the top of the newspaper.

"I'm perfectly sober."

"We need to talk."

"What's on your mind?"

"Are you going to get drunk again today?"

"If it pleases me…"

"What about tomorrow?"

"No drinking tomorrow. I'm going back to work."

"I'll believe it when I see it."

"You just watch."

***

On Monday morning, David was up early and got dressed to go to the theater. That afternoon, rehearsals were underway and, over the next three days, they went smoothly. David and the other players knew their lines to Usher's satisfaction and the play was ready to open again. On Thursday night, thirty minutes before the curtain was to rise, Usher was rushing around backstage making last-minute checks.

"Is everybody here? Richard? Gloucester? Queen Elizabeth?"

He looked around the stage and, when he didn't see David, he turned to Oliver.

"Where's David?"

Oliver gave his boss a sheepish look then motioned for him to follow.

Usher followed him to the property room where Oliver pointed out David slumped over dead drunk between a stack of stage props.

Usher stood over him.

"Poe!" he shouted. "David Poe!!!"

David, his eyes bleary, slowly raised his head.

"You talking to me?"

"Yeah. I'm talking to you. I'm telling you that you are fired. You are no longer part of the Charleston Players."

He glanced through the players gathered around him.

"Robert! Robert Sherman!"

The young man who had been playing David's understudy stepped forward.

"Yes, sir."

"Get into costume. You're going on as Richard III tonight. Do you know your lines?"

"Yes, sir!"

"Then get going!!"

Usher turned back to Oliver and another player.

"Get this piece of drunken garbage out of my sight!"

Minutes later, Oliver and another player were escorting the staggering David out of the theater. At the back door, they stopped. While one player held David erect, Oliver opened the door, then pushed him outside into the alleyway.

"Don't come back," Oliver said. "Mr. Usher will call the police."

David, through bleary eyes, watched Oliver and the other player disappear back into the theater, then he stumbled into a row of garbage cans and collapsed. Over the two hours, David slept in the alleyway behind the garbage cans. Once he awoke, he was sober enough to walk and started back to the apartment.

3
Aunt Muddy

When David entered the door, Eliza was nursing Eddie.

"What are you doing home?" she asked. "You're supposed to be rehearsing."

David collapsed on the couch.

"Luke fired me."

For a moment, Eliza stared, aghast.

"Fired? You don't have a job?"

"I was too drunk to go onstage."

Livid anger filled her face.

"You twit!! You empty-headed imbecile!! We have no income! We have a new baby and you come in here and tell me you've been sacked? As a husband, you are totally useless."

"Shut up!" David shouted.

"I'm just about finished with you, David Poe. I've had all I can take."

She got up from the chair and placed Eddie in the cradle.

"Are you sober enough to mind the children?" she asked. "I'm going out."

"Where are you going?"

"I'm going to talk to Luke. We must have some income. If you can't work, then I will."

David stared sheepishly at her.

"Go ahead! I'll mind the children."

***

Twenty minutes later, Eliza was backstage at the Strand talking to Luke Usher.

"I'm sorry," Usher said. "I've had all of David's shenanigans I can take. He's a good actor, but there is no end to the problems."

"I have a favor to ask…"

"What's that?"

"Now that David is fired, we don't have any income. Can you give me some sort of role so we'll have some money coming in?"

Usher studied her for a moment.

"Oh, Eliza," he said finally. "You're such a great actress. You've been such an asset to the company. A real trooper…"

"So can you give me something?"

Usher gazed at her.

"Yes," he said finally. "I need an understudy for the Queen Elizabeth role. It pays $30 a week. If you move into the part, I'll raise the pay to $45."

"Oh, thank you!"

"I can't afford to lose you. When we go to Philadelphia, I want to stage *Miss in Her Teens*. You're the belle of the ball in that role."

"Thank you! I'll report to work tomorrow."

***

Back at the apartment, Eliza announced the new arrangement to her husband. Eddie was in the cradle by the window and Henry was playing with his toy wooden blocks.

"Luke has given me understudy work so we can have some income. Do you think you can take care of the children while I work?"

"How am I going to care for the children? I can't nurse Eddie."

"Then I'll have to hire a wet nurse. Do you think you can cook and clean?"

"Don't be silly! I'm an actor. Not a housekeeper."

"Won't you try to cooperate with me?"

"Cooking and cleaning is a woman's work. I'm an actor, the greatest Richard III that ever lived…"

For a long moment, she stared at him, then suddenly burst into full-blown anger.

"You do well until John Barleycorn grabs hold of you. Then you turn into a quivering heap of useless mush. All of you Poes are just alike. You, your father, your grandfather. The whole bloody lot of you are drunken sots."

David got up and went to face her.

"You can't talk about my family like that!"

"Everything I said is true and you know it. You're a rotter! You're useless as a husband and I want a divorce. I'm going to the solicitor this afternoon."

"You're not divorcing me!"

"Just watch!"

For a moment, David glared angrily at her, then he reached out and slapped her across the face.

Fiery anger flashed across her face. She turned, grabbed a picture of William Shakespeare sitting on the table, and threw it at him.

David ducked and the photo crashed into little pieces against the apartment wall.

"Get out!!" she shouted. "Get out!!"

Now, at the loud commotion, the children were crying again.

"I'm gone."

Without another word, David went into the bedroom and began stuffing clothes into a suitcase. Fifteen minutes later, he reappeared carrying a suitcase. Without a word, he slammed the door behind him.

***

The following morning, Eliza interviewed Drusilla Jones, a slight, light-skinned black woman in her late twenties who had cared for Henry the previous year while the Charleston Players were in New York.

"Yes," Drusilla said. "I have plenty of milk and I can cook, clean, and care for the children. How much can you pay?"

"Five dollars a week."

"That will be fine."

"Can you start today? Right now? I need to be at the theater in two hours."

"Yes."

***

That afternoon, Eliza went to the Strand and began rehearsals as understudy for the role of Queen Elizabeth. That night, when she returned home, the apartment was clean and quiet. The two boys were sound asleep.

"Eddie has a clean diaper and was fed before I put him down. Henry played with his blocks and his books while you were gone."

Eliza smiled at Drusilla's work.

"Thanks so much!"

"You're welcome. There is a pot of beef stew and a pone of cornbread on the cook stove if you are hungry. I'll see you tomorrow at 8."

***

The following night, when Eliza came in from the theater, Drusilla was waiting at the front entrance to the apartment building.

"Drusilla!" Eliza said. "Why aren't you up in the apartment?"

"That husband of yours has gone crazy."

"What happened?"

"He busted into the apartment and started tearing up everything. He called me some awful names and told me to get out."

"Is he up there now?"

"Yes, ma'am. Drunk as a skunk."

Eliza studied the woman for a moment, then peered up the street, where she saw a policeman at the corner.

"Come on!"

Moments later, Eliza was explaining the situation to the policeman. After hearing her story, the policeman took quick action.

"Let's go up and have a look."

When the policeman opened the door, the apartment was in shambles. Henry was eating a piece of stale bread at the table. Eddie was in his cradle by the open window screaming at the top of his lungs. David was passed out drunk on the settee.

"David Poe!" the policeman said, standing over him with a truncheon. "Get up! You're under arrest."

David rolled over and, with bleary eyes, squinted up at the policeman.

"Go away!" he said and rolled over on the couch.

"Stand up!"

"Go away," David said again.

The policeman reached down, grasped his clothing, and pulled him to his feet.

"Stand up!! You're going to jail!"

"Huh?"

Then, the policeman, taking David's right arm and placing it around his neck, started to the door.

"All right, Mrs. Poe," he said. "He's going to jail. You won't have to worry now."

Once the policeman was gone, Eliza and Drusilla got the boys settled down again.

"Mrs. Poe," Drusilla said. "I'm sorry. I'm unable to work like this. I'm afraid I'm going to have to leave your employ."

"Oh, Drusilla, please don't do that. You're the only person I know that I can trust. Can you stay until I can find someone else?"

"Maybe a few days, but if he busts in here again and starts threatening and calling me names, I'm going to run."

"Do you know of anyone else who can help me take care of my children? Someone that can be trusted?"

"No, I don't."

"Tonight, I'm going to write a letter to my sister-in-law in Baltimore and ask her to come help me with the children. Can you please work until I hear back from her?"

"I'll try, but if your husband comes back in and starts mistreating me again, I'm going to run."

"You don't have to worry about him. He'll be in jail for at least a week."

"All right, ma'am. I'll try it for a few more days."

***

That night, Eliza sat down and wrote a letter to her sister-in-law Maria Poe.

February 7, 1809
Dear Maria:
  I hope this letter finds you well.
  Last year, when I visited with you and the other members of the Poe family in Baltimore, you said you were looking for childcare work. That is the point of this letter.
  At this moment, David and I are on the cusp of getting a divorce and I need someone I can trust to take care of our two children.
  I need a wet nurse for Eddie, the younger, and a caretaker for Henry, who is aged two. Also, I need an able person to cook and maintain the home while I am working.
  I can pay you $7 a week and you can take your meals and live at our apartment. Also, I will pay for your transportation costs to travel to New York.
  Our apartment is at Gotham Manor on 42nd Street on the second floor. Once you reach the top of the stairs, it will be the first apartment on the right.
  Please consider my offer carefully and respond as quickly as possible.
  I am in desperate need of your help.

Sincerely,
Eliza Poe

***

Two nights later, when Eliza arrived at the apartment, Drusilla handed her a letter. It was from Maria. Hurriedly, she opened it.

February 13, 1809

Dear Eliza:

I accept your offer of work.

I will arrive at your apartment Thursday afternoon.

The train ticket and the carriage ride from the station will be $11.

I hope that is satisfactory.

Thank you for the opportunity.

I will see you on Thursday.

Sincerely,
Maria Poe

***

Two nights later, when Eliza arrived at the apartment, Maria Poe was waiting with Drusilla. Eliza Maria Poe was a tall, twenty-two-year-old with a certain Puritan look. She had dark, unkempt hair, small piercing eyes, and a prominent nose. Her Mother Hubbard outfit would have been more appropriate for a fifty-year-old than a woman in her early twenties.

Upon seeing her, Eliza rushed to hug her.

"Oh, Maria, thanks so much for coming."

"I'm so happy to see you," Maria said.

Eliza showed her around the apartment.

"You'll be sleeping out here with the children. If you can sleep on the settee for a couple nights, I will buy a small bed for you. This will be your closet," Eliza said, indicating a small enclosure in the hallway. "You can put your personal belongings in here."

In the kitchen, Eliza explained, "If you need some things in here… food, pots and pans, and the like, just make a list and I'll get it."

After showing Maria the apartment, Eliza introduced her to Henry. Henry, who was just learning to talk, peered up uncertainly at his aunt.

"Henry," Eliza said, "I want you to meet your Aunt Maria."

"Aunt Muddy," Henry said happily, then went to Maria to hug her.

"No, dear," Eliza corrected. "Her name is Aunt Maria."

"Aunt Muddy!" Henry said again.

"No, dear."

Eliza started to correct the child again, then Maria intervened.

"It's all right," she said. "He's just learning to talk. If he wants to call me Aunt Muddy, then let him."

"Fair enough," Eliza replied. "Aunt Muddy it shall be."

***

Over the next week, Maria Poe settled in with Eliza and the children. Each morning, Eliza was up early and went to the theater. During the day, Maria would cook, clean, and care for the children. She nursed Eddie at regular intervals and entertained Henry by reading and playing children's games with him.

On Saturday night of the second week, when Eliza arrived at the apartment, she was exhausted from the night's performance. Upon arrival, Maria had a meal of beef stew, boiled potatoes, and cornbread waiting. Eddie was asleep and Henry was playing with his toys.

After the meal, Maria nursed Eddie and put him down. Over the next hour, Eliza read stories to Henry from a children's book. After an hour, Henry was tired and Maria put him to bed, then the two women sat down to relax.

"Oh, Maria," Eliza said when she sat down at the table. "You're a Godsend."

"I'm happy to help," Maria said. "You need some more toys for Henry. Also, I need some things for the kitchen."

"Make a list. I'll go shopping first thing in the morning and get what you need."

Suddenly, there was a knock at the door.

Eliza went to the door.

"Who's there?"

No answer.

"Who's there?"

Again, no answer.

Eliza unlatched the door and cracked it open.

Suddenly, David burst into the apartment.

"David!" Eliza said. "What are you doing here?"

"I need some money to go to Norfolk. I have not eaten in a day. Can you give me some money?"

"I'll give you $10. That's all I have."

"Then let me have it."

He looked across the room and saw his sister Maria.

"Maria! What are you doing here?"

"I'm helping Eliza."

David turned back to Eliza.

"Get me some money! Now!"

Eliza went to the table, opened her purse, and gave him a $10 bill.

He took it.

"I need more than that."

"I don't have it!"

"Don't you lie to me!"

He rushed across the room, grabbed Eliza's purse, and started dumping the contents on the settee.

"I told you that's all I have."

David rushed back across the room to face Eliza.

"You're lying! Get me some more money."

"I don't have any more."

Suddenly, David reached out, grabbed Eliza by the throat, and started choking her.

"David!" Maria shouted. "What are you doing?"

Maria rushed forward and, with both hands, tried to pull her brother's hands from Eliza's throat, but she wasn't strong enough. Quickly, she turned, hurried to the kitchen, and grabbed a frying pan. She came up behind David and, with both hands, swung the heavy frying pan and slammed it into the top of his head.

Instantly, David's body went limp. He released Eliza and collapsed on the floor.

Maria went to Eliza. Behind her, she could hear the children crying.

"Are you all right?"

"Yes," Eliza said, trying to regain her breath. "Stay here! Calm the children! I'm going to get the police."

Fifteen minutes later, two policemen arrived.

"Do you want to press charges?"

"I sure do," Eliza said. "I'll be down at the station tomorrow."

Moments later, Eliza and Maria, with a crying Eddie in her arms and a terrorized Henry clinging to her skirt, watched as the policemen carried the unconscious David out of the apartment.

***

The following morning before work, Eliza went to the police station and made an official report. Then she went to the solicitor's office and filed for a divorce action.

"The deed is done!" Eliza told Maria that night. "I filed for a divorce. The solicitor said the judge will issue an order preventing David from ever coming to the apartment again."

"Praise the lord!" Maria said. "Now maybe we can have some peace around here."

4
Consumption

Over the next six months, with Maria's help, Eliza's stage career soared to heights she could never have imagined. With Maria managing the children and household, Eliza could now concentrate on and put more energy into her roles. In early February, the actress playing Queen Elizabeth took sick and Eliza stepped into the role of Queen Elizabeth in *Richard III*. Almost overnight, she stole the show. After her many performances as Lady Macbeth, she now felt quite comfortable playing Shakespearean roles, which involved palace intrigue and the treachery of courtiers struggling against one another for control of the throne. Not only did she win rave reviews when she undertook the role, she continued to do so for the next six months until the end of the run. Finally, when the troupe left New York the following October, the *New York Advertiser* gave her a front-page farewell.

"With the closing of *Richard III* at the Strand last night, a precious jewel is now missing from the New York stage. Eliza Poe brought a welcome purity to the role of Queen Elizabeth that rendered forth subtle nuances of the character other players have not yet discovered. She will be sorely missed."

On the train from New York to Philadelphia, Usher visited Eliza, Maria, and the boys in their compartment.

"I want to stage *Miss in Her Teens* in Philadelphia," he said. "And I want you to work your magic once more. They loved you in that role last time. I see no reason they won't love you again."

***

In Philadelphia, Eliza, Maria, and the boys took quarters in the popular Commonwealth Manor apartment building on Baker Street. It was a two-bedroom unit with a large kitchen, a sitting room, and a parlor. When the family moved in, little Edgar had just turned eight months. He was an active, alert baby and, if he was crying, there was always a good reason. A month earlier, Maria had weaned him off breast milk and started feeding him "pap," a mixture of boiled water, bread, and mashed vegetables taken from a bottle. Each morning, Maria would buy fresh vegetables and fruits at the local market, then cook and crush them up into a creamy mush that could be swallowed by an infant.

Even at that young age, Henry delighted in tormenting his younger brother. Once Maria was out of sight, Henry would approach the infant Edgar in a loving way, then suddenly thrust his hands to his ears and make a goblin face. Instantly, little Edgar would jump back in terror and bawl at the top of his lungs.

"Henry, what's wrong with that child?" Maria would say.

"I think it's his diaper," Henry replied.

"I just changed his diaper," Maria would say, taking the infant into her arms and consoling him. "Did you do something to him?"

"I didn't do anything."

"Now don't you be scaring him. He's a good baby."

"Everybody likes Eddie. Nobody likes me."

***

For the Charleston Players' stand in Philadelphia, Usher rented the Chestnut Street Theater which, at the time, was the city's premier playhouse with 2,000 seats and a new gas-lighting system, which had been hailed by the local newspaper as "the latest achievement in theatrical illumination."

As expected, during the opening performance of *Miss in Her Teens*, Eliza brought down the house after singing "Missing Thee" and received three curtain calls once the play ended.

One reviewer raved "that Miss Poe's voice is pure silver and her bright future as a rising star on the American stage is assured."

Another reviewer quipped: "Miss Poe's melodious voice and interesting figure will not be soon forgotten."

Over the next six months, the troupe put on three performances a week on Friday, Saturday, and Sunday nights. Each night was a sell-out and, when the company left Philadelphia in January of 1810, Usher announced that the stand had been the "most profitable in memory."

***

On the train from Philadelphia to Baltimore, Usher discussed the upcoming Baltimore stand with Eliza.

"I want to stage August Kotzebue's *The Stranger* while we're in Baltimore," he said. "I want you to play Countess Waterson."

Quickly, Eliza turned to him.

"I hate this play," she said. "There is not one single moment of happiness. Playing the role of Countess Waterson is like stepping into a nightmare, and once it has ended, my mind, like the play, is a morass of darkness and sinister evil thoughts. I am so depressed after every performance."

Usher studied her for a moment.

"I really don't have a choice. Most of the theater-goers in Baltimore are Germans and they love dark, shadowy subjects with evil protagonists. Light, happy subjects don't play well with Germans."

Eliza inhaled.

"I'll try. But I'm not sure how long I can last."

"Do your best. I'm glad you told me," Usher said. "I'll rent the theater on a month-by-month basis."

Over the next four months, Eliza had to mentally prepare herself every night for the emotional darkness of the Countess Waterson role. It was not a happy time for her, but she had vowed to make the best of it. Not only were the play's themes depressing, but, in her role as a German aristocrat in the late 18th century, she had to wear huge, trailing gowns that flared out five or six feet and, in one scene, when the trailing gown got caught in a chair, the chair came with her when she exited the stage.

Finally, when the production ended in late in November of 1810, Eliza was more than relieved. On the night of the final production, she told Usher, "I have been fighting for my sanity these last few days. Don't ever ask me to play that role again because I will refuse!"

"I won't. I have seen how it affects you. Never again!"

***

Three days later, the Charleston Players left Baltimore and moved on to Richmond. On the train, Usher sat with Eliza.

"I want you to return to the role of Miss Biddy in Richmond. It's been my most profitable production and only because of you. So long as your voice is strong, I want to take full advantage of it."

"Fine with me."

"And I'm raising your salary to $75 a week."

***

When the Poe family arrived in Richmond, Eliza, with her new salary, rented a luxury apartment on the city's exclusive south side. It was a spacious affair with two bedrooms, a breakfast nook, a garden, and a parlor that could be used as a playroom. Eddie was now walking and talking and was nearing his second birthday. He was a sturdy child with an expressive face, keen eyes, and an obsession with books. He was unable to read, but he desperately wanted to learn. He would pick up his mother's complete works of Shakespeare and try to figure out which way to hold it for reading.

One day, Maria saw him.

"A book is read like this," she said, holding the book so the words were upright. "The words are upside down when you hold it like this," she said, holding the book to indicate.

"He can't read," said Henry, who was playing nearby. "He's just a baby."

***

It was early January of 1811. Once the Poe family was settled into their new Richmond home, Maria announced that she was going to throw a party for Edgar's second birthday. She scheduled the event for a Saturday morning when Eliza was free of the theater and she went all out by baking a large chocolate cake with vanilla ice cream and presents.

After Eliza, Maria, and Henry sang the happy birthday song, Edgar prepared to blow out the two candles.

"Go ahead, Eddie!" Eliza said. "Blow out the candles!"

Edgar smiled, took a deep breath, then drew back to blow out the candles. Suddenly, Henry lurched in front of him and blew out the candles. Edgar glared at his older brother angrily, then turned to his mother and began crying.

"Henry! Why did you do that?" Eliza said. "Eddie was supposed to blow out the candles! He's the birthday boy."

"He can't blow them out! He's just a baby."

Quickly, Eliza picked up the bawling Edgar, trying to console him.

"It's all right, baby. Hush up now. Mama's here!"

Moments later, after feeding Edgar a bottle of pap, Eliza laid him down for a nap. Then she returned to the living room to confront Henry. He was sitting at the table.

"Young man! Go to your room and stay there for the rest of the day."

Henry looked up sheepishly.

"I didn't do anything."

"You heard me!" the mother said again. "Get down from the table and go to your room!"

Henry began to whimper and got up from the table.

"Everybody loves Edgar," he said. "Nobody loves me."

"You know that's not true," Eliza said. "Maria and I both love you."

"You say that, but not really."

Livid anger flashed across her face.

"Go to your room!"

"But…" Henry said.

"Go! Go to your room!"

Henry turned and started to his room.

"And don't you ever again tell me again that I love Edgar more than you. It's just not true."

***

Now, at age two, one of Edgar's favorite pastimes was the weeknights when Eliza was at home and she would read stories from *Grimm's Fairy Tales* to the boys before they went to bed. Maria was always grateful for these times because it gave her a break from the boys.

One such night, Eliza, with both boys in night clothes and sitting in her lap, read the story of Hansel and Gretel. As she read, Edgar was engrossed in the story while Henry fidgeted.

Eliza was reading the part of the story where the evil old witch had lured Gretel to the big oven and was trying to entice her inside.

"But Gretel saw what the old witch had in mind, and she said, 'I do not know how to get inside the oven.'"

"'Silly goose,' said the old witch, 'the door is big enough. Just look, I can get in myself.'"

"Then the old witch crept up and thrust her head into the oven."

"Quickly, Gretel gave her a push that drove her far into the oven, then she shut the iron door and fastened the bolt. When the old witch began to scream quite horribly, Gretel ran away, and the Godless witch was miserably burnt to death. Then Gretel ran like lightning to Hansel, opened his little stable, and cried, 'Hansel, we are saved. The old witch is dead.' The End."

When Eliza stopped reading, the two children were quiet for a moment.

"Did you boys like the story?" Eliza asked.

"I liked it," Edgar said.

"Stupid story!" Henry said.

"I liked it, Mother," Edgar said. "Can you read another?"

"I'm hungry," Henry said.

"I knew you would like it, Eddie. You have interest in stories; Henry does not. Let's get up. Time for bed."

"I'm hungry," Henry said again.

"No! The food has all been put away for the night. Both of you get into bed and I'll be in in a minute to tuck you in."

Five minutes later, Eliza came into the boys' bedroom, holding a candle. Both were in bed.

First, she went to Edgar.

"Good night, Eddie. I love you. Sleep tight."

"Love you too, Mother. Good-night."

Then she went to Henry, checked his coverings, and kissed him on the forehead.

"Good night, Henry. Sleep tight!"

"Good night, Mother!"

Eliza turned and started to the door.

"Mother?" Henry called.

Eliza turned.

"Yes, Henry?"

"Why do you tell Eddie you love him, but not me?"

"He's younger. He's the baby."

"Do you love me too?"

"Of course, I love you too. Why would you even ask that? Now you two go to sleep."

Then Eliza closed the door.

Moments later, in the darkness, Eddie could hear Henry whimpering in the bed beside him.

"What's wrong?"

"Mother loves you, but not me."

"Mother loves you too; she just loves me more..."

Suddenly, Henry jumped out of bed and started cuffing Edgar. Instantly, Edgar was bawling.

Seconds later, Eliza, dressed in a nightgown, was in the room with a candle. When she burst in, she saw Henry socking Edgar with his fists. Instantly, she rushed forward and pulled Henry away.

"Henry! Why are you hitting your brother?"

"You love him more than me."

"That's not true. I've told you that."

Eliza glared at the child with livid anger.

"Now you have earned yourself a spanking."

"No!" Henry said.

Eliza, holding the candle in one hand and Henry's arm in the other, led him into the sitting room. After taking a belt from the closet, she began to spank Henry.

"Oh! Oh!" Henry yelled.

After some six licks, she stopped.

"Now if I see you hitting your brother again, the next spanking will be twice as hard. Do you understand?"

"Yes, ma'am!"

Eliza, still holding the candle, escorted Henry back into the bedroom.

"Now get into bed!"

Henry, staring angrily at Edgar, hesitated.

"Get into bed!"

"I'm going! I'm going!"

Moments later, Henry was safely under the covers again.

"Now go to sleep! If I hear any more commotion in here, I'm going to spank both of you."

"But, Mother, I didn't do anything," Edgar said.

"Go to sleep! Both of you! Now!"

For a moment, both boys were quiet again, then Eliza slipped out of the room.

In the darkness, Henry spoke.

"You little crybaby. I'll get you for this."

***

Nine months passed. During that time, Eliza's popularity in Richmond in the role of Miss Biddy surpassed that of Philadelphia. Night after night, the theater was jam-packed and the highlight of the show was the moment when Eliza sang "Missing Thee." Newspapers gushed about her talents and fans sent flowers stacked upon more flowers. When she left the theater each night, there would be up to 15-20 fans at the front entrance waiting to congratulate her and get her autograph. Sometimes, the crowd of attendees would start singing "Missing Thee" while waiting to buy tickets. Eliza was at the height of her theatrical career.

Then one night in early October, Eliza came home from the theater not feeling well. Maria could see the stress in her face when she entered the apartment.

"What's wrong?"

"I'm not sure. During the performance tonight, I felt so tired."

Then, without another word, she threw her purse in an armchair and collapsed on the settee.

"Oh, Maria, I think I'm losing my mind. The pressure of the theater and the fans. Trying to raise these two boys. It's too much for me."

"You're been working too much lately," Maria said. "Did you say anything to Mr. Usher?"

"Oh, no! If I've got a health problem, he will be the last to know. I'm going to be on that stage if my body will allow it."

***

The following week, after the Sunday matinee, Eliza was home early from the theater and having dinner with the boys. Maria had prepared beef stew, mashed potatoes, green beans, and cornbread.

Eliza took a seat at the table with the others. Maria blessed the food and began serving the family.

"So, what have you boys been doing today?" Eliza asked

She looked around the table at the faces, then suddenly stopped when she saw Edgar.

"Edgar! What is the red mark on the side of your face?"

"Henry cuffed me."

She turned to Henry.

"Why did you cuff your brother?"

Henry didn't answer.

Edgar spoke up.

"Because I told Aunt Muddy he had stolen the sausage from my plate," Edgar said.

Eliza looked to Maria for confirmation.

Maria nodded.

"Then you've earned another spanking," Eliza said.

Once the meal was finished, Eliza took Henry into the bedroom and spanked him. Maria and Edgar could hear the sound of licks and Henry screaming at the top of his lungs.

Later that night, after the boys were in bed, Henry told Edgar: "You little crybaby, I'm not finished with you."

***

On Saturday night of the following week, Maria could see the stress in Eliza's face when she came home from the theater. Once she closed the door behind her, she collapsed on the settee.

"Oh, Maria! I don't think I can make it another day. There's something wrong with me. Something is happening to my body."

"What is it?"

"I've got this pain in my chest and I have been suffering from shortness of breath."

"What do you want to do?"

"Let me see how long I can last."

***

The following morning, a Sunday, the Poe family was having breakfast in the garden. Maria had prepared scrambled eggs, ham, and biscuits with raspberry jam and fresh cow's butter. After breakfast, Eliza announced she was feeling tired and told Maria she wanted to rest. After an hour's nap, Maria went into the bedroom. Eliza was awake. She sat up in bed and started coughing into a handkerchief.

"Are you okay?"

Eliza looked at her ominously without answering, then coughed into the handkerchief again. Then she showed the handkerchief to Maria. There was a big splotch of red blood.

"Oh, no!" Maria said.

"Do you know what this means?" Eliza said.

When Maria didn't answer, Eliza blurted out the words.

"I have consumption."

"Let's not be too hasty," Maria said. "Let's have the doctor examine you."

***

An hour later, Dr. Carl McDermott, a tall, middle-aged man with glasses and a balding head, had finished his examination.

"Our worst fears are confirmed," he said. "You have consumption. And I must tell you it is advanced."

"How long do I have?"

"It's hard to say. Five, maybe six months. We may be able to arrest the advance with some ground peach pits, but there is no guarantee."

"What can we expect?" Maria asked.

"As the disease progresses, the coughing will become more frequent and you will become weaker and weaker until you are bed-ridden. In some cases, patients can remain in bed for a year or more. In other cases, the time in bed is less."

Eliza shook her head in dismay and looked upward.

"Oh, dear God! Why are you visiting this on me? Now, at a time when I have two little children to raise. Please, tell me why!"

"There is nothing we can do," Maria said. "We'll have to do the best we can."

"Oh, Maria! I don't know what I would do without you."

After the doctor left, Eliza turned to Maria.

"Let's keep this a secret. I don't want Luke to know about this until I am too weak to perform. We won't tell the boys until the very end. All right?"

"If that's what you want…"

5
Orphan

On Monday of the following week, Dr. McDermott returned to the Poe home and demonstrated the preparation of the peach pits remedy to Maria. He explained that the ground powder she made of the peach pits should be dissolved in hot water. Also, he recommended moving Eliza's bed closer to an open window for better air flow during her sleeping hours.

"No alcohol. No tobacco." he said. "Sometimes it's beneficial to take a quick stroll around the block once or twice a day. Any sort of exercise that will stimulate the lungs to open up and provide more air will help."

Once the doctor was gone, Maria set about preparing Eliza's medicine. Meticulously, she prepared the drink exactly like the doctor ordered, then had Eliza drink it down. Over the next four days, Eliza drank the brew each morning. As per the doctor's instructions, Maria moved her bed in front of an open window and Eliza began taking quick morning strolls around the neighborhood. When Eliza awoke Friday morning, she told Maria she felt better, much better, and was ready to go back to the theater.

"I can feel my strength returning."

"Praise the Lord!" Maria said.

On stage that night, her delivery of "Missing Thee" at the end of the second act gave no hint there was a problem. Near the end of the performance, however, the old feelings of fatigue returned and she wasn't sure she could make it. Twice, toward the end of the play, she couldn't remember her lines and, when the performance finally ended, she dragged herself backstage and collapsed.

When Oliver, the stage manager, saw Eliza sprawled on the floor, he immediately called Usher. Moments later, Usher appeared.

"Eliza! What's wrong?"

"I'm sick. I can't perform anymore."

"What can I do?"

"There's nothing you can do. I have consumption."

For a moment, Usher looked aghast at her.

"Oh God, no! Not you!! Not my star! Oh, Eliza, what will I do without you?"

***

During the month of October, Eliza became weaker and weaker and did not return to the theater. Her understudy assumed the singing role of Miss Biddy for the Saturday night performance and, while her renditions did not receive the rousing ovations Eliza was famous for, the show did continue its run. Usher was happy that no ticket refunds would be necessary.

Now, without income, the Poe family was in dire financial straits. First, they moved out of the luxury apartment to a small one-bedroom unit in southwest Richmond. Next, Eliza told Maria she could no longer pay her for her services with the children.

"That's all right," Maria said. "I can't desert you at a time like this."

"Oh, I am so grateful to you. We're going to have to watch every penny."

***

Four days later, Maria announced there was no food in the house and Eliza called Usher to her bedside.

"I'm sorry to trouble you about this, but we have no money for food. Can you help us?"

"Yes."

He reached in his pocket and withdrew a $50 bill.

"This will help you over the next few days. I'll stage a benefit performance for you next Saturday night."

***

The following afternoon, the *Richmond Enquirer* made a front-page announcement about Eliza's dilemma.

Earlier today (November 30), the Charleston Players and the Richmond Theater made public notice of a benefit performance on behalf of Eliza Poe, the actress famed far and wide for her singing performances in David Garrick's play, Miss in Her Teens. *The performance will be held Dec. 2 at Richmond Theater. Interested parties may obtain details at the theater. Those who wish to make outright contributions may visit the Poe home at 130 Commonwealth Street. Theater sources report Mrs. Poe is in dire need of financial help.* One such source said: "On this night, *Mrs. Poe*, lingering on the bed of disease and surrounded by her children, asks your assistance and *asks it perhaps for the last time.*"

***

Over the next few days, throngs of people, fans, well-wishers, neighbors, and curiosity-seekers came to visit. Some brought food, some brought gifts, many contributed cash, and still others, the curiosity-seekers, stopped by to witness the family's living conditions. Among those who visited was a small-statured, well-dressed woman in her early thirties. Her name was Mrs. Frances Allan.

When Maria greeted her, the woman announced that she had been one of Eliza's biggest fans. She said she had seen Eliza in New York two years earlier playing Lady Macbeth and twice in Richmond in *Miss in Her Teens*.

"I saw the newspaper notice and I wanted to help," Mrs. Allan said, pressing fifty dollars into Maria's hand.

Maria looked at the money.

"Not everyone is so generous. Would you like to meet Eliza?"

"Oh yes."

In the bedroom, Maria introduced Mrs. Allan.

"I must tell you that I abhor seeing you like this," Mrs. Allan said. "I always remember you as young, vibrant, and filled to the heavens with energy. I simply adored you in the role of Miss Biddy Bellair."

"Thank you!"

Then Eliza launched into a spasm of coughing.

"I'm sorry," she said. "I know my coughing isn't very pleasant."

"I understand."

"Would you like to meet my children?"

"Oh, yes!"

Eliza motioned to Maria to get the children.

Henry was first. Mrs. Allan shook his little hand and commented that he was a handsome child.

Moments later, Eddie appeared.

"Hello!" he said.

Upon seeing Edgar, a big smile crossed the woman's face.

"My! My! Aren't you a fine one? Such intelligent eyes and a pleasant smile. How old are you, Eddie?"

"Three," the child said, holding up three fingers.

"What do you like to do?"

"Listen while Mommy reads *Grimm's Fairy Tales*."

"Is that all?"

"I also like to eat the sugar cookies that Aunt Muddy makes."

"Tell Mrs. Allan about 'Hansel and Gretel'," Eliza said.

The child became very animated and acted out the scene where Gretel tricked the old woman to stand in front of the oven so she could shove her inside.

"I know that story," Mrs. Allan said. "I love it."

"Do you also like 'Tom Thumb' and 'Cinderella'?" Edgar asked.

"Oh yes. 'Tom Thumb' is one of my favorites."

Suddenly, Eliza had another coughing fit. Finally, it was finished.

"I'm sorry. I need to rest now. I wanted to say thanks for visiting and I hope you can come again."

"Yes, I hope so too."

Moments later, Maria was escorting Mrs. Allan to the door.

"What is her outlook?" Mrs. Allan asked.

Maria shook her head sadly.

"She doesn't have long. The doctor says just a few days."

"What will happen to the children when she passes?"

"I'm not sure," Maria said. "They will probably go to their grandparents or be put up for adoption."

Frances studied her for a moment.

"I wanted to say to you that my husband and I have no children. When the time comes, we might well be interested in taking little Edgar into our home and raising him. He seems to be such an intelligent child. Of course, I'll have to talk to my husband."

"I appreciate the thought. Can I ask a question?"

"Sure."

"You and your husband are well-off?"

"We own a plantation."

Maria quickly turned back to her.

"A plantation?"

"Yes, a plantation."

***

Two days later, Luke Usher appeared at the Poe home and presented Eliza with $425 in cash.

"The proceeds of the benefit," he said. "I hope it helps."

"Oh, thank you so much. We can survive a couple months on that. Maybe even longer. I could kiss you."

"I just wanted to help. You've been a good and faithful friend. I couldn't bear to see you in such a situation."

"My time is not long."

"I know that. I wanted to say thanks to you for your service to me and the company. Again, I'm sorry about what happened between me and your husband."

"I understand."

Usher took her hand, bent over the bed, and kissed her on the forehead.

"Good-bye!" Usher said.

"Good-bye! And thanks!"

***

When Eliza opened her eyes on the morning of Dec. 8, 1811, she knew her time was short. When she awoke, she was coughing violently and, at the sound, Maria was instantly in her room.

"How do you feel?"

"Oh, Maria, I don't have long. I want to say goodbye."

Maria, tears welling in her eyes, seated herself beside the bed and took Eliza's hand.

"I wanted to express my gratitude for your service over the past two years. My accomplishments in the theater would not have been possible without you."

"It was my pleasure."

"I no longer have earthly cares other than for the welfare of my children. Promise me you will ensure they go to good homes and be properly cared for."

"I promise."

"And mind Henry. He mistreats Eddie."

"You have my word."

"Now bring in Henry so I can say goodbye."

Moments later, Henry was at his mother's bedside.

"Remember to be a good boy, to love your brother, and to mind Maria. You're the oldest, so I expect more from you."

"I will, Mother. Are you going somewhere?"

"Yes."

"When will you return?"

Eliza looked at Maria.

"I'm not sure."

"But…"

Eliza motioned with her head for Maria to take Henry away.

"It's time to go," Maria said.

The child resisted.

"Where's Mother going?"

"It's time to go," Maria said again, hurrying him out of the room.

Moments later, Maria returned with Edgar.

"Oh, dear sweet little Eddie. I fear I must leave you to this mad world."

"Where are you going?"

"Away."

"When will you be back?"

"I'm not sure."

Eliza turned to Maria.

"Look in the drawer," she said, indicating the bedside table, "and get me the book of Byron's poems."

Maria opened the drawer and took out a signed copy of *Childe Harold's Pilgrimage*. Eliza took the book and turned to Edgar.

"This is my greatest treasure," she said. "I bought this two years ago when I was in London and heard Lord Byron read his poems. Now I want to give them to you."

She turned to Maria.

"Maria, read the note on the back of the book."

Maria read the note.

"To my darling son Eddie. May he never forget the immortal poems of Lord Byron."

Edgar took the poems.

"Thank you, Mommy!"

Then she lay back on the bed. Tears welled in her eyes.

"Oh, Maria. My time has come. The final curtain is ringing down on my life. Now is the end of the third act."

For a long moment, she launched into a spasm of coughing into one of the small towels Maria kept at her bedside. Finally, she stopped.

"Mommy, I love you," Edgar said.

"I love you too."

For a long moment, there was another spasm of coughing. Then, with seemingly helpless bewilderment, Eliza gazed into Maria's face. Her eyes closed, her body went limp, and she fell back into the nest of pillows.

"Mommy? Mommy?" Edgar said, taking his mother's hand and shaking it.

No response.

"Mommy! Mommy! Wake up!!

No response. Again, the child shook his mother's hand.

"Mommy! Wake up!"

He looked to Maria for an answer

"Aunt Muddy, why won't Mommy wake up?"

Maria did not answer.

For a long moment, Edgar turned to Maria for an answer. There was none.

"My mommy is dead, isn't she?"

Maria looked at him without speaking.

"Tell me! My mommy is dead. Isn't she?"

Finally, she spoke.

"Your mother has gone to a better world."

For a moment, the child looked into Maria's eyes. Then, at the realization of death's imminence, his eyes slowly filled with tears and suddenly, overcome with grief, he rushed into Maria's arms and began sobbing.

***

The following morning, the *Richmond Enquirer* published an obituary with the headline "By the Death of This Lady."

"Elizabeth Arnold Poe died yesterday morning [December 8]. Mrs. Poe was one of the actresses of the Charleston Players Company at present playing on the Richmond Boards. By the death of this lady, the stage has been deprived of one of its chief ornaments. And to say the least of her, she was an interesting actress, and never failed to catch the applause and command the admiration of the beholder."

***

Two days later, more than 1,000 people attended Eliza's funeral at St. Paul's church in southwest Richmond. There was not enough room inside for all of the mourners, so those who were unable to get inside milled around outside. They were friends, relatives, fans, politicians, fellow actors and actresses as well as curiosity seekers who only wanted to see the famous actress in her final appearance. Maria, who had left the boys in the care of a neighbor to attend the funeral, watched as Luke

Usher, Oliver, the stage manager, and four other members of the Charleston Players trudged up the muddy hillside to deliver Eliza's remains to its final resting place.

Once workmen began to lower the coffin into the cool, black earth, mourners stepped forward to drop mementos into the grave. There were bouquets of flowers, old ticket stubs, playbills, the lyrics to "Missing Thee," a piece of red cloth with Eliza's stitched image, and a copy of Byron's poems. Oliver dabbed his eyes at the spectacle, and Luke Usher, as he watched the outpouring of grief for his beloved star, broke down and wept like a little baby.

***

After the funeral, Maria retrieved the two boys from the neighbor and returned to the apartment. After some twenty minutes back at the apartment, she announced she had to go shopping and, before she left, she issued a stern warning.

"I'm going to leave you boys alone for about thirty minutes and I'm expecting you to behave. Now, Henry, when I get back, Eddie had better not be crying. Do you understand?"

"Yes, ma'am."

Satisfied that her orders would be obeyed, Maria took her purse and closed the door.

Some fifteen minutes after Maria left, Edgar withdrew the book of poems Eliza had given him.

Henry saw the book and studied it curiously.

"Where did you get that?"

"Mother gave it to me. She said it was her greatest treasure and she gave it to me to keep."

"Let me see that!" Henry said.

"No! Mother gave it to me. It's mine."

Suddenly, in a flourish of anger, Henry snatched the book from Edgar's hands.

"Give it back! Mommy gave it to me!" Edgar screamed, trying to take back the book.

Henry quickly pushed the smaller child away, then angrily began tearing out the pages.

"No! No!" Edgar screamed as Henry tore out more and more pages.

Again and again, Edgar tried to regain the book, but each time, Henry pushed him away. Once most of the pages were torn out, Henry threw the remainder of the book on the floor.

"You little crybaby!" Henry shouted.

Then he went to Edgar and began to choke the younger child.

Suddenly, Maria, her arms filled with sacks of groceries, appeared in the doorway. Once she saw what was happening, she dropped the groceries on the table and rushed to the children.

"Henry! Stop that!"

She wrested Henry's hands from around Edgar's throat.

"Henry! Why are you choking your brother?"

"I hate him!"

"Why?"

"Everybody loves him. Nobody loves me."

"Why, Henry, how can you say that?"

"Because it's true."

"You're going to get a spanking for choking your brother."

"You can't spank me! You're not my mother."

"You just watch, young man!"

Then, taking Henry by the arm, Maria escorted him into the bedroom.

In the parlor, Eddie could hear the loud claps of the belt on Henry's behind as he screamed in pain.

***

The following morning, while Maria and the boys were having breakfast, Mrs. Frances Allan suddenly appeared again at the front door.

"Can I have a word with you?" she said when Maria came to the door.

"Sure."

Once inside, Maria told the boys she wanted them to go into the bedroom while she had a conversation with Mrs. Allan.

"I discussed the subject of taking little Edgar into our home with my husband," she began, "and he is agreeable. Both my husband and I were orphans and we feel we should have sympathy for others in such a plight. Do you think my husband and I could get custody of little Edgar?"

"I'll have to talk to the solicitor."

"That will be fine."

"There is something else I think you should know."

Maria peered at her.

"What's that?"

"I saw something in the Norfolk newspaper this morning."

Mrs. Allan opened her purse and withdrew a newspaper clipping from the *Norfolk Gazette*.

"You should read this."

Maria unfolded the clipping.

"David Poe Jr., a Boston native and erstwhile actor with various theatrical troupes, including The Charleston Players, died last night (December 10) at the home of a friend in Norfolk. Donations are being sought from family, friends, and charitable-minded individuals to finance the burial. If burial expenses can be gained, Mr. Poe will be buried at the St. John's Cemetery in Norfolk."

Maria looked up from the clipping.

"Oh Lord! The bad news has no end."

"I'm sorry to be the one to tell you," Mrs. Allan said. "When can you talk to your solicitor?"

"Tomorrow."

"Please notify me as soon as possible."

***

When the family solicitor's office opened the following morning, Maria was there.

"I have communicated with the Poe family," he said. "They have agreed to take custody of both children."

***

Late that afternoon, while Henry was napping, Maria took Edgar aside.

"Now that your mother is gone, the solicitor says both you and Henry are going to live with your grandparents."

Edgar turned to her.

"No! I don't want to go! Please don't make me go."

"Why?"

"Henry is mean and base to me. He cuffs me when he is unhappy."

"Does he still do that?"

"Yes. And it hurts! I'm afraid of him."

Maria studied the child for a moment.

"So, you don't want to go live with Henry at your grandparents?"

"No. I hate him. I want to be away from him."

"You're sure?"

"Yes. I'm sure."

"Let me see what I can do."

***

The following Thursday afternoon, after receiving an invitation from Maria, Mrs. Allan was back at the Poe home.

"Before I make a decision," Maria said, "I want you to talk to Eddie again."

"That's fine."

"Eddie!" Maria called.

Moments later, when Edgar appeared in the living room, he politely took a seat in front of Mrs. Allan.

"Good morning, Eddie," she began. "Do you remember me?"

"Yes, ma'am. I remember you from last week. Aunt Muddy said you wanted me to come live with you."

"Yes. My husband and I have a big house on a plantation. And no children. We feel you would be quite happy."

"What's a plantation?"

"It's a big farm where we grow and harvest tobacco."

The child studied her.

61

"Do you have books in your house?"

"Oh yes, an entire library."

"Grimm's Fairy Tales?"

"Yes. 'Rumpelstiltskin,' 'Tom Thumb,' and 'Cinderella.' We could read them together."

The child's eyes lit up.

"I think I would like that…"

He paused.

"Do you have chocolate cake at your house?"

"We do. Our cook Dolina bakes big chocolate cakes with lots of icing and strawberries and blueberries on top."

The child's eyes widened again.

"Lots of strawberries?"

"Yes. Loads of strawberries. We could go for walks by the James River. You could go shopping with me and my husband in Richmond. We could do lots of things together."

"No other children. Only me?"

"That's right," she said. "You would have the entire fourteen rooms to yourself."

Edgar turned to Maria and smiled.

"Do you think you would like that?" Maria asked

"Yes, I would," Eddie said. "I think I would like that very much."

"Thank you, Eddie. I believe we will have quite a happy time together. Any more questions?"

"Yes," Eddie said. "Can I give you a hug?"

Frances smiled.

"Of course, I would love to give you a hug."

With that, Eddie went to Frances and gave her a big hug. After releasing the child, Mrs. Allan turned to Maria.

"Then we are decided?"

"We are decided."

***

At the solicitor's office the following morning, Maria announced the Allan's intention to take Eddie into their home.

"You'll need to change that in the legal papers," Maria said.

"Oh, it's really no problem," the solicitor said. "It's just a matter of rewording the documents. I will make the changes. We will appear before the judge and make everything legal and proper next Thursday."

***

The following Thursday morning, Maria, Edgar, and the family solicitor appeared in the Commonwealth's Children and Family Relations Court in downtown Richmond. Edgar, dressed in a blue sailor suit and carrying a small suitcase, was ready for his great adventure. Others in attendance were Mrs. Allan and her husband. John Allan was a short-statured man, five foot six, with a hawk-like nose and keen, deep-set eyes that peered out from under bushy eyebrows. His wife, when she stood beside him, was a full five inches taller.

After a series of brief exchanges with the family solicitor, the judge, a short, middle-aged man with a balding head and a red face, read the ruling.

"It is hereby decreed that, with these proceedings, the minor child Edgar Poe will be taken into the home of John and Frances Allan, noteworthy residents of Richmond, to live in said home until he has attained adulthood. It should be noted that the child is not being adopted and that the Allans have accepted said minor into their home out of the goodness of their hearts. With this enactment, let it be further decreed that the minor child formerly known as Edgar Poe shall henceforth and forever more be called by the name of Edgar Allan Poe."

***

Twenty minutes later, outside the courthouse, the Allan carriage was waiting at the street. As Edgar and his new family prepared to board, Mrs. Allan turned to him.

"Say goodbye to your Aunt Maria."

Maria bent down to embrace the child.

"I love you and will always remember you," she said.

"And I love you, Aunt Muddy."

Once the embrace was broken, Frances took the child's hand.

"Let's be going now."

With that, Edgar climbed up into the carriage with his new parents.

As the carriage lumbered away, Eddie turned back one last time to wave good-bye.

Maria returned the wave, then sniffled into a handkerchief as the carriage disappeared down the dusty road.

6

The Allans

Two hours later, as the Allan family carriage entered the grounds at New Dundonald, the Allan Plantation, Eddie sat up in the seat so he could gather in a full view. Along either side of the gravel road leading to the estate stood a row of aging white oaks whose sturdy, overlapping branches formed a long tunnel of rich greenery overhead. Once the carriage cleared the oaks, fallow fields for corn and tobacco stretched along either side of the road to the distant woodlands. Now Edgar could see the mansion itself, a massive, three-story brick structure with majestic Greek columns, high French-style windows, and two white marble lions guarding the entrance.

On one side of the mansion, some fifty yards away, stood three rows of ten slave cabins, unpainted, two-room clapboard structures with wood shingles. Nearby, adjacent to the cabins, was a giant dining hall where field slaves took their meals. On the opposite side sat barns, stables, and pastures for horses, mules, and cows and, even further back, stood giant storage and drying sheds for tobacco, fertilizer, grain, and plows.

Once the carriage stopped at the mansion entrance, the two footmen sprang into action. One held the carriage door for the family while the other gathered Edgar's suitcase, then mounted the steps and opened the door.

Dolina, a bulky black woman in her early forties with all-business eyes, appeared in the doorway.

"Afternoon, Mrs. Allan! How was your trip?"

"We had a good trip, Dolina. I want you to meet the new member of our family. His name is Eddie."

The woman peered down at the child.

"Hello, Mr. Eddie!"

"Hello!"

"Is his room ready?"

"Yes, ma'am. With clean sheets and pillowcases and towels. Everything just like you wanted."

"Go up and unpack his suitcase. We'll be up in a moment. I want to show him the house."

***

Over the next thirty minutes, Frances guided Edgar through the mansion. It was a sprawling structure with eight rooms on each of the first two floors, which included a gallery, a foyer, a sitting room, a formal dining room, a ballroom, and a large library. When they entered the library, Edgar lingered.

"You've got lots of books."

"Yes. I love to read."

Poe's eyes traced across the shelves.

"Is this where you keep the book you were telling me about?"

"Which one?"

"*Little May and the Letter A.*"

"It's here."

"Can I see it?"

Her eyes scanned the mahogany shelves. Seconds later, she took down a volume and handed it to Eddie.

Eagerly, he flipped through the pages.

"When can we read it?"

"Tonight. After dinner."

***

Two hours later, the Allan family and their newest member were waiting in the formal dining room, watching as slaves placed dishes of hot food on the table. The room was elegantly appointed with ornate ceilings, a renaissance oil painting on one wall and a giant gilded Italian mirror on the other. The oak dining table itself was a full twenty feet long with high-backed French chairs and a towering candle chandelier above. Once the table was prepared, John took a seat at one end with Frances at the other. Edgar looked around, trying to decide where to sit.

"Eddie, you sit down here by me," Frances said, indicating the seat to her right, "So I can help you with your plate."

"No," John said. "Sit him in the middle so we will look like a proper family."

"Why? I can't get up every time he needs something."

"Let Dolina help him. I want him to sit in the middle. That way, it doesn't appear that he is closer to you than me."

For a moment, Frances stared at him, frustration in her eyes.

"Oh, all right! Eddie, sit in the middle chair on this side."

As instructed, Eddie took a seat in the middle of the table exactly between them.

"Now we look like a family," John said, pursing his lips in satisfaction. "Why must you be so disagreeable?"

"I'm not being disagreeable," she said. "Sitting him that far away is just not practical. If he needs help with something..."

John raised his hand.

"Hush, woman!"

Frances shook her head in frustration.

"Forget I mentioned it."

John turned to Dolina.

"Serve the soup!"

Instantly, Dolina went around the table placing bowls of warm vegetable soup in front of each diner.

Once served, John unfolded his napkin, then took a large spoon, and began to eat.

Eddie, who had been watching, unfolded his napkin, then took a spoon and began to eat. As he took the first few spoonfuls, he made a slight slurping sound.

Annoyed, John turned to him.

"Edgar... did no one ever teach you table manners? You sound like a pig when you take your soup."

Edgar froze. He looked at Frances.

"Eddie," she said. "Don't suck your soup. Just spoon it into your mouth like this."

Then, using her soup spoon, she demonstrated. The child watched.

"Now you try it."

Edgar took the spoon, filled it with soup, then emptied it into his mouth.

There was still a slight slurping sound.

"This child is going to have to learn some manners," John said.

"Now leave him alone. He's only three and he's new to this household."

"He's going to have to learn table manners. I can't take him out in public if he slurps his food like a pig."

"Eddie and I will work on his manners. Just give us some time."

***

After dinner, Frances and Eddie retreated to his room. For more than an hour, they pored over the pages of the Little May book, reading and reciting each letter of the alphabet and pronouncing examples of words in which the letters appeared. Finally, she could see the child was getting sleepy.

"That's enough for tonight. It's time for bed."

Little Edgar, in his night clothes, crawled into bed.

Frances took a seat on the edge of the bed.

"I'm happy you have come to live with us."

"So am I! What shall I call you? Mother?"

"Call me Mother."

"All right, Mother. Can we read more Little May tomorrow?"

"Yes, but at the moment, you need to sleep."

She pulled the covers up to his chin, kissed him on the forehead, and got up to go.

"If you need anything, our bedroom is across the hall. Just rap on the door. Good night!"

She started to blow out the candle.

"Can you leave the candle lit?"

"Sure. Good night."

"Good night, Mother," said the child, then watched as she crossed the room and closed the door.

For several minutes, Edgar lay in the giant poster bed and, in the flickering candlelight, stared up at the flowing velvet drapery adorning its top and sides. Directly above the bed was a huge distinctly Italian painting of a troubled young mother suckling an infant. On the opposite wall was a French painting celebrating Napoleon's victory at Marengo and, in the corner, a massive fireplace with a white marble mantel featuring dancing cherubs with flaming torches carved into the support columns.

Curious about the view, Edgar got out of bed and went to the window. In the darkness beyond, he could see the lights of oil lamps flickering in the slaves' cabins and, even further away, the lights of downtown Richmond. Finally, weary and sleepy, he crawled back into bed, then, moments later, he was sound asleep. That night, he dreamed of Aunt Muddy.

***

The following morning, he was awakened by Frances' knock on the door.

"Time to get up," she said, poking her head in the door. "We're having breakfast on the balcony."

Ten minutes later, the Allan family was seated at a small table on the mansion's second floor balcony. They were having fried eggs, sausage, biscuits, and marmalade. John turned to Edgar.

"How was your night? Did you sleep well?"

"Yes. I slept well."

John took a sip of coffee, then dabbed his mouth with a napkin and turned to the child

"Edgar, I want to tell you that my wife and I have brought you into our family for some special reasons. First, since we have no children of our own, we want to be parents. We want to experience the joys of nurturing a child and watching it grow up. Most importantly, we want an heir, someone to carry on our name and legacy after we are gone. Do you understand?"

"Yes, Father!"

John smiled.

"I like that. It warms my heart to hear you call me Father."

He took another sip of coffee.

"To prepare you for your future role, I want to be assured that you have a good education. Over the next two years, Frances will be teaching you the rudiments of learning. Reading, writing, and doing sums. Once your basic instruction is complete, we will send you to a proper school. Do you understand?"

"Yes, Father!"

John motioned to one of the servants for more coffee. Once poured, he stirred in sugar.

"Edgar, do you see all of this?" he said, indicating the plantation grounds below with a sweep of his hand.

"Yes."

"I made all of this with my own two hands. I was a mere lad when I came to this country to live with my uncle. From him, I learned the value of hard work and perseverance. Now that you have come to live with us, I want you to learn those same values."

"What is perseverance?"

"Perseverance is the ability to remain with a task until it is finished. No shirking of duty. No dalliance. No quitting. Nothing worthwhile comes out of idleness. All success grows out of hard work."

"Yes, Father."

"This is the first step of a long journey. The years ahead will determine how well you apply these values."

John returned to his breakfast.

The family ate quietly for several minutes, then Frances spoke.

"The child is only three years old. You don't feel it's a bit early to be lecturing him?"

"It's never too early to teach a child the virtues which bring success. Now that he is part of the family, I want him to understand the principles that have made me who I am so that he can follow in my footsteps. An example is the best teacher."

"If you say so, dear…"

***

When fourteen-year-old John Allan arrived in Richmond from Scotland in the spring of 1794, all he owned were the clothes on his back, five English shillings, and a bountiful supply of ambition. As a clerk in his uncle William's mercantile store, he admired the elegance of the wealthy rice and cotton planters who rode into town on their thoroughbred horses, followed by the carriages of their equally elegant ladies and the wagons of their slaves. Seeing his uncle as a slave owner and landed gentleman, John wanted his own mansion, his own planation, his own horses, and his own slaves. And he found them.

During those early years, he drove the covered wagons to the docks at Norfolk and hauled back dry goods, whiskey, spices, ploughs, and barrels upon barrels of salted pork and beef. An able clerk, he stocked shelves, assisted customers, learned to rotate his stock, and keep out a keen eye for a clean, well-maintained establishment. When his uncle finally allowed him access to company ledgers, he quickly dug in to learn the mathematical calculations behind a successful business venture. These talents, along with his clear writing hand, his accurate figures, and his shrewd bargaining sense, quickly won the respect of others. Especially his Uncle William.

By the fall of 1802, at age 22 and spending money borrowed from his uncle, John opened his own mercantile business. Using techniques learned from his uncle, the business thrived and expanded. Three years later, he bought a majority interest in a Richmond bank, which allowed him to purchase New Dundonald. The previous owner, a bachelor, had been killed in a duel over a woman and, upon his death, the plantation, which was heavily in debt, was put up for auction by creditors. John was the high bidder. At the time of the purchase, the plantation consisted of sixty-two acres and fifty-four slaves. In 1805, John expanded the acreage to 185 acres and seventy slaves when he bought two adjoining parcels of woodlands, had it cleared, and began growing corn and tobacco. Now, in early February of 1812, he owned a thriving plantation, more than eighty slaves, four rental dwellings in Richmond, two banks, and a half interest in a gold mine. He was one of the wealthiest men in Richmond.

***

The first Sunday after his arrival, Edgar accompanied his new parents on a visit with William and Jane Stanard, their long-time friends who owned Magnolia Place, a cotton plantation some four miles away. Frances and Jane had been fast friends since childhood, both having grown up as wealthy Richmond socialites in homes less than a mile apart.

As young women, they attended and graduated together from the Staunton Institute for Women, Virginia's most prestigious women's college. Jane's father, a wealthy businessman and Richmond's long-time mayor, was a prime mover in local social and political circles and it was at a ball at her father's mansion where Jane had first introduced John and Frances and launched their courtship. Following their marriage in 1803, the two families grew close and John and William became business partners of sorts, each lending slaves to the other during harvest season.

When the Allans arrived at Magnolia Place that afternoon, they were greeted by their hosts at the mansion entrance. Jane Stanard was a petite twenty-eight-year-old with dark hair, piercing eyes, and a classic Greek face. Her husband William, nine years her senior, was a pudgy, medium-height man with a jowly face, a balding head, and a paunch.

"This is my new son," John said proudly when Edgar stepped out of the carriage.

"My! My! Aren't you a fine one," Jane said, bending down to brush Edgar's hair away from his eyes.

"I have a son too."

Edgar's eyes brightened.

"How old is he?"

"Three. Same age as you."

"Can I meet him?"

Jane smiled and took Edgar's hand.

"Come along."

Moments later, John and William retreated to the parlor for cigars and brandy while Jane, Frances, and Edgar strolled through the mansion to the rear terrace. Outside, playing on the carriage road adjoining the rear terrace, they found three-year-old Robert playing with a rolling hoop, a popular child's toy of the day in which a metal hoop was started rolling by hand, then kept rolling by striking the top with a metal baton.

"Robert!" Jane called.

The child stopped and looked toward her.

"Look!" Jane said. "You have a new friend."

Seeing Edgar, the child smiled, then, hoop and baton in hand, he rushed forward.

"This is Frances' new son Edgar."

Robert examined Edgar for a moment.

"Do you want to roll my hoop?"

"Will you show me?"

"Sure. Come on!"

Instantly, Robert turned and started rolling the hoop along the carriageway again while Edgar chased after him.

Seeing the children gone, Frances turned to Jane.

"Has your new book of poems been published?"

"Last week. I have a copy for you."

"Oh, I can't wait to read them. What's the title?"

"*Memories of Love.*"

Suddenly, Robert, who was the end of the carriageway, called,

"Mother!"

The women turned at the sound.

"Can me and Edgar go play in the field?"

"Yes, but don't get your clothes muddy. It rained last night."

"We'll be careful."

"Go ahead."

Moments later, Edgar and Robert were walking across the field of thick broom sage and rabbit-bitten grass.

Suddenly, Robert stopped.

"Look!"

He pointed into the grass.

"It's a turtle."

The two boys moved closer to examine the creature.

"Don't touch it," Robert said. "If it bites, it won't turn loose until it thunders."

"I'm not afraid."

For a moment, they studied the creature, then Edgar reached down. The creature withdrew its tiny head and feet into its shell.

"Let's capture it," Edgar said.

Then, very carefully, he placed his hands around the outer edges of the turtle's shell and picked it up.

"Come on!" he said. "Let's show it to our mothers."

The two boys raced back across the field to the mansion. Once they were within some fifty feet, Edgar suddenly stumbled and fell to the ground.

Robert peered down at him.

"Are you all right?"

Edgar, turtle still in hand, looked up.

"I'm fine."

Robert reached down and helped Edgar to his feet. Both knees of his trousers and the shoulders of his shirt were caked with mud.

"Come on!" Edgar said.

When the children arrived back at the mansion, John and William had joined their wives on the mansion's back terrace.

"Mother! Mother!" Edgar called.

Instantly, as the two children came rushing on the terrace, the adults turned their attention to them.

"Look what we caught," Edgar said, presenting the turtle.

"Yeeek!" Frances said. "Get that thing away from me!"

Then she saw the child's clothes.

"Look at you!!" Frances said. "Look at your clothes. You look like a mud hen."

John, a bit tipsy from the brandy, burst out laughing.

"He's a boy. Boys get dirty."

"Put down that turtle and let's go inside and get you cleaned up," Frances said. "We're going to have dinner soon."

John was still laughing.

"That's my son! He's all boy!"

***

An hour later, the two families were seated in the mansion's formal dining room waiting as slaves served the evening meal. Edgar had been washed and was wearing a clean set of Robert's clothing. Over the next hour, the Stanard and Allan families ate and chatted about business, politics, and friends. Once the main meal was finished, the group waited for dessert.

Finally, when it arrived, the diners prepared themselves to enjoy it. Suddenly, Edgar emitted a loud belch.

At the sound, annoyance flashed across John's face.

"You must forgive my son's manners," he said. "He has not yet learned to be polite at the table."

"No one is offended," Jane said.

"I'm offended," John replied.

"He's only three," Jane said.

"No matter. I want a son who is well-mannered."

His stern gaze returned to Edgar

"Edgar! Leave the table until we are finished."

Edgar looked to Frances.

"John," she said. "It's not worth making him leave the table. Like Jane said, he's just a child."

"The only way he will learn is to punish him."

He turned back to the child.

"Edgar! Leave the table!"

Suddenly, deep hurt in his eyes, Edgar burst into tears.

Frances got up and went to him.

"Come on, Eddie," she said. "Let's go sit in the parlor."

***

That night, after the Allan family returned to New Dundonald, Frances was tucking Edgar into bed.

"Mother. Why must Father be mean to me?"

"Your father is not a mean man. He is just strict. He knows what he wants and wants it exactly that way."

"But I couldn't help the belch. It just came out."

"I know, dear," she said. "But he is your father and you must learn to obey him. He wants to teach you the things he

75

believes you should know. I know it's hard, but you must obey him."

Edgar didn't answer. He was staring off into space.

Frances took his chin and turned his face to hers.

"Do you understand?"

"Yes, Mother."

"So will you follow your father's orders?"

"Yes, Mother."

7
Plantation Life

Over the next six months, Poe settled in with the Allans. In the mornings after breakfast, the family would sit together in the parlor, while Tea Cake, John's personal valet, trimmed his hair and sideburns. Tea Cake, an early thirties mixed-race man, was short-statured with a well-trimmed beard, gentle eyes, and a mischievous smile. John had paid $1500, a huge sum for a slave, to get Tea Cake from a plantation owner in Norfolk who claimed he was "the best personal valet in Virginia." During these "trimming" sessions, John, holding a mirror and watching Tea Cake's every move, would discuss business and make family announcements.

Once the sessions with Tea Cake were finished, John would leave the mansion while Frances and Edgar would retreat to the library or, weather permitting, on the mansion's rear terrace for his daily lessons. Frances had a slate and chalk on which she would drill Edgar on his words. She would write them, then have him write them over and over until he had mastered both the spelling and pronunciation. Once lessons were finished, she would read aloud from the popular children's books of the day. These included the *Life and Perambulations of a Mouse, Adventures of a Pincushion,* and the *History of Little Jack*.

Many afternoons, Edgar would accompany his foster father and Josias Gatewood, the plantation overseer and slave master, to inspect the fields. Josias was a hulking, barrel-chested man, a full six feet three tall and, when he walked, he had the lumbering appearance of a large bear. Next to John, whom the slaves referred to as "the master," Josias was the most feared man on the plantation. He was responsible for flogging errant slaves and enforcing the rules laid down by "the master." At the time, there hadn't been a flogging on the plantation in more than two years. This occurred when a stable slave received five lashes for failing to rub down a riding horse that had been ridden unduly hard.

The carriage carrying John, Josias, and Edgar would rumble across the fields as the slaves swung their hoes up and down, cutting away the weeds from the small tobacco plants. As they worked, they sang and, while Edgar watched, the rhythm of the hoes seemed to keep time with the rhythm of their songs. At sundown, Josias would ring the bell in the front yard of the slave quarters, signaling them to stop work. The slaves, shouldering their hoes, would file out of the fields and go to the big dining hall near the field slave quarters to eat. They would still be singing.

***

Some fifty yards behind the plantation mansion, nestled snugly among several magnolia trees, sat a white-washed two-story wood structure that served as quarters for the house slaves. Compared to the quarters for field hands, it had an overall well-maintained look. There was a good roof, high windows, and a long porch. Directly in front of the door was a well-worn grassless area where the small children could play in the daytime and the parents would sit and talk at night. A well-worn footpath led from the slaves' quarters across the carriage road to the rear entrance of the mansion.

One afternoon, while Frances was conducting Edgar's lessons on the back terrace, the child glanced toward the slave quarters where he saw an old man sitting on a nail keg and doing something with his hands.

"Mother, who is that?"

"That's Amos. He's Dolina's father."

"Why isn't he in the fields?"

"He's too old. He does light chores. Brings in firewood. Puts away clean clothing. Rakes the leaves. Nothing that requires too much strength."

"Can I go talk to him?"

"Just for a few minutes. I need to talk to Dolina."

Moments later, Edgar was trekking down the dirt path to the slave quarters. Upon arrival, he stopped several feet from the old man and examined him. Amos was sixty-two years old with a wrinkled face, sunken jowls, and snow-white hair and beard. Despite his age, he had an impish grin and a twinkle in his eyes.

"Morning!" Edgar said.

The old man smiled.

"Good morning. You must be Edgar. Dolina told me about you."

"That's me. What are you doing?"

"I'm carving an elephant."

The child's eyes widened with interest.

"Can I see?"

The old man held up what was once a solid block of wood. One end retained its original form, but the other had been carved to shape the head, ears, tusks, and front legs and feet of an elephant.

Eddie took the half-carved piece of wood and examined it.

"That's very clever."

Then he returned it and, for several minutes, watched as the old man continued carving.

Suddenly, from the mansion, he heard Frances calling.

"Eddie!"

The child turned.

"Yes, Mother."

"Come back in. We must continue your lessons."

Quickly, Edgar turned back to Amos.

"Will you carve an animal for me?"

"Which would you like?"

"A camel."

The old man smiled.

"One or two humps?"

Eddie laughed.

"Two."

"I'll have it for you tomorrow."

***

The following morning, Eddie could not wait to see the animal the old man had carved. The moment his lessons were finished, he bounded off down the dirt pathway to the slave quarters. When he arrived, Amos was seated on the nail keg waiting.

"Here you go!" Amos said, holding up the prize.

Edgar took the carving and examined it.

"Do you like it?"

"Oh, I love it! Can you do another?"

"Which animal?"

"A tiger."

"I carve good tigers. Give me a couple days. I'll do a tiger for you."

Eddie studied the old man.

"Where did you learn to carve?"

"From my granddaddy. When I was little on the plantation in Norfolk, I would watch my grandfather carve wood. He could carve houses and wagons. He would even carve out the spokes in the wheels."

Edgar listened with deep interest.

"How long have you been on this plantation?"

This single question launched the old man into a long diatribe about his life and he began telling Edgar about his boyhood days on a Norfolk rice plantation, his parents, and about how a cruel slave master had beaten his father to death.

***

That night at the dinner table, Edgar mentioned the incident about Amos' father.

"You can't believe everything that old darkie says," John said. "Slaves imagine things then tell them as if they were true."

"You don't think he's telling the truth?" Edgar said.

John turned to Frances.

"Why are you allowing Edgar to get friendly with the slaves?"

"What's wrong with him talking to Amos? Other than Robert Stanard, he has no friends."

"It's not a good policy for members of the master's family to be getting too familiar with slaves."

"He's just an old man. He can't cause any harm. And Eddie enjoys his company."

"What if he becomes friends with Amos and I decide to trade him?"

Quickly, Edgar looked up.

"Trade him?"

"Yes. Trade him."

"You wouldn't do that," Frances said.

"You never know," John said.

***

The Christmas of 1812 was Edgar's first Christmas with the Allans. On Christmas morning, when he awoke, he had a treasure trove of gifts awaiting. There was a chalk board, a bilbo catcher, toy wooden building blocks, a yo-yo, a rocking horse, pickup sticks, a toy wooden gun, and several new books. His favorite toy was the bilbo ball and he would spend hours attempting to toss the wooden ball into the cup. That afternoon, at the Stanards, Edgar received a rolling hoop from Robert and a matched set of shirt and trousers from Jane.

That night, back at home, the family was in the parlor. Edgar was playing with the bilbo catcher, Frances was reading a magazine, and John was examining his business ledgers. Finally, he closed the ledger and turned to Edgar

"Did you have a happy Christmas?"

"Yes, Father. I like all of my toys."

"You should feel fortunate that you are part of this family. You wouldn't have all of these toys if it hadn't been for us."

"What do you mean?"

"You should be thankful that we were kind enough to bring you into our home."

The child looked to Frances.

She nodded.

"I'm very happy to be part of your family. Thank you for all of the toys."

John smiled.

"Come sit on my knee."

Edgar arose, went to his foster father, and took a seat on his knee. John gazed admiringly at the child.

"How's he doing with his lessons?"

"Wonderfully well."

"He's learning to read and write and do his sums?"

"All of those."

John smiled.

"I'm very proud of you, Edgar. You're going to be a fine lad. You just need guidance. Lots of guidance."

***

One afternoon, while Edgar and Frances were finishing lessons in the library, the child heard music originating somewhere near the back of the mansion. Instantly, he went to the window and peered down at the slave quarters. There he saw Amos playing a banjo while several children held hands and danced in a circle.

"Can I go down to see Amos?"

"Yes. Lessons are finished for today."

Ten minutes later, Edgar was in front of the slave quarters listening to the banjo music and watching the children dance. For several minutes, he watched, then, deciding he wanted to join in, joined hands, and began dancing in a circle with the slave children.

Suddenly, the family carriage with John and Josias pulled up to the rear entrance of the mansion. Instantly, John glanced over and saw Edgar dancing with the slave children. Quickly, he got out of the carriage and stalked over.

"Amos!! Put away that banjo!"

Startled at his master's appearance, the old man stopped playing, then quickly gathered the children and started into their quarters.

"Amos!"

The old man stopped.

"If this happens again, I'll have you flogged."

"I didn't mean no harm, master."

"Go on!"

Amos and the children disappeared inside their quarters.

John turned to Edgar and glared at him.

"Father! What's wrong?"

"Come with me!"

Then he grasped the child's arm and started pulling him toward the mansion.

"What kind of child are you?" he said as they walked. "Dancing with the slaves. Don't you know that is beneath you?"

As they crossed the terrace to the mansion entrance, John saw Frances waiting at the door.

"What kind of child are we raising here? Has no one taught this child the basic social graces? A white child doesn't go dancing with black slaves!"

"He's just a child."

"There are certain basic social rules on a plantation. One of those rules is that members of the master's family does not consort with the slaves. It's beneath their dignity."

"He's only four. He does not understand such matters."

"Well, it's time he learned."

Frances looked down at Edgar.

There were tears in the child's eyes.

"Go on!" John said. "Get this child in the house."

For a moment, Frances hesitated.

"Now!"

Without another word, Frances took Edgar's hand and led him inside.

***

Nine months passed. In early September of 1813, the harvesting of the tobacco crop began. During harvest season, John was away from the mansion much of the time overseeing the gathering of the crop and ensuring that harvested tobacco was packed in hogsheads and delivered to Norfolk, where it would be shipped to England. Meanwhile, Frances and Edgar continued his morning lessons.

One afternoon, Frances announced that John had gone to Norfolk with two wagonloads of hogsheads. That afternoon, Edgar saw Amos sitting alone in front of the slave quarters.

"Can I go down and see Amos?"

Frances peered down from the second story window at the old man.

"It should be all right. Your father won't be back for two days."

Moments later, Edgar was with the old man, chatting and watching him carve. For almost an hour, the old man regaled Edgar with his stories.

"Can you play the banjo?"

"Mr. Edgar, the master will have a fit if he catches you down here."

"He's gone to Norfolk."

"I don't want to get in trouble."

"Father will never know."

For a moment, he looked at Edgar, then went inside the slave quarters and returned with the banjo. Moments later, he was strumming away and, at the sound, the children came out to dance and soon Edgar joined in. This continued for some ten minutes, then suddenly, a carriage with John and Josias pulled up to the rear entrance of the mansion. Instantly, John saw Amos playing the banjo and Edgar dancing.

Quickly, he lurched out of the carriage.

"Stop!" John shouted. "Stop right there!"

Upon reaching Amos, John snatched the banjo from the old man's hand.

"You were warned about this!"

Amos looked up submissively. By now, several house slaves had heard the commotion and gathered on the terrace to witness the proceedings.

"Josias!" John ordered. "Tie this slave to that drying rack and give him five lashes."

Seconds later, Josias was out of the carriage and leading Amos to the nearby drying rack. Then he proceeded to tie the old man's hands to the cross members of the drying rack. Once tied, he tore open the back of the old man's shirt, then went back to the carriage and took a whip.

"No! No!" Edgar screamed, running to his foster father. "I asked him to play the banjo. The fault is mine."

"Stand back!" John said. "Proceed with the flogging."

Suddenly, Edgar rushed to Amos and clasped his arms around the old man's waist.

"Father! Please don't do this! Please!" he sobbed, clinging to the old man's waist.

John stepped forward, grasped the sobbing child's arm and pulled him away.

"Proceed!"

The slave master uncoiled the whip and drew back to strike.

Suddenly, a voice called his name.

"Josias! Josias Gatewood!"

He turned.

It was Frances. She was rushing across the terrace to the drying rack.

For a long moment, Frances and Josias stared at one another. Then, suddenly, Frances reached out and snatched the whip out of his hand.

"That's enough of this madness!"

"What are you doing?" John shouted. "This is no affair of yours."

"I'm making it my affair."

Then, still holding the whip, she went to Amos and began untying his hands. Moments later, his hands were free.

"Go to your quarters!"

The old man obediently turned and started toward the slave quarters. Then Frances went to John, who was still holding the banjo in one hand and Edgar's arm in the other.

"You should be ashamed!"

Then she turned to Josias.

"And you should too."

Still holding the whip, she jerked Edgar's arm out of John's grasp, then turned back toward the house.

"Hold it!" John shouted.

"No! YOU hold it!" she shouted angrily.

Then she turned and uncoiled the whip.

"Let's see how you like it."

Then she made a half-hearted attempt to strike John with the whip. He threw up his hand to block the strike.

"Too much power can be total evil," she said. "And you have too much power."

Then, overcome with emotion, she shook her head in frustration and threw the whip on the ground.

"Come on, Eddie!"

She took the child's hand and started toward the mansion.

"Frances!" John called. "Come back here!"

She didn't break stride and disappeared inside the mansion.

Now John could see that the other house slaves had been watching the incident.

"Why are all of you standing around?" he shouted. "Get back to work."

***

That night, Edgar could hear loud voices coming from John and Frances' bedroom across the hall. He slipped out of bed and went to the door to listen.

"You made me look like a fool in front of the slaves today," John said.

"Somebody had to put a halt to your madness."

"Madness?"

"Yes. Madness! You should ashamed of yourself for flogging that old man."

"He's a slave and slaves must follow the master's rules."

"They are human beings. You're treating them like horses. Or dogs."

"I own them. They belong to me."

"No! They belong to God. You didn't create them. HE did. My uncle had slaves on his plantation, but not one time was one ever whipped."

"I'm not your uncle."

"Sometimes you are totally unreasonable."

"Unreasonable?"

"Yes. I know what's right and I know what's wrong. It's totally wrong to whip an old man for playing a banjo."

"Oh, you're just a woman. You don't understand these things."

"I know what's right and what's wrong."

"Hush up and go to sleep."

For several moments, there was quiet.

"Why didn't you go to Norfolk?"

"Two miles out, I got word the warehouses were full. There wasn't room to store my hogsheads. Josias and I are going next week."

Again, the bedroom fell silent. Edgar waited. After hearing nothing further, he tiptoed back across the hallway to his room.

***

In January of 1814, Edgar celebrated his fifth birthday. The following morning, the family was gathered in the parlor. Edgar played with his toy wooden soldiers, Frances was reading a magazine, and Tea Cake was trimming John's hair and sideburns. John, turning one way, then the other with a mirror, carefully inspected Tea Cake's work.

"Take a bit more off the top."

"Here?" Tea Cake asked, indicating.

"A little to the right."

Tea Cake carefully made the requested cut.

"How's that?"

John used the mirror.

"That's good. That's enough for today."

Tea Cake put away the scissors, clippers, and combs, and left the room.

John turned to Frances.

"How does it look?"

She got up and went to her husband.

"Looks good. Tea Cake did a good job."

Satisfied, John laid the mirror aside and turned to Edgar.

"Come talk with me."

Edgar arose and went to his foster father.

"Have a seat," John said, patting his empty knee.

The child took a seat on John's knee.

John peered thoughtfully at the child.

"How's he doing with his studies?"

"He can read, write simple sentences, do sums, and recite declensions of several Latin verbs," Frances said. "And he has read *The Adventures of Robinson Crusoe* and *Grimm's Fairy Tales* on his own."

"Very good!" John said. "I'm very proud of you, Edgar."

"Thank you, Father."

"Now it's time to start your formal education."

"What do you mean?"

"Next month, we're going to England to get you enrolled in school and I plan to open an office for my export business."

"Why am I going to England to go to school?"

"There are no good schools in America. These Americans are, by and large, an uneducated, illiterate lot. The schools offer very little in the way of education and culture. All of the good schools are in England."

"When are we leaving?"

"In two weeks. I have some business matters to attend to in town, then we'll be gone. While we're away, Josias will be living in the mansion and serving as master. He will be running the plantation as if I were here. There is no reason this plantation cannot run without me. Everybody knows their duties."

8

England

On the afternoon of January 11, 1814, the Allan family, along with twelve pieces of baggage, boarded a transport vessel that took them down the James River from Richmond to Norfolk. Upon arrival, they boarded the sailing ship, the USS *Martha*, and set sail for the British Isles. The thirty-four-day voyage was not only long but tiresome. For most of the journey, Frances was seasick and remained in bed in her cabin. Meanwhile, John complained about everything. The meat was too salty. The cabin was cold and crowded. The crew had to be called to remove small insects from his bed. The captain was less than cordial. Halfway through the voyage, a violent storm blew the ship off course and, for two days, John was so seasick, he was unable to eat.

Meanwhile, Edgar spent his time reading and watching the ship's sailors go about their duties. He was fascinated with the complex rigging system that was used to hoist and maneuver the giant sails in and out of the wind. For hours, he would stand on deck and wait to see the crew swing the yardarm and mainsail about for a new tack or trim a jib sail to match a gentle breeze. *Someday,* the five-year-old thought, *I may very well be a sailor myself and do the same thing these men are doing.*

Finally, on the afternoon of February 17, 1814, the USS *Martha* landed in London. Upon arrival, the Allan family and their luggage were loaded into a carriage and delivered to the Grosvenor Hotel in East London, where they would remain until they had permanent quarters. As the carriage rumbled along the cobblestone streets, the new surroundings were a visual feast for young Edgar. Everything was new and different. The people, the places, the accents, language, the dress, the culture, the food. England would be an adventure every bit as exciting as his going to live with the Allan family. He could not wait.

***

By the spring of 1814, England had outpaced both the French and the Dutch in exporting and importing goods to and from the colonies. Although America had won its political independence, it remained economically dependent on the British and its textile industry, the world's largest, to buy their cotton. By the same token, the colonies, which had little or no manufacturing, depended on England to provide goods such as machinery, textiles, farm implements, and medical supplies. As a result, the so-called "Atlantic economy" between the two nations was booming and John Allan intended to become a participant in those profits.

In London, the physical nerve center for shipping commerce was the Isle of Dogs, a tiny spit of land which was bordered on three sides by the winding course of the Thames River. Known as "the Docklands," it was a sprawling collection of docks, warehouses, shipping berths, and dray services. Meanwhile, directly north of the Isle of Dogs, a financial district consisting of banks, merchant houses, steamship companies, insurance brokers, commission agents, cargo handlers, and other such services had sprung up to provide both material and financial support for the shipping industry. It was here, in the immediate area north of "the Docklands," that John Allan settled his family for their new life in England.

First, he enrolled Edgar in the Thomas Burke Academy for Clever Children on Radcliffe Street just north of the financial district. It provided elementary education for both boys and girls aged 5-11 and, at the time, was the only private co-ed school in London. Adverts for the academy claimed students who attended Burke School were "near nobility" and represented the most prominent families in London.

Next, he rented a flat on Radcliffe Street. It was a spacious, two-bedroom apartment with a parlor, sitting room, and a large kitchen overlooking a garden. John liked it because it was only a fifteen-minute carriage ride to the Waterhouse building and only two blocks, easy walking distance, to the Burke Academy. Frances noted the new quarters was relatively small, but it was airy, had plenty of light, and there was an open-air market in the same block with lots of fresh meat and vegetables. Two days after the family moved in, she hired a housekeeper.

Lastly, John signed a lease with the landlord at the Waterhouse building in the financial district to rent a small office. This sprawling six-story brick structure was the most prestigious building in the shipping district. All of the major import/export businesses, including East India company and Caledonian Steam Lines, had offices there. The space consisted of two rooms, a reception area in front and a small office area in the rear for meeting clients.

The same afternoon the lease was signed, Frances, who would serve as John's secretary, was in the office cleaning, hanging curtains, and preparing the office for use. Next, John signed a contract with an insurance underwriter to sell shipping insurance and applied for a permit from the National Maritime Board to become a commissions agent and sell cargo space on outgoing ships. Once that was complete, he bought an advert in the *London Times,* and Blue Anchor Maritime Services, John's new company, opened for business.

***

Five years passed. It was early September of 1819, and John, Frances, and ten-year-old Edgar had carved out a new life for themselves in the suburbs of East London. Edgar had completed the first four levels of grammar school at the Burke Academy. An excellent student, he now had a firm grasp of reading, writing, and Latin verb and noun declensions. As he was now about to enter the fifth level, he would start learning the Greek alphabet and begin his studies into Greek and Roman history. Also, during those five years, Edgar had become fast friends with classmate Nathan Hughes. Like John, Nathan's father was in the shipping business and had an office in the Waterhouse building. Frequently, Edgar would spend weekends with Nathan and the Hughes family. Likewise, Nathan was a frequent weekend visitor at the Allan home. Thanks to Nathan, Edgar had become a competent rugby player.

During those five years, John's shipping business, Blue Anchor Maritime, struggled to survive. The first year, which was 1814, the business earned 3,400 pounds, mostly through insurance contracts. Early on, John discovered that selling cargo space was very competitive and, in order to turn a deal, profit margins had to be cut to the bone. As the year 1815 drew to a close, it appeared the company was going to make a huge profit, but, at Christmas, when one of the company's insured ships and fifty-five lives were lost off the coast of South Africa, the company had to pay up and lost over 11,000 pounds. The following year, the company broke even and, in 1818, it made a paltry 2,100 pounds. Now, nine months into the year 1819, the future of the company appeared uncertain.

***

It was Sunday night, September 7, the night before Edgar was to begin his fifth term at Burke academy. In anticipation of the following day, he had gone to bed early but was unable to sleep. Finally, he got out of bed, lit an oil lamp, and began reading. He overheard John and Frances talking in the adjacent bedroom. As was his habit, he slipped quietly out of his bed, into the hallway, and went to their bedroom door to listen.

"I received the annual letter from Josias today about the state of affairs at New Dundonald," John said. "He said this year's tobacco crop brought in $18,700, the largest profit ever."

"Then why are we here in England slavishly devoting ourselves to this silly shipping business that's going nowhere? We have plenty of money and a comfortable home back in America. I miss Dolina's cooking. I miss Jane. And I hate these winters… the constant rain, the fog, the cold. I long for the warm days and bright sunshine of Virginia."

"Now, be patient, dear," John said. "I want to give it one more year. Today, I talked to a woman who is co-owner of

Churchill Shipping Enterprises. She says she believes we can merge our businesses so both companies can reap the profits. She is coming to dinner Saturday night. Be sure the housekeeper puts on a good spread."

"What's her name?"

"Rosalee Bradford Churchill."

***

The following morning, Edgar walked the two blocks along Radcliffe Street from the family home to the Burke Academy for the first day of his fifth term. The building that housed the school was a single-story brownstone structure with high French windows, a portico, and a statue out front depicting a small child reading a book. In front, there were two entrances, one into the boys' section of the school and another for the girls. Once he arrived, as always, Edgar waited at the boys' entrance for his friend Nathan and, once he appeared, they would go to class together.

On this particular morning, as Edgar waited for Nathan, he saw a strange-looking carriage stop in front of the girls' school. He watched closely as an expensive-looking, middle-aged woman stepped out, then held the door while a young girl, slim, well-dressed with a pretty face and curly ringlets of brown hair showing under the edge of her bonnet, got out of the carriage and started toward the girls' school entrance. As she strode across the schoolyard, Edgar was unable to take his eyes off her.

As Edgar watched, Nathan arrived. Nathan Hughes was a ruddy-faced ten-year-old with a quick smile, hay-colored hair, and alert blue eyes.

"Morning, mate!"

Edgar was still watching the girl.

"Who is that girl walking with the older woman?" Edgar asked, nodding toward her with his head.

Nathan turned.

"That's Catherine Anne Caldwell. Her father owns Caldwell manufacturing in Hanover."

"My! My! She's so beautiful!"

"Come on," Nathan said. "Mr. Burke will tan our hides if we're late to class."

Edgar lingered a moment longer as the girl made her way up the school house steps, then disappeared into the building.

"I think I'm in love!" Edgar said.

"Come on! We've got to hurry!"

***

The classroom was a large, high-ceilinged room with the pungent smell of burned coal. In the front, behind the headmaster's desk, hung a huge picture of King George III in all his regal glory, and along the walls on either side were strung small placards displaying the printed letters of the English alphabet. Each desk was a small table 48x24 inches with an inclined top for writing. When students entered, there were books on the desks with slabs of slate and clay chalk. In the corner sat a stool with a dunce cap and hanging at the edge of the blackboard was a cane for whippings.

As Edgar and Nathan sat among the other students, the classroom was atwitter with boys' voices, laughing and talking, excited about the first day of the new school year. Suddenly, Edgar was hit in the back of the head with a spitball. Edgar rubbed his head, then turned, and his eyes met those of a redhaired boy with a sneer and a what-are-you-going-to-do-about-it grin.

"That's for you, Yank," the redheaded boy said.

"Low-life scoundrel!" Edgar said.

"Ha!" the other boy said with a sneer.

Edgar turned to Nathan.

"Who is the redhaired kid?"

Nathan glanced across the crowded classroom.

"That's Neville Bullard. I was in pre-school with him at Shardwell. He's a meanie. Best to stay away from him."

Suddenly, Nathan looked up.

"Uh-oh, here comes the headmaster."

Thomas Burke, a tall, unsmiling man in his fifties with a balding head and wire-rimmed glasses, strode into the room. Instantly, the students fell quiet. For a moment, Mr. Burke's eyes glanced solemnly across the classroom. Then he tapped a ruler on the desk.

"Students! Hear me and hear me well! I have a firm set of rules in my class. I would advise each and every one of you to heed them well. You will not speak in class unless called upon. Whispering during class is forbidden and any student found guilty will be punished with five licks with a ruler across the open palm. For the dullards in the class, I have a dunce stool," he said, pointing to the corner. "For the incorrigibles, I have this."

Then he reached up and took down the whipping cane.

"Do all of you see this?"

"Yes, Mr. Burke!" the class said in unison.

Suddenly, without warning, he whacked the cane across the top of the desk and it made a loud cracking sound. At the sound, the boys jumped in fright.

"The first lick will bring tears. Does everyone understand?"

"Yes, Mr. Burke!" the class said in unison.

"Then we shall begin today's lessons."

***

An hour later, Edgar, Nathan, and the other boys were on the playground playing rugby. The other team had just scored a goal and it was time for Edgar and Nathan's team to kick off. Poe took the ball, walked back to the starting line, and prepared to kick.

Suddenly, Neville Bullard, who was on their team, rushed up.

"Give me that, Yank!" he said, snatching the ball from Edgar.

Anger flashed across Poe's face and, before Neville could kick it, Edgar gave chase.

"Give it back!" Edgar said, running after him. "Give it back!"

"Let me see you take it, Yank!"

Suddenly, Nathan came up behind Neville, threw a body block into him from behind, and the redheaded boy went sprawling on the ground. As he did, the ball came free and Edgar scooped it up. Then Edgar returned to the starting line to kick again. The moment he prepared to kick the ball again, Neville went charging after him. As Neville reached Edgar, Nathan stuck out his leg in Neville's path and the redhead crumpled to the ground. Quickly, Edgar kicked the ball into play again and, as the rest of the team ran down the field, the angry, frustrated Neville sat helplessly on the ground.

"I'll get you two for this!" he shouted after Edgar and Nathan. "I'll have my own back with both of you."

***

Some forty minutes later, the recess was near its end and Nathan was ready to return to class. He looked around the playground for Edgar, then finally spotted him at the divider, a wire mesh opening in the wall between the boys' playground and the girls' playground. Edgar was peeking through the wire as the girls did flips on the monkey bars.

Nathan rushed up to him.

"What are you doing?"

Edgar did not answer at first. His eyes were fixed on the girls as they did flips.

"Catherine Anne Caldwell is wearing white knickers with pink ruffles."

"How do you know?"

"Watch!"

Nathan waited, then watched as the girls did more flips, exposing their bottoms in the process.

Nathan burst out laughing.

"Yeah. And Gloria Hollister is wearing yellow knickers."

Suddenly, they heard the bell signaling the end of recess.

"Come on!" Nathan said.

"Wait! I want to see Catherine's knickers again."

"I'm going in!" Nathan said.

He turned and started racing across the playground.

Seconds later, Edgar, after seeing Catherine's knickers one last time, was right behind him.

On Saturday night, promptly at 7 p.m., Rosalee Bradford Churchill arrived at the Allan residence for dinner. She was a bosomy, pudgy little woman with a pretty face and an overall expensive look. Once inside, she and Frances exchanged pleasantries and, when Edgar was introduced, she looked at him and commented, "He is a lovely child!" and didn't speak to him again for the rest of the evening. Once food was served, the conversation immediately turned to business.

"John, you seem to prefer many small deals to a few big ones," Rosalee said as she served herself some shepherd's pie. "I would rather negotiate four large deals in a month than fifteen smaller ones. The large transactions take longer to negotiate, but they are more profitable."

"So what do you propose?" John said.

"First, you should not offer shipping services; you want to be the shipper. Shipping services are competitive, and, for that very reason. have low profit margins. The biggest profits in shipping have always been in moving goods from a cheap market to a more profitable venue. You aren't doing that."

"So what do you propose?"

She paused to take another bite of scalloped potatoes, then, after some chewing, she spoke.

"In a warehouse on Canary Wharf, there are 800 American-made riding saddles that were confiscated by the Royal Navy from American ships during the War of 1812. They are owned by the King, but since they are American saddles, there is no market for them here in England. They have been sitting in the King's warehouse for over six years. The English doesn't want them, but they should sell well in America."

"What's the price of the saddles?"

"There is no price," she said. "They are sold at auction. At the last auction, there were no bids."

She paused for a moment, helped herself to more scalloped potatoes, then continued.

"The next auction is in May. If we could get those saddles for say… five pounds each, we could make a good profit if we had a distributor in America."

"I have a mercantile business in America where we could sell them."

"How much does a new riding saddle sell for in America?"

"Anywhere from $20-$50."

Quickly, Rosalee turned to him.

"You can get up to $50?"

"Yes. For a well-made leather riding saddle."

"So if we could buy the saddles for five... even seven pounds, we could make a handsome profit."

John studied her for a moment.

"Brilliant," he said. "Absolutely brilliant. Then I suggest we bid on the saddles at the next auction."

"I'll start the application tomorrow," Rosalee said.

Once the business talk was finished, Rosalee turned to her personal life.

"I grew up in a wealthy family in Dorchester," she said. "My father was the owner of a machine company that made textile looms. I went to the best schools."

"What schools did you attend?"

"Oh, since you're American, the names would mean nothing to you. Also, I have a title, but I don't often mention it."

"What is your title?"

"I'm the Countess of Cornwall. My older sister Claudia was married to Sir Francis Wallace, the Earl of Dorchester. When she died three years ago, the King passed her title to me."

"So I am entertaining royalty tonight?" Frances said.

"You could say that," Rosalee said with a proud smile.

Finally, once the meal and business talk were concluded, John, Frances, and Edgar accompanied their guest to her carriage at the front of the residence. It was a fine carriage, with gold door handles, wide steel wheels, and drawn by a sturdy-looking black Arabian horse. Once she boarded it, the Allan family waved a final good-bye then watched as the carriage rumbled off down the street.

"What about her husband? Why didn't he accompany her?"

"He's very old and bed-ridden."

Frances peered at him for a moment, then they went back inside.

***

On Wednesday afternoons, after classes were dismissed, Edgar and Nathan would walk the seven blocks from Burke School to the War Memorial Park across from the Waterhouse building. The one-block-square park featured a statue of three British sailors wielding sabers and pistols clashing with attacking Spanish sailors. Nearby, there was a large fountain with pigeons, fast food vendors, and street entertainers. The park had been built several years earlier to celebrate the British naval victory over the Spanish armada some two hundred years earlier. On the south end of the park was a large, grassy field where Edgar and Nathan would play rugby with their friends. Many Wednesday afternoons, after playing rugby, Edgar would ride home with Nathan and his father George in the Hughes family carriage since the two families lived less than three blocks apart.

Nathan's father was the portrait of a true British gentleman. Medium-height and in his early forties, he had a lean, oval face, a well-trimmed mustache and goatee, and attire that spoke of wealth. This included a top hat, silk shirts with a tailored waistcoat, and deerskin pantaloons with silver-buckled shoes. Sometimes, he carried a cane.

On one Wednesday afternoon, some two weeks after John's meeting with Rosalee, Nathan's father mentioned Rosalee during their ride home.

"I understand your father is joining forces with Rosalee Churchill in the shipping business."

"Yes. She was a guest at our home recently for dinner. My father says she has a good mind for business."

"I'll give her that, but that's where her talents end."

"What do you mean?"

"You can't believe a word she says."

"She claims she has a title. The Duchess of Cornwall… or something like that."

Mr. Hughes laughed.

"She owns no more of a title than I do. She grew up in the slums of east London. She was a dancehall girl at Coventry Garden when old man Churchill walked in one night, saw her dance, and took a fancy for her. Three months later, they were married. He was 63 and she was 32. She would still be swinging her bum in the follies if it hadn't been for old man Churchill."

"Father says Mr. Churchill married her because she is a good businesswoman."

Mr. Hughes laughed again.

"I guess you can find a little goodness in everyone. You can put face rouge on a pig."

Now the carriage was slowing to stop in front of the Allan residence.

"Also, from what I hear, she loves to cock a leg," Mr. Hughes said as an afterthought.

Then he turned to Edgar.

"Here we are at your home, Edgar. Good afternoon."

"See you tomorrow, Eddie!" Nathan said.

"Goodbye!"

Edgar got out of the carriage, waved once again, and started up the steps to the family home.

***

At the Burke School the following morning, when Nathan arrived to meet him, Edgar asked him about his father's comment of the previous day.

"What did your father mean yesterday when he said Rosalee Bradford Churchill likes to cock a leg."

"He means she likes sexual intercourse," Nathan replied. "You know. Amorous congress."

For a moment, Edgar studied him and thought about his answer, then they rushed off to class.

***

Three months passed. During that time, John started coming home from the office later and later each night. Since

Tea Cake hadn't accompanied them on the trip, the weekly task of trimming John's hair and sideburns fell to Frances and Saturday mornings would usually find the three of them in the parlor with Frances trimming her husband's hair and Edgar listening. On one such Saturday morning, Frances mentioned the subject of Rosalee.

"You've been spending a lot of time with Rosalee Churchill lately," she said. "Over this past week, you were late three nights and your dinner got cold."

"Now don't be getting any ideas," he said. "It's all business. I have no interest in her other than business. Negotiating deals takes time and effort."

John stopped then held up the mirror to inspect her work.

"Take a bit more off the top," he said. "And even up the sides."

Frances returned to her trimming.

"We made 9,000 pounds on the riding saddles," he said. "Now we are negotiating to buy four looms for a textile firm in Boston. If we can buy them at the right price, we can make at least 10,000 pounds."

9
The Secret

The following morning, ten-year-old Edgar was waiting for Nathan at the entrance to the Burke School. When Nathan arrived, Edgar was all eyes as he watched Catherine Anne Caldwell stroll along the walkway from the family carriage to the girls' school entrance.

"I have some news," Nathan said.

Edgar waved him away, indicating he wanted to finish watching before he engaged in conversation. Moments later, when Catherine disappeared into the school building, he turned to Nathan.

"What news?"

"News about your father."

"What could that be?"

"I fear to tell you."

"Tell me anyway."

"I saw your father and that Rosalee woman leaving the office yesterday. My father says she is cocking a leg for him."

Edgar drew back. His face screwed up in anger.

"It's a lie! My father would never betray his marriage vows to my mother."

"I'm just telling you what my father said. He's not in the habit of lying."

"I tell you it's not true."

"If you don't believe it, that's your business."

"Well, I don't believe it."

Nathan shook his head and laughed.

"Come on! Let's go to class."

***

During the morning recess that day, Edgar played rugby with the other boys for most of the period, then, for the last fifteen minutes, he went to the dividers to see what color knickers Catherine Anne Caldwell was wearing that day. During the entire time he was watching, she did not go to the monkey bars a single time. She spent the time playing on the swings with the other girls. On the swings, Edgar was unable to get a good look at her underwear.

Suddenly, Nathan rushed up.

"What are you doing?"

"Watching Catherine Anne," Edgar said, still peering through the divider.

Suddenly, the two boys heard the sound of the first bell at the girls' school. As the girls abandoned their play, Edgar's eyes followed Catherine Ann Caldwell as she raced across the schoolyard.

"She's going into the girls' loo," Edgar said.

Quickly, he turned to Nathan.

"Come on!"

He left the divider and started racing across the schoolyard toward the bathrooms.

"What are you going to do?" Nathan said, taking stride beside him.

"I haven't seen Catherine's knickers today!"

Moments later, they were inside the boys' restrooms.

"The girls' room is on the other side of this wall," Edgar said, pointing to a gray wall beside the latrines. "See that window up there?"

"I see it!"

Edgar pointed to a trash can.

"I want you to hold this trash can while I stand on it and peek through the window into the girls' loo."

Nathan laughed.

"You might see Gloria Hollister. See what color knickers she's wearing."

Nathan set the lid on the metal trash can and tried to hold it steady. Edgar put one foot on the lid, then started to raise himself.

Suddenly, the trash can gave away under him, and Edgar, seeing he was about to fall, jumped off.

"You've got to hold it steady," Edgar said.

"It's no fault of mine if you can't keep your balance. Let's try again."

Once again, Nathan reset the lid on the trash can, then held it tightly while Edgar climbed on top. On top again, and feeling secure, Edgar grasped the window ledge and pulled himself up so he could see through the window.

Nathan waited.

"See anything? Do you see Gloria?"

With their backs turned to the restroom entrance, they did not see Neville Bullard suddenly walk in. For a moment, Neville stopped, sized up the situation, then quickly turned and darted back out.

"Do you see Gloria Hollister?" Nathan said.

"Catherine is going in one of the stalls, but there's a door on it."

"Let me see!" Nathan said.

"Now she's coming out of the stall…"

"Do you see Gloria?"

Suddenly, behind them, they heard the sharp, rasping voice of Mr. Burke.

"Aha! Caught in the act!"

Both boys whirled around to face Headmaster Burke. As they did, in their fright, Nathan released the trash can; the trash can fell one way, Edgar the other, and both Edgar and the contents of the can spilled on the floor.

"You two shall pay full measure for this!"

He grabbed each of the boys by the earlobes, then led them down the hallway to his office. Neville walked behind them, chortling with delight at every step.

***

Ten minutes later, in the headmaster's office, the two boys were staring across the desk at the stern face of Mr. Burke.

"You are naughty, naughty boys for trying to peek into the girls' loo. You know such things are against the rules of God and this school. I could give both of you a good caning for what you did, but I fear it would have little effect on the evil thoughts in your minds. Your parents must know what a dastardly deed you have committed."

Then he began writing notes with a graphite pencil.

Edgar looked at Nathan. They feared the worst.

Finally, Mr. Burke stopped writing.

"These are notes to each of your parents. Tomorrow, which is Wednesday, both of you are expelled. If you return the notes to me with your parents' signatures, you may return to classes on Thursday."

He handed each of the boys the notes.

***

That afternoon, after classes ended, Edgar and Nathan were walking down Radcliffe Street. Edgar withdrew the note Mr. Burke had given him.

December 9, 1819
Dear Mr. Allan:

Your son, Edgar is being expelled for one day for an act unbecoming a student at the Burke Academy for Clever Children.

"I must press upon you the importance of addressing your son's miscreant behavior. Discuss with your son the vile act he has committed and I urge you to dispense whatever parental punishment you deem necessary."

This document must be signed forthwith by you and returned to me before your son will be allowed to return to classes.

Sincere regards,
Thomas Burke, Esquire.

Edgar looked up from the note.

"What are we going to do?"

"I'm not going to show this to my father," Nathan said. "He'll blister my bum. I'm going to sign it and return it and say my father signed it."

Edgar studied him for a moment.

"That's a good idea. Old man Burke won't know the difference."

***

That night, after the evening meal, John asked Frances to trim his beard and hair for the bank meeting he had the following day. Edgar sat nearby and listened.

"I won't be in the office tomorrow," John said. "The Hanover-Newcastle board is considering a new set of regulations for making loans. The meeting will last most of the day."

"That's fine. I shall close the office at one. Should I keep your dinner warm or will you make other arrangements?"

"I'll have dinner with the other board members at the Excelsior."

"Then I won't wait up for you."

***

The following morning, Nathan was waiting for Edgar at the appointed place on Radcliffe Street.

"What do you want to do today?" Nathan said.

"Let's just roam around."

"Where do you want to go?"

"Let's walk all the way down Morant Street to the docks and look at the sailing ships."

"Father says it's rough down there. Nothing down there but whorehouses and dance halls."

"Whorehouses? Have you ever seen a whore?"

Nathan paused thoughtfully.

"No."

"Neither have I. I want to see a whore."

***

Over the next hour, the boys walked the twelve blocks along Morant Street to the shipping wharves on Front Street. As they walked further and further south, the surroundings became less and less hospitable. While the street's north end featured dignified public buildings, well-maintained residences, and rows of respectable businesses, the south end quickly became a rambling shantytown of dilapidated dwellings. Scruffy-looking men sat in doorways drinking, playing cards, and throwing dice as women openly suckled babies, while other hungry children tugged at their skirts. In an alleyway, the boys watched as hungry feral cats and stray dogs prowled through overturned garbage cans. The sickening smell of rotting food and human waste lingered in the air.

"Whew!" Nathan said. "Let's get out of here."

Moments later, upon reaching Front Street, the two boys saw a long row of weather-beaten wooden buildings facing the docks. High atop one, a sign blared "Mollies Follies" and featured several frowsy-looking women dancing in colorful, scanty costumes. Although it was only 9 a.m., loud music, women's laughter, and the sound of clinking glasses could be heard from inside.

Suddenly, Nathan stopped and pointed to a two-story wooden structure and a sign at the corner. The sign, in large red letters, read "Love Emporium." On the ground floor, men were intermittently passing in and out the door. On the balcony above, several women, in various stages of undress, were smoking, chatting, and sipping drinks.

"I think that's a whorehouse," Nathan said.

The boys edged closer, then peered up at the women.

"Aye! What are you young blokes doing on this end of town?" said a dark-haired woman who was smoking a cigarette. "You're not old enough for what we're offering."

This brought a twitter of laughter from the other women.

Edgar stared up curiously at her.

"Are you a whore?" he asked.

The dark-haired woman looked at the others, then the entire group erupted in raucous laughter.

"No!" she said. "We're bloody nurses. We care for mankind's most basic need."

Edgar looked to Nathan.

"What's she talking about?"

"I don't know," Nathan said, shrugging.

Suddenly, a stocky middle-aged man wearing a blue uniform emerged from the front door. As he was leaving, he was fastening the top buttons on his shirt.

"Wilfred!" one of the women called.

The man looked up.

"Hope to see you again soon!"

Wilford smiled.

"Oh, you shall!"

Once his shirt was buttoned, he swept back his hair and put on his cap. Once the headpiece was comfortably on his head, he spotted Nathan and Edgar.

"Hey! You two fartlings! Why aren't you in school?"

Instantly, the two boys turned.

"Who are you?" Nathan asked.

"I'm the truant officer."

Nathan turned at Edgar.

Suddenly, their faces filled with fright.

"You lads better run!" said shouted one of the women.

Instantly, the two boys broke into a full run back north on Morant Street.

"Stop! You little devils! Come back here!"

Instantly, he went tearing up the street after them.

Over the first two blocks, the boys outran the older man. In only a matter of seconds, they had streaked the two blocks back north on Morant Street, then ducked into an alleyway and hid behind several trash cans. Moments later, from their hiding place, they watched as the truant officer, huffing for breath, stopped briefly to check the alleyway, then, upon seeing nothing, turned and continued north on Morant.

"We gave him the slip," Nathan said. "Let's go down two blocks to Blackpool, then we'll double back to Morant."

Over the next ten minutes, the boys walked quietly along Blackpool Street. They felt they were safe now.

Suddenly, the truant officer, face red and breathing hard, jumped out of an alleyway in front of them.

"There you are! Now you're mine!"

Instantly, the two boys turned and broke into a full run.

Seconds later, the truant officer was right behind them.

"Run!" Nathan said.

Edgar looked back.

"He's gaining! Run!"

Both boys were running as fast as their legs would carry them.

Suddenly, the truant officer caught up with them, grabbed Nathan's shirt from behind, and spun him around.

"Now I've got you!"

Edgar stopped running and turned to watch as Nathan tussled with the officer.

"Unhand me!" Nathan screamed. "Unhand me!"

Edgar stepped forward and delivered a mighty kick to the officer's shin. The officer's face contorted in pain. He released Nathan's arm and grabbed his shin.

"Run!" Edgar said.

In a flash, the two boys were in a full run again, the officer close behind.

"We've got to make it back to Saltwell Street," Nathan said.

"Why Saltwell?"

"He has no authority there. It's out of his district."

"Are you sure?"

"Trust me! Run!"

Now, with renewed effort, the boys were once again outpacing their pursuer.

Seconds later, at Saltwell Street, the two boys dodged between several carriages, dray wagons, and pedestrians to get to the other side of the street. Safely across the dividing line, the two boys, gasping for breath, stopped running and looked back. Across the street, the truant officer had given up the chase and was shaking his fist at them.

"Whew! That was a close call," Nathan said, breathing heavily.

"What do you want to do now?"

"Let's go back to the war memorial and watch the old women feed the pigeons."

"That's too boring," Edgar said. "Let's see what's on the other side of the Waterhouse building."

"What time is it?" Nathan said.

Edgar glanced at the clock on a nearby bank building.

"Almost one."

"Our mates won't be at the rugby field until after three."

"Let's go watch the old women feed the pigeons and wait for them."

***

Fifteen minutes later, the two boys were at the War Memorial Park, laughing at an organ grinder and his monkey. Finally, bored, they bought two apples, then took a seat on one of the benches surrounding the fountain. For several moments, they sat quietly eating the apples and watching the midday pedestrians pass through the park.

Suddenly, Nathan pointed toward a couple passing near the monument.

"Look! It's your father!"

Edgar turned.

"Where?"

"There!" Nathan said, pointing. "The couple behind the statue about to go through the gate. It's your father and that Rosalee woman."

Edgar's eyes turned to the place Nathan was pointing.

Then his eyes fell upon his father and Rosalee Churchill walking hand-in-hand through the park gate toward the Waterhouse building.

"Oh my God!" he said. "I cannot believe my eyes!"

"What are you doing to do?"

"I'm going to follow them. Come on!"

Several minutes later, the boys watched as John and Rosalee, still holding hands, passed through the park gate. At the street, they stopped momentarily and shared a kiss.

"That low-life dog!" Edgar said. "He told Mother he would be at a bank meeting all day."

His eyes followed them as they crossed the street to the Waterhouse building.

"Come on!" Edgar said. "Let's see where they're going."

Over the next ten minutes, at a safe distance, the two boys followed John and his paramour. Once they had crossed the street, they strolled past the main entrance to the Waterhouse building and headed down to the next block.

"Where are they going?" Nathan said.

"We're going to find out."

The two boys watched as the couple passed a vegetable market, a blacksmith's shop, and a saddlery. Then they went into a small tavern. The sign above the door read "Hangman's Pub."

"What are we going to do now?" Nathan said.

"We're going to wait and see where they go."

"They could be in there for hours."

"I'm going to wait," Edgar said.

For some thirty minutes, the boys waited outside the tavern at a safe distance. Finally, impatiently, Edgar turned to Nathan.

"Go inside the pub and pretend like you're looking for someone. See what my father and that woman are doing."

"You go."

"He'll recognize me. He doesn't know you. Go in and ask the saloonkeeper if he has seen your father today. While he's answering, you can see what they're doing."

Moments later, Edgar watched as Nathan walked up the street and disappeared into the tavern. Five minutes later, Nathan came out again.

"They're in one of the back pews drinking ale and kissing."

Edgar gazed at his friend thoughtfully.

"What are you going to do?" Nathan asked.

"I'm going to wait and see where they go."

"Our rugby mates will be gathering in the park in another hour."

"I'm going to wait."

***

Twenty minutes later, John and Rosalee emerged from the tavern and started up the street toward the Waterhouse building. Edgar and Nathan, keeping a safe distance, followed them. At the Waterhouse building, John and his paramour took the side entrance.

"I think they're going to the office," Edgar said.

"I thought the office closes at one on Wednesdays."

"It does," Edgar said. "Let's give them some time, then I want to go up and see what they're doing."

Several minutes later, the two boys passed through the side entrance and were tromping up the stairs to the second floor.

Quietly, they approached the office of Blue Anchor Maritime and stopped in front of the door. They listened. They heard Rosalee's voice.

"Oh yes, Johnny! That's what I like! Yes! Yes, Johnny! Yes!"

Nathan whispered to Edgar, "Does that sound like they're discussing business?"

"I know what they're doing," Edgar said. "Come on! Let us go back across to the street to rugby field and wait for our mates."

"What are you going to do?"

"I'm going to tell Mother."

***

Two nights later, Edgar and Frances were alone in the parlor of the family home. They had finished their evening meal and Edgar was doing his lessons while Frances was poring through shipping manifests. John had not yet come in from the office.

"Mother!" Edgar began. "I have something to tell you."

Distracted, she turned to him.

"Are you in trouble at school?"

"No. It's another matter."

"Then tell me."

He waited, trying to decide how to frame the words.

"You know Father and this Rosalee woman have become very friendly."

"They have business to discuss."

"I fear to tell you they are more than friends."

"What do you mean?"

Poe hesitated, then blurted out the words.

"They have become lovers."

Frances stopped stone cold and peered at him.

"Now do not be playing with me," she said. "I've got to have these manifests ready for a sailing tomorrow."

"Mother, it's true."

Frances inhaled, then spoke.

"My husband is an egotistical tyrant who thinks he owns the world, but he would not renege on our marriage vows. I know him too well."

Edgar did not know how to reply. He knew he was unable to tell her outright what he and Nathan had witnessed. It would be too embarrassing.

"Mother?"

"No! Don't bother me!" she said. "I'm busy and don't have time for your foolishness."

"But…"

"Quiet!" she said, raising her voice. "I've got to work."

***

"She didn't believe me!" Edgar said when he met Nathan at the Burke school the following morning. "She acted like I was making it up."

Nathan laughed.

"What are you going to do now?"

"I'm going to make her believe it."

"How are you going to do that?"

"I have a plan."

***

On the following Wednesday after school, Edgar went to the War Memorial Park and played rugby with his school friends. All the while, he kept an eye on the Waterhouse building across the street for John and his paramour. At 4 p.m., he saw them come up the street from the Hangman's Pub and go through the side entrance into the Waterhouse building. The following Wednesday afternoon, he was back again playing rugby with his friends. Again, like clockwork, Edgar watched as his foster father and the woman went through the side entrance at the Waterhouse building at 4 p.m.

On the playing field, Edgar turned to Nathan when he saw them.

"There they are again," he said. "Right on time."

"You're a good detective," Nathan said. "A truly good one."

***

The following Wednesday morning, as Edgar was saying good-bye to his mother before school, he asked a favor.

"Mother, can you meet me at Patrick's Shoe Emporium near the office today? I found a new pair of shoes I want."

"You don't have enough shoes?"

"Not like these."

"Just tell me which ones you want and I'll get them after I close the office."

"I want to try them on again."

Frances could see there was no need to continue the argument.

"Oh, all right. What time?"

"At four."

"I'll be there."

***

That afternoon, Edgar was waiting in front of the shoe store when Frances arrived in a cab carriage. They went into the store, Edgar tried on a pair of new shoes, and, once he approved them, Frances paid the clerk and they walked out. Back out on the street, Frances started to hail a cab carriage.

"Mother! Can we go up to the office for a minute?"

"Why? It's closed."

"I need to use the loo."

"You can't wait until we get home?"

"No."

Ten minutes later, Edgar and Frances were inside the Waterhouse building climbing the stairs to the second-story office. As she approached, she withdrew a key, but before she did, she checked the knob.

"It's unlocked," Frances said. "Now who...?"

She looked ominously to Edgar.

"There's somebody in there..."

Then, without another word, she swung open the door.

Rosalee's bosomy, pudgy body, legs spread wide apart, was sprawled across the red settee in the reception room and John was thrusting his body into hers with the utmost ferocity.

"Hello!" Frances said.

"Oh, my god!" Rosalee said.

John saw his wife.

"Frances!"

Quickly, they halted their coupling and scrambled to hide their nakedness.

Calmly, Frances examined the scene.

"So... this is the business which has been keeping you away from home so much lately? What about the bank meeting today? You lying dog!"

By now, John had donned his breeches and Rosalee had managed to pull a flowery dress over her head.

"It's not what you think..." John said.

"I don't have to think anything. I have two eyes to see."

Frances turned to Edgar.

"Come on!"

Then she stopped and turned back to her husband.

"I'll be at home in one hour and we shall discuss our divorce."

Then she slammed the office door.

***

John did not arrive at the Allan home until 9 p.m. that night. When he entered the door, Frances looked up from her reading, then turned to Edgar.

"Eddie, you remain in here. Your father and I are going into the bedroom to discuss some matters."

John and Frances went into the bedroom and closed the door. Once they were inside, Edgar went to the door to listen.

For several moments, there was total silence. Then he could hear Frances starting to weep softly.

"I want a divorce," she said finally. "Eddie and I are going to return to America and let you have your little tart all to yourself."

"Oh, my dear Frances," he began. "I'm sorry for what I have done. I have no lasting love for this woman."

"You seemed to be enjoying yourself when I opened the door to the office this afternoon."

"But it's you I love. It's you that owns my heart."

"Why didn't you think of that earlier?"

"It was a mistake. I'm sorry."

A long silence.

"You reneged on our marriage vows. I trusted you and you violated that trust. How can I ever trust you again?"

"It was all just a whim. It's you I love."

Another long silence.

"Only a divorce will give me the satisfaction I require."

"A divorce? We cannot get a divorce. Look at our history. We have been happily married for thirteen years. What will our friends say?"

"I want a divorce."

"Don't do this!! You can't just throw away all the years of happiness we've had together."

"Divorce or nothing. I'm going back to Richmond."

Another long silence.

"Where are you going to get the money for passage?"

Edgar could hear the anger in his voice.

"You bloody fool! Don't you know I keep a cashable bank draft for $1,000 with me at all times on my uncle's bank in Richmond."

She laughed.

"I can go into any bank in England and instantly have $1,000 cash, more than enough for passage back to the States for me and Eddie."

All was quiet for a moment.

"If you force me into a divorce," John said. "I will do everything in my power to destroy you and your family's reputation. I know people in high places in Richmond who will believe anything I tell them."

"You wouldn't do that!"

"Oh, yes I would! I would fight you with every resource I have to destroy you and your family's reputation."

"You low-down, lying dog!"

A long silence.

"What life would you have without me?" John asked. "Truth is, you wouldn't have a life. You're not going to let something like this destroy our years of happiness?"

"Something like this? You make it sound so innocent. You have crossed a line. The love I had for you has turned cold. Now all I feel toward you is hatred and bitterness."

A long silence.

"So what are your plans?"

"I'm going back to America. You can stay here with your fat little tart."

"What about the divorce?"

"I'll let that matter lie. At least for a while."

"Thank you!" John said.

Edgar could hear the relief in his voice.

"Give me a week," John said. "I'll settle up everything and we'll go back to Virginia."

Another long silence.

"How did you know Rosalee and I were at the office?"

"A little bird told me."

"Who? I demand that you tell me."

"That shall remain a secret."

"You can't keep a secret from me."

"I can and I will. It is my secret and shall remain as such."

Another long silence.

Edgar could hear John moving around the room.

"Sweet darling Frances! Permit me to show you how much I love you."

"No! Get away from me! You traitorous dog! You can sleep on the settee in the parlor tonight."

***

On Sunday of the following week, the Allan family, along with eighteen pieces of luggage, boarded the USS *Lothair* bound from London to New York, then to ports south, including Norfolk. John and Frances had separate berths for the return trip. As before, Edgar occupied himself with reading and watching the sailors move the ship's sails in and out of the wind. For the return trip, with a strong westerly wind behind them, the mighty ship required a total of twenty-eight days to reach New York. Finally, four days later, when it entered Norfolk Harbor, Frances was beside herself with joy.

"I have not the words to describe to you how happy I am to be back at home," she said as she and Edgar stood at the ship's railing. "This is one of the happiest days of my life."

Edgar turned to her.

"You must never reveal to Father that I was the one who led you to him and Rosalee. He will kill me."

"Don't worry, dear. It is our secret and I shall go to my grave with it."

Edgar smiled.

"If it had not been for you," she continued, "I would never have known the truth. Thank you, Eddie!"

"I love you, Mother."

"I love you, Eddie."

10
Jane Stanard

It was December of 1821. It had been two years since the Allan family returned to America and resettled into plantation life. John had Tea Cake again and ceased to complain about his haircuts; Frances was once more ordering slaves to perform household duties rather than doing them herself. After some discussions, she and John had reached a livable truce about his dalliance and were sleeping together again. Poe, now a tall, strapping twelve-year-old, was finishing his second year at Richmond's Old Brook School, the 1820s equivalent of high school. During those years, Poe had renewed his friendship with Jane Stanard's son Robert. At Old Brook, both boys were named to the academic honors list; both participated in several after-school sports, including boxing and rugby. Almost every Sunday would find the two boys together at either Moldavia or New Dundonald.

During Sunday family visits, each member of both families knew the drill. Frances and Jane would pair off to go sit on the back terrace, sip tea, and chat; John and William would retire to the drawing room for cigars, brandy, and a heated discussion about politics; Edgar and Robert would dash off to the fields along the banks of the James River, where they would swim, fish, and raft. It was a practiced routine that each family member expected and adhered to.

Then, one Sunday in late April of 1821, during an Allan family visit to Moldavia, something happened that would change Edgar's life. Edgar and Robert had spent the morning playing at the river when they returned to the mansion for lunch. On the back terrace, they found Frances listening to Jane read poetry. When the boys rushed up, Frances put her finger to her lips, indicating they should remain silent until Jane finished. The boys stopped to listen.

Jane was reading:

So, we'll go no more a-roving
So late into the night,
Though the heart be still as loving,
And the moon be still as bright.

For the sword outwears its sheath,
And the soul wears out the breast,
And the heart must pause to breathe,
And love itself have rest.

Though the night was made for loving,
And the day returns too soon,
Yet we'll go no more a-roving
By the light of the moon.

Once Jane was finished reading, Edgar turned to her.

"Who wrote that poem?"

"That's Lord Byron's 'We'll Go No More A-roving.'"

"Can you read the last stanza again?"

Jane reread the last lines.

"Such beautiful words," Edgar said. "They take me into another world."

"That's the power of poetry," Jane said.

"I would give anything to be able to write a poem like that," Edgar said. "How do you become a poet?"

"Oh, silly boy! You learn to write poetry by writing poems."

He studied her for a moment.

"You think I could be a poet?"

"Of course, and a good one. Like me, you have a natural inclination for language."

"How would I get started?"

"You write. You write letters, you write notes, you write poems. For a young poet, the best training is to keep a personal journal. A daily record of what you say, what you do, what you think, the people and influences around you. This daily recording of your life will train your mind to translate thoughts into words. I started my journal when I was twelve years old."

For a long moment, Edgar peered thoughtfully at her. In that single instant, Jane had awakened a secret part of himself. She had struck a special chord somewhere deep within his soul.

***

That night, when Poe arrived back at New Dundonald, he went straight to his room, sat down at his desk, and took quill and paper.

April 27, 1821. Today, on this date, with these words, I begin the first steps of my writing journey. In the days ahead, I shall make every effort to record my daily activities, thoughts, plans, and activities on these pages.

***

Over the following week, Poe made four entries in his new journal. Each day at school, whether he was reciting Latin declensions, taking boxing lessons, chatting with Robert about girls, having breakfast… whatever he was doing, he made a mental note that would be entered into his journal that night.

The following Sunday, the Allan family was back at Moldavia. Upon arrival, Poe announced he had written a poem, "The Coming of Spring," and asked Jane to critique it. Over the next hour, Jane and Edgar sat in her study while she explained the rhythms, the rhymes and the dos and don'ts of good poetry.

"Do you see this line?" she said.

Edgar followed her finger.

"You have 'da-da-da-da-da-da-da'," she said, keeping time with the syllables like a musical conductor does with beats. "Seven das."

Again, Poe's eyes followed her finger.

"In the next line, you have da-da-da-da-da-da-da-da-da," she said, once again keeping time with the syllables. "There are nine das rather than seven. The beats of the two lines are not coordinated."

Suddenly, his eyes lit with recognition.

"Let's take Robert Herrick's poem 'Julia'," she continued, taking down a small volume from her bookshelf. After flipping through several pages, she began reading.

"Listen to this. 'When as in silks my Julia goes,' there are eight beats. "Da-da-da-da-da-da-da-da."

Edgar was listening.

"Now count the beats in the next line. "Then, then, methinks how sweetly flows...' again, eight beats."

"I see your point," he said. "The beats of each line are perfectly matched."

"Poetry is essentially music. You should study the beats of every line to understand how the beat of one line works, then even predicts, the beat of every other line."

She paused.

All the while Jane had been conducting the impromptu lesson, Robert had been waiting to go out and play.

"Eddie!" he said, during the pause. "Let's go back to the river."

"Wait a minute!"

Jane thumbed through the pages to a new poem.

"Lord Byron's 'She Walks in Beauty' is one of my favorites," she said. "Listen to the beats and compare them line by line."

As Jane proceeded to read the poem, Edgar was mesmerized not only by the beauty of the words, but by the beauty of the reader. Somehow, up until now, he had not noticed what an exquisitely beautiful woman Jane was. Now he was suddenly aware of her well-formed face, chiseled cheekbones, a pert nose, chestnut brown eyes, and raven black hair. The proportions of her body, breast to hips, the slope of her neck, the slim legs, and her dainty feet were such that the most beautiful of Greek goddesses would be envious, he thought. *This is the face of Helen of Troy.* This was the face that launched a thousand ships. *Hereafter, I will call her Helen.*

Once Jane was finished, she handed the book to him.

"Take this home and read these," she said. "It will be a good exercise in rhythm and rhyme."

"Come on!" Robert said. "Let's go to the river."

"That's enough for today," Jane said. "We'll continue next Sunday."

With that, Edgar and Robert bounded out of the house for the river.

Fifteen minutes later, as the two boys sat fishing on a fallen log jutting out into the James River, Edgar turned to Robert.

"Your mother is such a beautiful woman."

Robert studied his friend.

"I never think of her that way," he said, "but I see why you would say that."

***

Over the next few weeks, Poe began reading more and more poetry. At the Old Brook library, he read the works of Samuel Taylor Coleridge, Christopher Marlowe, and Robert Herrick. Then he started writing more poems of his own. As Jane had promised, the daily exercise of keeping the journal made him more aware of words, their meanings, their uses, their nuances, the way they could be arranged for differing effects, the usefulness of first lines, the purpose of closing lines. During his daily activities, he trained himself to remember the events in his daily life. Then, each night after dinner, with great anticipation, he rushed to his journal to record them. Thanks to Jane, he was becoming a poet.

***

The years 1822 and 1823 flew past. Edgar's summers were spent with Robert and their school friends on the James River fishing, rafting, and swimming. The boys would hold swimming contests to determine who could swim the greatest distance, and, in one contest, Edgar won out over all the others by swimming a total of six miles upstream. The other boys were amazed at his swimming prowess.

Meanwhile, Edgar's foster father still carried the hope that Edgar would someday take an interest in managing the plantation. In late July of 1822, Edgar accompanied him to Norfolk to a slave auction. During the auction, Edgar met Hezekiah Reynolds, one of John's old friends and a Norfolk slave owner. At dinner that night, Reynolds told John his prize golden retriever had had a litter of pups and asked if he wanted one.

"I don't care for dogs," John said.

"What about your son?"

"He wouldn't know what to do with a dog."

"I would."

"Do you want one of the pups?"

"No!" John said.

"Please, Father."

"Oh, all right," John said.

On the journey home, John asked what he was going to call the dog.

"Reynolds! After his owner," Edgar said.

Back in Richmond, Edgar built a small doghouse, and, with the help of Amos, nurtured and cared for the animal. After a year, Reynolds had become a splendid animal and a perfect companion for the boys at the river, where they would spend endless hours fetching and retrieving balls and tree limbs from the river.

***

At Old Brook, Poe continued to develop his boxing skills. Richard Bryson, the headmaster, had been a prize fighter as a young man and took a special interest in Poe's boxing skills. He would spend hours as Edgar's sparring partner, coaching him on defensive moves, counter moves, and tactics for winning a boxing match.

"Keep that left hand in your opponent's face," he would say, "then when you see an opening, come in with the other hand to make a knockout punch. You have quick, nimble hands and a solid right hook."

Each year, Bryson would stage boxing matches between students in varying weight classes. Each year, Poe would win not only his own weight class, but sometimes classes above his own against opponents who were much older and heavier. During one sparring session, when Poe, who weighted only 130 pounds, knocked out an opponent who was well over 200, the coach was amazed.

"My! My!" Bryson said. "That's a vicious right hand you've got."

***

On January 19, 1824, Edgar celebrated his fifteenth birthday. For the occasion, Frances and Jane threw a party at Moldavia complete with a huge chocolate cake, colorful garlands, and gifts. In attendance were Robert and Edgar's friends from Old Brook as well as friends of both the Allan and Stanard families. Once festivities were ended, Jane and Edgar retired to her study to discuss writing and poetry. As part of the session, she read cantos from Lord Byron's *Childe Harold's Pilgrimage.*

"In his poetry, Byron has a clearer, more magnificent vision than all of the other romantics," she said.

"Yes," Edgar said. "His words seem to reach deeper into the heart."

"Did you know that the leaders of the Greek rebellion have asked Byron to join their fight for independence against the Ottoman Turks?"

"How do you know this?"

"I receive the London newspapers every week off the packet ships. The news is over a month old, but some news is better than no news. Let me show you."

She arose from her seat and went to a nearby stack of newspapers. All were from London. The *Daily Times*, the *Telegraph*, the *Daily Mail,* and others. After shuffling through several, she withdrew one.

"Look at this!"

It was the *London Telegraph* dated December 12, 1823. The headline read: "Greek rebels seek Byron's support in fight for Independence."

Jane took the paper and started reading aloud.

"During a recent visit to Italy, George Gordon Lord Byron, the vaunted poet and well-known rake, met with leaders of the Greek rebellion and praised their efforts to liberate their country from the iron hand of the Ottoman empire.

"Byron, a well-known philhellene, told the warriors: 'No cause could be more noble than to rescue Greece from the grasp of the heathen Turks. Greece represents the cradle of western civilization and that legacy should remain forever free of tyranny and heathen control.'"

Edgar looked up from the newspaper.

"Has Byron accepted?"

"Not yet," Jane said. "London's literary community is holding its breath waiting to hear his answer."

"Where is Byron now?"

"He's in the Lake District of England with his mistress, Countess Teresa Guiccioli. No one has heard from him for a month."

Poe stared wistfully off into space.

"What a noble undertaking! What on God's earth could be more romantic? A famous poet going to Greece to fight for their independence."

"Oh yes," Jane said. "The glory, the majesty of such an enterprise. If Byron accepts, it will be forever remembered. He will not only have become a great poet but a hero to the English-speaking world."

***

Thirty minutes later, Edgar and Robert were at the river, and Poe, using a long stick as a play sword, was pretending to be Lord Byron. Standing poised, his play sword at ready, Poe pretended to be Byron addressing Greek soldiers before leading them into battle.

"I, Lord Byron, have come to lead the noble Greeks against the savage heathens who have been ruling your land."

Then he turned, pointed his play sword toward the tall bushes along the river's edge, and shouted, "Charge!"

Suddenly, he turned and limped toward the bushes, stabbing, thrusting, and slashing the greenery with his play sword.

"Die! You heathen dogs! At the point of my sword, you shall die an inglorious death! The glory of Greece must be restored. The land of Plato, Aristotle, and Sophocles must be liberated. Die like the heathen dogs you are. Long live Greece!"

Out of breath, he stopped.

Robert, who had been watching this display of heroic pretense, turned to him.

"Why are you limping like that?"

"Lord Byron has a crippled right foot."

"Oh," Robert replied.

***

The following Sunday, when the Allan family carriage arrived at Moldavia, Poe saw Jane waiting at the mansion door. Quickly, he jumped out of the carriage and rushed to her.

"Did Lord Byron accept the rebel leaders' offer?"

"Yes!" she replied. "He has committed his life and fortune to the Greek cause. He has left England for Greece to join the fight."

"Hallelujah!" Poe said, raising his fist in triumph. "Long live Lord Byron and the glory of Greece."

"Come on in; we'll read about it."

Over the next hour, Jane and Poe were poring over the London newspapers for the latest developments on Lord Byron.

"Here's one!" Jane said.

She began reading excerpts:

"With this single act, the name George Gordon Lord Byron, already the most famous of romantic poets, will become forever enshrined in the annals of our great national heroes."

After she finished the article, she looked to the London newspapers for another headline.

"Here's another!"

She picked up the next newspaper

Before she started reading, she turned to Edgar.

"Listen to this."

She began reading aloud.

"For what greater cause could a romantic poet commit their life? Nothing could be more noble than liberating Greece from the Ottoman savages.

"To fulfill his commitment, Byron has set sail from England to Greece to join the Greek rebellion. He is expected to arrive in Genoa, Italy, the staging area for rebel operations, on February 13."

"Hallelujah!" Poe said. "He is not only a great poet, but a true adventurer."

Once their excitement over Byron's commitment to the Greeks had ended, Jane critiqued Edgar's latest poem and commented that his sense of rhythm and rhyme was improving. When that was finished, they discussed Shakespeare's sonnets; Jane gave an impromptu lecture on iambic pentameter, and finally, Jane pasted a map of Europe on a blackboard in her study so she and Poe could track Lord Byron's trek across Europe to Greece.

When darkness fell that afternoon, the usual signal it was time for the Allan family to return home, Jane and Edgar were still in her study discussing literature and poetry.

Frances, who had been sitting nearby listening to their conversation and trying to entertain herself, told Edgar it was time to go home.

"Just a little longer, Mother."

Frances did not push the matter.

Ten minutes later, John appeared.

"Edgar. It is time for us to depart."

"Can I talk to Jane a bit longer?"

"No! It's dark and I have some matters to attend to at home," the foster father said

Edgar, annoyed, turned to Jane.

"I'm sorry. I must be going now."

***

In the carriage, on the way home, John Allan questioned Edgar's relationship with Jane.

"It's not natural for a teenage boy to spend so much time with a grown woman. What's the purpose of it?"

"She's a poet," Frances said. "And a good one. Eddie wants to write poems. She's trying to help him learn."

"Poems? Poetry? What a bucketful of pig swill. Total idiotic trash. Can a poem buy you anything? What is a poem good for?"

"They express thoughts," Edgar said. "They pass culture from generation to generation. They are an art form…"

John interrupted.

"Jane Stanard is putting crazy ideas in your head. I was hoping someday you would be able to run the plantation. Writing poems is not contributing to that goal."

"Father! You must allow me to lead my life the way I choose."

"You little ingrate! Remember! You are not adopted. I can have you removed from my house any time I like."

"You never let me forget that, do you?"

"Nor do I intend to."

***

April 3, 1824. I am in love with Helen. Beautiful in both mind and body, she fascinates every fiber of my being. Unlike most women, whose minds could best be used as haylofts, Jane is a deceptively wise woman who feels quite comfortable exploring the realms of gold. The sudden shifts of her mind, like a skate impulsively changing directions in mid-flight, is a spectacle to behold. From Goethe to chemistry to astronomy to iambic pentameter, her mind traverses a vast universe of separate compartments. And the sheer wonder of her body. Exquisite bonbons, beautifully sloping neck, high firm lilies resting magnificently, not too large, not too small. Oh, to be her physician and have the right to explore every nook and cranny of her pulchritudinous form, including that abiding mystery at her thighs.

***

Over the next month, the Allan family was at Moldavia every Sunday. The moment the family carriage would arrive, Edgar would quickly exit and dash into the mansion to meet Jane. Once inside, they probed through the London newspapers for the latest on Lord Byron's fight for Greek independence. Once they had gone through the entire stack of newspapers, they would select the articles they wanted to read. Then Jane would begin reading excerpts.

"Here we go!" Jane said, then she began reading.

"February 19, 1824. Lord Byron recruits army, marches on Cephalonia. Article says: 'Lord Byron and his army of 3,000 mercenaries have surrounded the island city of Cephalonia and are demanding unconditional surrender from the Turkish forces trapped inside.'

"February 26, 1824. Byron's Troops Claim Victory in Cephalonia. Article says: 'Two days ago, Lord Byron and his combined army of mercenaries and partisans claimed a resounding victory at this island city after routing Turkish forces and driving them into the sea.'

"March 9, 1824: Lord Byron's Army Claims Victory at Vasiliki! Article reads: 'Lord Byron's seemingly invincible army marched victoriously into the besieged city of Vasiliki today after a combination of withering artillery fire and frontal assaults sent the heathen Turks fleeing back to their ships.'

"April 6, 1824. 'Lord Byron's Army Awaiting Reinforcements!'" read the *London Gazette* headline.

"After resounding victories in the Turkish-occupied cities of Cephalonia and Vasiliki, Lord Byron's army is now bivouacked at Missolonghi awaiting to join a rebel force of 10,000 soldiers under the command of General Alexandros Ypsilantis. Once united, the combined armies are expected to launch a major attack on the Turkish-held City of Missolonghi."

Jane, after finishing the final article, looked up from the newspapers.

"What a great victory for Lord Byron and the western world," Edgar said.

Jane looked away. Her eyes began to fill with tears.

"Why are you weeping?"

"Somehow I sense that Byron's fate will be connected to my own death."

"Why do you say that?"

"Just a woman's intuition."

***

On Friday afternoon of the following week, when Edgar arrived home from school, Frances met him at the door.

"I have horrible news!" she said.

"What is it, Mother?"

"William Stanard is dead. He was killed in a runaway carriage accident in town."

"Oh, no!" Edgar said. "I feel so bad for Jane and Robert."

"Can you take a dress to Jane for me? She wants to borrow a black taffeta dress to wear to the funeral."

Ten minutes later, Tea Cake, Poe, and the black dress, neatly folded and encased in protective wrap, were in the family carriage headed to Moldavia.

Upon arrival, Edgar, dress in hand, went to the door. Jane was waiting. Edgar could see she has been weeping.

"You have my most sincere condolences," he said.

"Thank you!" she said, taking the dress. "Can you come help me bring some wine up from the cellar?"

"Where is Robert?"

"He's visiting friends in town."

Five minutes later, Jane, wine cellar key in hand with Edgar close behind, was going down the mansion's backstairs to the wine cellar. After going down two flights, she stopped in front of a heavy wooden door. Once she unlocked it, Poe dutifully followed her inside. Then she relocked the door. Poe wondered why.

John Isaac Jones

Moments later, they were walking among long rows of wine bottles stacked neatly on racks on either side. Finally, at the end of the rows, near the rear of the cellar, she stopped and turned to him. For a long moment, she gazed into his eyes, then kissed him on the lips and began unbuttoning his shirt.

"I've been longing to do this for some time," she said. "Now I'm free to do so."

Moments later, Poe's shirt was off. Jane's lips made a trailing course of kisses across his chest, his neck, and finally, his lips. He could hear her breath coming hard and fast on his cheek. With each successive kiss, he could feel his need rising. Somehow, he was unable to believe what was happening, but he made no attempt to resist. Suddenly, the kisses came to an end and Jane took his hand.

"Come with me."

Then she led him through another door to another part of the wine cellar.

"These are old servant's quarters in here," she said. "There is a bed."

Once inside, she closed the door, then she knelt on the floor to remove his shoes and stockings, then his pantaloons and undergarments. Once he was undressed, she sat him on the edge of the bed, then began to undress herself. As she removed one garment after another, Edgar was now viewing the hips, the shoulders, breasts, and thighs he had dreamed of so many, many nights. Once she was naked, she crawled into bed and beckoned to him.

"I want you to be as my husband. I want you to surrender to me."

Moments later, Poe was in the bed joining his body to hers in amorous congress.

***

April 16, 1824. On this day, Helen awakened a dark mystery which had been hiding all these years in the hinterlands of my soul. Oh, great wonders of the universe, but dreams do come true. The beautiful lover of my fantasies seduced me into her arms today. In that single moment, we

132

were Tristan and Isolde, Romeo and Juliet, Lancelot and Guinevere. I shall forever remember this day.

***

At William Stanard's funeral two days later, John Allan and Edgar served as pallbearers while Frances remained at Jane's side to comfort her. After the services ended, Frances accompanied Jane back to the family carriage.

As they walked, Jane suddenly stopped and began taking deep breaths.

"What's wrong?" Frances said.

"I've got to rest a moment. I feel faint."

"I've never seen you like this. There has to be some reason."

Jane paused before she spoke

"When I was born, one of the chambers of my heart was smaller than the others. Doctors said it would not be a problem while I was young, but as I grew older, it would begin to affect me."

"Is there anything I can do?"

"There is nothing anyone can do. I must live with it."

"Take my arm," Frances said. "I'll help you to your carriage."

***

A week passed. Then, one Saturday morning, Frances watched a carriage pull up at the front entrance at New Dundonald. Immediately, she recognized the driver as Jeremiah, a slave at Moldavia. His passenger was Ruth, another slave at the plantation. When Frances opened the door, she could see the woman had been weeping.

"Ruth? What's wrong?"

"Oh, Mrs. Allan. Miss Jane is sick unto death. She has asked that you and your son come to her bedside."

"What's wrong?"

"I don't know, but you've got to hurry. She's not long for this earth."

***

Thirty minutes later, Frances and Edgar were at Jane's bedside. The moment Poe saw her, his heart flew into his mouth. Her face was drawn and deathly pale. There were dark circles under her eyes and her breath was labored. A nurse waited nearby.

"Oh, I'm so happy to see you two," Jane said. "Edgar, will you go up and check the London newspapers and see where Byron is? I have been too sick to get out of bed. The newspapers are on the top shelf beside the works of John Milton."

"I'll find them."

"What has happened to you?" Frances said.

"The physician says the problem with my heart is manifesting itself greater than ever before. He says I must remain quiet and undisturbed or I will surely die."

Moments later, Edgar returned to her bedside.

"Where's Lord Byron?" Jane asked.

Poe inhaled, then shook his head sadly.

"Terrible news! Lord Byron contracted malaria fever and died while fighting at Missolonghi."

"Oh no!" she said. "I feared as much. Now I must lay down the mantle of my own life."

Suddenly, the nurse stepped forward.

"I'm sorry, but you must be going now."

Frances turned to Jane.

"Can I take a lock of your hair?"

"Yes! There are scissors in the bedside table."

Once Frances had the lock of hair, Jane turned to Poe and offered her hand. Edgar took it.

"Someday you'll be a great poet."

"I hope so."

With that, the nurse stepped forward.

"You must be leaving now."

***

The following morning, the slave Ruth appeared in a carriage to New Dundonald a second time. When Frances, with Edgar behind her, opened the door, both knew the news was going to be horrible.

"Miss Jane died in her sleep last night," the slave said, wiping away tears. "The funeral will be day after tomorrow."

"Thank you!" Frances said.

Once Ruth was gone, Edgar turned to his mother.

"She said Lord Byron's death would be related to her own. I wonder how she knew."

***

Two days later, Edgar, Frances, and John attended Jane's funeral at St. Paul's Church in south Richmond. Once services were finished, they watched solemnly as pallbearers carried Jane's coffin up a muddy hillside to a crest overlooking the James River.

"Ashes to ashes.... dust to dust," said the minister, a tall, gray-haired man in a black frock, as he threw a handful of dirt into the open grave. "All things that live must one day come to an end."

Frances and Edgar wept like little children as they watched their friend's remains being lowered into the cold, damp grave.

***

That night, back at New Dundonald, Poe poured out his grief in his journal.

April 21, 1824. Never shall I forget the beautiful Helen. She of the splendid mind, the exquisite face, and gracious manner. The majesty of her loveliness embodied the glory of Greece and the grandeur of Rome. As if it were a dream, the Gods sent her to me to serve as mentor. I shall forever remember her for not only instilling in me my love of poetry, but for awakening my manhood.

11
Widening Rift

The deaths of both Jane and William Stanard over a period of only three weeks changed the lives of every member of the Allan family. First, Frances lost her lifelong friend and soulmate. There would be no more Sunday visits to Moldavia to share personal secrets, chit-chat about family and friends, and remember their childhood years together. John no longer had his business-savvy friend to discuss politics, share brandy and cigars, and loan out slaves at planting and harvest time. Then there was Edgar. When Jane's father arrived the following week to take Robert back to Boston, the fifteen-year-old had now lost not only his closest friend, but his literary mentor and confidante as well. Finally, the most far-reaching impact of their deaths was that Edgar would be spending more time with his foster father.

***

In early May of 1824, Edgar finished his final term at Old Brook. At the graduation ceremony, the headmaster praised Poe for his "hard work, first-rate academics, and his excellence in boxing, debate, and ancient languages. Master Poe has a bright future ahead of him."

In the carriage, on the return trip to New Dundonald, John turned to his foster son.

"As I have told you many times, the main reason I brought you into this family was to have an heir. Now that your education is complete, I want you to start working with Josias and learn plantation operations."

"Father, I want to further my education by going to college."

"I see no reason for you to attend college. I only finished level seven in elementary school. I have needed no further education."

"But, Father…"

John held up his hand for Edgar to remain quiet.

"Tomorrow, Josias and I are going to Norfolk to the slave auction and I want you to accompany us. You must learn to measure the value of a slave so you can buy them at a profit. A successful plantation operation begins with good slaves."

Poe shook his head.

"Father, I fear that my heart will not allow me to learn the business of buying and selling human beings. I see all people as living, breathing creatures who have feelings and want to be loved and accepted."

"That's going to change," John said. "If you refuse to learn to manage this plantation, I no longer want you at New Dundonald."

Immediately, Frances turned to him.

"How can you say such a thing? He has expressed to you he has no interest in running the plantation. He wants to be a poet and a writer."

"I don't have room for a poet at New Dundonald."

"Edgar is not one of your slaves," Frances continued. "He's been a member of this family for twelve years. I'm not sure about you, but I love Edgar."

John glanced sullenly at her, then turned to Edgar.

"You be ready to go with me and Josias to Norfolk on Monday morning."

***

That night, after he was in bed, Edgar heard loud, angry voices coming from his foster parents' bedroom. Quickly, he slipped out of bed, went across the hallway, and eavesdropped under the door.

"No!" Frances was saying. "You shall not come into my bed. All the hurt and misery I suffered in England has now returned with this new revelation."

"I didn't know Rosalee was pregnant," John said. "We left England in such a hurry."

"And you've been paying $300 a year to support this bastard child?"

Long silence.

"I didn't want you to know," John said. "I had hoped you could forgive me that unfortunate incident. I have tried to make amends for my mistake."

"I did forgive you. I felt, once I did that, we could be happy again. Now I learn about this."

"I can't change what has happened."

"So many times, I have dreamed of being a mother to your child. Now you have gone and had a bastard child with that slut in England."

"The fault is not mine if you are unable to conceive a child."

Frances was quietly weeping.

"I have explained to you it was a mistake," John continued. "In my heart, it's you I love. Please forgive me."

"Those are only empty words. You do not truly feel that in your heart. Go back to your own bed and go to sleep. I loathe your touch."

"Then grant me a divorce. I want a wife who will share my bed."

"I will do no such thing. You have not suffered enough. I want you to be hurt to the depths I have been. Now get away from me!"

Long pause.

"Hereafter, I want my own bedroom," she said.

"Then you shall have it. Perhaps that will give me new freedoms."

Moments later, Edgar could hear John's footsteps plodding across the floor to his own bed.

Long silence.

"Who was it that told you Rosalee and I were in the office?"

"You'll never know that, so quit asking. It is my secret and shall be for all time."

"Someday I'll discover who it was."

"Blow out the candle and go to sleep."

Seconds later, under the door, Poe could see the light go out in the room.

***

The following morning, John, Josias, and Edgar were in the family carriage heading eastward to Norfolk. Following behind them were two wagons, one loaded with seven slaves to be sold and another containing food, clothing, equipment, and supplies for the trip. Around nightfall, the group arrived in Norfolk and took rooms in a hotel while the slaves were quartered in holding pens at the auction house.

At the auction the next morning, Poe followed behind as John and his slave master inspected the rows of slaves. Men, women, and children were chained like dogs to wooden platforms. Once the auction began, bidding was fierce. When one slave, a young, coal-black male with broad shoulders and a narrow waist, was put on the block, three plantation owners launched into a fierce bidding war and the price soared to over $1,800. When one owner suddenly jumped the bid to $2,000, the others withdrew. By the end of the day, John had sold all seven slaves he had brought to the auction and purchased five new ones.

That night, during dinner in the hotel dining room, John asked Edgar for his thoughts about the auction.

"It makes me sick to my stomach. You should be ashamed to participate in such a barbaric practice."

John looked knowingly at Josias.

***

Over the months of May and June, John and Frances became strangers in their own home. After house slaves moved Frances' bedroom furnishings – bedstead, clothes and personal items – across the hallway adjacent to Edgar's room, the husband and wife began ignoring one another. John, who now spent the majority of his time with Josias, ate in the main dining room while Frances took meals in her new bedroom. On weekend nights, John would arrive late to the mansion, often tipsy, sometimes staggering from drink. John and Frances had become like ships passing in the night.

***

One night, a month after the bedroom move, Edgar was sound asleep in his room when he heard a rap on the door. Quickly, he got out of bed, lit a candle, and went to the door.

"Who is it?"

"It's me… your mother."

"Mother, what do you want?"

"Would you like for me to give you a warm bath?"

"Mother! We talked about this. I am fifteen now. I'm too old for you to be giving me baths."

"Then can I come in and talk?"

Edgar opened the door.

Once inside, she took a seat at a small writing desk. For a long moment, she stared at him, then suddenly burst into sobs.

"Mother, what's wrong?"

"Oh, Eddie! I am so lonely. No one to touch, to talk to, to share my life with. Now that Jane and my father are gone, I have no one to turn to but you."

"Mother! What's happening to you?"

"Your father's infidelity has destroyed my life. All the values I was taught to believe in as a child – love, marriage and family – have all been shorn away. There are no foundations in my life now. I feel threatened at every turn."

"You and Father cannot reconcile your differences?"

"We're finished. I have much love to give, but nowhere to give it. I have hands to give love, there is no one to receive it. My soul is filled with love, but there is nowhere for it to go.

"Oh, Mother! I can't bear to see you like this."

"I feel I should tell you something horrible."

"What?"

"I think I'm losing my mind."

"Oh, Mother! You're just distraught."

"It's far more than that."

Then she reached in her pocket and withdrew a green medicine bottle containing the lock of Jane Stanard's hair.

"I want you to have this. I know how much Jane meant to you."

Edgar took the bottle.

"Mother, why are you doing this?"

"Because something terrible is happening to me."

"Mother! You're overwrought."

"No. I'm slipping away."

"Mother. I really must sleep. I'm going to the fields again tomorrow with Father and Josias."

"Then I'll be leaving."

She got up to go.

"Are you certain you wouldn't like for me to give you a warm bath?"

"I am certain!"

"Good night!" she said.

"Good night."

Moments later, Edgar heard her footsteps in the hallway, then the closing of her bedroom door.

***

The following morning, Edgar was back in the fields with John and Josias in the family carriage as it trundled over the narrow dirt road that skirted the plantation grounds. Now, in mid-June, the tobacco fields were a sprawling sea of lush greenery across the plantation landscape. At one point, the carriage came to a halt and Josias got out to inspect a long row of tobacco plants. For several minutes, he walked expertly among the rows, then stopped and tore away a single large tobacco leaf.

"Edgar!" he called, motioning for Poe to come to him.

Edgar dutifully left the carriage.

"Look at this," Josias said, tracing his finger across the young tobacco leaf to indicate long black streaks. "This is black shank disease. Do you see the black streaks?"

"I see them."

"These infected plants must be shorn away or the entire crop could be lost."

Moments later, they were back in the carriage, moving to a new part of the field. Finally, the carriage stopped again.

"Edgar, come with me," Josias said.

Together, they got out of the carriage and began walking among the tobacco rows.

"Here," Josias said, pointing to spaces between the tobacco plants, "is where the seeds didn't germinate because they were planted too deeply. For tobacco seeds to germinate, they need some sunlight. Do you understand?"

"I understand."

After two hours in the fields, the family carriage headed back to the mansion. As it trundled back along the narrow road to the mansion, John turned to Edgar.

"Did you learn anything from Josias's words about growing tobacco?"

Edgar looked up sullenly.

"I'm hungry. Can we hurry back to the mansion so I can make a ham sandwich?"

John looked knowingly at Josias.

***

Late that night, after Edgar was in bed, he heard a rap on his door. It was Frances.

"Edgar?"

"Yes, Mother."

"What day is it?"

"It's Tuesday."

"Can I give you a warm bath?"

"Mother, we've already discussed this."

"It would mean so much to me."

"No, Mother! For the final time, no."

For a moment, he waited. Then after several minutes, he heard her footsteps returning to her own bedroom.

An hour later, he was awakened again. Again, he went to the door.

"Edgar?"

"Yes, Mother."

"Can I give you a bath?"

"No, Mother."

A long silence.

"What day is today?"

"I've told you. It's Tuesday."

"Please let me give you a warm bath."

He did not answer.

"Please! Please allow me to bathe you."

Over the next ten minutes, he heard her sobbing outside the door, pleading that he permit her to bathe him.

"Please! Please, Edgar!" she wailed again and again. "Please allow me to bathe you."

Finally, after he failed to go to the door, he heard her footsteps returning to her own bedroom.

***

Two months passed. It was now early August and, on Monday of the following week, John and Josias were having breakfast in the mansion's main dining room.

"Tomorrow, I'm going to Roanoke with four wagonloads of furniture for a mercantile store," John said. "While I am gone, I want you to show Edgar the ledgers. Show him the columns and rows and explain how to reconcile the balance sheet. Let him do the calculations himself. I'll be back on Friday."

***

The following morning, Edgar was having breakfast in the main dining room when Dolina suddenly came rushing in.

"Mr. Edgar! Mr. Edgar!"

"Dolina! What's the matter?"

"Come quick! There something wrong with Mrs. Allan!"

Moments later, Poe was following Dolina out of the mansion into the slave quarters at the rear of the home. Inside, he saw his foster mother sitting on one of the beds.

"Mother! What are you doing?"

"I want to be a slave," she said.

"Mother! You must return to the mansion. You have your role and slaves have their role. Please come back inside with me."

"I'm staying here. We have bought, sold, raped, and abused these poor people for too many years. Now I want to be a slave. I want to know how it feels to be a slave."

"Mother! You must return to the mansion. That is your proper place."

"Do you truly believe so?"

"Yes."

Suddenly, she burst into tears.

For several moments, Edgar let her weep. Finally, she stopped and peered up at him.

"All right! If you say so."

Poe gently took her shoulders, then helped her to her feet and they started out of the slave quarters as Dolina followed

Once Edgar had returned Frances to her bedroom, he turned to Dolina.

"You must never mention this to anyone."

"I won't, Mister Edgar. I promise."

***

On the following Friday at noon, John returned from his Roanoke trip to New Dundonald. The moment he saw Josias, he asked about Edgar.

"Did you show him the books?"

"I did."

"What happened?"

"I explained each row and column of numbers as you instructed and he said he would do the calculations. When I got back, he was looking out the window."

"Had he done the calculations?"

"No."

"What had he done?"

"On the page where I requested that he make the calculations, he drew a picture of a fire-breathing dragon with huge claws and a pointed tail."

John inhaled, then shook his head in disgust.

"I'm finished with him. He is totally useless to me. His head is in the clouds. Beautiful damsels. Fire-breathing dragons. Don Quixote charging windmills. He is bleeding me dry and providing nothing in return."

"You've known that for some time. What are your plans?"

John studied his slave master.

"I'm going to get rid of him," John said finally.

"How do you intend to accomplish that?"

"I'm going to send him away to college."

"And when he returns?"

"I will not allow him to return unless it's on my terms."

For a moment, the slave master studied John, then burst out in raucous laughter.

***

Late one afternoon three days later, Edgar was reading in his room when there was a knock on the door. It was Dolina. When he opened the door, he could see she had been weeping.

"Oh, Mr. Edgar. My poor father is dying. He has asked that you come to his bedside."

Ten minutes later, Poe was seated at Amos' bedside in the slave quarters behind the mansion. Some twenty to thirty other slaves were solemnly gathered around the death bed. Edgar could see the old man was not long for this earth. Poe took his hand.

"Oh, Amos," Edgar said, tears welling in his eyes. "I want to express my gratitude for your friendship, all the animals you carved for me, and all the stories you told me about your days on the rice plantation in Norfolk."

Slowly, Amos raised his head.

"It made me happy to do it, Mister Edgar."

Amos smiled, then took a deep breath.

"Oh, Mister Edgar," he said. "It's getting dark. Real dark. I can see the sun setting in the west."

A short pause as he stared up at the ceiling, then he turned back to Edgar, who was still holding his hand.

"May God bless you and keep you," Amos said, then his body slumped over in the bed. For a long moment, Poe could feel the old man's hand tighten its grasp on his, then suddenly go limp.

"Oh, dear Lord!" Dolina wailed. "My father has gone to heaven."

***

August 11, 1824. Today I watched the slaves bury Amos in the cemetery behind the field slaves' dining hall. As his body, encased in a crude pine box, was lowered into the grave, all of the other slaves, some sixty or seventy strong, gathered around the grave and, to the pounding beat of native African drums, melded their voices together in a single farewell song. As I listened to their mournful cries, I would hear the glory, the pain, the grief, the collective voice of Africa screaming out for mercy for all the years of persecution and enslavement. I have always sensed a deep spirituality in black people. Today, I witnessed its essence.

***

The following morning, when Edgar came down the stairs, he saw John and Josias having breakfast in the main dining room.

"Morning, Edgar," John said.

"Morning, Father. I fear something terrible is happening to Mother."

John gazed at him for a moment, then calmly took another sip of coffee.

"She is no concern of mine. She has requested to be alone and I have honored her wishes."

"She's not herself. She continues to ask me what day it is when I have already told her five times. She sits in her room all day staring out the window and mumbling to herself."

John shook his head.

"The problem is not mine."

"She is your wife."

"Not anymore. She is in this house, but she's not my wife."

"How can you say that?"

John stared at him for a moment, then changed the subject.

"Sit down! Have a cup of coffee. I want to talk to you about another matter."

Edgar took a seat. A slave poured coffee for him.

"I'm very disappointed in you," John began.

"Father, what do you ask of me?"

"I have asked you to be my heir, but you have shown no interest."

"I'm not naturally inclined to plantation work."

"That's because your head is filled with all of this balderdash about poetry. Beautiful, dying young women. Shadowy figures with daggers. Nightly encounters with ghosts. Can you not understand all of this poetry business is totally without worth?"

"You have no appreciation of language."

Anger flashed across John's face.

"Don't tell me what I have appreciation for. I took you into my home and gave you a life you could never have imagined otherwise. If it had not been for me, you'd be living on the street or in some state-run institution."

"I appreciate all the things you have done for me."

John was not finished.

"You spend far too much time eating the bread of idleness. And your moods are mostly sour and brooding. There seems to be no happiness in your heart."

"Even though I'm not a spectacle of joy every moment does not signify that I am ill or depressed."

"You're wasting your time and mine," John said. "Reading Don Quixote and all the kissy-kissy romance books from Walter Scott. All the while, you're spending my money and giving me nothing in return."

A long pause.

"Father, it appears that we are at an irretrievable impasse," Poe said. "What shall you have me do?"

"I've made a decision."

"What decision is that?"

"I'm going to send you to college."

Poe was taken aback by the words.

"College? The University of Virginia?"

"Yes. When the new school year opens in January, I want you to enroll."

Poe peered at him.

"When did you change your mind?"

"After reconsideration, I've decided you should have a good education."

"Oh, Father! That makes me so happy. Thank you so much."

***

The next four months flew past. The tobacco harvest, Thanksgiving, and Christmas came and went quickly. John hired a live-in nurse for Frances, who had become a hermit, hiding in her room day after day, mumbling to herself.

On the morning of January 2, 1826, seventeen days shy of his sixteenth birthday, Poe was in the mansion foyer ready to set off to the University of Virginia. His bags were packed, his credentials were ready, and he was anxious for the new adventure to begin.

John was waiting to say his farewell.

"Before I go," Edgar said, "I want to say goodbye to Mother."

Seconds later, he was upstairs in Frances's room. When he opened the door, she was seated in front of the room's bay window, gazing down on the plantation grounds and mumbling to herself.

"I told her she should never have married him. My mother said he was given to drink, gambling, and loose women. I told her she was making a mistake when she accepted his proposal...."

"Hello!" Edgar said.

Frances turned at the sound.

"Dear brother Uriah! What are you doing here?"

"Mother, I'm not your brother. I'm your son Edgar."

"Oh, I'm so glad to see you, Uriah. How is Henrietta? Is she still teaching school?"

Edgar did not know how to respond.

"Mother, I'm going off to college. I will not be seeing you for a few months. Perhaps even longer."

"College? Oh, dear brother, you're much too old for college."

"Mother…"

He stopped, at a loss for words. Then he strode across the room and kissed her on the forehead.

"I'm sorry," he said. "I have no words for this."

He turned to go.

"Uriah! Where are you going? Come sit with me and we shall chat."

"Bye, Mother!" he said sadly.

He turned and left the room.

A few minutes later, back in the mansion foyer, Edgar was saying goodbye to his foster father.

"Here is a bank draft for $300 to deposit in the Commonwealth bank in Charlottesville. I am expecting that sum to cover your expenses for the first year."

Edgar took the bank draft, examined it, then secured it in one of his bags.

"Thank you, Father!"

For a long moment, Edgar stared at his foster father, afraid of the question he was about to ask.

"What do you intend to do with Mother?"

John did not answer at first.

"You know she's mad as a hatter," he said finally.

"I know."

"I'm going to keep her here. It is cheaper to keep her here with a nurse than to put her in one of these state-run homes. I really don't want the world to know that my wife has lost her sense of reason."

Edgar nodded solemnly.

"Don't you think you should be going?" John said. "Your transport is waiting."

"Oh, yes! Well, thank you again, Father. I shall be writing. Good-bye!"

"Good-bye!" John said.

Edgar gathered his bags and started to the door. As he strode down the walkway to the waiting carriage, he suddenly heard the mansion door slam behind him. For a moment, he stopped and wondered why. Then, thinking it was nothing important, he continued down the walkway to the waiting carriage.

12
Rowdy Row

By the spring of the 1825, Thomas Jefferson, stateman, former president, author of the Declaration of Independence, and one of the most influential men of his time, was in his declining years. At age 86, he told friends he was going to put the madness of Washington politics behind him and return to education, his first love. Ten years earlier, he and a band of vested associates had bought 200 acres of land at Charlottesville, a farming community high in the Blue Ridge Mountains of southern Virginia, to establish a university. The following year, he organized a campaign in the legislature for a university charter and, once it passed, he set about designing the buildings, planning the curriculum, and hiring instructors. When it finally opened in June of 1825, Jefferson appointed himself the university's first rector. Upon assuming the position, Jefferson told a trusted friend, "Of all my accomplishments, the one for which I hope to be best remembered is as founder of the University of Virginia."

***

Now, in early January of 1826, the university was in its second year and, as rector, Jefferson insisted that he personally approve each new candidate for enrollment. On one particular morning, the interviews had been particularly tiresome. He had interviewed six candidates and accepted only two. Two of the candidates were woefully unprepared for higher education and the other two had had felonious run-ins with the law. One, in fact, had been charged with armed robbery.

When Jefferson's assistant Emily, a smallish, early twenties, dark-haired woman, came into his office that morning with names of the latest candidates, he looked up at her.

"How many more candidates?"

"Four."

"Do any of them look promising?"

"I wouldn't know, sir. I have not seen their credentials."

"Very well. Send in the next one."

Moments later, Emily was back in the waiting room adjacent to Jefferson's office. She called the next name on her list.

"Poe. Edgar Allan Poe."

Moments later, inside the rector's office, the sixteen-year-old Poe stood at attention in front of the former president.

"Have a seat," Jefferson said. "I am perusing your application."

As he waited, Poe studied the former president. A slight man, maybe five feet, eight inches, Jefferson had a thin, serious face, piercing blue eyes, and long gray hair that hung about his shoulders.

Finally, Jefferson looked up.

"I see you've studied history, social systems, governments, and languages. Especially Latin and Greek."

"That is correct."

"Then I assume you feel you are qualified to answer my questions?"

"I hope so."

"Then I shall proceed. Who was Caesar's counterpart in *Plutarch's Lives*?"

"Alexander the Great."

"Who famous poet did Tacitus write about?"

"Homer."

"Conjugate the Latin verb amicus."

"Singular. *Amico, amici, amicus, amicum.* Plural. *amici, amicorum, amicis, amicos.*"

"Very good. What was the famous book written by Pliny?"

"Pliny the younger?"

Jefferson laughed. "Pliny the elder."

"That would be *Naturalis Historia*."

"Which of Keats poems were written under a mulberry tree?"

"'Ode to a Nightingale.'"

Over the next fifteen minutes, Jefferson continued asking questions about astronomy, philosophy, mathematics, Greek drama, and Roman history. Once finished, he studied Poe for a long moment.

"I'm impressed!" he said. "You have an excellent grounding for higher education."

"Thank you, sir!"

Jefferson arose from his chair, walked around the desk, and offered his hand.

"Welcome aboard!" he said, shaking Poe's hand. "It is candidates of your caliber we're seeking here at the university. So many students who apply here are the offspring of wealthy, spoiled aristocrats who feel they are privileged. Too often, this leads to sloth and intellectual laziness. You are truly a breath of fresh air."

***

An hour later, Poe was in the registrar's office to pay for his expenses. The bursar was a stocky, sallow-faced man in his early forties with a thick mustache and glasses.

"Student housing ranges in price from $25 to $18 for the four-month term. East, South, and North Range rooms are the expensive ones at $25, while West Range rooms run $18 a term."

"What's the difference?"

"There is no difference in the rooms."

"So why the price difference?"

"Students in the West Range have a reputation for unruliness."

"And they're $18 for a semester?"

"Plus $12 for rental of the furniture."

"Furniture rental?"

"Some students have been known to burn the furniture for firewood."

"I would never do that."

"If you want the room, you must pay for use of the furniture."

"Oh, all right!"

The bursar prepared to add up Poe's bill.

"Let's see," he said. "We have a room and furniture at $30, $100 for four courses, and $80 for dining hall privileges. That's a total of $210."

"Dining hall privileges are $80 for a semester?"

The bursar nodded.

"I hadn't counted on that."

"You can pay for half of the term, then pay the second half when due."

"That's what I'll do," Edgar said.

"Then, presently, you owe $184. The remaining $40 for continued dining hall privileges will be due on February 28."

"That's fine."

Moments later, the bursar took Poe's bank draft, then turned to an assistant.

"Stephen! Will you show Mr. Poe to his dormitory room?"

***

Ten minutes later, Stephen and Poe were strolling across the university grounds.

"Where is your room?" the assistant asked.

"No. 13 Range West."

"That's rowdy row."

"Rowdy row? How did it get such a name?"

"Students residing in that section have a reputation for brawling, gambling, and taking intoxication liquors."

"It is all I can afford."

"Then you have no choice."

Moments later, they arrived at the dormitory building. In front of them stood a massive, rectangular brick structure. Once they entered the rectangle, Poe could see that all of the dormitories had been built along four separate walls of the rectangle and looked out on an expansive grassy area in the center. The green expanse was some seventy yards long and thirty yards wide at the center.

"This is the college lawn," Stephen said, indicating the grassy area.

"What's it used for?"

"On warm days, students like to sit in the grass to study or just relax. Some students like to go there for picnics. Mr. Jefferson believes that a love of nature is part of a good education."

Moments later, Poe and the bursar's assistant were walking along the colonnaded walkway in the Range West section of the building.

"Ah! Here we are at number 13!" Stephen said.

Poe opened the door. It was a sparse, unadorned room with a small bed, a writing desk with a straight-back chair, a fireplace, and a wash basin.

"The dining hall is in the building on the other side," Stephen said. "The library and rotunda are adjacent."

Poe thanked him then went inside.

***

Thirty minutes later, Edgar was moving his trunk from the college storage area into his dormitory room. Once his belongings were situated, he decided to explore the campus. The moment he exited the door, he saw another student, a ruddy-faced teenager with blue eyes and a shock of unruly blonde hair, coming out of No. 14, the adjacent dormitory room.

"Hello!" the other student said. "Aren't you Edgar Poe? From Richmond?"

Edgar turned. He recognized the face.

"I remember you at Old Brook," he said. "Your name is Luther Riddle. Your father owns a tavern in Richmond."

"That's right. At Old Brook, you were the best boxer in the school. Are you headed to the dining hall?"

"Yes."

"I'll walk with you."

Moments later, as they strolled, Luther explained he was in his second term and hated college. During his first term, he had failed to pass Greek.

"I only came to college because my father insisted. He said all he had ever been was a saloon keeper and he wanted me to have opportunities never afforded to him. I would rather be waiting tables at the tavern than listening to some stuffy professor talk about Caesar and his campaign in Gaul. Oh God! You could never know how I struggle with Greek."

"Maybe I can help you," Poe said. "I'm quite proficient in the language."

"You think you could help me?"

"Sure."

***

Ten minutes later, they stepped into the dining hall. It was alive with the voices of students scattered about in groups. First, they went through the cafeteria serving line, bought ham sandwiches, then proceeded to look for a table. Luther's eyes scanned the area, then, in the corner, he spotted a group of three other students.

"Let's sit over here with the Roanoke boys."

As they approached the table, Poe studied the group. At the head of the table was a tall, gangly youth, obviously older than the other two, wearing a three-cornered hat and a shabby shirt. He was clean shaven and had a deep scar, which ran from the bottom of his right eye to the tip of his chin. He was eating a bowl of beef stew. To his left sat a medium-built, light-haired youth wearing a brown leather vest. To his right was a dark-haired, chubby youth with a round face and bulging jowls.

As they took a seat, Luther spoke to the blonde-haired youth.

"Afternoon, Turner!"

"Howdy, Luther," the other student replied.

Quiet settled across the table as Edgar and Luther took a seat and began to unwrap their sandwiches. By this time, the student in the three-cornered hat had finished his beef stew.

"Luther!" he said. "Who is your friend?"

"His name is Poe. Edgar Poe. He's in Range West."

Luther turned to Edgar.

"Edgar! I want you to meet Jack Blow."

"Hello!"

Then Luther turned to the others.

"This is Turner Dixon," he said, indicating the youth in the leather vest. "And this is Dabney Matthews."

Poe acknowledged their presence with polite hellos.

Suddenly, a snarl crossed the face of Jack Blow.

"Poe! What happened to your hair? Looks like somebody gave you a haircut with a hay baler."

Turner and Dabney laughed.

"I've noticed nothing amiss with my hair."

"I've seen better haircuts on stray dogs."

"I didn't come here to be insulted," Poe said.

"Who's insulting you?" Jack said. "I'm just making conversation. Where you from, Poe?"

"Richmond."

"Richmond? All they got in Richmond is stray dogs and whores."

"You are nobody if you are not from Roanoke," Dabney said.

Jack Blow turned to him.

"Shut up! I'm doing the talking."

Dabney pulled back.

"I was in Richmond once," Jack Blow continued. "I almost beat a man to death in a bar there one night after he cut me with a knife. See this scar?"

Edgar did not respond.

"Poe! I am talking to you. I asked you if you see this scar?"

"I see it."

"Since then, I never liked anybody from Richmond."

"Sorry for your misfortune."

A pause.

"Poe! You ever had the living daylights beat out of you?"

"Not recently."

"Well, just watch your step. I am the man that runs things around Range West."

"I have no intention of encroaching on your powers."

"What's the word you used?" Jack Blow said.

"He called you a roach," said Dabney.

Fresh anger crossed Jack Blow's face.

"You want me to cut your throat?"

"I meant no harm," Poe said. "What is meant was that… if you are the leader at Range West, I will not challenge you."

"You just remember that!"

Satisfied, Jack Blow stood up to leave.

"Come on, boys! Let's go!"

Instantly, the other two were on their feet.

"See you later, Luther," Jack Blow said. "Tell your friend Poe to watch himself. And get a decent haircut."

The three turned and started walking away. Suddenly, Jack Blow stopped and turned back to Luther.

"You going to be at Maude's on Saturday night?"

"If I've got the money."

"Got some new women down there. A pretty little redhead, heavy bristols," he said, placing both hands under his breasts and pushing upward.

Dabney and Turner giggled at Jack's comment, then the three left the dining hall.

Ten minutes later, Luther and Edgar were chatting as they walked back to the dormitory.

"The Roanoke boys are a bunch of ruffians and Jack Blow is their leader," Luther said. "If you fight one, you have to fight all of them. I am still shaking my head about how he was ever accepted for enrollment."

"I was wondering the same thing. How old is he?"

"He's twenty-two and meaner than a snake. Be sure to keep your doors locked at night. It's dangerous. There will be fights and drunken brawls."

They walked quietly for a moment.

"What is Maude's?"

"It's a brothel outside of town where they have women and drink and high stakes card games."

"Have you been there?"

"Yes. It's wide open. Anything goes."

January 8, 1826. Luther Riddle is such a fine fellow. Kind, well-tempered, and honest as the day is long, he is the sort that will be a close friend for a lifetime. Not particularly intelligent, but a patient soul. I am happy to help him with his Greek translations. Unlike myself, he has not had a grounding in languages. No matter. He is so extremely grateful for my assistance.

January 10, 1826. After only two days, the majority of the funds Father gave me is dangerously depleted. Out of the $300 he provided, I have only $60 remaining. Tomorrow, I must spend another $24 for books, which will leave me with a paltry $36 to my name. At the minimum, I am blessed with housing and a constant source of food. Considering this, I shall delay my requests to Father for more money until the very last moment.

***

The following Friday night, Poe and Luther were in Poe's room translating Greek, when suddenly, they heard loud cursing and shouts. Instantly, they were outside. The south end of the "university lawn" was illuminated with torches and they could see three horses with riders about to commence a race across the grassy area. They immediately recognized one of the riders as Jack Blow. One of the students was leading the horses to a starting line. Nearby, several other students, bills in hand, were shouting their bets.

"Twenty dollars on the roan!" said one.

"Ten dollars on the black horse!" said another.

Finally, the wagers had been placed.

Then the student who was holding the horses shouted, "The finish line is the flagpole at Range North."

The bettors were impatient.

"Come on! Get them started!"

Taking his cue, the student holding the horses stepped away and withdrew a flintlock pistol.

"Ready! On your marks! Get set! Go!"

At the sound of "go!", the student fired the pistol into the air and the three horses and riders bolted across the college lawn to the delighted shouts of the bettors. Suddenly, the sound of stampeding horses' hooves echoed between the dormitory walls. Seconds later, the horses had reached the designated finish line.

"I won!" shouted Jack Blow.

"No! I won!" said the other rider, a short, stocky student known as Wilson.

"You're a liar!" Jack Blow said. "My horse was a full neck ahead. You owe me $20."

"You son of a whore!" Wilson replied. "Who are you calling a liar?"

Now Jack Blow was off the horse and headed toward the other student with a hunting knife in his hand.

"You want me cut out your liver and feed it to the dogs?"

"Try it!"

The two students circled one another.

"Stab him, Jack!" someone shouted. "Let him have it! Right in the heart!"

Suddenly, Wilson withdrew a pistol from his belt, pointed it at Jack, and pulled the trigger.

It clicked.

"Now I'm going to kill you," Jack said.

Suddenly, Wilson threw down the gun, turned, and ran.

Jack laughed.

"You better run... you son of whore," he said. "Nobody crosses Jack Blow."

***

The months of January and February flew past. All that time, Poe was busy attending classes and studying for examinations. On Friday nights, he helped Luther with his Greek translations. Saturdays would be spent in the library researching subjects such as Cicero, Plutarch, and Herodotus. On Sundays, he would invite other students to his room to listen to ghost stories he had written. He was preoccupied with his studies and, since his housing and food was paid for, he had no need for cash money. Finally, he decided to ask his foster father for more money.

March 3, 1826
Dear Father:
    I fear to tell you that the $300 you provided for my expenses has fallen far short of my requirements.
    At this moment, I have only $36 remaining.
    Please find it in your heart to send me another $100 so I can concentrate on my lessons without worry of finances.
    Please send the requested funds soonest as I am in the direst of straits.

Affectionately yours,
Edgar

***

March 6, 1826. There have been many student fights lately. Last night, the faculty expelled Dabney Matthews, one of the Roanoke ruffians, for biting the arms of Jeremiah Caldwell, the student he was fighting. I witnessed the entire foray since it happened in front of my door. Matthews was the much stronger of the two, but he was not content with that. After wrestling Caldwell to the ground, Matthews began to bite huge chunks of flesh out of the other student's arm from the shoulder to the elbow. Pieces of flesh as large as my hand were dangling from Caldwell's arm by the time other students could pull the two apart. Caldwell is from Kentucky and quite often boasted about the readiness of Kentuckians to engage in a man-to-man skirmish. Before this incident, he had been on suspension twice.

***

On the afternoon of March 9, a representative of the bursar's office was waiting at Edgar's dormitory room when he returned from classes.

"A total of $40 is due for continued dining hall privileges."

"I'm afraid I don't have it."

"Then I must inform you that your dining privileges are suspended."

"Can I receive dining privileges on credit?"

"That is not part of our policy."

***

The following morning, when he checked his mailbox, there was a letter from his foster father. *Hallelujah! I am saved!* Hurriedly, he opened the letter.

March 10, 1826
Edgar:
 There will be no further money from me to finance your sojourn in college.
 My disappointment with you is saturated beyond all limits.
 If you have the resourcefulness you claim, you should seek gainful employment to meet your expenses.
 I have no intention of putting further money into your ill-advised adventure.

John Allan

"That low-life scoundrel!" Poe said aloud. "He has abandoned me to my fate."

***

March 11, 1826. Now I am desperate. I no longer have a constant source of food. What shall I do to sustain myself? I have become an outcast and can only associate with those whose lot is the same as mine. How can I peruse my faculties for studies when my mind is aflame with worries about money? My foster father has abandoned me to my fate. Perhaps I can draw upon the generosity of my friends.

***

The following morning, as he was leaving ancient history class, he sidled up to his friend Harley Granger.

"Harley, can you let me borrow $5?"

"When can you pay me back?"

"A couple weeks."

Harley withdrew a bill from this pocket and handed it to Poe.

Later that afternoon, after Latin Literature, he borrowed another $5 each from Timothy Ruskin and James Watson.

When he arrived back at his room that night, Luther was waiting.

"I have news," he said. "Yesterday, I received a letter from my father telling me I must return to Richmond immediately. He has taken ill and is in desperate need of my assistance in the tavern."

"I'm sorry to hear about your father. I shall miss you."

"And I will miss you. Next time you are in Richmond, come visit me. Riddle's Tavern. Corner of Oakmont and Fourth."

"I'll do that.

Luther offered his hand.

Poe shook it.

"One more thing," Poe said. "Can you lend me five dollars?"

Luther put his hand to his pocket, withdrew a five-dollar note, and handed it to Edgar

"Remember! You'll find me at Riddle's Tavern."

"I'll remember!" Poe said. "Thanks for your generosity!"

***

The following Friday night, Poe was back at Maude's. During two earlier visits, he had lost $2 on the first night and won $13 on the second. That night, the game was seven-card stud and, in early hands, Poe won a total of $17. As the night waned on, he had several good hands, but winning a big pot seemed to elude him. Finally, near the end of the evening, cards started to fall his way.

163

When he saw two kings dealt in the hole, he sensed he was looking at a good hand. His next card was a seven of spades and the next four cards were another king and two threes. Full house, kings over threes. This was the hand he had been waiting on.

As bets went around the table, the other players folded and the game came down to Poe, Jack Blow, and an older man wearing a white hat. Watching the play were Turner Dixon and Dabney Matthews. Although Dabney had been expelled for trying to bite off another student's arm, he remained in Charlottesville to be near Jack and Turner.

"I'll bet $40," Jack said.

He turned to the man in the white hat.

"Forty dollars to you," Jack said.

"Too rich for me," the man said, throwing in the cards.

"All right, Poe," Jack Blow said. "It's $40 to you."

"I call and raise $100."

A snarl crossed Jack's face.

"One hundred dollars? What in hell do you have?"

For a long moment, Jack peered at what cards Poe had showing.

He reached into his pocket and took out a wad of bills. He counted out eighty dollars, then he turned to Dabney.

"Give me $20."

Dabney produced a twenty-dollar bill, then threw the money in the pot.

"All right, Poe!" Jack said. "What you got?"

"Full house. Kings over threes."

"Ha!" Jack said, turning over his cards. "Full house. Aces over nines. I win!"

Jack reached out and started raking in the chips. Suddenly, he stopped and turned to Poe.

"Where's the $140 you called with? Did you put it in the pot?"

Poe paused before he spoke.

"I'm afraid I'll have to put you on the cuff."

Livid anger flashed across Jack's face.

"On the cuff? You are not supposed to be in the game unless you have cold cash."

"I have every intention of paying you."

"When?"

"I'm not sure, but rest assured you will get you money."

Jack motioned to Dabney Matthews, who was standing nearby with Turner Dixon. It was a signal. Instantly, Dabney stepped behind Poe and pinned his arms behind his back.

"What are you doing?" Poe said.

Jack stepped forward and started emptying Poe's pockets. Moments later, he had withdrawn a small pocketknife, a room key, an unused graphite pencil, an old receipt, and $7 cash.

"I'm keeping this as interest," Jack said, holding the $7 in Poe's face. "I'll be expecting my money. You can run, but you can't hide."

Jack drew his hunting knife. Then, as Dabney continued to hold Poe, Jack held the weapon to Poe's face. Edgar peered nervously at the cold steel.

Suddenly, Turner Dixon stepped up.

"Jack! He will pay you. His father is one of the richest men in Richmond."

Jack looked from Turner to Poe.

"Is that right?"

"My father is a very wealthy man."

Calmer now, Jack stepped back.

"Let him go!" said Jack.

Dabney released Poe's arms.

"If you don't get my money, you're a dead man. Understand?"

"You shall have your money," Poe said. "I promise."

***

March 17, 1826. Oh, great heavens! I have lost all my money. All I have remaining is $20 in the Commonwealth bank account. I have no available source for sustenance and I need more firewood quickly or I shall surely freeze to death.

***

That afternoon, he withdrew another $5 from the bank account, then went to the local baker and spent $2 on four loaves of bread and two jars of strawberry jam. Back in his room that night, he ate half a loaf of bread and tried to read Tacitus's essays, but the room was too cold for him to concentrate. Crazy with cold, he got up from the desk, emptied the desk drawers, then broke them up into small pieces and built a fire. The four drawers brought a bright flame, but, after an hour, they were little more than glowing ashes and the room was cold again. Giving up on studying, he went to bed and covered himself with clothing to keep warm. Finally, he dozed off to sleep. At 3 a.m., he awoke shivering with cold. Instantly, he was out of bed and added the wooden chair for the writing desk to the ashes. A few minutes later, with a fire roaring in the fireplace, he drifted off to sleep again.

***

The following night was bitterly cold. Three feet of fresh snow had fallen during the day and, at sunset, temperatures had fallen into the low twenties. Back in his room, Poe ate most of the second loaf of bread, but had no wood to make a fire. To stay warm, he crawled into bed and piled heaps of clothing atop himself, but he was still shivering. Finally, he got out of bed and began breaking up the shell of the desk and built a fire. Then he drifted off to sleep. Around 3 a.m., he woke up shivering. Quickly, he got out of bed again and threw the wooden slats for the metal bed into the fireplace. These were the last pieces of burnable wood in the room. Moments later, he had a cheery fire and the room was warm. He went back to bed and slept peacefully through the night.

***

That afternoon, once classes were finished, Poe went to the Range West woodyard to determine the feasibility of pilfering firewood. The woodyard for the Range West rooms was located directly behind the dormitories. The gatekeeper was an old, white-headed slave who sat at the entrance counting the pieces of wood and collecting the money as students made purchases. Although the yard was fenced to prevent theft, there was a large oak tree in a rear corner whose strong limbs jutted over the top of the fence. Immediately, Edgar concluded that one could gain entry by climbing the tree, then dropping into the woodyard on the other side.

March 21, 1826. Tonight I have no choice but to pilfer firewood from the university's stockpile. Such a catastrophe my life has become. I came to this institution to be a scholar and now I will become a thief because my dastardly foster father has abandoned me.

***

That night, after darkness fell, Poe trudged through the snow to the Range West woodyard. The night was bitterly cold and no one was about. Stealthily, Poe went to the rear fence, shinned up the oak tree, and swung himself down into the enclosure.

For a moment, he waited. After seeing no one was about, he began picking up chunks of wood and gently dropping them over the fence into the deep drifts of snow. After twelve pieces, which he knew to be an armful, he pulled himself back up into the tree, then dropped back outside the enclosure. After checking again for witnesses and seeing none, he filled his arms with wood and started back to his room. Once he reached the hallway and started down the colonnade to his room, he heard a shout.

"Ho! You there! Stop!"

Poe stopped and turned.

It was the university security officer.

"What are you doing with that armload of firewood? Are you stealing? The woodyard closes at 5. You're under arrest."

***

Edgar spent the night in the Charlottesville city jail. The following morning, he was hauled before the local magistrate, a fat, balding man with large jowls and glasses. After reviewing some documents, he turned to Poe.

"This offense does not fall within the jurisdiction of the state court. Take the defendant to the university proctor and let Mr. Jefferson mete out his punishment."

An hour later, the proctor and a Charlottesville policeman escorted Poe into the university administration building, then into Jefferson's office. When the proctor announced the charges against Poe, the former president stood aghast.

"Poe! You are the very last student I would have expected to be brought into my office on such a charge. I am shocked that a student with his credentials would be caught committing such a vile act."

"I have not money to buy even a meal."

"No matter!" Jefferson said. "A lack of funds is no reason for you to lower yourself to steal."

"But…"

Jefferson held up his hand for silence.

"You are hereby expelled from the University of Virginia, never to return to this institution again."

He turned to the proctor.

"Draw up the expulsion documents! Get this miserable piece of human vermin out of my sight."

13
Kidnapping

The seventy-five miles from the University of Virginia back to Richmond was one of the longest journeys of Poe's life. The following morning, as the B&O train rumbled ever northward, Poe felt a deep sense of foreboding at seeing his foster father again. Now he remembered the strangeness of his departure two months earlier. The sudden decision to send him to college. The slamming of the mansion door. The shortness of funds for his expenses. *Was the entire episode part of a conspiracy to remove me from the mansion?* he asked himself. Each of these considerations was weighing heavily on his mind as the train drew nearer to Richmond. Somehow, deep inside, he felt this meeting would resolve the long-standing differences between him and his foster father.

Upon arrival in Richmond that afternoon, Poe took a cab carriage to New Dundonald. At the mansion door, he was greeted by Dolina.

"Good afternoon, Mr. Edgar," she said. "Wait right here while I get Mr. Allan."

"I'm not allowed inside?"

"Mr. Allan said if you came here, you were not allowed to enter and I was to get him soonest."

Moments later, John appeared. He seemed surprised.

"What are you doing here? You're supposed to be in Charlottesville."

"I was expelled."

At first, John was not sure he heard correctly.

"Expelled?"

Poe explained what happened.

Once he was finished, the foster father studied him for a moment, then broke into raucous laughter.

"Why is this so funny?"

"Your entire life is a story of failure. Your worthlessness is evident in everything you do."

"Why did Dolina refuse to allow me entry?"

"I no longer want you in this house. You may only return when you decide you want to be a part of this plantation."

"Are you saying I have no right to expect anything further at your hands?"

"Under the circumstances, yes! You shall not return to this house until you can make a contribution."

"Then I shall make my own way."

"What manner of work do you propose to undertake? You have never worked a day at gainful employment in your entire life."

"I intend to be a poet, a man of letters."

John shook his head in amusement.

"Where will you find work for such an enterprise?"

"Of that, I am not sure, but I shall discover it."

"Leave this house and never return. From the first day I saw you, you were a disappointment. Then you say you wish for a collegiate education, but you are not resourceful enough to continue when the funds run short."

Hot anger flashed across Edgar's face.

"Now I know the truth."

"What truth?"

"In the past, at times when you little thought I was listening, I have heard you say that you had no affection for me. Now I know it is true."

John did not reply.

"May I see Mother?"

"No. She won't recognize you. She sits in front of the window all day and mumbles to herself."

"What about my room?"

"It is being occupied by your mother's nurse."

"I cannot remain in this house? Even for one night?"

"No! Be gone!"

"Somewhere in this wide world there is someone who will treat me humanely, not as you have treated me. Dragging your wealth in front of me as if I were a dog. With me all the while hoping that someday I would be good enough to receive your acceptance and become a certified member of the family. Have you any recollection of how times you have reminded me that I was never adopted? That I was nothing more than a wayward waif you took in only because of your generosity?"

John was visibly stung by the words.

"You ungrateful little whelp! Depart these premises! Now!"

For a moment, not moving, Poe studied his foster father.

Suddenly, out of the corner of his eye, he caught sight of a strange woman at the top of the stairs.

"Is that Mother's nurse?"

"She is a personal friend."

Poe stood aghast at the realization.

"You would dare bring some other woman into this house, some cheap, low-life floozie, while my mother is here?"

"It is my house; I shall do as I please."

"You low-life scoundrel! You immoral dog!"

"Get out! Go on! I shall not allow you to call names me in my own house."

"I have no money for food or lodging."

"That is not my problem. Get out!"

"Someday you shall pay for the way you have treated me."

"How so?"

"What you sow, so shall you reap…"

John laughed.

"Maybe you should take up the ministry! Now get out of my house!"

Poe shook his head in frustration, then turned and walked out.

"And don't ever return!" the foster father shouted.

As Poe strode down the mansion walkway, he heard the mansion door slam behind him.

***

Ten minutes later, Edgar, suitcase in hand, was walking along the main road into downtown Richmond. Darkness had fallen and a drizzling rain had descended upon the land. *Where can I go?* he thought. *What shall I do? With no money, where shall I spend the night?* Over the next thirty minutes, he walked into town. By the time he reached Main Street, the rain was coming down in buckets and he ducked under the awning of a pawn shop. As he stood watching the rain fall, he suddenly remembered his friend Luther. Perhaps all was not lost. Over the next few minutes, he walked the five blocks to Oakmont and Fourth Streets where he saw the sign for Riddle's Tavern. Upon arrival, he could see it was dark and closed. He ducked under the front stoop to escape the pouring rain. Tired and frustrated, he was soon sound asleep.

***

When he awoke the following morning, he was looking into Luther's eyes. His friend had arrived at the tavern for another day of business.

"Edgar!" he said. "What are you doing here? I thought you were in college."

"Not anymore."

"What happened?"

"It's a long story. I have been disowned by my family. I have no money to buy food and nowhere to stay. Do you have some work I could do?"

"Do you know how to wash dishes? Serve tables? Sweep the floor?"

"Yes. To all of those."

"Then come inside. I think I can help you."

Thirty minutes later, Poe was in the tavern storage room helping Luther move around heavy barrels of beer so Edgar would have a place to sleep.

"You can make yourself a bed here," Luther said. "It won't be much, and you'll have to endure the smell of stale beer, but you will have a roof over your head."

***

Riddle's Tavern was a neighborhood watering hole on Richmond's north side that served food, drink, and provided entertainment for patrons such as darts, checkers, and backgammon. Luther, with the help of barmaid Margie, a dumpy, frowsy, middle-aged woman, tended the bar and collected the money. A former slave named Nicodemus, an old white-haired man, served as cook and, once food was prepared, it was Edgar's job to serve it. Tips were good and Edgar seemed to get along with patrons.

***

Two months passed. Over that period, Poe became an expert tavern employee. Every day, when the business opened, Poe was at Luther's side helping with the business. He slept in the stockroom, ate out of the tavern kitchen, and washed his clothes in the tavern's washpot. At night, when the business closed and the barmaid and the cook were gone, Edgar was there to help Luther clean up and prepare the premises for another day of business. The hours were long, but Luther was a good boss and Edgar thrived. The pay was $3 a day, but tips often exceeded that amount. During those two months. Edgar managed to save $28.

***

In late May, with the approach of summer, customer volume at Riddle's began to rise. This surge in new customers brought in many of Poe's old friends.

One night, Harley Granger, who had been a fellow student at the university, showed up. He was surprised to see Poe.

"You're working here now?" Harley asked.

"That's right."

"Then pay me the $15 I loaned you at the university?"

"I'm sorry. I don't have it."

"When I let you borrow it, you promised to pay it back in two weeks."

"I can't pay you."

Harley went to Luther.

173

"Your employee owes me $15. Can you make him pay?"

Luther shook his head.

"That's strictly between you and Edgar. I don't get involved in such matters."

Miffed, Harley finished his drink and walked out.

***

Two nights later, James Watson and Timothy Ruskin, two more of Poe's university friends, appeared in the tavern. Once they saw Edgar, they asked about the money he had borrowed.

"You owe me $10!" Ruskin said.

"You owe me $20!" added Watson.

"I can't pay you!"

"I took you at your word when I loaned you the money. Now I see you're not as honorable as you pretend to be."

"I don't have your money."

An hour later, after Watson and Ruskin left, Luther went to Edgar.

"How many people did you borrow money from?"

"I don't recall exactly."

"There seems to be no end to them."

***

Two nights later, Edgar was busy waiting tables when Turner Dixon showed up. Like the others, he was surprised to see Poe.

"I wondered what happened to you," Turner said. "One day, you just disappeared."

"I had some problems."

"You best not let Jack Blow find out you're here. He's never forgotten you owed him $140."

"I told him I would pay him."

"He'll hunt you down to get his money."

Poe studied Turner for a moment.

"You're not going to tell Jack I'm working here, are you?"

"Oh no! I would never do that!"

Two nights later, Luther and Edgar were closing the bar. It had been a long, tiring day and Poe, who had worked fourteen hours, was ready for it to end. Luther was ushering the last few customers out the door while Edgar was placing all the chairs on tables so he could sweep the floor. Once the customers were gone and the front door was locked, Poe was outside on the street sweeping off the front entrance.

Suddenly, a carriage stopped on the street in front of the tavern. Two shadowy figures, their faces hidden by black cloths, emerged from the carriage and headed straight to Poe. Edgar looked up, but it was too late. Before he could defend himself, one of the figures rapped him across the head with a truncheon, then, as he slumped over, they grabbed him and hauled him into the carriage. Then it sped off into the night.

***

When Poe awoke, his head was aching. He looked around. It was night and he was in an old barn. He could smell fresh hay and horse manure. Somewhere in the distance, he could hear rushing water. He was seated on the barn's earthen floor, his hands tightly bound behind him to one of the barn's upright wooden columns. Nearby, sitting in front of a fire, were Jack Blow and Dabney Matthews.

"Look, he's coming around," Dabney said.

"Oh, my head! My aching head!" Poe said.

"Poe, you didn't think you were going to get away without paying the $140 you owe me?" said Jack.

"I told you I would pay you."

"Well, where's my money?"

"I don't have it."

"You've been working in that tavern. What do you mean you don't have it?"

"He hasn't got a red cent," Dabney said. "I've already been through his pockets."

A pause as Jack added more wood to the fire.

"What are we going to do, Jack?"

"Didn't Turner say his father was one of the richest men in Richmond? Said he owned a plantation?"

"Yeah."

"Let's see if we can collect a ransom."

"That's a good idea!"

Jack turned to Edgar.

"What's your father's name?"

"I have no intention of telling you that. He wouldn't give you money anyway. He has disowned me."

"You liar! You're just saying that to spoil my plan."

"It's true. He could care less if I lived or died."

Instantly, Jack was on his feet. Not to be outdone, he grabbed a piece of flaming wood from the fire.

"Maybe you'd like for me to burn your hair off," he said. "I never did like your haircuts anyway."

Then Jack moved closer and held the flaming piece of wood within inches of Poe's face. He recoiled at the intense heat.

"No! No! Don't burn me!"

"Then tell me your father's name!"

Poe hesitated, then Jack jammed the burning piece of wood into Poe's cheek.

"Yow!" Edgar screamed, shaking his head to ward off the pain.

"What's your father's name?"

"Allan. John Allan."

"What's the name of the plantation?"

"New Dundonald."

Jack stepped back and turned to Dabney.

"You ever heard of New Dundonald plantation?"

"No."

"I'm going to write a ransom note and take it to this John Allan. If he wants to see you alive again, he is going to have to pay $1000."

"You're wasting your time," Poe said.

"Shut up!" Jack said.

"What are we going to do with him after we get the money?" Dabney asked.

"We'll kill him and throw him in the river."

"Yeah," Dabney said, turning to leer at Poe. "I would like that."

Moments later, Jack was writing the ransom note. Once finished, he told Poe to sign it.

"I shall not sign such a document."

Jack turned back to the fire and grabbed another piece of burning wood.

"No! Not that! I'll sign it."

Then, taking the graphite pencil Jack had been using, Poe signed the ransom note.

"Now we're getting somewhere," Jack said, shoving the note into his pocket.

He turned to Dabney.

"I don't know when I'll be back, but you keep close watch on him. Here! You keep the pistol."

Jack withdrew a flintlock pistol from his belt and handed it to Dabney.

"Now be careful! It's got a hair trigger. The smallest bump will cause it to fire. If he tries to escape, blow his head off."

"I'd love to."

"And lay off that joy juice while I'm gone. If he escapes, you're going to answer to me."

"Don't worry! That will never happen!"

Moments later, Poe could hear Jack in the stall behind him talking to a horse.

"Easy, boy!"

Then Poe could hear the sounds of a horse being bridled, saddled, and led out of the barn.

"I'm thirsty," Poe said. "Can I have some water?"

Dabney laughed.

"What do you need water for? We're going to kill you anyway."

"And what about food? You aren't going to hold me here without food or water?"

"Looks that way."

Then Dabney pulled a bottle out of his pocket and took a swig.

"You know that you and Jack will not get away with this," Poe said. "The moment the constable learns about it, he is going to arrest both of you. You will probably get life in prison."

"How are they going to catch us?" Dabney said, taking another swig. "If you're dead, who's going to tell the constable?"

"Oh, rest assured you'll be apprehended and punished. The constable will discover who owns this barn. They find out how you and Jack received access to it…"

"Shut up!" Dabney said, reaching for the pistol. "Shut up or I'll blow your brains out."

***

Three hours later, Poe could hear the hoofbeats of a horse nearby. Then he could hear the barn door open as Jack led the horse back into the stall behind him.

"What happened?" Dabney said.

"When I knocked, a slave came to the door and said John Allan wasn't home. When I asked where he was, she said Norfolk. I asked when he would be back and she said she didn't know."

"What did you do then?"

"What could I do? If he is not there, there's nothing I can do."

"He's probably in Norfolk shipping tobacco," Edgar said.

"I'll try again tomorrow."

"Can I have some water?"

"You don't need water," Jack said.

"The two of you are going to spend your life in prison for this."

"Shut up!" Jack said.

Then he stood up and delivered a sharp kick to Poe's leg. Edgar grimaced in pain.

***

The first night, Poe was unable to sleep. The pain in his head and now his leg was keeping him awake. Nearby, wrapped up in an old blanket, Jack Blow was snoring. The pistol was in his belt. The fire was a mound of glowing ashes. Dabney, his back propped up on the barn wall, was sound asleep.

Edgar was crazy with thirst. Behind him, he heard the horse's tail swishing about to ward off the flies. Then he stretched as far as he could to see behind him. As he did, he found that, if he stretched far enough, his lips could almost reach the water in the horse's trough. Then he discovered, by moving his bound hands higher up the column, he could shift his body and his lips could reach the horse's watering trough. Now, in the new position, he drank his fill of water. Moments later, he was sound asleep.

***

When he awoke, he could see sunshine peeping in through the eaves of the barn. He smelled food. Nearby, Jack and Dabney were sharing a loaf of bread, several pieces of fried chicken, and a bowl of green beans.

"Are you going to feed me?"

Jack and Dabney laughed and continued eating.

Once finished, Jack stood up.

"I'm going back. Maybe he'll be home this time."

***

Two hours later, Jack reappeared.

"What happened?" Dabney asked. "Was he home?"

Jack shook his head in frustration.

"He was home. I showed him the ransom note and he read it."

"Then what?"

"He started laughing. Then he wadded up the ransom note and threw it on the ground. He said, 'Go ahead and kill him! I could care less!'"

"Then what?"

"He slammed the door in my face and went back inside."

Dabney shook his head slowly, then turned back to Jack.

"What are we going to do?"

179

"Let's take him out in the woods and kill him," Jack said. "Then we'll throw him in the river. Nobody ever comes around these parts."

Dabney untied Poe's hands.

They led him out of the barn into the thick woods between the barn and the river. Now Poe knew where he was. In the distance, some 100 yards away, he recognized the James River. He was somewhere south of the Stanard plantation. If he could get to the river, he would be safe.

With Jack holding one of Poe's arms and Dabney the other, they were leading him through thick undergrowth. The pistol was in Jack's belt.

"Where do you want to do it?"

"Let's get close to the water. We don't want to have to carry his dead carcass too far to throw it in."

Suddenly, Poe jerked his arm out of Dabney's grasp, then turned to face Jack. Knowing the pistol had a hair trigger, he kicked the pistol in Jack's belt with all his might. Instantly, the single-shot pistol went off harmlessly.

As it did, Poe jerked away from Jack and dashed off through the woods.

"You son of a whore!" Jack said. "Come back here!"

Some twenty yards ahead of them, Jack could see Poe streaking toward the river.

"Come on, Dab! We can't let him get away! He'll tell the constable and we'll go to prison."

Instantly, they dashed off.

Poe had reached the water's edge, but his path was blocked by a stand of thick bramble bushes. He looked for an escape. Behind him, he could see Jack, hunting knife in hand, and Dabney in hot pursuit. Then he tore through the brambles toward the river, snagging his arms and legs on the thorns. They were too thick for him to pass. When he started back out, Jack and Dabney rushed up.

"Now we have him!" Jack said. "Grab him and I'll put this knife in him."

Dabney lunged at Poe, but Edgar quickly stepped aside and Dabney fell into the mass of bramble thorns.

"Ooow!" he screamed in pain.

Poe turned to face Jack. They circled one another, then Jack rushed at Poe, swinging the knife wildly. Poe, knowing he would be safe if he could reach the river, suddenly turned and started running again. He ran some thirty yards, then, seeing a clearing at the water's edge, he rushed forward and dove in.

Moments later, he looked back to shore and saw Jack and Dabney, tired and frustrated, shaking their fists after him. Poe knew they were no match for his swimming skills.

***

The next morning, Poe was waiting at Riddle's Tavern when Luther appeared to open.

"What happened?"

"I was kidnapped by Jack Blow and Dabney Matthews."

"Kidnapped?"

"They held me in an old barn for the past two days. They tried to collect a ransom from my foster father, but he laughed it off."

"Are you going to report them to the constable?"

"No time for that," Poe said. "I'm leaving. I want to get my things, my last bit of pay, and I'll be gone."

"Where are you going?"

"When I was a toddler, my mother said, 'Remember the city of Boston. The birthplace of you and your father.'"

"The city by the River Charles?"

"That's right."

"What will you do there?"

"I have no earthly idea."

"Good luck!" Luther said, offering his hand. "Remember that I shall always be your friend."

May 10, 1826. My life has reached a turning point. I fear that the legacy I created at the University of Virginia will haunt me for the remainder of my days. I would happily pay my creditors if I had the funds, but my paltry income will not allow it. I must escape and create a new life and a new identity. I must flee the debtors, the cheats, the liars, and others who seem to be forever hounding me. I shall make my own way. Somehow. Some way. Some day.

***

That afternoon, suitcase in hand, Poe paid the $2 to take a launch down the James River to Norfolk. Upon arrival, he went straight to the docks and began canvassing shipping lines for the cheapest fare to Boston.

After the first three, he was quoted prices ranging from $12 to $16. At the fourth one, after quoting a price of $14, the clerk offered to help.

"How much do you want to pay?"

"As little as possible."

"Go to piers 110-118. That is where the cattle boats are docked. Usually, you can get passage for $8. You'll have to endure the stench of cow manure and bawling calves at night, but it's cheap passage."

Poe could smell the cattle boats before he arrived. Out of the seven to eight ships tugging at their moorings, Poe's eyes stopped on the USS *Guernsey*. Directly in front of the ship, he could see a small hut with a clerk inside.

"How much for a ticket to Boston?"

"Eight dollars for a single hammock."

"Is that the cheapest?"

"Yes. Three days to Boston."

Poe handed over the payment.

"What name should I put on the ticket?"

"Perry. Edgar A. Perry."

14
Incognito

Two months passed. In early June of 1826, Poe was living a new life in Boston under the assumed name of Edgar A. Perry. Upon arrival in the city, he had first found work as a painter in the renovation of an old hotel near Boston Commons. There he met an out-of-work stevedore who said he would be returning to the docks at the end of the week. When Poe asked if other workers were needed, the man invited Edgar to accompany him. The following morning, Poe began work loading and unloading cargo for an international shipping company called Wentworth Lines. It was strenuous work and he had to deal with the constant complaints of ship captains, but it paid well and he could easily manage the $10 a month he was paying for a small garret room at the nearby Shawmut Hotel. His nights were spent writing poetry and, when he arrived, Poe had a total of thirteen poems he felt were worthy of publication.

One day, while Poe was having lunch and reading a book, another Wentworth employee from the nearby office building approached to ask about some cargo that had been loaded that morning. He was Poe's age, well over six feet tall with blonde hair, a ruddy face, and a well-trimmed mustache. After Poe answered his questions, he asked about the book Edgar was reading.

"Famous battles in history," Poe said. "At the moment, I'm reading the chapter on the battle of Thermopylae."

"Oh, yes. Three hundred Spartans held off the entire Persian army. Do you aspire to be a soldier?

"No. I just love history, especially Greek history."

"My name is Thomas Pickering Jones," he said, offering his hand. "Soon I'm going to be a professional soldier. Like you, I love to read about famous battles. My favorite is Waterloo, where Wellington outmaneuvered Napoleon across the grassy knolls of eastern Belgium."

"I too am a fan of Lord Wellington. He also showed his mettle at the Battle of Vitoria in Spain."

Poe studied him for a moment.

"What did you mean by you said 'I will be a professional soldier soon.'?"

"You have to be eighteen to enlist. I'll be eighteen in two more months."

"What made you decide that soldiering was your calling?"

"My father and my grandfather were military men. The thrill of risking one's life to lead troops into battle has always appealed to me."

"Sudden death is your likely end."

"Such is the life of a soldier."

Over the next fifteen minutes, they discussed the battles of Waterloo, Hannibal's siege of Rome, and Napoleon's famous battle against Austrian forces at Marengo. Once Poe's lunch was finished, Jones returned to the office. Over the following week, he was back three more times to engage Poe in conversation about famous battles.

***

A week later, the Wentworth office manager, a tall, thin balding man wearing thick glasses, came to the docks to meet Poe.

"I've been talking to Thomas Pickering Jones. He says you're quite brainy."

"I would like to think so."

"Ever do office work?"

"Oh yes!" he lied.

"We need another clerk in the manifest office. Would you be interested?"

***

Once Edgar started work in the manifest office, he and Thomas quickly became close friends. Day after day, they would pore over piles of shipping manifests. A cargo manifest was an official record of a ship's cargo and every Wentworth ship that left the harbor had to have one. It was a passport for goods rather than passengers and customs officials at each port of call required one.

Over the following days, Poe and Thomas would spend most Saturdays together, shopping at Fanueil Hall or loitering at Boston Commons eyeing passing women, enjoying the street entertainers, or simply lazing in the summer sun. During these times, Thomas would drone on and on about his dreams of being a professional soldier and fighting in a famous battle like his father at Bunker Hill.

***

One Saturday, Thomas said he wanted Poe to meet his cousin Eleanor. After a ten-minute walk from the commons, Thomas led Poe to a small restaurant on the south end of River Street. As they approached, Poe could see a petite woman, pretty face, early twenties, raven-black hair, and dressed in a fashionable summer smock, sitting at a table. She reeked of elegance and wealth.

Thomas introduced her as Eleanor. She offered her hand. Poe took it, then seated himself.

"Thomas says you are a poet," she began.

"I've been known to traipse down the paths of rhythm and rhyme."

She smiled.

"I write poetry myself," she said. "I also read quite a bit of poetry. Just finished the works of Samuel Taylor Coleridge."

"He is one of my favorites," Poe said. "His poem, 'The Rime of the Ancient Mariner,' is one of the finest poems I know."

A pause while they ordered food.

"Thomas says you work for Wentworth," Edgar said.

"I audit the books for the company up and down the Atlantic seaboard. My degree is in finance."

"I would think company officials put quite a bit of trust in you."

"I'm the boss's daughter," she said. "My father owns the company."

Poe laughed.

"Sounds like you've lived a life of privilege."

She turned, apparently annoyed.

"I would rather not discuss my personal life."

Poe glanced at Jones, then dropped the subject.

Moments later, their food was served. As they prepared to eat, Poe examined her every move. Up close, he could see her eyes. They were a dark violet color, like new irises in bloom.

Thirty minutes later, they had finished their meal, then arose from the table to say their good-byes. Eleanor turned to Poe.

"Will you be at the party next Saturday?"

"Party?" Poe said, turning to Thomas.

"The company's Fourth of July party is next Saturday."

"Do I have to dress up?"

"You'll need a dinner jacket."

"I don't have one."

"I'll lend you one."

Poe turned back to Eleanor.

"I'll be there," he said.

Eleanor seemed amused.

"You don't like to dress up?" Eleanor said. "You don't like to flout your social self?"

"I'm not much of a social animal," he said. "I prefer being alone."

"I can identify with that."

Poe offered his hand as a parting gesture.

Eleanor took it.

"Do you prefer to be addressed as Eleanor?"

"My full name is Eleanor Jane Wentworth. That is far too many words to identify any one person. Please call me Lenore."

Upon leaving the restaurant, Poe questioned Thomas about her.

"She's 22. Took a degree in business finance at Wheaton last year, but she is quite adept at subjects outside of finance. Especially literature and history. Her father is Thaddeus P. Wentworth, owner of the company. He is my uncle."

They walked quietly.

"She must have a strong constitution," Poe said. "Usually it is men who take degrees in business finance."

"Eleanor is not your average woman."

"Those purple eyes are mesmerizing."

Thomas laughed.

"I know. Since the first day I saw her, I am still fascinated by them."

They walked quietly.

"Why doesn't she like to talk about herself?" Edgar said.

"That is her way. She loves to create a sense of mystery about herself. Once you get to know her, if she likes you, she'll open up."

"How long will she be in Boston?"

"Five, maybe six weeks."

"Do you think she liked me?"

"Oh, yes."

"How do you know?"

"Her eyes lit up when you mentioned that you preferred to be alone."

***

June 16, 1826. Never have I encountered a woman with the same carriage and countenance as Tommy's cousin Lenore. Unlike most women, who are little more than twittering songbirds, she is quite reserved in her speech and mannerisms. Her most distinctive quality is her eyes. They are a soft purple hue, which, coupled with the black hair, gives her an unearthly appearance. When I look into her face, her eyes seem to be looking far, far away as if she were seeing a world far distant from this one; a world which others cannot discern. There is a delicious, undefinable mystery about her. I shall dream about those unearthly, violet eyes.

***

The following Saturday, Poe and Jones were in attendance at the company's July fourth celebration in the company's luncheon hall. Poe, decked out in his borrowed dinner jacket and new shoes, followed Thomas around as he moved among guests making introductions and engaging in small talk. Finally, bored with the trite party conversations, Poe wandered out to the terrace overlooking the harbor. There he found Lenore sitting alone, sipping her drink and gazing across the water.

"Good evening!" she said.

"Why aren't you inside with the revelers?"

"I am not one to seek the din and the glare. Have a seat."

Poe took a seat.

"The moon is laughing tonight," she said, peering up at the golden mound shining down on the harbor. "It has discovered a new lover among the heavens and is celebrating."

"Yes." Poe said, looking up. "I can discern its joy. The new lover has delivered a new garden of earthly pleasures."

She smiled.

"Tell me about your poems," she said. "What have you written lately?"

"'Summer Love' is the title of my latest poem. It is a quality poem, but somehow I feel it could be improved."

"Subject matter?"

"A story of love gained and lost. The oldest story known to man."

"I too have delved into that subject," she said. "My latest poem falls into that category."

"What's the title?"

"'Love's Reply.' The entire poem is love's attempt to explain its elusiveness. Would you like to read it?"

"If your poetry is as interesting as you, I would be delighted."

"Would you like to return with me to my quarters? I could show you the poem. I have stimulants."

"What kind of stimulants?"

"All kinds."

***

Thirty minutes later, Lenore was leading Edgar up the stairs at the luxurious Excelsior Hotel on Boston's fashionable east side. Once inside her room, she prepared drinks, then withdrew a loose-leaf folder containing various single sheets of poems. She withdrew one. Poe took it and read it.

"Excellent poem," he said. "The images are strong and vivid. They dance across the stage of the reader's imagination. That is the mark of good poetry."

"Did you truly like it?"

"I would not have said it if I had not meant it."

She studied him for a moment.

"Come! I shall show you my stimulants."

She went to a small table and pulled back a covering. There was a line of six bowls on the table.

"What do you have here?"

"Here," she said, pointing to the first bowl, "We have a stimulant from South America called marijuana. It is best for a quiet, mellow afternoon."

She moved to the next bowl.

"Here we have mescaline from Mexico; users proclaim they can see God while intoxicated on this one. Next, we have pure opium from Shanghai; it is the grandfather of all stimulants; next is cocaine from Peru, black hashish from Persia, and over here, we have magic mushrooms from Siam. Each of these can deliver you to new and different worlds beyond this one."

Poe stood staring at the row of bowls. He had never seen anything like this.

"Have you used stimulants to improve your writing?" she asked.

"No, but I have always been interested in exploring the landscape of my mind to the fullest."

"It is been said that Samuel Taylor Coleridge wrote 'Rime of the Ancient Mariner' while intoxicated with opium."

"I have heard that. How did you obtain these?"

"I have sailor friends who travel the world and bring them to me."

Then, she turned and withdrew a clay pipe from a drawer and began sifting opium powder into the bowl. Once filled, she reached for a candle on the table, lit the pipe, and inhaled deeply.

"Would you like to join me?"

Poe took the pipe, studied it curiously, then put it to his mouth and inhaled deeply. He handed it back to her.

"No! Have another. It takes two, maybe three to bring forth the fullness of the new world."

Poe took two more draws, then handed the pipe back. Taking the pipe, she placed it on the table, then turned back to Poe

"Come! Let us be as Bacchanalian revelers. Let us throw our cares to the wind and bathe in the pleasures of the flesh."

She went to a nearby closet, retrieved a cotton blanket, and spread it on the floor. Then she began removing her clothes.

As he watched the garments slip away from her lithe body, he could feel the initial effects of the stimulant. She stood naked in front of him.

"Come!" she said, kneeling on the blanket and beckoning to him. "Lie with me. Let us blend our bodies into one. Life is but a dream within a dream. Let the priests and the lawyers and the bankers have their logical worlds while we bathe in a dream of our own making."

Almost immediately, he was undressed and lying on the blanket beside her. As he gazed into her purple eyes, his head began to swim. One moment, her face was moving closer to his, then, seconds later, vanishing further and further away. The room began to sway. The curtains were waving in the breeze, although there was no wind. The beige colors of the hotel room began to form liquid droplets, then beads of beige began to roll down the hotel room walls like tears and form puddles of brown liquid on the floor. *This is opium intoxication*, Poe told himself. Moments later, he was coupling his body with hers.

***

Thirty minutes later, their amorous desires sated, they lay naked in one another's arms. As the opium started to take full effect, Edgar's mind was filled with a universe of dark, macabre, otherworldly images. Ghosts, goblins, black cats, ghouls, bats, haunted houses, grave robbers, wandering spirits, moonlit graveyards, hunchbacks, and horrible scenes of medieval torture danced across the stage of his imagination. The stimulant had opened a part of his hitherto unknown self. Until now, the principal subjects of his work had been dying young maidens, lovely summer days, and satires about the foibles of his friends. Now he sensed these ghosts, goblins, and graveyards would become the new building blocks for his work. The simulant had brought the new images to the forefront of his consciousness.

***

The following night, back in his hotel garret, Poe sat down at his desk to write. At the top of the blank sheet, he wrote the title "A Dream within a Dream." For several minutes, he pondered the lines he was about to write, then suddenly, he remembered his thoughts of the previous night while intoxicated on opium. Magnificent, vivid images came spewing forth, like torrents of rushing water over a waterfall. Frantically, he struggled to capture them before they escaped his mind. Finally, after an hour of feverish composition, he had the rough draft of a new poem. He read it.

Take this kiss upon the brow!
And, in parting from you now,
This much let me avow —
You are not wrong, who deem
That my days have been a dream,
Yet if hope has flown away

In a night, or in a day,
In a vision, or in none,
Is it therefore the less gone?
All *that we see or seem*
Is but a dream within a dream;

I stand amid the roar
Of a surf-tormented shore,
And I hold within my hand
Grains of the golden sand —
How few! yet how they creep
Through my fingers to the deep,
While I weep — while I weep!
O God! Can I not grasp
Them with a tighter clasp?
O God! can I not save
One *from the pitiless wave?*
Is all *that we see or seem*
But a dream within a dream?

"Finest poem I've ever written," he said to himself.

***

The following weekend, Poe was back at Lenore's hotel room.

"Tonight," she said, "we shall visit another world beyond the one we know. We shall touch the brows and feel the hot breath of those who are no more."

Poe watched as she stirred a brown powder into a glass of water.

"What do we have tonight?"

"Magic mushrooms. The ancient Mayans used these for thousands of years in religious ceremonies. It is said one walks among the spirits of the dead when intoxicated."

She took a drink of the brown liquid, then handed the glass to him.

"Drink!"

The following night after work, Poe seated himself at his desk. His mind was filled with fantastical images from the previous night's stimulants. Taking quill in hand, he wrote the title "Spirits of the Dead." As he started to write, the images began to pour out. Furiously, he scribbled the words. As each new line emerged from his mind, it was perfectly formed to match every other line. Finally, after over an hour, he had a rough draft. He read it.

Thy soul shall find itself alone
'Mid dark thoughts of the gray tombstone—
Not one, of all the crowd, to pry
Into thine hour of secrecy.

Be silent in that solitude,
Which is not loneliness—for then
The spirits of the dead who stood
In life before thee are again
In death around thee—and their will
Shall overshadow thee: be still.

The night, tho' clear, shall frown—
And the stars shall look not down
From their high thrones in the heaven,
With light like Hope to mortals given—
But their red orbs, without beam,
To thy weariness shall seem
As a burning and a fever
Which would cling to thee forever.

Now are thoughts thou shalt not banish,
Now are visions ne'er to vanish;
From thy spirit shall they pass
No more—like dew-drops on the grass.

The breeze—the breath of God—is still—
And the mist upon the hill,

Shadowy—shadowy—yet unbroken,
Is a symbol and a token—
How it hangs upon the trees,
A mystery of mysteries!

He looked up from the poem. A satisfied smile crossed his face.

***

June 28, 1826. I never dreamed there was a woman in this world like Lenore. Over the past few days, I have fallen into a magical dream where this beautiful woman has awakened the fullness of my imagination. The masses of women I have known seek marriage, having a family, and growing old together. Lenore has none of those desires or expectations. She seeks only to explore the great intellectual heights; to bathe in the pleasures of the flesh and is shameless in doing so. She wants only to sail the seas of the human spirit and bask in the savage delights of carnal pleasures. As a lover, she transports me to a state of total amorous satisfaction. Oh, dear God, when I pass from this earth, lay my soul to rest in this woman's arms. No man could ask for more than Lenore. Absolutely no man!!

***

At the end of July, while working in the office one day, Thomas made a major announcement.

"The day has come," he said.

"What day is that?"

"My birthday is tomorrow. I'll be eighteen and I'm going to the U.S. Army enlistment office and sign the papers."

"I'll miss you."

"Why don't you accompany me?"

Poe peered thoughtfully at his friend.

"I don't believe I would like the life of a soldier. It would be too rigid and structured for my taste."

"That's part of the military. Good soldiering grows out of strict discipline."

"It's not for me."

"The military would be perfect for you. You would have a roof over your head every night, three square meals a day, and all the time you could desire to write. It would be ideal for you."

"Do you really think so?"

"I know so."

"Let me contemplate it."

***

Two days later, Poe and Thomas met Lenore at the docks where she was waiting to board a ship to Halifax, Nova Scotia, and her next auditing assignment. Decked out in a fashionable gray V-neck bustle dress and matching hat, she could have stepped off a women's magazine cover.

"Quite fashionable," Poe said.

"Thanks for the compliment!"

"I shall miss you. Thank you for your friendship."

"Stay in touch!" she said. "You can always reach me through Thomas."

"I'll do that. Thanks again."

Then, shouldering her personal bag, she said good-bye to Thomas, and they watched as she strode up the gangplank and disappeared among the other passengers.

Moments later, they were walking back to the office.

"You're going to be lonely in that office without me," Thomas said. "Are you sure you don't want to enlist?"

"I think not."

"I dare you!"

Poe stopped and stared at Jones, pure annoyance in his face.

"You dare me?"

"I double dog dare you!" Thomas said. "For all of your intelligence, I don't believe you have the qualifications to succeed in the U.S. Army."

Firm resolve settled across Edgar's face.

"We'll just see about that!"

"What do you mean?"

"Tomorrow I'll go with you."

Thomas smiled, then hugged him.

August 3, 1826. I shall always remember the beautiful, mysterious Lenore. The dream lover with the purple eyes and the scintillating mind who unleashed the myriad forces of darkness within me. Jane Stanard showed me my love of poetry, but it was Lenore who unlocked the deep, dark mysteries hidden within the caverns of my soul.

15
U.S. Army

It was late March of 1829. Over the past three years, Poe had been serving in the U.S. Army at Fort Independence near Boston under the assumed name of Edgar A. Perry. Located on Castle Island just north of the city, the garrison served as a first line of defense against enemy warships advancing into Boston harbor. During the War of 1812, in a skirmish with five British man-o-wars, the fort's proudest moment came when its mighty forty-eight-pound guns sank two of the vessels and drove the others back out to sea.

During those years, Poe discovered military life agreed with him far more than he had imagined and he thrived as both a soldier and a poet. In the fall of 1828, he was promoted to the rank of sergeant major for artillery, the highest rank he could attain as an enlisted man. In that capacity, his job was to oversee the loading, storage, and transport of artillery shells and, as leader of Battery H of the First Artillery, he had won high praise from both his commander and fellow soldiers.

The rigid discipline and organization of military life proved to be a boon for Edgar's writing. As Thomas had predicted, he had plenty of time to devote to his poetry and did not have to worry about where his next meal was coming from. In late February, he had spoken to a local printer about publishing *Tamerlane*, his first book of poems.

"New books of poems are usually forty-eight pages long with a separate poem on each page," the printer said. "Cost of printing the interior will be $15 plus $2 for binding. If you would like to add a cover illustration, that's another $3."

"I'll go with the plain cover."

"Then your total cost is $17 for fifty copies."

Poe paid in cash.

"Who shall be named as poet?"

"Just list the author as 'By a Bostonian.' When will the book be ready?"

"Within the next week."

***

Meanwhile, Edgar's friendship with Thomas Pickering Jones grew stronger than ever. Like Poe's, Jones' star had risen rapidly at Fort Independence. After proving himself an expert marksman, he was well-liked, he excelled at hand-to-hand combat training, he drew high marks at inspections, and he proved himself as an able artillery man. Now, with a rank of sergeant major, Jones was a highly respected drill instructor and answered directly to the garrison commander.

***

Two nights after speaking with the printer, Poe was having drinks with his fellow soldiers at the One-eyed Sailor, the local watering hole for Fort Independence soldiers, when he announced the forthcoming publication of his book of poems.

"Congratulations, Poe," said Joshua Gibson. "You've been saying you were a poet. Now you can prove it."

"I'll buy one!" said Harley Hood. "I've always enjoyed reading good poetry."

"You know you can count on me to buy one," said Jones.

"I'll take a copy," said Robert Hobson, a Battery H member.

"Me too!" said a Battery D member.

"Same here!" said several other soldiers.

Later that night, when the tavern was closing, Jones looked around for Edgar. He was nowhere to be seen.

"Where's Eddie?" Jones asked.

"I'm not sure," said Gibson. "He was here a few minutes ago."

Moments later, Jones and the others were outside as the tavern keeper locked the door behind them. As they started back to the garrison, Thomas glanced into the thick bushes beside the tavern. He saw a pair of legs sticking out. He went to investigate and instantly recognized the figure as Poe.

"Eddie? Eddie?" he said, bending over Poe and shaking him. Poe sat up and rubbed his eyes.

"I had too much to drink," he said.

"Come on," Jones said. "Me and Gibson will help you back to the barracks."

***

Two mornings later, in route to the noonday mess, Jones made his own announcement.

"I wanted to tell you something, but it must remain a secret."

"My lips are sealed."

"I've applied to West Point."

Poe drew back.

"How did you do that?"

"Quite simple. I requested an application, filled it out, and sent it back."

"When will you know if you're accepted?"

"It will be a while. If they approve my application, then I will have to be recommended by an influential person to the Secretary of War and the academy commander. You must have an unblemished record to get an appointment."

"What influential person would you get to recommend you?"

"My uncle Thaddeus."

They walked quietly for a moment.

"What's the name of the Academy commander and the address?"

"Are you interested?"

"Absolutely."

"You must understand that the discipline and structure at the academy is far more rigid than the regular army. They expect 24-hour dedication. Chances are, you will have little or no time to write."

"I'll find time to write," Poe said. "I can always find time for that."

They had reached the mess hall.

"Why do you want to keep it a secret?"

"If I announce it and don't get accepted, I'll have egg on my face."

Poe nodded his understanding.

"I'll get the addresses for you."

***

March 18, 1829. Today, I picked up my books from the printer. In my entire life, nothing, absolutely nothing, has delivered the level of satisfaction I felt when I held that first book of poems in my hand. Contained therein lay the result of many years of hopes and dreams. As I studied the thin volume, I was confident it was adequate proof for my foster father and all other doubters that I am a poet. The publication of this volume demonstrates that I can make my way in this world as a writer rather than buying and selling my fellow human beings.

***

The following morning, a Saturday, he was promoting and selling books to his fellow soldiers.

"Some of the finest verse you will ever read," Poe told barrack mate Samuel Farlow, presenting him with one of the books. "If you like Byron and Shelly, you'll love these poems."

Farlow took the volume and examined it.

"By 'a Bostonian'? Why isn't your name on it?"

"I like an air of mystery about my work."

Farlow laughed, then shelled out $1.25.

"Looks kind of thin!" said Alfred Murphy, a member of Battery H.

"Great things come in small packages," Poe said. "You won't realize how great it really is until you read it."

Murphy reached in his pocket and paid for a volume.

"So, this is it?" said Jones, examining one of the volumes. "I can't wait to read it."

"I've heard about your poems," said Silas Merchant. "I'll take one."

By the end of the day, he had sold forty-one of the fifty copies that were printed. That night, back in the barracks, he counted out more than $50 in sales proceeds. "Who says I can't make a living writing poetry?" Poe said to himself.

***

The following Monday morning, Poe knew his fellow soldiers would have had time to read his book over the weekend. He could not wait to hear their adulation and admiration. As he strode to morning mess, he saw a group of soldiers coming toward him. Two of them, Tom Murphy and Silas Merchant, had bought his book.

"Murphy!" Poe called. "Did you read my poems?"

"Biggest load of rubbish I've even seen."

"I'm sorry you didn't like it," Poe said.

Murphy and Merchant dismissed Poe with a wave of the hand and continued walking.

Before drill that day, he saw a group of Battery D soldiers who had bought the book entering the parade ground. He asked for their opinions.

"It was a damn cheat," said one soldier. "I want my money back!"

"You bought the book in good faith," Poe said. "I can't return the money."

"Then I'm never speaking to you again. And I shall tell all of my friends what a thief you are."

Poe turned to another member of the group.

"Harriman! What about you?"

"I threw my copy in the River Charles." Harriman said. "Maybe the fish will like it."

"I used mine in the toilet this morning," said another soldier.

"Useless rubbish!" said still another.

Poe could not believe what he was hearing.

"None of you liked my poems?"

"If you're a poet, I'm the man in the moon," said Harriman.

With that, the group waved him away and continued walking.

Later that day, he saw other soldiers who had bought the book. Upon seeing Poe, they skirted around him as if they did not know him.

***

March 24, 1829. Today was the most miserable day of my life. Only two people, Tommy and Joshua Gibson, expressed appreciation for my book of poems. The others either mocked my efforts or explained that they downright hated them. Their cold rejection has cut a gaping wound in my pride. Perhaps I am a fool. Perhaps the life of a poet is not for me. Perhaps I am leading myself down a pathway of self-delusion, thinking I could walk in the footsteps of Byron or Shelley. Tonight, I wish to disappear from the face of this earth and the ill feelings of my friends. Perhaps prose, in the form of short stories, would be a better path for me.

***

The following morning, Poe received the application from West Point. The minute he opened the letter, he went straight to Thomas for advice about how to answer the questions and the ramifications of each. When Poe started to fill out the application as Edgar A. Poe, Thomas pulled back.

"Who is Edgar Allan Poe?"

"That's my true surname."

"You're not Edgar Perry? The name I have been addressing you as all this time?"

"I had to change my name to escape my creditors. All the stuff about growing up in Philadelphia and being the son of a printer was made up."

Thomas burst out laughing.

"You played an excellent masquerade. "

"I assure you no harm or ill will was meant."

"I'm sure of that," Jones said, laughing again. "Edgar, you are truly a strange sort."

"That's what makes me interesting."

Jones chuckled again.

Finally, after two hours of Poe's questioning and cross-questioning of Thomas, they completed the application. Poe sent it off the following morning.

***

March 27, 1829. I have become a pariah with my fellow soldiers. Those who did buy my book have turned against me. Further, they have told those who did not buy the book that I am a thief. Other than Tommy and Joshua Gibson, those who were my friends before the book was published, now skirt around me or ignore me upon my approach. I am shunned on every hand. It is as if I have leprosy. Oh, how I long to escape this cold rejection of my friends.

***

That night, he dreamed of Aunt Muddy. In the dream, he remembered their days together when he was a toddler. The kind, loving smile. The soft, reassuring voice. Always nurturing, always playing the loving mother, Muddy was a haven against a world that showed no pity. Before he reported for inspection the following morning, he penned a letter to her.

April 3, 1829
Dear Muddy:

It has been sixteen years since I last saw you. While I am happy to receive your occasional letter, nothing would make me happier than to look into your kind, motherly eyes.

Currently, my plans are to get away from army life for a time, so that I may refresh myself from some recent malicious experiences.

May I pay you a visit?

Affectionately yours,
Edgar

***

Five days later, he received her reply.

April 8, 1829
My Dear Edgar:

    I was happy to receive your letter.

    Yes. It has been sixteen years since I laid eyes on you. While I fondly remember your days as a toddler, I recognize full well that you are an adult now.

    Since the last time I saw you, I have become a wife, a mother, and a widow. In the fall of 1817, I married William Clemm Jr., a local hardware merchant and, in 1822, I bore him a daughter. After he died last year, my daughter and I have been living with Grandma Poe in the old family home in Baltimore.

    It would thrill my very soul for you to pay a visit. I want you to meet my daughter Virginia. She is pretty as a picture and smart as a whip.

    You may visit anytime you like. Grandma would be happy to see you. She has never met you.

Affectionately,
Maria Clemm

The following morning, before going to the mess hall, he was in the commander's office requesting a 21-day leave of absence. That afternoon, he was notified by an adjutant that the leave had been granted.

***

Two days later, when Poe's carriage arrived in Baltimore at the old Poe family home on Amity Street, it was the first time he had seen the dwelling. An aging, two-story clapboard structure, it had a wood shingle roof and four rooms on the bottom floor and three on the top. Nestled among a grove of white oak trees, the home was surrounded by open fields on three sides and, on the fourth, by the Patapsco River. It was built in 1793 by Poe's grandfather, David Poe Sr., a career military man. During the Revolutionary war, Poe had served as a field commander at the battles of Brandywine and Ticonderoga and, when he retired in the spring of 1813, he had the rank of general and was serving as Assistant Deputy Quartermaster General in Baltimore. He died of scarlet fever in 1828, the previous year.

As Poe exited the carriage and started to the door, he saw Maria waiting on the porch. Without a word, he went straight to her and hugged her.

"Oh, dear Lord!" she said. "Let me look at you. You're not three years old anymore."

She stepped back to examine him.

"You're so handsome, Eddie. If your mother were here, she would be so proud. Come on in."

As they started inside, Poe examined her. Now, at age 35, he could see she had changed little. She still wore the same black and white Mother Hubbard outfits with a white ruffled regency cap. During her waking hours, she had a flowery apron tied around her waist with a handkerchief, a box of snuff, and a folded copy of the Lord's Prayer in the pocket. The only noticeable difference was the deepened lines in her face, especially around the eyes and the lips. They were testimony to a life of devoted motherly love.

Once inside, Maria prepared tea and they chatted about their lives and the latest family news. Poe asked about his brother Henry; Maria said he was in Norfolk. When tea was finished, Maria took him into one of the first-floor bedrooms to meet his grandmother, Elizabeth Carnes Poe, for the first time. When Maria opened the door, the old woman turned her bulky, gray-haired frame to face them.

"Mother! This is Edgar Poe. He is David's youngest son."

The old woman put on her glasses, then squinted to view him.

"Oh, yes! I've heard about you," she said. "You are every bit as handsome as your father. Maria has spoken to me many times about your toddler days."

After a brief chat with his grandmother, Maria led Poe out of the bedroom.

"Mother doesn't get out anymore," Maria said. "She's sixty-nine. She sleeps most of the day and takes only two meals."

Now, back in the kitchen, they heard footsteps on the back porch and a young girl's voice.

"Mother! Mother!"

Suddenly, a young girl of seven, her arms laden with fresh green ferns, burst into the kitchen.

"Look!" she said, unable to contain her excitement. "Today I found three peacock ferns. They were growing on a log jutting out into the river."

Seconds later, she laid the fresh ferns on the table. Then she saw Edgar.

"Virginia, this is your cousin Edgar. He'll be visiting for a while."

"Hello!"

Then, very adult-like, she walked over and offered her hand. He took it.

"Come look, Edgar!" Virginia said, turning back to the ferns. "Do you see how finely the bottom leaves of the peacock fern are filigreed? It is as if they were tiny fingers."

Poe arose from his seat to examine her prize.

"Now," Virginia said, expertly pointing to another fern. "Compare the peacock fern to the gladiator fern. See the difference?"

She held the two ferns side-by-side for Poe's inspection.

"Oh yes," he said. "I would never have noticed. What do you do with these?"

"I collect and classify them. Each species has its own peculiar set of natural properties. It is called pteridomania, also known as fern collecting."

She withdrew a small volume from her pocket.

Poe took it and read the title.

"*Fern Fever: The Story of Pteridomania.* Very interesting."

"All right," said Maria. "Take your ferns up to your room so I can clean off the table. We'll be eating soon."

Virginia started to gather her prizes.

"Cousin Edgar, would you like to go fern hunting with me one day?"

"Oh yes. I would like that. Perhaps then I could learn to discern the difference between the peacock and the gladiator fern."

She laughed.

"Can we go tomorrow?"

"Sure!"

***

That night, Poe decided he wanted to get out of the house, so he wandered down to Ryan's Tavern, the neighborhood bar at Amity and Hartwell Streets. After a few drinks, he struck up a conversation with the barmaid, a smiling, light-haired woman in her early twenties with a pretty face. Her name was Sophia.

"Haven't see you around here before," she said. "New in town?"

Poe explained he was visiting with relatives. It was a weeknight and there were few patrons, so they chatted while she attended to the occasional customer.

"I grew up in the mountains of Western Kentucky," Sophia said. "After my father was killed in a mining accident, my mother passed shortly afterward and left me and three other small children on the mercies of the world. After a year in an orphanage, I was adopted by a family in Baltimore."

She stopped, wiped away a tear, then continued.

"Being adopted and brought to a big city was the best thing ever happened to me. If I had not been adopted, I'd still be living in the desolate hills of Kentucky."

A pause as she went to serve a drink. When she returned, she explained that she was an aspiring artist and had been drawing illustrations for magazines.

"I send them out," she said. "But they are sent right back. It's a tough business."

A pause.

"Are you married?" she asked. "You aren't wearing a ring."

"I'm single. I have not yet met the woman who could steal my heart."

She laughed.

"You're such an attractive man. I'm surprised some woman hasn't latched on to you."

"I'm flattered," he said.

"It's true. You are a very handsome man."

Over the next two hours, they chatted about themselves until closing time. When the tavern owner began to herd patrons out the door, Sophia turned to Poe.

"I'm going to be up late tonight," she said. "Would you care to come up to my apartment? I could show you my illustrations."

"I better not," he said. "I'm a guest in a home and I don't want to come in too late."

She peered at him.

"I have some laudanum," she said.

He smiled.

"Well, in that case…"

That night, Poe arrived back at the old Poe home at 3 a.m. Everyone was asleep and Poe had to rap on Maria's bedroom window to get into the house.

16
West Point

The following morning after breakfast, Edgar and Virginia were in the fields behind the family home searching for fern specimens. As they made their way to the Patapsco River, they saw a large chinaberry tree standing alone in the field, not more than 100 yards from the water's edge. As they moved closer, Poe could see the tree had once been part of a home. Nearby, scattered among the tall weeds and bushes, were the remains of a concrete foundation, a well, and a falling chimney.

Virginia, wearing a smocked dress and a white regency cap, led the way along the river's edge while Poe, in knee-length breeches and army boots, carried the collection basket. He watched as she darted from bush to bush and fallen tree to fallen tree in search of her prizes. After two hours, they had collected four gladiator ferns, three will-of-the-wisps, and a strange-looking specimen Virginia had not seen before. As they probed through the book looking for the unidentified fern, it started to rain.

"We better get out of this rain," she said. "Let's run to the chinaberry tree."

Moments later, they were standing under the chinaberry tree watching the rain fall. As she looked out at the rain, Poe looked down at her. Flat-chested, boyish hips, skinny legs, and eyes wide open, Virginia was a portrait of a beautiful, prepubescent young girl. Her development as a young maiden had not yet begun.

***

Later that afternoon, back at the old home, Virginia asked Edgar if he played chess.

"As a matter of fact, I do," he said.

"I must warn you, Edgar," Maria said, "she's an excellent chess player."

In the first game, Virginia check-mated him in nine moves. Poe was baffled.

"How did you do that?"

"You were following a classic knight's thrust pattern," she said. "I know all of the countermoves. Shall we play again?"

Over the next two hours, they played eight more games of chess and Virginia won every one. In the last game, Virginia check-mated him in thirteen moves.

"What happened that time?"

"Knight's gambit is one of the oldest traps in chess. I offered the bait and you came rushing right in."

Poe shook his head in disbelief.

"Amazing!"

***

The following morning, when Poe came down the stairs for breakfast, Maria was waiting.

"I have bad news," she said. "Today I received a letter from your brother Henry saying Frances Allan was dead."

"Oh, no," he said.

"Whatever differences you have had with your foster father in the past should be laid aside at a time like this. Do you not feel you should visit the plantation to show your last respects?"

Poe inhaled.

"Perhaps you're right."

***

Two days later, when Poe's carriage pulled up at New Dundonald, his heart was filled with trepidation.

Dolina answered the door.

"Mr. Edgar," she said. "Please wait here!"

Moments later, John appeared.

"What business do you have here?"

"I heard the news that Mother had passed."

"Yes! She was buried two days ago at Shockoe Hill."

A pause.

"So, I shall ask you again, what business do you have here?"

"I thought perhaps, out of respect for Mother, we could be civil with one another."

John Allan inhaled, then studied him for a moment.

"Perhaps you are right. Come in!"

Over dinner that night, alone in the mansion's main dining room, they discussed their lives. John said he planned to be married again. Poe said he had been a soldier for the past three years and had made application to West Point.

"West Point?" John said. "How did you arrange such an event?"

Poe explained his friendship with Thomas Pickering Jones.

"I wish you well with your appointment."

"Can I ask you a favor?"

"If it's about money, no."

"Money has nothing to do with it."

"So what is the favor?"

"I need a person of influence to recommend me to the secretary of war and the West Point commander for an appointment."

"You want me to make those recommendations?"

"Yes."

He studied Poe for a moment.

"Do you have the necessary addresses?"

"I do. They're here."

Poe withdrew a sheet of paper with the information.

"Leave them with me and I will see the deed is done."

"Will you forget our past differences and give me high praise? I must have an unblemished record to be accepted."

"I will."

"When will your letters go out?"

"Tomorrow afternoon."

"Thank you, Father! Thank you very much!"

When Poe left that night, John Allan shook his hand and wished him well.

***

Two days later, Poe was back in Baltimore and, over the next two weeks, his days would find him with Virginia playing chess, gathering ferns, reading poems, and making frequent visits to the library. Nights would find him drinking ale at Ryan's Tavern and, after closing time, in Sophia's apartment ingesting stimulants and fornicating.

On the night of June 18, Maria prepared a sumptuous meal of fried chicken, potatoes, and black beans with biscuits.

"I'll be leaving tomorrow," Edgar said. "I wanted to say thanks for allowing me to visit. My stay has been quite pleasant."

"I hope you can come and visit again," Virginia said.

"I hope so too."

***

That night, Poe was back at Ryan's Tavern to say good-bye to Sophia.

"Thanks for the nights we had together," she said. "If you're in Baltimore again, I hope you will come visit me."

"I shall do so. I too have enjoyed myself."

Before he left, she gave him a long kiss.

"That's so you'll remember me the next time."

Poe smiled.

She looked into his eyes.

"My! My! You are so handsome. I would do anything to have you for my man."

He smiled.

"I'll see you again!"

Then Poe waved good-bye and strode off down the street.

***

That afternoon, on the train, he could feel himself being pulled back to the old Poe home. He was not sure why, but it seemed the spirits of his ancestors were tugging at him to return to the old clapboard structure and honor the legacy of the past. The first night he had slept there, in the attic, he had the same feeling. It was as if the house had some sort of magnetic attraction for him. He could escape it, but he could still feel it tugging at him. How could a simple wooden house have such an effect?

***

Three days later, upon his return to Fort Independence, Poe went straight to his mailbox. There were several letters. One was from The United States Military Academy at West Point, New York.

The following morning, in route to the mess hall, Poe saw Thomas rushing toward him.

"Guess who's going to West Point?" Thomas said.

"Guess who else is going to West Point?" Poe replied.

Jones stopped and peered at him.

"You got an appointment?"

"I did."

"When are you due to report?"

"August 3."

Jones laughed out loud.

"Me too! We shall report together."

***

June 9, 1829. What a lucky fellow I am. Just in the nick of time, I am saved from the mockery and rejection of my friends. I will no longer have to endure their cold-shouldered comments, their derisive insults, and their falsified social graces. I shall move to the next level of soldiering while they remain in the regular army as mere enlisted men. The best revenge, as they say, is success. Such a lucky fellow I am!

***

On August 3, 1829, Poe, at age 20, entered the United States Military Academy. Well-schooled and quick-witted, he proved to be an exemplary cadet over the first six months. He excelled in his classes, especially French, and won high marks for his lucid recitations and near-perfect pronunciation. He was prompt for drills and inspections and was praised for his performance on the parade ground. By fall, however, Poe began to buckle under the harsh discipline, long marches, and miserable food. His primary complaint was the lack of time to write.

***

January 11, 1830. As an author, my talents are rotting at West Point. During my tenure at Fort Independence, I could walk away from daily military life and cast myself into my poetry. I am totally, inexorably unable to do that here. Each time I sit down to write, I am notified of some new demand by my superior officers. Report for inspection. Be on the drill field in ten minutes. Parade dress in one hour. There is no end to the demands and the study requisite is incessant. Minimum of four hours study each night. I am like a rat trapped in a hole. I must escape from this confinement so I may return to my writing. Otherwise, I shall go mad.

***

Two days later, while Poe and Jones were on the parade ground preparing for drills, Poe confessed his unhappiness.

"I must remove myself from this place," he said. "I am suffocating from the constant demands."

"I warned you that the discipline was much more rigid here than in the army. In our days at Wentworth, I could see you were an exceptionally brilliant fellow, but buckling down to the strict discipline of the academy is not within your personal repertoire. That is the element which is keeping you in an unhappy frame of mind."

Poe peered at his old friend for a long moment.

"I'm not certain what is required, but I must remove myself."

214

The following morning, when members of Company C showed up on the parade ground for inspection, Poe was wearing nothing but his helmet, an ammunition belt, and a smile. When the drill sergeant faced him, he demanded an explanation.

"Cadet! Where is your uniform?"

"I don't have one, sir."

"You had a uniform yesterday."

"But I don't today, sir."

"I can see that."

Anger flashed across the drill sergeant's face.

"Fall out! Return to quarters. This behavior will result in ten demerits in your monthly report."

Poe broke ranks, his lily-white behind shining in the morning sunshine, and trotted across the parade ground toward his quarters. Several other soldiers chuckled as he passed.

***

Over the month of January, Poe was absent from classes, parade, reveille, roll calls, and chapel every day. During that time, outside of mess hall visits, he remained in his quarters and wrote short stories.

"Have you just given up?" Jones asked one day at mess. "I heard about your appearance at drill stark naked."

Poe did not answer right away.

"I shall have my freedom one way or another," he said finally. "I can no longer endure this imprisonment."

"You're going to be court-martialed."

***

On February 5, 1831, four weeks after he appeared naked at drill, an adjutant in the commander's office arrived at his quarters and presented him with court-martial papers. Poe opened the document and read it.

From the Offices of John W Eaton, Secretary of War, relating to the court-martial proceedings against Cadet Edgar A. Poe:

> • *Charge 1st: – Gross neglect of duty.*

> • *Specifications 1st – In this, that he, the said Cadet Edgar Poe, did absent himself from the following parades and roll-calls between the 7th January and the 27th January, 1831, Viz., absent from evening parade on the 8th, 9th, 15th, 20th, 24th, and 25th January 1830; absent from reveille call on the 8th, 16th, 17th, 19th, 21st, 25th and 26th January 1830; absent from reveille call on the 8th, 16th, 17th, 19th, 21st, 25th, and 26th January 1830; absent from class parade on the 17th, 18th, 19th, 20th, 24th and 25th January 1831.*

> • *Specification 2nd. –In this, that he, the said Cadet Edgar A. Poe, did absent himself from all his academic duties between the 15th and 27th January 1831.*

> • *Directive: The court, after mature deliberation on the testimony adducted, find the prisoner guilty of the 1st Specification of the 1st Charge and adjudge that he, Cadet Edgar A. Poe, be dismissed from the service of the United States and cease to be considered a member of the Military Academy after the 6th March 1831.*

By Order of the Secretary of War,
John W. Eaton

Poe looked up from the document.
"Hallelujah!" he said to himself.

***

That afternoon, Poe paid a visit to Thomas.
"I see you finally accomplished your goal," he said. "I got the news this morning."

"I had to free myself," Poe replied. "I was unable to breathe."

"So, what do you plan to do?"

"I'm not sure. To be honest, I would like to have my old job back at Wentworth Lines. Can you talk to your Uncle Thaddeus?"

"If there is nothing in the office, you can always find work on the dock. I shall talk to him."

"Thanks!"

"Good luck and goodbye."

***

A month later, Poe had returned to his old life. Once again, he was living in his old garret room at the Shawmut Hotel and writing every night. After a month working on the docks, the company office manager invited him to return to the manifest office and he accepted. He enjoyed the work, his fellow employees were pleasant enough, and the pay was fair. His new daily routine was virtually identical to the life he had known before entering the military.

***

In late April, he received a letter from his foster father.

April 22, 1831
Edgar:

Today I received letters from the commander at West Point and the Secretary of War notifying me of your expulsion from the academy.

It seems that no matter the opportunity presented to you, you manage to corrupt it and fall far short of the trust and expectations others have placed in you.

You have humiliated me and my efforts to help you gain admittance to the academy. I placed my reputation at stake for you and, once again, your actions have led to abject disappointment. I have believed in you for the last time.

Hereby, I am retiring from any further efforts to assist you and I wish it to be understood that our relationship is at an end. Now and forever.

As of today, rest assured you shall never again hear from me.

John Allan

***

Over the next three years, Poe worked for Wentworth lines. By day, he processed cargo manifests and argued with ship captains about cargo being loaded on incoming and outgoing vessels. By night, he wrote short stories and sent them off to magazines. One story, "MS. Found in a Bottle," a tale of mystery and suspense, was sent to *Graham's Magazine.* Another short story, "Hans Pfaal," a macabre science fiction tale, was dispatched to *Godey's Lady's Book.* It prompted a reply from the editor who complained that the story was "far too ghoulish" for his readers' taste. "The Man of the Crowd," a work Poe deemed to be his finest short story theretofore, was sent to *Burton's Men's Magazine.* All were returned with rejection notices.

17
Lilies in the Rain

It was the spring of 1834 and the twenty-three-year-old Poe, disgusted and disillusioned with his futile efforts to earn a living as a writer, was more than ready for a change. Any kind of change. Then, one morning in early April, he received it in the form of a letter from Maria.

April 9, 1834
Dear Edgar:

I am writing this letter because you are my final hope.

Since the death of my mother last month, my daughter and I have been left destitute. With her death, we are no longer receiving the monthly pension from my father's military retirement. This means we have no income to sustain ourselves.

Can you send $20 so we can buy food?

I have pawned my wedding ring and my Witherspoon silver tea service to buy food. Tomorrow, I will take my last silver tea set to the pawn broker. After that, I am uncertain as to how we shall survive.

I wish to say, if you can make any sort of financial contribution to the household, you are welcome to come here and live.

Should you decide to do so, you could have the attic room on the second floor which you occupied during your stay five years ago.

Now that Mother is gone and Virginia is in school, you would have more than adequate peace and quiet for your writing efforts.

If you can contribute, please send soonest because we are desperate.

All my love,
Muddy

As he read the letter, he knew he had no choice but to comply. Maria was the closest thing to a mother he had ever had. She had cared for and nurtured him when he was unable to perform those duties for himself. In his heart, he knew he could not deny her in this hour of desperate need.

That afternoon, he penned a reply.

April 14, 1834
My Dear Muddy:
I am deeply wounded to learn you and Virginia are in such dire financial straits.
I am enclosing $20 in this return letter.
Make good use of it until I arrive.
I need a few days to clear up some business matters here in Boston, then I will travel to Baltimore to take up residence in the old family home. I will arrive at your home on the morning of April 20.
For all of the blessings you bestowed upon me as a toddler, I cannot ignore your heart-felt requests for assistance.

Affectionately yours,
Edgar

***

Once Poe arrived back at the old family home, the first order of business was to get the attic room set up as a writing parlor. First, he needed some sort of desk. Maria did not own a bona fide writing desk, but she had a small table that could be used as one. That first morning, Maria cleaned out the attic room, then Edgar and Virginia managed to bring the table up the stairs and place it in front of the attic window. Poe began to unpack his writing equipment, his quills, ink, paper, old poems and short stories, and associated materials. Included was a stack of letters with publishers' names at the top.

"What are these?" Virginia asked.

"Those are rejection notices for my short story 'William Wilson'."

Virginia picked up several and scanned through them.

"*Godey's Lady's Book. Graham's Magazine*, the *New York Gazette, Burton's Men's Magazine, Childers Modern Homemaker.*"

She took special interest in the one from *Godey's*.

"Why would you submit a ghoulish story like 'William Wilson' to *Godey's*? Their readers have no interest in horror and death. They are wealthy socialites who are interested in fancy clothes, the theater, exotic vacations, and French perfume."

Poe shrugged.

"I thought they might possibly be interested."

"Your stories are being woefully misplaced," she said.

By late afternoon, Poe's new quarters had been set up. Maria did a final inspection.

"Looks good," she said.

Then she turned to Edgar.

"Can you go with Virginia to the market and help her carry back the groceries? She is buying a twenty-pound sack of flour and it's too heavy for her to carry."

***

An hour later, laden with groceries, Poe and Virginia were trudging back to the old Poe home. As they passed several businesses, Virginia caught sight of a stack of old magazines and newspaper at the top of a trash can in an alleyway.

"Wait!"

Poe stopped. Virginia's eyes scanned through the publications. There was *Godey's Lady's Book, Burton's Men's Magazine,* and several other old copies of popular magazines of the day. Virginia looked around to confirm no one was watching, then she grabbed a handful.

"What are you going to do with those?" Poe asked as they continued walking.

"I'm going to read them," she said.

He laughed.

Back at home, once the groceries were put away, Virginia took a seat on the settee with the magazines. Poe studied her as she paged through them. Now, at almost age twelve, she was already a blossoming young maiden. She was not pretty in the traditional sense, he thought. Although she had large, brown eyes and a pert nose, her beauty expressed itself in the way her eyes lit up upon discovering something new. It was the sparkle in her eyes when she laughed; it was the innocent way she approached life that made her attractive, Poe thought. After some twenty minutes, Virginia arose from the settee and came to him with one of the magazines.

"Here's the one you should be sending your ghoulish stories to."

She held up a copy of the *Southern Literary Messenger*, then she took a seat beside him and indicated the headlines on the front page.

"Look at this!" she said, pointing to the story titles. "'Rappaccini's Daughter' by Nathaniel Hawthorne. 'The Legend of Sleepy Hollow' by some author named Washington Irving. Apparently, their readers love ghoulish stories or they wouldn't be printing them."

Poe peered at her.

"Why did I not realize that?" he said absently.

***

April 21, 1834. I had forgotten how much I enjoyed the comforting presence of Aunt Muddy. She has this special talent for calming the violent storms in my soul and, in her presence, my worldly cares seem to vanish into nothingness. I remember feeling the identical sentiment during my toddler days. And her daughter Virginia is such a delight. No longer is she the gangly, tree-climbing tomboy I knew when I visited five years ago. Now she is blossoming into a beautiful young damsel with a handsome womanly shape that is already turning men's heads. And such a sharp acumen. She fully grasps the meaning of Plutarch's work at the tender age of twelve. An amazing young woman, this Virginia.

***

The following morning at breakfast, Poe asked Virginia what she had planned for the day.

"It's too muddy to go fern hunting. I'm in no mood for the library."

She paused, then turned to him.

"Would you like to follow a funeral?"

"Why would I follow a funeral?"

"Funerals can be quite entertaining. Mourners wear their emotions on their sleeves at funerals and you never know what might occur. Some people have been known to go mad at funerals."

Poe laughed.

"Then we shall follow a funeral."

Instantly, Virginia reached for the *Baltimore Herald*, then began flipping through the pages.

"At Simpson's Funeral Parlor, there are four funerals today, but it's on the other side of town. Too far."

She probed further.

"At Winkenhoffer's, three funerals are scheduled for today. It is only four blocks away. Funerals are scheduled at 10, 1 and 3."

"Shall we catch the one o'clock funeral?" Poe said with a laugh.

***

That afternoon, shortly before one, Edgar and Virginia were waiting in front of Winkenhoffer Funeral Parlor. As they waited, a two-horse wagon bearing the flower-laden coffin of the deceased emerged from the rear of the building and stopped at the front door. Moments later, mourners began to fall in line behind the wagon to follow it to the burial ground. Poe and Virginia fell in line with them. As the procession began moving, a young boy, not more than thirteen, marched at the head of the procession playing the death march on a flute.

Twenty minutes later, the mourners and the wagon had reached the cemetery. As Poe and Virginia watched, the coffin was unloaded and carried to the graveside by pallbearers. The mourners, including Edgar and Virginia, gathered quietly around the open grave as the minister began speaking.

"Ashes to ashes and dust to dust. Man born of woman is but of a few days and full of trouble. He cometh forth and is cut down, like a flower; he flees life as if it were a shadow, and never continues in one stay…"

Suddenly, the minister's solemn words were interrupted by a man's frantic voice.

"Help! Help! For God's sake, someone please help me!"

Instantly, the minister and mourners broke their supplicant poses and began looking around for the source of the voice. Finally, the minister's eyes fell on a fresh grave, not more than thirty feet away.

"It's coming from that grave over here," he said.

Moments later, the minister and several mourners were standing over the grave where the voice was emanating. They could see a large speaking horn had been installed beside the headstone, indicating the grave had been outfitted with an apparatus to prevent someone from being buried alive, a popular device of the day.

The minister bent down to the speaking horn.

"Hello! Hello!" he said. "Is this…?"

He stopped and glanced at the grave marker.

"Joseph P. Watson?"

"Yes! Yes! It is I!" the voice replied loudly. "I've been buried alive. Please get me out."

The minister turned to the mourners.

"Will someone call the sextons," he said. "We've got to get this poor man out of his grave."

Instantly, several mourners, upon seeing two sextons nearby digging a fresh grave, summoned them. When they arrived, the minister explained the situation. The sextons immediately began digging and throwing fresh earth out of the grave. Finally, after ten minutes, they had reached the coffin. One of the sextons rapped on top of the coffin with a shovel.

"Hello! Hello!"

"I'm still in here," the voice shouted. "Get me out!"

Seconds later, one of the sextons was in the grave and opened the coffin lid. Then, the mourners, the sextons, and the minister drew back in horror when a middle-aged man, dressed in funeral attire, stood up in the coffin. He was elated.

"Oh! Thank you so much," he said. "I feared that I was destined to remain in there for all eternity."

At the sight, Poe began to laugh uproariously.

The others turned and stared at him.

"I think we should be going," Virginia said.

***

That night, at the dinner table, the only thing they could talk about was the incident at the graveyard. Once the meal was finished, Poe and Virginia played chess for almost two hours, then Poe retired to his garret room and sat down to write. He took quill in hand and a blank piece of paper and wrote the title for a new short story: "The Premature Burial." Once he started writing, he was unable to stop. The words poured out of him in great avalanches. Feverishly, he wrote through the night and, around 3 a.m., he was finished.

The following morning, he showed the story to Virginia.

"I enjoyed the story," she said. "Now send it off to the *Southern Literary Messenger* and you'll get it published."

"Do you really believe that?"

"Of course. Those are the stories their readers love."

Poe stared at her.

"And don't address it to just anybody. Get the name of the editor and send it directly to him."

"I don't have the editor's name."

Virginia got up, went to the stack of old magazines she had found in the trash, and pulled out a copy of the magazine in question.

"His name is Thomas White."

Poe laughed at her resourcefulness.

The following morning, Poe posted the story to the *Southern Literary Messenger* in Richmond, addressed directly to the editor.

***

Over the next few weeks, Poe began spending more and more time with Virginia. They helped Maria with household chores, went fern hunting, played chess, and attended lectures at the local library on phrenology and hypnotism. One of their favorite pastimes was picnicking on the Patapsco River. There they could watch the passing boats and while away their time. During one picnic, Poe asked about her ability to play chess.

"I learned from my father," she said. "As a military man, he said soldiers spent a lot of time playing chess. After he retired, we would play chess at his hardware store. When customers came in, he would get up to help them and this would give me plenty of time to plan my next move. He always said, to master chess, you have to plan at least six moves ahead."

"He was a good teacher."

"We would spend hours and hours playing, and he would explain the possibilities of every move. Before he died, he gave me his book on mastering chess."

"When did he die?"

"When I was six," she said. "Nothing that has ever happened to me hurt me like losing my father."

Suddenly, she began to weep.

"Even now, after more than six years, I still miss him. Being around you reminds me of being with my father."

"Do you wish to return to the house?" Poe asked, upon seeing her tears.

"No!" she said, wiping her eyes. "I'll be fine."

***

April 26, 1834. With each passing day, my heart is becoming inextricably intertwined with that of my cousin Virginia. Every moment I am with her, this attraction grows stronger. Now I know what Elizabeth Browning meant when she wrote "the heights my soul may reach." With every smile, her eyes light up with love and kindness. Although she is not yet twelve years old, she has the heart and mind of a fully-grown woman.

***

The following day, Virginia retrieved the mail from the mailbox. There was a reply from the *Southern Literary Messenger*. Virginia waited for Edgar to open it.

May 3, 1834
Dear Edgar Poe:
I am pleased to report that your short story, "The Premature Burial," has been accepted for publication in our magazine.
Currently, it is scheduled for our August issue.
Enclosed you will find a bank draft for $25.
Your offering is a perfect match for our readers' literary tastes and I encourage you to submit other such stories in the future.
Thank you for your contribution.

Sincerely,
Thomas White, Editor

"Hallelujah!" he said, looking up from the letter. "This is the opportunity I've been waiting for."

***

The following morning, Virginia and Edgar were in the fields hunting for ferns. Virginia, wearing a smocked dress and a white regency cap, led the way. Poe, in knee-length pantaloons and army boots, followed close behind, carrying the collection basket on his shoulder.

"I wanted to express my gratitude to you for my success with the short story. I fear I could not have achieved it without your help."

"You are welcome. It makes me happy to help you."

Near the river's edge, she spotted a fallen tree trunk jutting out of the water, a prime locale for ferns.

Moments later, as they neared the tree, it started to drizzle rain.

At the fallen tree, she stopped. Her eyes scanned its entire length.

"Look! A thespian fern," she said. "Three of them!"

Quickly, she moved to the ferns and clipped the stems, then handed them to Edgar, and he placed them in the collection basket. Now the rain had suddenly quickened and was pouring down.

"Let's run to the chinaberry tree," she said. "It will provide some shelter."

Moments later, they were huddling under the chinaberry tree. The tree provided some shelter, but they were still getting wet. Poe peered up at the tree, trying to decide the driest place. He changed positions.

"Come over here," he said. "There is more shelter."

She moved to his side. Poe peered down at her as she watched the pouring rain. Five years earlier, he had stood with her at this exact spot. Then, she was a gangly, prepubescent tomboy of seven. Now at age twelve, she was a young maiden in flower. She was not wearing under garments and, through the wet cotton dress, he could see the outline of her nubile, pear-shaped breasts. Sensing he was staring at her, she turned. Their eyes met. Unable to control himself, Poe bent down and kissed her on the lips.

She held the kiss for a long moment, then withdrew and looked away. Then she turned back to him.

"Why did you do that?" she said.

"I'm not sure. I think we're falling in love."

"Do you really think so?"

"Yes."

"Can we do it again?"

This time, they held the kiss for a long moment. Then, suddenly, as if she was frightened, Virginia broke the kiss again and looked out into the rain.

For a long moment, she did not speak.

"The rain is almost stopped now," she said. "We'd better get back."

Then, with Edgar holding the collection basket in one hand and Virginia's hand in the other, they raced across the field to the old family home.

***

May 22, 1834. Today, as I stood under the chinaberry tree in the rain with Virginia, I spied the virginal young lilies resting upon her chest. They were the size of small melons with their tips pointing to God. Such a beautiful sight. Someday, somehow, some way, I shall make those lilies mine. They shall be mine and mine alone.

***

Two days later, they were at the library. They had spent the last two hours reading passages from the life of Cicero and Plutarch.

"Why do you think Plutarch chose Caesar to be the match for Alexander the Great in *Plutarch's Lives*?"

"Alexander was the greatest military man in Greek history. Of all the Roman military leaders, Caesar was the greatest. It was only logical."

"Very good. Why do you think Cicero hung on to his republican principles during the civil wars?"

She peered thoughtfully at him for a moment.

"I don't know."

"Republican principles were what had brought Cicero to the Roman senate in the first place. He could not abandon the tenets upon which his entire reputation had been based."

She smiled.

"Oh, Edgar. You're so smart."

For a long moment, he studied her.

"Will you marry me?"

Instantly, she drew back at the question.

"Marry you?"

"I want you to be my wife."

She laughed nervously.

"Will you say it again?"

"I want you to be my wife."

She smiled then looked into his eyes.

"Oh Eddie. I would adore being your wife, but we will have to discuss it with Mother."

***

Back at home that afternoon, they found Maria in the sitting room, sipping tea and reading the Bible.

"Muddy, Virginia and I would like to speak with you."

"You sound serious."

"Come sit at the table," he said.

Moments later, Maria was comfortably seated at the table. Edgar spoke first.

"I've grown very fond of Virginia these past few months."

"I can see that."

"I think we've fallen in love."

Maria drew back at the sound of the word.

"Love?"

"We want to get married, Mother," said Virginia.

Maria looked from one to the other, then took a deep breath, trying to collect her thoughts.

"She's not even 12."

"Age has no meaning to a loving heart," Edgar said.

Maria turned to Virginia.

"Do you love him?"

"With all my heart."

Maria shook her head doubtfully, then turned to Virginia.

"Virginia, can you go into the parlor while I talk to Eddie in private?"

Virginia arose from her chair and left the room, then Maria turned back to Edgar.

For a moment, she studied him before speaking.

230

"You can't marry her without some form of steady income. These little payments of $15 and $10 for your stories here and there won't support a household."

"I'll find steady income."

"Furthermore, she's too young,' Maria said. "At age twelve, a young girl's body cannot comfortably accept a man. My mother was married at the age of twelve, but she said a hundred times she wished she had waited another year."

"We don't want to wait."

"No. I want you to wait until she is 13, then you can marry her."

"That's more than a year away."

"That is my decision. And I want you to promise me there will be no amorous congress until you are married."

Poe inhaled.

"So shall it be. I always respect your opinion."

***

The following morning, there was another letter from the *Southern Literary Messenger*. Once Poe had the letter in hand, Maria and Virginia waited for him to read it.

June 3, 1834
Dear Edgar Poe:

The Southern Literary Messenger *is currently in need of an able assistant editor.*

The duties involved include original contributions to the publication, the ability to review poems, novels, and short stories, as well as the ability to substitute for the publisher in his absence.

I feel the expertise and felicity with words you displayed with your recent submission, "The Premature Burial," qualifies you for this position.

Can you come to Richmond to discuss the details?

Sincerely,
Thomas White, Editor

Poe looked up from the letter to Virginia.

"My destiny is calling," he said.

"This is our beginning."

"I shall take the position and begin building a foundation for our future," Poe said.

"Ask and ye shall receive," Maria said. "That what it says in the Bible."

***

An hour later, Poe sent off a return letter to the *Messenger* editor that he would arrive in ten days. That afternoon, he and Virginia returned to the library and checked out the poems of William Wordsworth. Back at home, they sat in the white swing in the garden and read the poems. After glancing through several poems, Poe stopped.

"Oh, here's a beautiful little poem," Poe said, "It's about daffodils."

"Read it to me."

Poe began reading.

I wandered lonely as a cloud
That floats on high o'er vales and hills,
When all at once I saw a crowd,
A host, of golden daffodils,
Beside the lake, beneath the trees,
Fluttering and dancing in the breeze.

Continuous as the stars that shine
And twinkle on the milky way,
They stretched in never-ending line
Along the margin of a bay:
Ten thousand saw I at a glance,
Tossing their heads in sprightly dance.

For oft, when on my couch I lie
In vacant or in pensive mood,
They flash upon that inward eye
Which is the bliss of solitude,

And then my heart with pleasure fills,
And dances with the daffodils.

Poe looked up from the poem.

"Such a vivid, free-flowing poem."

"I quite agree."

"We must celebrate the beauty of this poem," Poe said. "We must commemorate the magnificence, not only of the words, but the pure grandeur of its message."

"How shall we do that?"

"We shall plant a host of daffodils here in the garden by the white swing. It shall be a celebration of Wordsworth's poem and our love."

That afternoon, they visited the local horticulturist and purchased a planter filled with young daffodils. Then, back at home, Poe dug a hole at one end of the white swing while Virginia, getting down on her knees, placed the young sprouts in the black earth.

"Now! Look at that!" Poe said. "Each time we see the daffodils, we shall be reminded of our love."

***

Four days later, Poe was on the train to Richmond. Before leaving, he had explained to Maria and Virginia that, once he accepted the editor's position, he would write them a letter and they could make plans from there.

"I have no intention of moving to Richmond unless you two are married," Maria had said. "We have a home here."

"First, let me determine the living circumstances," Poe said. "Then we'll make a decision."

18
Magaziner

By the mid-1830s, America's fledgling magazine industry was expanding with enormous leaps and bounds. With the advent of steam-powered presses and faster delivery methods such as railroads and steamships, readers were quietly extending their reading time beyond daily newspapers to the more leisurely content of periodicals. Rapid urbanization was feeding a growing literary rate, and rather than satisfying themselves with the staid, hard news of local newspapers, magazines appealed to a wider, more general audience and offered a wider array of subjects, which included humor, puzzles, insightful criticism, political analysis, and a generous amount of fiction and poetry. In Richmond, the major player in this nascent industry was a publication called the *Southern Literary Messenger*.

***

When Edgar's carriage stopped in front of the *Messenger*'s offices that morning in mid-August of 1834, he saw a white two-story brick structure on East Grace Street jammed between the Red Dog Saloon and a harness shop. On the façade, high above the second-story balcony, a huge sign in bold red letters proclaimed: "Southern Literary Messenger" and underneath, in smaller red fonts: "Devoted to Every Department of Literature and the Fine Arts."

Poe, suitcase in hand, stepped down from the carriage, paid the driver, then turned and started toward the entrance. As he approached, he saw a medium-height man, fiftyish with thinning gray hair, spectacles, and a stern countenance, standing in the doorway.

"Are you Edgar Poe?" the man asked.

"That is correct, sir."

The older man stepped forward and offered his hand.

"I am Thomas White, publisher of the *Messenger*. Come inside."

Ten minutes later, the two men were seated in White's office in a back corner on the building's first floor. The editor sat behind a wooden desk stacked high with books, yellowed magazines, and personal memorabilia.

"First, I wanted to say that your short story, 'The Premature Burial,' caused quite a stir among our readers this last month. They are not accustomed to stories about people arising from the grave. Grisly, but entertaining."

"So what are you seeking in an employee, Mr. White?"

"In a word... a right-hand man. Someone to do poetry criticism, provide stories and poems for the publication, do an occasional political analysis, and deal with poets and writers. You know writers can be a nasty lot."

Poe smiled.

"I can fill those needs."

"Most of all, I want controversy. I want to hear people's opinions. I want people to get mad and air their complaints about what's happening in the world around them."

"You mean editorial essays?"

"That's exactly what I mean."

"How much does the position pay?"

"Forty dollars a month."

"I'll be expecting a salary of $50 a month."

The editor cocked his head to one side.

"I have never paid that much to an employee."

"Let me say to you, sir, that you have never had an employee like me."

White studied him for a moment.

"You seem quite confident."

"If I do not believe in myself, who will?"

"All right, you seem firm. I shall pay you $45 a month."

"Agreed."

"Now I want it understood that I run a tight ship. No wastage. All oil lamps are to be extinguished after work. If you need another quill, you must bring me the old one. Each new bottle of ink must be signed for. Is that understood?"

"It is."

"When can you start work?"

"In the morning."

***

That afternoon, Poe took a room at a boarding house some two blocks from the *Messenger* office. It was a cramped, second-story, one-room affair with a bed, a writing desk, and wash basin that overlooked a blacksmith shop. Once he was settled, he wrote a letter to Virginia.

August 21, 1834
My Dear Sissy:
Glorious news!
Today I was hired as an assistant editor at the Southern Literary Messenger. *This is the dream we have awaited, since it represents steady income and future financial stability in our lives.*

I am assuming my duties immediately, so I cannot return to Baltimore to retrieve my personal belongings. Please put together two more suits of clothes in the old army trunk and post to me, care of the Southern Literary Messenger.

I trust that both you and Muddy are in good health.
I miss you so!

Affectionately yours,
Eddie
P.S. Please remember to include my book on Tacitus in the package. It is a small, black-bound volume on the top shelf of the bookcase.

***

The following morning, White gave Poe his first two assignments. The first was to critique James Fenimore Cooper's new romance novel, *Mercedes of Castile*; the second was to review a book of poems, *The Far Shallows*, penned by one Edward Wingate. Both were for the upcoming September edition.

Two days later, Poe had read the poems, written his critique, and submitted it to the editor. Once White had read it, he immediately came out of his office.

"Edgar! You don't feel this is overly critical? You called these poems 'oatmeal for children and simpletons'?"

"That was my honest opinion."

"This is one of the most scathing reviews I've ever seen."

"It speaks the truth of the poems."

"I'm going to print it, but I'm not sure of the consequences."

***

Three days later, Poe submitted his review of Cooper's novel. Again, he was unrelenting in his criticism and White came out of his office.

"You don't feel this review of Cooper's novel is rather harsh?"

"That's my opinion."

"Of his novel, you wrote: 'I must say that the *Mercedes of Castile, A Romance,* is the worst novel ever penned by Mr. Cooper. He is incapable of writing believable characters because that is not his forte; with that in mind, would we expect that his heroine would be anything more than an inanimate object that plods through the story?'"

White looked up from the review.

"Do you feel that's an appropriate criticism? James Fenimore Cooper is the premier novelist in America today."

"The heroine is an inanimate object passing in front of the reader. He is incapable of creating believable, full-dimensional female characters."

"I'm going to print it, but he is not going to be happy. Come into my office. I want to talk to you about your next assignment."

Moments later, Poe was sitting in White's office.

"Next Tuesday," White began, "the Richmond County Commission is going to hear a proposal about the Hawkins Valley Dam Project. The commission's plan is to flood a valley in the western part of Richmond County to provide water for a canal to transport goods and passengers to the far western counties of the state. The sponsor of the project is commissioner Samuel P. Lipper."

***

The following Tuesday afternoon, Poe was present at the commission meeting. He listened to the various arguments for and against the project and, once the meeting was over, the body decided to take a vote at the next monthly meeting.

When Poe left the meeting, he was met outside the commission building by a shadowy figure.

"You must go to the county land records office and see who owns most of the land in Hawkins Valley," the man said. "You'll blow the lid off the project."

"Who owns it?"

"The family of the man who's sponsoring the project."

***

Two days later, Poe had written his copy and submitted it to the editor. After White read the copy, he came out of his office.

"Poe! How do you know that Samuel Lipper's family owns 13,000 acres of land in Hawkins Valley?"

Poe reached for a document on his desk. It was the public deed record for land owned in Hawkins Valley by Commissioner Sam Lipper's family. White took the document and read it.

"Jumping Jehoshaphat!" White said. "There it is! In black and white."

The editor turned from Poe, calculating numbers in his head.

"That means, at $2 an acre, the going price for land in that part of the county, Fuller's family would receive $26,000 if the project is approved. That's a small fortune."

"That's correct," Poe said.

"I'm going to print it, but we're going to catch hell from the commission."

***

Eight days later, the September edition of the *Messenger* was on the streets. After only a day, White was receiving letters from readers about the Hawkins Valley Dam project. He called Poe into his office.

"Readers love the exposé on the Hawkins Dam Project. They say that is the kind of reporting the *Messenger* should have in every edition. All of them are now calling for the dam project to be cancelled. Good work, Poe!"

***

The following Monday, Poe was back in White's office.

"More letters from readers today," White said. "After reading your critique of Wingate's poems and Cooper's novel, they are calling you 'the tomahawk editor.'"

"What does that mean?"

"Like a savage Indian, you take no prisoners with pieces you dislike. You scalp each and every one."

"I know quality writing when I see it. Both poetry and prose. You hired me to deliver an honest opinion. And that I did."

***

The following Monday morning, a short, shabbily dressed man in his late thirties appeared in the *Messenger*'s office. Poe greeted him.

"Morning, sir. How can I help you?"

"I'm looking for Edgar Poe."

"That would be me."

"I'm Edward Wingate. Are you the one that wrote the review of my book of poems *The Far Shallows*? You called them 'mere oatmeal for children and simpletons'?"

"That is correct."

"You termed them vile, tasteless, and of no literary merit?"

"That sounds right."

The man leaned over Poe's desk, staring angrily into his face.

"I'm inviting you to step out into the street so I may give you a good thrashing."

White, who had been watching, stepped out of his office.

"Hold on there!" he said. "There will be no violence in this office."

Wingate turned to face White.

"This low-down scoundrel has humiliated and insulted me in front of my readers and my friends. I demand satisfaction."

"It shall not be in this office."

Wingate looked from White to Poe, then, fists raised, he rushed at Poe.

Instantly, Poe was on his feet, fending off the blows.

"Leave this office!" White shouted. Now!"

As if he had not heard, Wingate rushed at Poe again, fists first. As he did, Poe's right hand suddenly shot out and sent Wingate to the floor. White bent over him.

"He's out cold. Were you a boxer at some time in the past?"

"In secondary school."

White looked down on the unconscious man on the floor.

"I'll call the constable."

***

The following week, White received a letter from James Fenimore Cooper.

In part, it stated: "Your new assistant editor is a shallow buffoon. It appears he is unable to discern the difference between literature and the label on a laxative bottle.

"Hereby, I cancel my subscription to your magazine and I shall inform my friends and fellow scribes that it is operated by nothing less than morons and imbeciles."

***

On Thursday of that week, there was a new visitor to the *Messenger* office. This time, it was Richmond County Commissioner Samuel M. Lipper, a medium-height, fiftyish man with a sallow face, thinning hair, and a paunch. The moment he entered the office, he went straight to Poe.

"Good day, Mr. Lipper," Poe said.

The man did not waste time with civilities.

"What harm did I ever bring to you? What foul mischief did I ever commit upon you?"

"Why would you ask such questions?"

"Why did you reveal the details of my family's ownership of land in Hawkins Valley?"

"That was my job. The public has a right to know."

"You have ruined my reputation in Richmond for all time. Now I'm a laughingstock."

"My job is to report the truth."

For a long moment, Lipper glared at Poe, pure hatred in his eyes.

"Now it is time for me to do my job."

Then he reached inside his coat and withdrew a flintlock pistol.

White, who had been watching from his office, rushed out of his office.

"Wait! Wait!" he shouted.

But it was too late.

As Lipper cocked the pistol and took aim, Edgar dove under the desk.

Blam!

The sound of the pistol shot reverberated across the office, then Lipper turned and darted out the door.

Quickly, White went to Poe.

"Edgar! Edgar! Are you hurt?"

Poe peeped over the top of the desk.

"I'm fine."

"I'm going to get the constable. It won't be difficult to find Lipper."

***

Later that afternoon, White called Poe into his office.

"I've made a decision," he started. "We're going to have to tone it down. We are becoming much too controversial."

"Controversy is what you said you wanted."

"Not like this. Over the past two weeks, one contributor tried to thrash you. The premier novelist in the nation called you an imbecile and a county commissioner has attempted to kill you. The constable has been in this office five times. We must tone it down. No more scathing reviews or explosive political exposes."

"You're the boss. Is that all?"

"No. You left an oil lamp burning when you left the office last night. And it burned all night. Do you realize that whale oil costs fifty cents a gallon? You must become more aware of expenses in this office."

"I shall be more careful in the future."

***

September 22, 1834

My Darling Virginia:

A great loneliness has descended over me these past two months. My poor heart is an empty shell without you and I long for the moment I can reach out to touch you and see the smile in your eyes.

My nights are an empty room with no pleasure or amusement. Oh, how I long to sit in the parlor with you and Muddy, singing songs and playing chess.

My new occupation happily consumes me, but I long for your smile and your gentle touch during the nights.

242

Oh, I miss you so!

All my love,
Eddie

***

The following night, as the office was closing, Oliver Highsmith, the *Messenger*'s typesetter, stopped by Poe's desk. Oliver was a gangly, freckled-faced twenty-two-year-old, a full six foot three with a shock of curly red hair and a constant smile.

"Want to meet me at the Red Dog for a few ales after work?"

"That should be more entertaining than sitting alone in my room."

An hour later, Poe and Oliver were at the rail at the Red Dog knocking back some ales. Before the night was over, they had had more than a few. When the tavern closed, the proprietor had to shove them out the door. The next morning, Poe did not appear at work until 10 a.m.

White was furious.

"Edgar, where have you been? I told you I needed that Lockman piece by 10 today. What are you doing coming into work at 10?"

"Oliver and I had a few too many last night at the Red Dog."

"He was at work on time. Why can't you do that?"

Poe shrugged.

"I'm sorry, Mr. White. It shall not happen again."

***

September 30, 1834
My Darling Sissy:
This miserable loneliness that has pervaded my soul is driving me to drink. During the day, my mind in occupied with my work, but at night, the only remedy for this terrible loneliness is spirits.

Oh, how I long to see and be near you.

All of my love,
Eddie

***

The following morning, Poe was seated at his desk when White passed him in route to his office.

"You were out consorting with John Barleycorn again last night," White said.

"How do you know?"

"I can smell it when I pass your desk."

"Is it offensive?"

"Very much so. When will you have the new poetry reviews ready?"

"By this afternoon."

***

On October 3, when the new issue of the *Messenger* hit the street, it was the largest selling issue the publication had ever had. It featured Poe's short story "William Wilson" on the front page and three of Poe's poems on inside pages.

When Poe arrived at work at ten minutes past 11, White called him into his office.

"What in God's name are you doing coming to work at 11?"

"Sorry, Mr. White. It was a late night again."

"I'm at my wit's end with your drinking. Either you or John Barleycorn must go. You have been late to work seven times this month. Your copy has become sloppy and filled with errors. Why all of sudden have you put your nose in a bottle?"

"I miss my family. My fiancée and her mother remain in Baltimore."

"Why didn't they come with you?"

"My fiancée and her mother have their own home. Furthermore, at the time, we could not afford it."

"They can't come to Richmond now?"

"I'm not sure."

"You're a good writer and I'm happy to have you as an employee, but this drinking must stop. If it continues, I no longer want you as an employee. Is that understood?"

Yes, sir."

***

Over the month of November, Poe remained sober, he was at work on time every morning and, in that month's issue, he had one short story, "The Oval Portrait" and two poems, "Dream within a Dream" and "To Helen" in the issue.

During the first week in December, White congratulated him on his behavior.

"You've done well this past month. I congratulate you on your sobriety and your work. The November issue has been the largest in our history."

"Thank you!"

"Do you still miss your family?"

"More than you could know."

***

During the first week in December, when White arrived at work early one morning, he saw a pair of legs sticking out of the bushes between the Red Dog Saloon and the *Messenger*'s office. He moved closer to investigate.

Poe was sound asleep in the bushes, wearing the same clothes he had worn at work the previous day. White bent over him.

"Edgar? Edgar?"

Poe slowly rolled over and opened his eyes.

"Mr. White?"

"What in God's name are you doing sleeping in the bushes?"

"I didn't make it home last night."

"I can see that," he said, shaking his head in disapproval. "Come on inside. we need to talk."

Ten minutes later, Poe was in his editor's office.

"I'm made a decision," White said. "I want you to take two weeks off at Christmas. I want you to go back to Baltimore and see if you can bring your family here. If you can do that and the drinking comes to an end, I want you to continue in my employ. If not, I no longer want you."

"Thank you for your fairness."

"My words are not an empty threat. Last week, I received a letter from a young novelist named Thomas English who wishes to join the *Messenger*. I want you to know that you are not the only fish in the sea. Am I making myself clear?"

"Yes, sir."

***

On December 20, 1834, Poe boarded a train from Richmond to Baltimore. On the train, he was delighted at the prospect of seeing Virginia and Muddy again. When they met him at the station, Poe ran to Virginia and swooped her up in his arms. Back at home, he told them of White's proposal.

"Moving from the family home is a big decision," Maria said. "We can't just pull up stakes and leave without some financial assurance."

"Muddy, I have an excellent position with the magazine. I enjoy my work and I earn a good salary. All that I am lacking is you and Virginia."

"How would we live?"

"In the same manner we lived here. We could contract a room at a boarding house. At the moment, I'm paying to support two households."

Maria turned to Virginia.

"What do you say?"

"I want to be with Eddie. I want us to be a happy family together again."

Maria inhaled.

"So do I," she said solemnly. "Then we'll move to Richmond."

"If you move to Richmond, what will happen to the old home?"

"It will be claimed by the state. Taxes have not been paid in five years."

"Then let us make haste to move to Richmond."

Maria turned to Poe.

"Edgar, you understand, if we move to Richmond, the original agreement remains in place. Virginia will sleep in my room until you two are married."

"Agreed."

***

The Christmas of 1834 was a happy time for the Poe family. Poe bought Virginia the peach colored bustle dress she had been yearning for. Maria received a new Paul Revere tea service. Virginia's favorite gift that Christmas was a daffodil-shaped silver pendant and necklace Poe had had made in Richmond.

"Oh, Eddie!" she said as she opened the little white box. "I love it."

Poe removed the necklace, then, as Virginia waited, he placed it around her neck.

"There it is!" he said.

Virginia went to the mirror.

"Thank you, my darling," he said.

"I love you!" she replied.

"And I love you."

***

December 28, 1834: Now that I have my beloved Sissy, I am a man in full once more. My soul is centered; my heart is singing. The tie that binds me to the universe is with me once more and I feel the return of my full power as a man of letters. The year 1835 shall be a glorious year in my life.

19
Child Bride

It was late July of 1835. For the past seven months, Poe, Maria, and Virginia had been living in Richmond at Sarah's Manor, a small boarding house on the city's south side. The family's new quarters were a small, two-bedroom unit on the second floor overlooking a garden. Virginia and Maria took the large bedroom while Edgar slept in the smaller one. Maria complained it was cramped, but Poe promised they would move to larger quarters when he got a raise.

Only days after they moved in, Maria met Mrs. Sarah Yarrington, the boarding house proprietor, and the two quickly formed a fast friendship. Both had been widowed, both were deeply religious, and both had grown up in Baltimore. A bulky, jovial, round-faced woman in her late forties, Mrs. Yarrington was an astute businesswoman and had a thriving business in the boarding house. On Sunday afternoons, she and Maria would regularly have tea, swap recipes, talk about the Bible, share family gossip, and play cards.

Now that Poe had his beloved Virginia at his side, his star rose rapidly at the *Messenger*. He stopped drinking, was at his desk bright and early each morning, and his stories and poems were regular features in the publication. His novel, the *Narrative of Arthur Gordon Pym,* had been serialized in the *Messenger* for the past three months and had gained a huge reader following. Subscriptions were at 7,000, an all-time high. Needless to say, White was overjoyed.

One day in late July, Poe brought Virginia into the *Messenger* office to meet his editor.

"Edgar, is this your daughter?" White asked, upon seeing Virginia the first time.

"This is my betrothed."

"Oh!" he said apologetically. "It's a pleasure to meet you."

After several minutes of small talk, Virginia left the office and White pulled Poe aside.

"You're going to have a devil of a time marrying that girl. You don't feel you're robbing the cradle?"

"We're in love. Love doesn't see age."

"In the state of Virginia, you can't marry a girl under 18 unless her father signs an affidavit."

"She doesn't have a father. Her mother will have to sign."

"A mother can't sign."

"I wasn't aware of that."

"So how do you propose to marry her?"

"We'll have to devise a plan."

"Good luck."

***

With Virginia's thirteenth birthday less than a month away, Poe discussed the matter with her that night and they decided to go to the Commonwealth Courthouse the following morning to buy a license.

The clerk was a middle-aged man wearing thick glasses.

"We want to buy a marriage license," Poe said.

The clerk looked from one to the other.

"How old is the bride?"

"She's 18."

The clerk laughed.

"No!" he said, shaking his head. "She's not a day over 12. Does she have a birth record?"

"One was never recorded."

"Then the only way you can buy a license is to have her father sign an affidavit."

"She doesn't have a father. Her mother can't do it?"

"No."

"So what are we supposed to do?"

"You can wait until she turns 18."

"That's not going to happen."

"Then I can't help you."

***

The following morning, Poe talked to his solicitor. When
he heard Poe's dilemma, he shook his head.

"That's a problem in the state's law," he said.

"Her mother can't sign an affidavit?" Poe asked.

He laughed.

"The state of Virginia takes a dim view of a woman signing
anything, especially an affidavit."

"So what can we do?"

"You can go to North Carolina. Their laws are less
restrictive."

"That's out of the question."

"Then the only other choice is a common law relationship."

"You mean living together without the benefit of
matrimony?"

"That is correct."

"We want to be married."

"I don't know what the solution is."

***

Back at the office, Poe discussed it with Oliver Highsmith.

"My brother had the same problem," Oliver said. "He had
to go to Chester County. It's easy to get a license over there."

"What are you talking about?"

"There are two branches of the Commonwealth
Courthouse in Chester County. The first one is in downtown
Chesterfield and it is the one most people use. The second one
is out in the countryside and it's run by an old woman who is
nearly blind."

"Nearly blind?"

"Yeah. She can't see more than a few feet in front of
herself."

"So how does she judge the ages of people getting
married?"

"Her daughter does it, but sometimes the daughter is not
there."

"How do you know this?"

"My brother did it. I was with him. When he was married last year, his bride was only fifteen. When the daughter is not there, the old woman lets anybody that has $2 buy a license. She's more interested in the money than the law."

Poe studied him for a moment.

"How do you know when the daughter's not there?"

"You have to go and check."

***

The following Friday afternoon, after the August issue was put to bed, Poe and Oliver took the horse-drawn train to Chesterfield, twenty-five miles to the south. Once they arrived, a cab carriage took them to the outskirts of town. There Oliver pointed out the vital records office. It was a private home with a sign out front which read: Commonwealth Vital Records Office, Chester County, Virginia.

Inside, they saw a young woman seated at a desk.

Upon seeing her, Oliver turned to Poe.

"That's her!" he whispered. "She's the one that verifies ages."

"Good afternoon!" Poe said.

"Hello! How may I help you?"

"What hours will you be open next week?"

"We'll be open Monday through Friday."

"Will you be here?"

"I'll be here every day except Friday. That is when I'm going to Hopewell to visit my aunt. My mother will be here. She will be happy to help you."

***

A week passed. On the following Friday, Poe, Oliver and Virginia were on the horse-drawn train back to Chester County. On the train, Poe coached Virginia about their undertaking.

"Now, when she asks for your birthday, you must give the date which matches the age you state. If you say you're 22, you must give a birthday in the year 1813."

"I know what to say."

Upon arrival, they took a cab carriage from downtown Chesterfield to the records office. Once inside, they saw an old woman alone behind the desk.

"How can I help you?"

"We want to buy a marriage license."

"Have a seat," she said, indicating two chairs in front of the desk. Once they were seated, she took quill in hand, dipped it in ink, then turned to Poe.

"Name?"

"Edgar Allan Poe."

"Father's name?"

"David Poe Jr."

"Birthdate?"

"January 9, 1809."

She turned to Virginia.

"Name?"

"Eliza Virginia Clemm."

"Father's name?"

"William Clemm Jr."

"Date of birth?"

"August 15, 1813."

"Then you're 22?"

"Correct."

The old woman stopped writing, pushed her glasses up on her nose, and squinted at Virginia for a long moment.

Poe and Virginia held their breath.

Satisfied, the old woman entered the birth date, then put the official Commonwealth of Virginia seal on the license.

"That will be $2."

***

The next morning, Maria announced to Mrs. Yarrington that her daughter and Edgar were going to be married.

"Oh, I love weddings," she said. "We shall put on a wedding they will never forget. We shall make her a wedding dress. We'll bake a cake. We'll hold the wedding at my home and we'll put on a wedding feast with all the trimmings."

***

Three days later, Poe was at his desk when a young woman, tall, early twenties, and well-dressed, came into the office.

Upon seeing Poe, her eyes instantly lit up with interest.

"Hello!" she said. "Are you Thomas White?"

"He's in his office," Edgar said, pointing behind him.

Moments later, the woman went into White's office and the door closed. When she came out twenty minutes later, Poe watched as she strode past his desk to the door. Seconds later, White came out of his office.

"Who is that?" Poe asked.

"Her name is Elizabeth Lummis Ellet. She has some poems to sell, but she is asking too much. Remember her poem 'To a Whippoorwill'?"

"I remember. Absolute sentimental rubbish."

"In the past, we've published her poems. Many of our readers love them."

"How much is she asking?"

"She wants $10 each, but I would never pay that. She'll return tomorrow and I want you to talk to her."

"Why me?"

"She's interested in you. I saw the way she was looking at you."

"What do you want me to do?"

"Get friendly, very friendly, with her. See if she will come down on the price."

"You know I'm engaged to be married."

"You don't have to tell her that."

"How much do you want to pay?"

"Ten dollars for all five poems. Not a penny more. See what you can negotiate."

"I say you're wasting your time and your money."

"Just do as I ask."

"You're the boss."

***

The following morning, Elizabeth Lummis Ellet was back in the *Messenger* office.

"Hello again!" she said, "You're Edgar Poe?"

"Yes!"

"Mr. White said you were the person to talk to about my poems."

"Have a seat. We like five of your poems," Poe began. "Since we're only using them for fillers, however, we cannot pay the total of $50 you are requesting."

"I fail to see why not. My work has always been well received by your readers."

"That's my best offer."

She smiled and studied Poe for a moment."

"Perhaps I could lower the price for a personal favor."

"What might that be?"

"Are you married?"

"No."

"Then perhaps we could have a luncheon date to explore the realms of gold. I have read several of your poems and I feel I could learn some fine points of poetic composition. Your mind could embrace mine in an intellectual union."

"If I agreed to such a proposal, what would the price of the poems become?"

"A total of $10."

***

An hour later, they were at Ingram's Dining Emporium having corned beef hash, fried potatoes, and boiled cabbage. Poe listened patiently as she droned on about her childhood in Baltimore; she said her father was a professional soldier and her older brother George was following in his footsteps. She detailed her struggles with iambic pentameter and the state of the weather in Richmond. As she spoke, Poe studied her. She was tall for a woman and dressed in a fashionable summer

254

smock complete with curly ringlets that hung about her shoulders. Although she had the dainty appearance of a woman, there was no softness, no gentleness in her face. She had the cold, indifferent eyes of a man. Finally, after an hour, Poe was relieved it was over.

When Poe and Ellet returned to the office, Ellet prepared to say good-bye.

"I took great pleasure in our meal," she said. "Perhaps we could do it again."

Poe smiled.

"That would be nice."

She turned to leave.

"Good day!" she said, then strode out of the office. Once she was out the door, White rushed over.

"How did it go?"

"You're getting the lot for a total of $10."

"Ten dollars for all five poems?"

"Correct."

"Marvelous!" White said, rubbing his hands together. "Good work, Poe!"

***

Over the next two weeks, Maria and Mrs. Yarrington were busy preparing for the wedding. First, there was the wedding gown. Mrs. Yarrington, an expert seamstress, bought the cloth, and together, she and Maria conducted four fitting sessions with Virginia to stitch together a wedding dress. Then a total of fifty invitations were sent out to a select group of family and friends. Finally, the night before the wedding, they baked a giant chocolate cake and prepared an array of meats, vegetables, and desserts for the wedding feast.

***

On the morning of August 16, 1835, one day after the bride's thirteenth birthday, Edgar and Virginia were married in the parlor of Mrs. Yarrington's home, located next door to the boarding house. The bride was radiant in a white taffeta wedding gown with tufted shoulders, an empire waistline, and matching veil. Rev. Amasa Converse, a tall, crane-like man in his late forties, conducted the ceremony. Oliver Highsmith, his lanky frame dressed in an ill-fitting gray suit, served as best man. Editor Thomas White was in attendance. As the minister started to read the vows, the couple's appearance suggested they were father and daughter rather than husband and wife.

"Do you, Edgar Allan Poe, take this woman to be your lawfully wedded wife, to have and to hold from this day forward, for better, for worse, for richer, for poorer, in sickness and in health, to love and to cherish, till death do you part, according to God's holy ordinance."

"I do."

Then he turned to Virginia.

"Do you, Virginia Eliza Clemm, take this man to be your wedded husband...?"

As Rev. Converse read the vows, the old women sniffled into their handkerchiefs and gushed about what a beautiful bride she was. After the ceremony, there was a wedding feast and dancing. Once the feast was finished, guests threw handfuls of rice as the couple, suitcases in hand, boarded the cab carriage that would take them to the train station for a three-day honeymoon.

***

That afternoon, the newlyweds arrived in Petersburg, a small country hamlet some twenty-five miles south of Richmond, then took a carriage to the Oakbrook Inn and booked a room. Before entering the bridal suite, Poe carried her across the threshold. The next morning, they remained in bed until noon, then had breakfast and strolled leisurely about the town. As they passed a church cemetery, Virginia peered through the iron fence at several tombstones.

"You know every grave marker tells the story of a life. You see the one over there," she said, pointing to a tall, moss-encrusted marker.

Suddenly, she stopped.

"Look! A flotilla fern is growing out of that grave. I want to pick it."

Poe turned and followed her as they walked around the cemetery fence to the front of the church and entered the graveyard gate. At the grave they had seen earlier, Virginia picked the flotilla fern.

"Look at that," she said as she examined her prize. "I haven't seen one of those in a while."

Suddenly, the late afternoon sun slipped behind dark clouds and it started to rain. At first, it was only a drizzle, then rapidly, it became a downpour.

"Come on!" he said. "Let's run for the church."

Moments later, they were standing under the stoop at the church's front entrance. For several minutes, they watched the rain come down, then Poe turned and tried the door. It opened.

"Let's go inside," he said.

There was a sinister air about the silent, darkened church. Their eyes scanned the pews, the pulpit, the altar, and the huge cross standing against the back wall. Virginia turned to him.

"I want to join my body with yours in this place."

"In a church?"

"Why not?"

"Where?"

She looked around.

"In one of the pews," she said.

Then, suddenly, she changed her mind.

"No. On the altar," she said decisively. "I want to do it on the altar."

She started to remove her clothing.

Poe smiled.

"Oh, you naughty, naughty girl!"

Then he started to remove his clothing.

***

The following morning, they went shopping in downtown Petersburg, attended a lecture on phrenology, and in the afternoon, they returned to the hotel.

"I want to make love among the dead tonight," Virginia said.

Poe laughed.

"There is no end to your mischief."

"Death is an aphrodisiac," she said. "Tonight, I want to take an old quilt and return to the cemetery. I want to make love among the grave markers."

***

That night, before dusk, they took a blanket from the hotel closet and started back to the cemetery. As they moved among the grave markers, Virginia looked for one suitable for her purpose. Finally, they came upon a sheltered grave with a flat slab of marble sitting at ground level.

"This is the one," she said.

Then, as darkness fell, she spread the old blanket across the top of the white marble slab and they began removing their clothes. Some twenty minutes later, their carnal desires satisfied, they lay naked together on the marble slab. Night was closing in.

Suddenly, they saw a light approaching.

"Hello! Hello!" they heard a man's voice call. Then a sexton, a middle-aged man carrying a lantern in one hand and a shovel in the other, appeared in front of the grave. He could see what they had been doing.

"A bit randy? Eh?" he said. "You two couldn't wait to get home?"

"We're newlyweds," Poe said.

The sexton laughed.

"I understand. I was young once."

"You won't say anything?"

"No. Just get your clothes on and be on your way."

***

As they walked back to the Oakwood Inn, Virginia turned to him.

"Bringing our bodies together is such a special part of my life with you."

"It is now and shall forever be," Poe said.

"You must never reveal my twisted side that is attracted to death."

"My dear, my own attraction to death has inspired some of my greatest poems."

"You are a man. Others will accept that. But for me, a woman, it would seem twisted and unnatural."

"I promise to never say a word."

"I love you, darling Eddie."

"I love you, darling Virginia!"

***

August 20, 1835. Over these past few days, the virginal lilies I spied under the chinaberry tree last summer were made mine and mine alone. Like Vulcan, I claimed my virginal Venus. Over those same days, I have witnessed the furthermost heights and depths of my beloved Virginia and know her more intimately than ever before. As a lover, she has exceeded my most ardent expectations. As a woman, she is a study in opposites. On one hand, she has the sweetness and innocence of a thirteen-year-old child, yet, on the other, the heart and soul of an old woman.

***

Back in Richmond that night, Maria came out to meet them when the cab carriage pulled up in front of Sarah's Manor. Inside, she had a meal waiting and, afterward, they sat down for a family talk.

"Eddie, you're a married man now and you have new obligations," Maria said. "We cannot continue to live in this cramped boarding house. There is not enough space in my bedroom to curse a cat. We've got to have larger living quarters."

"At the salary he's paying me, we can't afford it."

"Then you need to ask for a raise."

***

The following morning, Poe was in White's office arguing about a raise.

"I have made thousands of dollars for you over the past year," Poe said, "And now you refuse to share those profits with me. My stories and poems have been the heart of the *Messenger*. Why should I continue to provide you with that when you see no need to compensate me?"

"I know! I know!" White said. "You've done an outstanding job these past few months."

He studied Poe for a moment.

"This is what I will do. In November, after I pay the annual rent on the building, I will raise your salary to $60 a month."

"Only $15 a month?"

"That's all I can afford."

"That's not enough. I am a married man now and I have new responsibilities. I want a salary of $75 a month."

"Now you're being unreasonable."

"I shall not allow you to put me off. Tomorrow, I shall begin seeking new employment."

White studied Poe for a long moment.

"How much did you say you want?"

"A salary of $75 a month."

White inhaled.

"In November, if the revenue continues as it is now, I will pay you $75 a month."

Poe stood up and shook the editor's hand.

"I shall depend on that."

***

Over the next three months, Poe continued his duties, churning out new poems, short stories, and critical essays. During the month of October, subscriptions failed to grow as they had over the previous months, but they were still holding steady at 8,000 on the first day of November. When Poe saw the new subscription numbers, he went back to White.

"Today is November 3," Poe said. "This is the week I'll be expecting my pay raise."

"I'm sorry, Edgar," White said. "The press breakdown last month as well as the ongoing libel suit is preventing me from giving you the raise. I know I promised it, but I can't live up to it now."

"Then I shall be seeking other employment."

"Suit yourself."

***

The following Friday, White and Poe were busy all morning with the press run. Oliver had run off 3,000 copies, then the press broke down and more than two hours were needed to repair it. Finally, once the press was running again, they took seats at their desk for a break.

"Look who's coming," White said, nodding toward the front door with his head.

It was Elizabeth Lummis Ellet.

"She's got some new poems she wants to sell," White said. "She's all yours. Remember, don't tell her you're a married man."

Now she was approaching Poe's desk.

"Good day, Edgar!" she began. "I wanted to say thanks for the prominent display of my poems in the recent edition. Can we have lunch again?"

"Will it result in a discounted price on your new poems?"

She smiled.

"Probably."

Twenty minutes later, Poe and Ellet were back at Ingram's Dining Emporium.

"I believe you will like my new poems," Ellet said. "Three were published in *Graham's Magazine* last month. They paid me $5 each."

"The *Messenger* won't pay that. Mr. White is a skinflint. He won't pay a penny more than he has to."

"That's what I have heard," she said. "Are you unhappy there?"

"I'm being robbed."

"*Burton's Men's Magazine* in Philadelphia is seeking an editor," she said. "I saw a big page three advert in this month's issue. They have published several of my poems and they pay far better than the *Messenger*."

***

That afternoon, Poe was in the local mercantile store and bought a copy of *Burton's Men's Magazine*. The moment he opened it, he saw the advertisement. The following morning, Poe penned a letter to the publisher outlining his qualifications.

***

Two weeks later, he received a reply.

November 19, 1835
Dear Edgar Poe:
  My sincere gratitude for your earlier correspondence.
  I am hereby offering you the editor's position you have applied for at Burton's Men's Magazine.
  I have been fondly reading your work in the Messenger for the past year and feel your poems, short stories, and essays would be a viable asset to my publication.
  The position pays $80 per month and includes an assortment of personal perks including season theater tickets, an expense account, and a two-week paid vacation each year.
  Please respond with a date when you can report to work.

Sincerely,
William Evans Burton, publisher

20
Four Silver Tea Sets

By the 1830s, the spirit of freedom that had grown out of the Revolutionary War had sparked a cultural movement in Philadelphia which earned the city its nickname, the *Athens of America*. During those years, Philadelphia became a thriving, pulsating beehive of artistic creativity as architects, painters, sculptors, authors, and craftsmen of all types arrived from other states and England to leave their marks. There was money and reputations to be made. Public art galleries, a natural history museum, a public library, as well as numerous theaters and concert halls, offered instant culture and artistic expression to all who sought it. Buildings, including Congress Hall, Independence Hall, Christ Church, the State House, the Philadelphia Museum of Art, and the Bank of Pennsylvania sprang up throughout the city to celebrate the architectural glory of ancient Greece. In April of 1834, British-born architect Henry Latrobe told members of the city's Benjamin Franklin Intellectual Society that "Philadelphia is the most cultured city in America. Its public library is open eight hours a day."

***

On the morning of January 9, 1835, when Poe's carriage arrived at the offices of *Burton's Gentlemen's Magazine*, he saw a sprawling three-story brick building at the corner of 12th and Chestnut Streets with a bakery on one side and a tannery on the other. Suitcase in hand, Poe stepped down from the carriage, paid the driver, then turned and went inside.

263

"I'm Edgar Poe," he told the receptionist. "I'm here to see Mr. Burton."

"Go right in," she said, indicating a large corner office.

William Evans Burton was a medium height, broad-shouldered man in his late thirties, well-groomed with impish brown eyes, dark hair, and long sideburns. Upon seeing Poe, he arose and walked around his desk.

"Good day, Poe!" he said, shaking Poe's hand and slapping his back. "I've been looking forward to meeting you. Have a seat!"

Poe seated himself in front of the desk.

"Welcome to my team! Where shall we start?"

"First, I would like to know what my duties will be."

Burton smiled, then began speaking.

"I advertised the position for an editor, but essentially what I'm looking for is a front man. Someone to represent the face of the publication. Your title will be editor, but I see no reason for you to spend your days behind a desk editing stories, chasing reporters, and arguing about contributor's fees. I have other people for that. I want you to be the face of the magazine. People know you and your work. I feel you will be well-received."

"You want me to make public appearances, lectures, mostly public relations work."

"Correct. That is not to say that I don't want you to contribute to the magazine. Along with your publicity chores, I want you to write short stories. Scary, macabre tales that will make the hair rise on the back of the readers' necks. When they read your stories, I want them to scream in fright in mid-sentence and have nightmares."

"No poems?"

"Our readers are mostly men and they have little or no interest in poetry. They're interested in short stories and articles about tobacco, guns, fishing stories, coin and stamp collecting, and sports, especially boxing and horse racing."

"I can provide that."

"That's what I wanted to hear."

A pause.

"Have you always been in publishing?" Poe asked.

"In a word, no. When I came to this country from England six years ago, I didn't know where my life was going. I'd been an actor, a stage manager, and an entrepreneur, but publishing had always been my first love. When I heard Philadelphia's reputation, I knew this was where I wanted to start a magazine. People here want to better themselves; they are open to new ideas and want to grow as human beings. I'm glad I came to Philadelphia."

He paused.

"I understand there is an employee discount for living in your hotel," Poe said.

"Yes. Also, the position includes season tickets to the Chestnut Street Theater and an expense account for entertaining customers. You already know the position pays $80 a month."

"That's a very generous salary."

"I like for my employees to be happy."

Poe nodded his agreement.

"Is there anything else?"

"No, Mr. Burton. I believe that's it."

"Please call me Billy," he said. "That's what all my friends call me."

"All right. Thanks, Billy."

That afternoon, Poe took custody of a sixth-floor unit at Burton's hotel, the Roxborough. There were two huge bedrooms, a full kitchen, a parlor, a sitting room, and a view that overlooked the city. With the employee discount, it cost a total of $25 a month and was an easy two-block walk to the office.

***

Over the first week, Poe's new life as front man was a whirlwind. On Monday morning, dressed in gym wear, he worked out and hobnobbed with the other men at Harwell's gymnasium, the city's premier physical fitness outlet. That afternoon, he gave a lecture to the Philadelphia Society of Useful Information about the importance of magazines in the modern world. Tuesday found him at city hall with Burton attending a city council meeting about a new dam project that was due to begin soon on the Brandywine River. On Thursday, there was a speech to the Philadelphia Society of Practical Women, and on Friday, he was a judge at a shooting contest. Edgar was on his way.

***

At the end of the second week, Maria and Virginia arrived with the family furnishings. When Poe opened the door to their new home in the Roxborough, both were beside themselves with excitement.

"My! My! Look at this!" Virginia said as she swept through the rooms. "This is high society."

"First thing is we're going to get a piano," Maria said. "I miss our singing together."

"Oh, Eddie, I can't believe all this is happening," Virginia said.

"Why shouldn't it happen? We deserve it. We've waited long enough."

***

On Monday of the following week, Poe was working at his desk when his old friend Elizabeth Lummis Ellet and a strange man came into the office.

"Edgar Allan Poe!" she said, as she approached his desk. "I heard you were working for *Burton*'s."

"I've been here almost a month now. Are you selling poems today?"

"My work does not fit well in men's magazines," she said. "But my friend here has some poems."

She turned to the man beside her.

"Edgar, this is my friend Rufus Griswold."

"Hello!" Poe said.

Poe stood up from the desk to shake the man's hand.

"Good day, sir!" Griswold said with a big smile.

He was a medium-height, thick-chested man in his late thirties with stooped shoulders, shifty eyes, and a face encircled with hair.

"Rufus is a poet," Ellet said. "He would like to speak with you about them."

"We aren't publishing much poetry, but I'll be happy to take a look."

"Perhaps you would be interested in subscribing to my Registry of American Poets," Griswold said.

"Registry of Poets?"

"Every year, I publish a compendium of all the poets in America. It lists poets, their works, where their works can be purchased, and a current address where poets may receive letters from readers."

"I do need some publicity for my poems. Will I receive a copy of your registry every year?"

"It is printed in early July of each year and will be posted to you upon publication."

"How much does it cost?

"A mere $5 a year. It will mean publicity for your poems and you will receive letters from your readers. This will help sales."

"Sign me up!" Poe said.

***

Over the next six years, Poe settled into his new position. When he was not making public appearances, he was at his desk busy writing critical reviews and short stories. During that period, Poe's literary creativity would blossom like never before and he would write his most famous short stories. Everywhere he turned, there seemed to be the germ of an idea for a new short story.

One night after dinner in the summer of 1835, he was sitting in the parlor with Virginia when she mentioned the daffodils they had planted in Baltimore. Suddenly, for no apparent reason, he remembered how, after he left the old Poe family home to return to Richmond after the first visit, he could feel the old homeplace pulling him back. He wondered if a house could be a valid character in a story. If a house could intentionally move the plot of a story forward.

That night, he sat down and wrote "The Fall of the House of Usher," a chilling tale about a man who takes custody of the estate of a friend, then discovers the dwelling is possessed with an evil spirit that causes anyone who enters to become ill.

In the spring of 1836, Virginia brought a cat into their house, a black tabby named Catterina, which took the habit of sleeping at the foot of their bed. One night, after Poe determined the cat was an annoyance, he ordered Virginia to lock the feline out of their bedroom. She did as instructed, but the following morning, the cat was curled up asleep at the foot of their bed.

"Did you let the cat in last night?" Poe asked.

"She knows how to open the latch. Didn't you know all black cats are witches?"

Poe peered at her but did not reply.

The next morning, he sat down and wrote "The Black Cat," the chilling tale of an alcoholic who blames his addiction on Pluto, his pet cat. In a fit of rage, he hangs the pet, then, out of nowhere, a stray black cat, the ghost of the creature he killed, follows him home and proceeds to drive him insane.

During early May of 1837, while reading Shallowford's *History of the Spanish Inquisition*, Poe gasped in horror at the cruel methods of torture used by inquisitors to extract confessions from their unfortunate victims. There were iron maidens, metal pincers, thumbscrews, and other devices designed to burn or mutilate hands and feet. That night when he went to sleep, he dreamed about them. The following morning, he woke up and wrote "The Pit and the Pendulum."

In the early fall of 1838, Poe delivered a speech to the Philadelphia Abolitionist Society and, in the process, he told a story he remembered from his days as a soldier. While serving at Fort Independence, Poe had heard the story of two lieutenants, Robert F. Massie and Gustavus Drane, who held a duel after arguing over a card game. Drane, whom nobody liked, killed the popular Massie in the duel, and that night, a group of soldiers who disliked Drane kidnapped and entombed him alive in the walls of the fort.

The following morning, Poe wrote the "Cask of Amontillado," the tale of a man who seeks revenge against another whom he feels has insulted him. After meeting his victim at a carnival, the avanger lures his victim into the catacombs of his home and entombs him alive.

During the days before Christmas of 1839, Poe and Virginia were in the local food market waiting to pay for groceries they wanted to purchase.

Ahead of them, two women who were also buying groceries chatted as they waited for their bill.

"He thought he was going to get away with murder," one of the women said. "Sooner or later, your sins with find you out."

That night, he sat down and wrote "The Tell-Tale Heart," a macabre yarn about an unnamed narrator who murders an old man, then hides the body under the floorboards of his home. Finally, the narrator's guilt manifests itself when the murderer imagines he can hear the victim's heart still beating under the floorboards.

In the spring of 1840, Poe read the *Memoirs of Eugene Francois Vidocq*, a famous French criminal whose exploits had been the subject of numerous articles in magazines. It was a first-hand narrative of Vidocq's criminal career, detailing how he hid bodies, stashed away robbery cash, wiped out his enemies, and eluded police for more than thirteen years.

The next morning, Poe wrote "Murders in the Rue Morgue." In the story, he created the character C. Auguste Dupin, the first Sherlock Holmes, and laid out full-blown the conventions of the modern detective story. The brilliantly deductive inspector, his slow-witted partner, police baffled by conflicting clues, and the famous drawing room confrontation with the suspect were all defined once and forever. It would later become the most important short story of the nineteenth century.

***

The six years Poe worked for Burton would be the wealthiest days the Poe family would ever know. Their standard of living had never been so high and would never again be as such. They enjoyed luxurious living quarters, they frequently dined out at restaurants, they purchased expensive clothing, attended plays and operas at the famous Chestnut Street Theater, took Sunday afternoon picnics in the countryside, attended the Saturday afternoon horse races at Hampton Downs, rubbed elbows with world-famous people, and bought expensive gifts for themselves. Poe bought a gold watch, a silver cravat pin, and an opal pinky ring. Virginia filled up her closet with fashionable dresses and, since she loved shoes, she purchased a total of nine pairs, four with silver buckles.

Maria, who measured her wealth by the number of silver tea sets she owned, had never been so rich. In the past, when times were good, Maria would purchase high quality tea serving sets and store them away for lean times. Her favorites were the expensive Paul Revere sets, but occasionally, she would buy a downscale Witherspoon set. Then, when hard times arrived, she would begin to pawn the tea sets one at a time to make ends meet. Previously, the most tea seats she had ever owned was two. Now, in Philadelphia, she had a total of four silver tea sets, three Paul Revere and one Witherspoon. Times had never been so good.

***

One night, when Poe arrived at the hotel from the office, Maria was waiting at the door. She was holding out a letter.

"Who is it from?"

"Your foster father."

"Why am I suddenly receiving a letter from him?"

"Read it!"

Poe took the letter and began reading.

March 13, 1841
Edgar Poe:

I wanted to say to you that you are the most vile, loathsome, dishonorable dog I have ever known.

I curse the very day I allowed you to enter my home and my family.

You took my name, my wealth, my home, and my honor and provided nothing in return.

You are the lowest piece of human garbage I can conceive of.

I hope you burn forever in the hottest flames of eternal hell.

Rest assured, you cancerous dog, you shall never hear from me again.

John Allan

Poe looked up from the letter.

"What is the source of the hatred? When we last parted, he shook my hand."

"Some people, when they grow old, are unable to forget the injuries of the past."

"Each of the last two letters stated he would never write me again. Yet he continues to send letters."

"He must protect his hatred. It's all he has."

Poe shook his head.

"So, what should I do?"

"Ignore it."

***

Four days later, Rufus Griswold, the slight little man with the stooped shoulders and the hairy face, appeared in the magazine office.

When Poe saw him coming in the front door, he greeted him before he reached his desk.

"Rufus Griswold! Is my subscription due again?"

"Oh, no! You are all paid up," he said, offering his hand. "I just stopped in to say hello."

After small talk, Griswold asked Poe about his position at the magazine.

"Oh, I still enjoy my work," he said. "I get tired of listening to men brag about their wealth, their recent European vacation, and how beautiful their wives are, but everything considered, I'm quite happy."

"You know, all of the big literary movers and shakers have left Philadelphia. They're in New York now."

"Why do you say that?"

"Because it's the truth. Didn't you tell me you wanted to own your own magazine? There are far more opportunities for new publications in New York than in Philadelphia."

Poe shook his head thoughtfully.

"I shall remain at *Burton*'s, at least for a while. As I said, the pay is quite adequate and I enjoy the work."

"Suit yourself!" Griswold said.

***

Six weeks later, on the morning of May 3, 1841, the newfound wealth the Poe family had been enjoying came to a sudden end. On that morning, as usual, Poe left the Roxborough Hotel and walked the two blocks to the magazine offices. When he arrived, the company's employees were milling aimlessly about in front of the building. The doors were locked, the windows had been shuttered and barred and a legal notice on the front door proclaimed "Bankrupt!" in big, bold letters.

"His high living, easy come, easy go lifestyle finally caught up with him," said one employee.

"That scoundrel," said another. "He didn't pay me for my last month's work!"

"Same here!"

"He owes me money too!" said still another man. "If I could find him, I would take it out of his hide."

"I haven't been paid for last month myself!" Poe said.

"I'm going to sue," said another employee. "I'm going to talk to my lawyer!"

Moments later, Poe hailed down a cab carriage and went to Burton's home on the city's exclusive east side. Poe had been there many times before for parties, business meetings, and get-togethers. A black woman, apparently a housekeeper, answered the door.

"Is Mr. Burton in?"

"He's not been here for four days."

"Do you know where he might be?"

"He said he was going back to England."

"Do you have an address?"

"No!" the woman said.

***

So, once more, the Poe family had to readjust to their new economic fortunes. First, they moved from the spacious unit at the Roxborough Hotel to a small farmhouse on the outskirts of town. The piano was abandoned because it was too expensive to move. Also, they abandoned most of the expensive clothing they had accumulated for their nights at the theater and the opera. Of the nine dress suits he owned, Poe took the three newest, two pairs of shoes, and four shirts, and everything else was left behind. Virginia took four of the expensive dresses, three hats, and, of the nine pairs of shoes, she took three.

"Why should I take them?" Virginia said as she stuffed the keepers in an old trunk. "We won't be going to the theater or the opera again any time soon."

Poe laughed out loud.

Ten minutes later, as the carriage containing their worldly possessions trundled across town to their new quarters, Virginia turned to Poe.

"We have proven that material wealth alone cannot bring happiness," she said.

"That we have!" he said.

"Amen!" said Maria.

***

So, for the next eleven months, the Poe family lived in the farmhouse outside of town and survived on the occasional $10 to $15 bank drafts Poe received for old poems and short stories. He applied for editorial positions in New York and Boston, but a recent economic downturn had resulted in no offers. Little by little, the material goods they accumulated during the good times slowly but surely slipped away. The gold watch, the silver cravat pin, the opal pinkie ring all were sold or pawned. Maria began to pawn off her silver tea sets. During each of the months of January, February, and March of 1842, she pawned one of her Paul Revere tea sets. Then, in early April of that year, just as Maria was taking her last tea set to the pawn shop, a strange-looking carriage pulled up in front of the farmhouse.

The driver, a well-dressed, middle-aged man wearing glasses and a three-cornered hat, was sitting in the carriage seat.

"Are you Edgar Poe?" he asked.

"That I am! Who might you be?"

"I'm George Rex Graham, new owner of *Burton's Men's Magazine.*"

"New owner? What does that mean?"

"It means I'm going to be publishing a new magazine and I want to know if you want to come to work for me?"

"Editorial work?"

"Correct. Can you report to work tomorrow?"

"Where?

"Same place. Same building."

"I'll be there."

***

The following morning, bright and early, Poe was sitting in Graham's office, the same office Burton had occupied during his tenure.

"*Graham's Ladies' Magazine* will appeal to women of all ages," Graham said. "I want short stories and articles about travel, fashion, housekeeping tips, recipes, music, and art."

"No poems?"

"My intention is to stay away from poetry for a while. I want to try upfront, hard-hitting informational pieces first."

A pause.

"Anything else?"

"How much does the job pay?"

"Sixty dollars a month."

"That's much less than I was earning with Burton."

"That is all I can afford."

"I guess I have no choice."

***

From the very first, the working relationship between Graham and Poe was strained. On Poe's third day at work, they argued about the spelling of the word "gray."

"The word 'gray' is spelled g-r-a-y in America," Poe said. "In England, the common spelling is g-r-e-y. But that's only in England."

"At my publication, it will be spelled g-r-e-y."

"You're spelling it wrong!"

"That's the way I want it."

"You're the boss."

"That's right! And don't you forget it!"

***

Over the following year, Poe and the cantankerous Graham crossed swords on numerous occasions. They argued about the press run, the size of illustrations on inside pages, circulation, and design of the front page. Then, one day in late September of 1843, they had a major clash.

After Graham's niece performed in a piano recital at the local library, he decided the story should go on the front page.

"That's filler material," Poe said. "You can't put a namby-pamby story like that on the front page."

"Who says I can't?"

"Is it because the subject is your niece?"

"That's beside the point."

"That is THE point. You are putting your personal preferences ahead of the interest of your readers."

Graham turned to him.

"Look, Poe! I have had just about enough of your contrariness. I'm the owner of this magazine and you shall do as I direct you or you will no longer be employed here."

Poe glared at him.

"Go ahead and sack me."

"If I knew where I could find another one like you, I would do it in an instant. The piano recital piece is going on the front page exactly the way the publisher wants it."

Poe did not reply.

"Do you understand?" Graham continued. "The publisher, that's ME, wants it that way. Have you forgotten I own the whole damn shooting match?"

Poe took a deep breath and shook his head disapprovingly.

Graham turned, stalked back into his office, and slammed the door.

***

The next morning, Rufus Griswold showed up to collect the annual fee for his poetry registry. As always, when he entered the office, he had a big smile and a glad hand.

"Edgar! What's the problem? You seem to be unhappy today."

"I've had my fill of this blasted magazine and its publisher. I am sick to death of writing about cleaning floors, mid-width crinolines, the latest French perfume, empire waistlines, and frilly, ruffled bonnets. They do nothing for my soul."

"Why don't you come up to New York? I told you the bloom is off Philadelphia as a literary mecca. New York has taken it away."

"Do you really think so?"

"I'm certain of it."

"Bookstores in New York sponsor book signings and author salons. The Lyceum movement is in full swing. If you are an adept public speaker, you can make more money giving lectures than you can writing."

Poe studied him.

"Your reputation is firmly established," Griswold continued. "I'm sure Nathaniel Parker Willis would love to hire you for the *Evening Mirror*. Last month, he published one of my short stories and three of my poems and paid me $100."

"That's good pay."

"You're wasting your time in Philadelphia."

A pause. Poe changed the subject.

"Where is your friend Elizabeth Lummis Ellet? I haven't seen her in a while."

"She's in New York. Just published a new book titled *Women in the American Revolution*. I understand the book is doing quite well."

"Is she your paramour?"

Griswold peered curiously at Poe.

"Why would you ask that?"

"You two seemed quite friendly the last time you were in the office."

"Let's just say we are just friends," Griswold said with a big smile. "Now, shall we talk about renewing your subscription?"

That afternoon, Poe saw Griswold off at the train station. He promised to be in touch.

***

After dinner that night, Poe reported his conversation with Griswold to Maria and Virginia.

"I want to move to New York," he said.

"What's in New York?" Maria asked

"More opportunity than I am finding here."

"Do you believe this Griswold?" Maria asked.

"I have no reason not to."

"If you feel it's worth it, I'm in agreement," Virginia said. Maria inhaled.

"Eddie, if you feel it's necessary, we shall move to New York."

21
New York

In the 1840s, New York's lower Manhattan was a far cry from the expansive, bustling beehive of a metropolis the world knows today. The commissioner's grid of 1811 had mapped out the future city's 155 streets and twelve avenues, but, by 1844, the vast majority of the surveyed lands remained empty and uninhabited, resulting in a patchwork of mostly dirt streets, scattered farms, estates, clusters of modest wood and red brick homes, and commercial districts featuring the businesses of the day. Several recent shipping ventures promised a host of new economic opportunities to the city. The Erie Canal project of 1821 brought in lumber, coal, and hay from upstate while Robert Fulton's steamship line accelerated the movement of cargo and passengers up and down the Hudson River to Albany, Buffalo, and points north. In 1818, the city opened the world's first regular packet service to England with the Black Ball Line and, by 1830, it dominated the nation's merchant marine and helped spur the massive influx of immigrants which would double the city's population between 1820 and 1840. Meanwhile, the Buttonwood Agreement of 1792 had brought a consortium of banks, insurance firms, underwriters, and brokers to Wall Street, which would serve to support the future New York Stock Exchange. Each of these ventures contributed in its own way to creating a hotbed of commercial activity, which promised wealth and prosperity to all newcomers.

***

On the morning of January 6, 1844, the Poe family, along with three trunks, two wooden boxes filled with books, and an empty bird cage, boarded a train that would carry them and their belongings from Philadelphia to New York. Over the four-hour journey, Maria was sick most of the time from the constant jerking motion of the train.

Upon arrival in New York that afternoon, Rufus Griswold was waiting at the station.

"Glad to see you, Edgar," he said, offering his hand as Poe stepped off the train. "You made the right decision."

"I hope so," Poe said, pressing his hand.

Griswold caught sight of Virginia as she stepped off the train.

"Is this your daughter?"

"This is my wife Virginia."

"You wouldn't be out robbing the cradle, would you?"

Peeved, Poe glared at him.

"Mind to keep your personal opinions to yourself."

Griswold laughed.

"I didn't mean any harm."

Griswold stepped forward.

"It's a pleasure to meet you, Virginia," he said, bending down to take her hand.

Virginia shook his hand.

"A pleasure to meet you, Mr. Griswold."

"You can just call me Rufus. I'm a very modest man."

Griswold laughed again.

"Thank you, Rufus."

Then he saw Maria.

"And this is your mother?"

"My mother-in-law. Her name is Maria."

"A pleasure to meet you, Maria," Griswold said with a polite bow.

"Hello!"

"We've got to get our belongings," Poe said, motioning to a nearby black porter.

"Come on," Griswold said. "I'll walk with you."

Moments later, with Poe and Griswold in front, the group was slowly making their way to a line of waiting cab carriages at the street while a porter, pulling a trolley with their belongings, followed.

"You'll be glad you came to New York," Griswold said. "I can make you famous. I can put your poems and short stories in the hands of every reader in this town. It may cost a little money, but I can make you famous."

"How much money?"

"Oh, we'd have to sit down and calculate the expenses for my various services, but I can do it. Also, you'll need to join my society."

"Society?"

"The New York Society of Extreme Literary Enthusiasts. It is my group that brings together authors and readers. As president of the group, I sponsor lectures and other author events to promote members and their work. My group has had some of the most famous writers in New York as its members."

"Like whom?"

"James Fenimore Cooper, Washington Irving, and Nathaniel Hawthorne. There were others, but those are the most noteworthy."

Poe was impressed.

"In truth?"

"Of course, in truth. I'm telling you, as your promoter, I can make you famous."

Upon reaching the line of waiting cab carriages, Poe motioned for one to come forward.

Moments later, the porter was loading the family's belongings into the carriage. Poe helped the porter heft the trunks into the carriage while Griswold held the door for Virginia and Maria. Once they were safely inside, he closed the door.

"Virginia! Maria!" he said. "It was a pleasure meeting you."

Then he turned to Poe.

"You have a beautiful family, Edgar. I shall meet you Monday morning at the *Evening Mirror* offices on Ann Street."

Then he waved good-bye and the carriage started off down the street.

Suddenly, Griswold rushed forward and started running after the carriage.

"If you will join the society this week, I will waive the induction fee. That's a savings of $10."

"We'll discuss it on Monday," Poe said.

"Just wanted to tell you!"

Then Griswold, out of breath, stopped running and watched as the carriage disappeared down the street.

In the cab carriage, the three rode quietly for several minutes, then Maria turned to Poe.

"What did you say his name was?"

"Griswold. Rufus Wilmot Griswold."

Maria shook her head.

"I don't trust him."

"Why do you say that?"

"He's got shifty eyes. And he talks too much."

***

The Poe family spent that first night in the Algonquin Hotel, and the following morning, after some two hours of searching, rented quarters in a boarding house at 130 Greenwich Street, which was located between West Houston and Spring streets in lower Manhattan. It was an airy, one-bedroom apartment with a garden, a combination kitchen/living room, and a private parlor for Edgar's writing. At $10 a week, a huge sum for a one-bedroom, it was in the heart of the city's literary and artistic community. Poe complained that fishmongers brought an unpleasant smell to the street during daylight hours, but they would call it home for the moment. Muddy had requested a two-bedroom unit so she could have her own bedroom, but Poe said the quarters were only temporary and he would find something more spacious once he had additional income.

***

The following Monday morning, Poe met Griswold in front of the *New York Evening Mirror* building, a three-story red brick structure jammed between a brewery and a saddlery at 22 Ann Street. Once inside, they went straight to the office of Nathaniel Parker Willis.

Nathaniel Parker Willis was a stocky, late-thirties, dapperly dressed man with shoulder-length hair, a well-kept mustache and goatee, and a certain military bearing. One of the most popular authors of his day, Willis had won the hearts and minds of readers of all ages with his novels *Letters from under a Bridge* and *The Coquette*.

"Glad to have you aboard," Willis said, offering his hand. "I'm familiar with your work and I feel you'll be an asset to the *Mirror* as an editor and critic. Your salary will be $1200 a year. Is that agreeable?"

"Yes. Will there be expenses?"

"For certain occasions."

"And working hours?"

"Nine until 6 except on Thursdays when we put the publication to bed. There will be a few last-minute details which need attention. You'll have a desk beside Rufus."

Willis stopped, glanced across his desk, and picked up a sheet of paper.

"Here's your first assignment."

Poe took the paper and glanced at it.

"Perfect."

"I'll look for you in the office tomorrow morning around 9."

***

Once they left the *Evening Mirror* offices, Poe went to Griswold's home at West 72nd Street and Broadway. It was a modest, two-bedroom home and Griswold, who was single at the time, kept a typical bachelor's home with dirty dishes and empty wine bottles strewn about the floor.

"You should join my society as soon as possible," Griswold said. "Once you're a member, I can arrange for lectures, book signings, and other author events."

"Is there payment for lectures?"

"Of course! When I schedule a lecture, I take care of all the arrangements including renting the hall, printing programs, and publicizing the event in the newspapers. The society charges 50 cents per person to attend. Often we have over 200 paying guests in attendance."

"How much to join?"

"Ten dollars for an induction and $2 a month thereafter. If you join today, I will waive the induction fee."

"What would I lecture on?"

"Anything you like. Usually lectures deal with literary subjects, such as poetry, novels, essays. Tell you what... If you want to join today, I'll arrange for you to do a lecture on the state of American poetry next week at Blackstone's."

"The big book seller on Broadway?"

"That's right. Just one more way the city's readers can become aware of your work."

"I'm sold," Poe said. "I'll sign."

"Wise move. You won't be sorry."

***

That night over dinner, Poe told Virginia and Maria about the deals he had struck with Griswold.

"I sense we are about to experience a new reversal of our financial fortunes," he said as he took a bite of roast chicken. "I have my first assignment from the *Evening Mirror* and I feel my participation in Griswold's group will improve sales of my poems."

Both Virginia and Maria were quiet for a moment.

"I tell you I don't trust that man," Maria said.

"Muddy, he is already arranging for me to deliver a lecture."

"A lecture?"

"Yes. I am delivering a lecture next week at Blackstone's Books on the state of American poetry. Rufus says, with my reputation, I shouldn't have any problem filling the lecture hall."

"Will you make money from it?"

"I get half of the door proceeds once expenses are paid."

283

Muddy looked at him.

"When will you be paid?"

"On Tuesday following the lecture."

"We need groceries and stove wood. Also, you need a new pair of shoes."

"I'll bring the money to you once I collect it."

Poe took another bite of green beans.

"When can we get another piano?" Virginia said.

"When we get a bigger place."

They ate quietly.

Finally, Maria spoke.

"Maybe I should change my opinion of this Rufus Wilmot Griswold."

***

A week later, on the night on January 14, 1844, Poe was preparing to make his first public appearance in New York as a lecturer. For the occasion, he had new shoes and Maria had pressed his suit. Virginia, who was decked out in a black Hemet full circle dress and matching shoes, was radiant. As they were about to leave, Maria made a final inspection.

"Fingernails clean, matching belt and shoes, coat shoulders smooth," she said as she went around him.

"You fuss after me too much, Muddy."

"This is your big night," she said as she brushed the lint off the shoulders of his coat. "I want you to look good."

Finished with the brushing, she checked the straightness of his cravat and made certain his shirt cuffs did not extend past his coat sleeves. Finally, she stood back to look at him. She was satisfied.

"Now you're ready."

***

An hour later, when Poe took the podium, a crowd of almost 100 people were in attendance. Griswold introduced the speaker as a "brilliant poet and well-known figure in American poetry" and explained that, after the lecture, there would be a question-and-answer session. Once the introduction was finished, Griswold took a seat beside Virginia in the reserved section in the front row.

On the podium, Poe struck a handsome figure as a speaker. All six foot one of him stood perfectly erect with an almost military bearing; he spoke with a clear, concise voice and presented himself with a definitive air of sincerity and expertise.

"It pleases me to see my fellow New Yorkers appearing here tonight," he began. "I trust that, once you leave, you will have a deeper understanding and appreciation of American poetry than when you arrived. Let me begin by saying that American poetry has always stood in the shadows of British poetry. In short, American poetry is in its infancy when compared to that of England. The literature of a nation is little more than an extension of its history, culture, and moral values. Since America is a much younger nation than England, the gentle observer cannot expect our poetry to be as mature and polished as that of the British. That is not to say America does not have some fine poets in men like Ralph Waldo Emerson and William Cullen Bryant, but we have not yet produced a Tennyson, a Wordsworth, or a Lord Byron."

Over the next hour, Poe briefly traced the history of American poetry from early practitioners such as Anne Bradstreet and the slave Phillis Wheatley to the better-known poets of the day. He elaborated at length on Bryant's Thanatopsis and Ralph Waldo Emerson's "Ode to Beauty." Finally, he settled on the work of Byron and Keats, spending the last half-hour quoting and analyzing passages from Byron's *Childe Harold's Pilgrimage*.

"In conclusion," he said, "American poetry is a work in progress. It evolves year after year as each new and old poet brings their latest work to the fore. At present, America's leading poets are yours truly, Bryant, Emerson, and Holmes. Also, I must say that America has some fine women poets, especially Frances Sargent Osgood, who has a rosy future in American poetry. In particular, her poem 'Rivulets of a Dream' is a masterful piece. She has a fine ear for rhythm and a discriminating eye for details."

Poe stopped and took a sip of water.

"That concludes the lecture portion of the event. I will now open the floor to questions."

A middle-aged man wearing a fedora raised his hand. Poe acknowledged him.

"Do you feel you have written your greatest poem?"

"My talents as a poet have been honed quite keen, but my greatest poems have not yet been written."

Another hand went up.

"Who do you consider the best American poet at present?"

"Yours truly!" he said quickly. "But, as noted earlier, we have other fine poets."

"What about Longfellow?"

Poe shook his head in disapproval.

"That's reading for school children."

"You don't like Longfellow's work?"

"Useless rubbish."

"Mr. Longfellow would take issue with that."

"Let him take issue."

"Mr. Poe, what is your favorite poem?" asked a young woman in a flowery dress sitting in the front row.

Poe pondered for a moment.

"I have several favorites. Lord Byron's 'She Walks in Beauty,' Robert Browning's 'My Love is Like a Red, Red Rose,' but if I had to choose a favorite, it would be Shelley's poem 'Ozymandias.' How many know the poem?"

Several hands went up.

"For those of you who have never heard the poem, it goes like this."

Poe cleared his throat, then began quoting.

I met a traveler from an antique land,
Who said - "Two vast and trunkless legs of stone
Stand in the desert. Near them, on the sand,
Half sunk a shattered visage lies, whose frown,
And wrinkled lip, and sneer of cold command,
Tell that its sculptor well those passions read
Which yet survive, stamped on these lifeless things,
The hand that mocked them, and the heart that fed;

And on the pedestal, these words appear:
My name is Ozymandias - King of Kings;
Look on my Works, ye Mighty, and despair!
Nothing beside remains. Round the decay
Of that colossal Wreck, boundless and bare
The lone and level sands stretch far away.

Once he had finished quoting the poem, the audience erupted in loud applause. When the applause died away, Poe continued.

"If it had been my poem, I would have written the last line as 'far, far away,' but it was not my poem. In this work, Shelley is saying that no matter the magnitude of power, wealth, and fame one may attain in this world, ultimately, your life will be nothing more than useless dust. A perfect parable for the romantic age."

He paused for a moment and took a sip of water.

"Any more questions?"

No hands went up.

Poe looked at the clock.

"I see that I have held you for two hours. That's sufficiently long enough for anyone to listen to an old poet's ramblings about his craft. Thank you for your time and I will be available afterward for more questions and conversation. Thank you!!"

With that, loud applause coursed across the room.

As Poe stepped down from the podium to the auditorium floor, a throng of attendees, mostly young women, flocked forward to greet him.

"Oh, I so enjoyed your lecture," said one young woman with a bright smile and hay-colored hair. "Please sign my program."

"Oh, Mr. Poe," said a bulky, middle-aged woman in a frilly dress. "Can I have your autograph?"

"Me too!" another starry-eyed young woman said.

Over the next thirty minutes, Poe signed autographs, answered questions, and chatted with attendees. Finally, once the crowd thinned out, a smallish woman in her early thirties with large grey eyes and black hair approached Poe.

"Mr. Poe?"

He turned.

"I'm Frances Sargent Osgood. I wanted to say thanks for your kind words about my poetry."

"Oh, it was my pleasure," he said. "I love your work. It would please me for you to come to my office at the *Mirror* so we could discuss your work for publication."

"I would like that."

He turned.

"Please allow me to introduce my wife Virginia."

Osgood turned to Virginia, smiled, and shook her hand.

"A pleasure," Virginia said.

Suddenly, Elizabeth Lummis Ellet, her signature ringlet curls dancing about her shoulders, appeared and elbowed Osgood aside.

"Edgar, I have an urgent need to speak with you."

An annoyed expression flashed across Poe's face.

"Can you not see that I am conversing with Mrs. Osgood?"

"Yes, but I didn't think she would mind."

"But I do mind," Osgood said.

Poe looked from one to the other.

"Do you know her?"

"She's my neighbor," Osgood said. "And a very poor one."

Annoyance flashed across Ellet's face

"People who live in glass houses shouldn't throw stones."

"Please! Please, ladies!" Poe said. "We're in a public venue."

He turned to Ellet.

"How can I help you, Elizabeth?"

"I wanted to ask you to review my new book on *Women in the American Revolution* for your publication."

"I'm not disposed to discuss such matters here. You will need to bring this to my office."

"Monday morning?"

"That will be acceptable," Poe said.

"Thank you!"

Then she glared angrily at Osgood and left.

Poe turned back to Osgood.

"Now we may continue," he said. "Will you now be attending the society's events?"

"I shall. You have brought new attention to my work."

"The pleasure was mine," Poe said.

A pause.

"We must be leaving now," Virginia said, turning to Osgood. "I'm so happy to have met you. You must pay us a visit. I will show you my fern collection."

Osgood's eyes alighted with interest.

"You collect ferns?"

"Oh, yes, since I was a small child."

"I collected ferns as a young girl," Osgood said. "All of my albums are now stored in the attic with old pictures, family heirlooms, and such. I have not looked at them in years. I would be happy to accept your invitation."

"Say next Sunday afternoon. Around 3."

"That will be perfect," Osgood said.

"I won't be there," Poe said. "I'll be at the office."

"Then it will just be me and you," Virginia said.

"That's perfectly fine."

***

Later that night, back at the boarding house, Poe and Virginia were preparing for bed.

"I must be the luckiest woman in the world," she said, slipping her naked body under the bedcovers.

"Why do you say that?" he said, crawling under the covers with her.

"I saw the way all those women flocked around you tonight. They were like flies after honey. All of these women chasing you and yet you are all mine."

"My darling, I am yours and yours alone for all of my life."

He kissed her, then blew out the candle on the bedside table and took her into his arms.

***

January 28, 1844. Frances Sargent Osgood strikes a unique incarnation of womanhood. Medium height, slender even to fragility, graceful whether in action or repose;

complexion unusually pale; hair very black and glossy; eyes of a clear, luminous gray, large, and with a singular capacity of expression and a deep, rich intellect. In no respect can she be termed beautiful (as the world normally understands the epithet), but the question, "Is it really possible that she is not so?" Her lustrous eyes remind me of my foster mother's. Soft, kind, gentle. When I converse with her, her grey eyes seem to be reaching into my soul.

22
Flight of the Raven

The following Monday morning, at the *Evening Mirror*'s weekly editorial meeting, Willis was explaining the magazine's need for top-notch poetry to bring up the paper's circulation.

"You are a magical poet," Willis said. "Your sense of rhyme and measure is without equal. Your grasp of high poetic subjects stands head and shoulders above the others, but the *Evening Mirror* needs a truly great poem for its readers. A poem for the ages. A poem that will stagger the reader with its brilliance. A poem that every reader will always remember."

"Such poems only arrive once or twice in a lifetime."

"I'm sure you have some more great poems living inside you, Edgar. You must discover them and put them on paper."

"I'm writing every day."

***

On Tuesday, when Poe arrived at his desk at the *Evening Mirror*, he asked Griswold about his proceeds from the previous week's lecture.

"There were more than seventy-five people at the event," Poe said. "At fifty cents per person, I should have at least $35 due me."

"I'm afraid only $14 is left. There was a total of sixty-two paying attendees. After paying the costs of renting the hall for $10 and printing programs, which came to $7, this leaves only $14."

Griswold plopped a stack of papers before Poe.

"Only $14?" Poe said.

"Only $14. You have the bills in front of you."

***

That night, Poe gave the money to Maria.

"Fourteen dollars? That is all? I thought you said more than eighty people were in attendance."

"Perhaps my numbers were a bit exaggerated. Rufus said there were sixty-two attendees who paid. He said some arrived after the lecture began and attended without paying."

***

The following Sunday afternoon, after the midday meal, Poe left Maria and Virginia alone at the boarding house and went to the *Evening Mirror* office. At 3 p.m., Frances Sargent Osgood arrived at the Poe home.

"Oh, please come in," Maria said when she answered the door. "You're Frances Sargent Osgood. My daughter told me all about you."

Inside, Osgood was cordially greeted by Virginia and, once they were seated in the parlor, Maria hurried to serve tea.

"I'm so happy you came to visit," Virginia said. "Should I call you Frances?"

"No. Call me Fanny. That's what my friends call me."

"Thank you, Fanny," Virginia said. "My husband has enormous respect for your poetic talents. You seem like such an interesting woman. Please tell me about yourself."

"There's not a lot to tell. I was born in Boston, a child of well-to-do parents. When I was 22, I sat for a portrait by the painter Samuel Stillman Osgood. By the time the picture was finished, we were engaged and married. We have two daughters, but currently, we are estranged. He lives and paints in Boston. I live and write poetry in New York."

"Are the daughters in New York?"

"They live with their father in Boston."

"Do you miss Boston?"

"I don't miss the cold weather. With the snow every winter, you spend an inordinate amount of time inside. Some nights are so cold, you just cannot get warm. I prefer warm weather."

"I've seen winters like that in Baltimore."

"Tell me about you," Osgood said.

Virginia proceeded to tell about her childhood days in Baltimore, the loss of her father at an early age, meeting Poe, and their eventual marriage. She concluded with the statement they were very happily married.

"Do you think you and Edgar will have children?"

"I'm not sure. It seems that every few years, we pick up and move. I do not think I would want to subject a child to the constant moving around. Shall I show you my fern collection?"

"Please."

Over the next two hours, the two women went through three albums of Virginia's fern collection.

"Oh, I love the thespian fern," Frances said. "Once, when I was a small girl, my mother and I found a clump of thespians growing under an old tree stump in an open field. The way my mother was gesticulating and carrying on, you would have thought we had discovered a gold mine."

"I know the feeling," Virginia said. "I collected ferns for two years before I found a cinnamon fern. Then, one day before Edgar and I were married, we found a stand growing along the banks of the Patapsco River. I cannot tell you how happy I was."

Suddenly, Osgood looked at the clock.

"My goodness," she said. "It's five o'clock. How time flies when you are enjoying yourself. I must be going."

"Thank you for visiting my home," Virginia said. "I hope to see you again."

"Will you be at the authors' salon at the Lyceum next Saturday?" Osgood asked.

"I shall."

"Then I shall see you there."

***

Six months passed. In late August of 1844, at Maria's constant requests to have her own bedroom, the Poe family moved from Greenwich Street to an old farmhouse at the intersection of what is now West 84th Street and Broadway. The home was owned by Patrick and Mary Brennan, long-time friends of the Poe's whose family owned a string of successful dry goods stores in lower Manhattan. The dwelling, the most spacious home the family had ever lived in, was a six-room, two-story wood structure with three fireplaces, three bedrooms, and a separate ground floor writing parlor that looked out through latticed French doors to a small garden. Edgar's writing desk, his books, writing quills, and personal items were moved into the room. Adjacent to the French doors, Virginia said they needed a piece of furniture to place along the wall. Maria suggested that a picture of Grandmother Poe would work in the space, but Virginia said it was not quite right.

"I'll find something," Virginia said. "Can we get another piano? We have plenty of room now. I miss our singing and playing together."

"So do I," Poe said. "I've already got one picked out. "It will be delivered at the end of the month when I receive my *Evening Mirror* pay."

***

Two days after the move, a Saturday, Poe and Virginia were leaving an open-air vegetable market on Fourth Avenue when Virginia saw a sign in front of a home for an estate sale.

"Eddie, let's go in here for a moment."

Inside, an auctioneer was barking out bids for a huge painting of a sailing ship. Again and again, as the auctioneer barked out the bids, hands would go up to meet the price.

"Sold to the man in the red fedora for $25," the auctioneer said.

The auctioneer turned from the crowd, wiped his brow, took a sip of water, and turned to the next item.

"Here we have a bust of Pallas, the Greek goddess of wisdom. The little cherry table you see will be sold with the bust."

Bidding began at $2. After several moments, the bids reached five dollars.

"We can't afford something like that," Poe said.

"It's the perfect piece to sit beside the French doors. I want it."

Poe turned from her to the auctioneer.

"Eight dollars!" he said.

Suddenly, the bidding stopped. The other bidders looked around at Poe.

For a long moment, the auctioneer peered across the crowd.

"Going once! Going twice! Sold to the tall gentleman with the drooping mustache."

***

Back at home, Virginia placed the bust of Pallas and the table along the wall beside the French doors in Edgar's writing parlor. Then, as Poe and Muddy watched, she stood back to inspect her creation.

"Perfect!" she said. "Now we need some curtains over the French doors. Maybe some yellow or green."

"I like purple," Muddy said. "I'll make some purple ones."

***

Over the next week, Poe worked five days at the *Mirror*. On Friday, September 4, 1844, which was the day the new edition was put to bed, Poe worked more than eleven hours and arrived at the farmhouse home at 9 p.m. When he left the office and took a carriage home, it was a gloomy, foggy night with drizzling rain. Upon arrival at the farmhouse, he stopped at the mailbox, took several letters, then trudged through the mud along the little dirt pathway leading to the house. Once inside, he thumbed through the letters. His eyes lit up when he saw one was from Thomas Pickering Jones.

"Tommy!" he said to himself. He tucked the letters inside his coat and opened the door.

Inside, Virginia and Muddy greeted him, then he flopped down in a chair.

"I have roast turkey, mashed potatoes, green peas, and biscuits," Maria said.

"Give me a few minutes. I am tired. I want to eat, read the mail, then go to bed."

***

After finishing his meal, Poe went to his writing parlor and took a seat at the desk. Then he took out the letters and thumbed through them. There was a bill for clothes cleaning, a notice from a dentist asking him to become a patient, and an advertisement from a bakery. At the bottom of the stack was the letter from Tommy. He picked it up.

The return address read:

Lt. Col. Thomas Pickering Jones,
Fort Moultrie, S.C.

August 31, 1844
My Dear Friend Edgar:

It is with a heavy heart that I must report this sorrowful news.

Eight days ago, your close friend and my beloved cousin Eleanor Jane Wentworth passed from this earth.

While conducting a vacation tour on the luxury steamship the USS Faithful *near Bermuda, an uncontrollable fire suddenly erupted onboard and the vessel sank in less than fifteen minutes.*

Our beloved Lenore and 67 other hapless souls perished when the ship capsized and sank.

I trust that she and her spirit are now in the hands of almighty God.

I am sorry to have to report this to you.

Sincerely,
Tommy

Poe looked up from the letter. Then, as the thought registered fully, he burst into tears. Suddenly, the tiredness had left him. His mind was aflame with a thousand thoughts of the days and nights he had spent with Lenore, their sexual encounters and their use of exotic stimulants. For a long moment, Poe put his head in his hands. Then suddenly, he got up, went to the bureau drawer, and took out a bottle of peach brandy. Finally, he sat down at the writing desk, took quill in hand, and began to write. At the top of the page, he penned "Lenore." Then he paused.

Outside the window, rain continued to drizzle in the foggy, moonless night. He took a drink of brandy, then got up and opened the French doors to let in some air. As he did, intermittent flashes of lightning crackled across the night sky. For a long moment, he waited for the brandy to take hold, then he returned to the writing desk. For several more moments, he stared off blankly into space, then began writing.

Once upon a midnight dreary, while I pondered, weak and weary,
Over many a quaint and curious volume of forgotten lore—
Though my heart was filled with sorrow, I could...

He stopped writing. Then, bottle in hand, he got up from the desk and, while taking intermittent sips of brandy, began pacing the floor.

Suddenly, he heard a mysterious tapping at the French doors. He went to them and peered out into the night. Nothing but wind, drizzling rain, and thunder. The fresh breeze after the rain felt good and he opened the doors a bit wider. Finally, satisfied it was nothing, he returned to the desk and began writing again.

While I nodded, nearly napping, suddenly there came a tapping,
As of someone gently rapping, rapping at my chamber door.

"'Tis some visitor," I muttered, "tapping at my chamber door—
Only this and nothing more."

Again, he stopped writing. The fire in the fireplace burned brightly. The purple curtains Maria had made for the French doors fluttered gently in the night breeze. He returned to his desk.

Ah, distinctly I remember it was in the bleak December,
And each separate dying ember wrought its ghost upon the floor.
Eagerly I wished the morrow; —vainly I had sought to borrow
From my books surcease of sorrow—sorrow for the lost Lenore—
For the rare and radiant maiden whom the angels name Lenore—
Nameless here for evermore.

For a moment, the memory of the night he and Lenore had ingested the opium flashed across his mind. He laughed out loud with pure pleasure at the thought. Suddenly, he grew gravely serious again and put quill to paper once more.

And the silken, sad, uncertain rustling of each purple curtain
Thrilled me—filled me with fantastic terrors never felt before,
So that now, to still the beating of my heart, I stood repeating
"'Tis some visitor entreating entrance at my chamber door—
Some late visitor entreating entrance at my chamber door—
This it is and nothing more."

Now the poetic images were flooding rapidly into his mind.

Presently my soul grew stronger, hesitating then no longer,
"Sir," said I, "or Madam, truly your forgiveness I implore,
But the fact is I was napping, and so gently you came rapping,
And so faintly you came tapping, tapping at my chamber door,
That I scarce was sure I heard you"—here I opened wide the door;—
Darkness there and nothing more.

Again, Poe ceased writing, got up from his chair, and went to the French doors to peer out into the night. Nothing more than drizzling rain and a dreary, moonless night. For a moment, he lingered, then rushed back to the writing desk.

Deep into that darkness peering, long I stood there wondering, fearing,
Doubting, dreaming dreams no mortal ever dared to dream before,
But the silence was unbroken, and the stillness gave no token,
And the only word there spoken was the whispered word, "Lenore?"
This I whispered, and an echo murmured back the word, "Lenore!"—
Merely this and nothing more.

Again, he heard the tapping. It was louder than before. What could it be? The night wind bumping a tree limb against the house? A small animal seeking shelter from the rain? Then a flood of new images flashed across his mind.

Back into the chamber turning, all my soul within me burning,
Soon again I heard a tapping somewhat louder than before.
"Surely," said I, "surely that is something at my window lattice,
Let me see, then, what the treat is, and this mystery explore—

Let my heart be still a moment and this mystery explore;—
'Tis the wind and nothing more!"

For a long moment, he waited, listening to the tapping sound. Then, as if it were a visitation from on high, a black raven flew into the room through the French doors and alighted on the bust of Pallas. For a moment, Poe trembled at the sight. *The powers of darkness are speaking to me,* he thought. *The spirit of Lenore is trying to reach me from beyond the grave.* Suddenly, his mind was filled with a new rush of poetic images. Quickly, he returned to the desk and picked up the quill.

Open here I flung the shutter, when, with many a flirt and flutter,
In there stepped a stately Raven of the saintly days of yore...

Feverishly, he continued writing and, over the next hour, he wrote the first draft. Then he read it over and over aloud for rhythm and melody. Just as the morning sun was peeping over the horizon, he read it one more time, then collapsed sound asleep on the parlor floor.

***

The following morning at 7 a.m. Virginia knocked on the parlor door. When there was no answer, she went inside and found Poe sound asleep on the floor, holding a writing quill in one hand and the new poem in the other. Nearby was the empty peach brandy bottle.

She strode across the floor and knelt beside him.

"Eddie? Eddie! Are you all right?"

He continued to sleep soundly.

Then she looked up and saw the French doors were open. The floor in front of them and the bust of Pallas was wet from the blowing rain.

Quickly, she closed the French doors and drew the purple curtains. Then she knelt beside him again.

"Eddie!"

Slowly, Poe opened his eyes, rubbed his face, then raised himself on one elbow.

"What time it is?"

"Past 7. Why didn't you come to bed last night?"

"Oh, my darling. I had a poem to commit to paper. Probably the greatest poem I have ever written."

"Where is it? I want to read it."

"Can I get some coffee?"

"Go into the kitchen. Mother has a fresh pot brewing."

Poe got up and left the writing parlor while Virginia read the poem.

Fifteen minutes later, she appeared in the kitchen.

"This is your greatest work, but the title should not be 'Lenore.' The title should be 'The Raven'."

***

Over the next few days, Poe was plagued with doubts about the quality of his new poem. On Monday of the following week, he sent it to British Poet Richard Horne, whose epic poem "Orion" Poe greatly admired, to ask for this opinion.

"A well-written and conceived poem," Horne replied. "The lines dance across the page and the sense of the narrator's near-madness with grief shines bright and clear. A poem to be remembered."

The following day, Poe sent the poem to William Ross Wallace, author of "The Hand that Rocks the Cradle," who, in his reply, termed the poem "fine, uncommonly fine."

"Fine?" Poe wrote back. "Is that all you can say about this poem. I tell you it's the greatest poem ever written in the English language."

***

Finally, a week after the poem was written, Poe told Virginia and Maria over dinner he had made a decision.

"I fear I shall have to throw my beautiful child upon the mercies of the world to discover its true worth. Tomorrow I

301

will present it to Nathaniel for publication in the *Evening Mirror*. Then I'll know its true value as a work of art."

The following morning, Poe took the poem to the *Evening Mirror* offices. When he arrived just after eight, Willis was not yet in and Poe left it on his desk in clear sight, then went about his regular duties. When Willis arrived shortly afterward, he greeted Poe with a passing hello, then went directly into his office. Suddenly, around 10 a.m., Willis burst out of his office.

"You've done it, Edgar," he said, unable to contain his excitement. "You have truly outdone yourself. This is one of the greatest poems ever written. This will make you famous!"

***

On September 9, 1844, "The Raven" was published in the *New York Evening Mirror*. With the publication, in an editor's note, Willis wrote: "In my opinion, this poem is the most effective single example of 'fugitive poetry' ever written in this country. Every reader will empathize with its spirit of desperate grief."

Willis was right. Over the next few weeks, the poem took the world by storm. Not only was it copied in countless newspapers at once, but within two weeks, the words "The Raven" and "Nevermore" were on the lips of every American reader.

"No poem ever established itself so immediately, so widely, and so imperishably in men's mind," said Horace Greeley, editor of the *New York Tribune*. "This work will stand the test of the ages."

"This poem is unsurpassed in English poetry for subtle conception, masterly ingenuity of versification, and a consistent, sustaining imaginative lift," commented scholar Samuel M. Woodbury. "It will stick in the memory of everyone who reads it."

"This poem is greater than we know," said author Charles Fenno Hoffman. "It is despair brooding over wisdom."

References to the poem started to appear in advertisements. One newspaper ad for a Staten Island saddle manufacturer proclaimed: "The Raven promises Stillwell's double-stitched saddles are the finest saddles made in America."

"Nevermore will you suffer a sleepless night," proclaimed an *Evening Mirror* ad for the popular Dr. Coventry's Sleeping pills.

There were numerous parodies in both newspapers and magazines. First, "The Owl" in the *New York Tribune*.

But the owl he looked so lonely, saying one word and that only,
That a thimbleful of whiskey I did speedily outpour...

Then "The Veto" in *Godey's* women's magazine.

Once upon an evening dreary, the council pondered weak and weary,
Over many a long petition which was voted down a bore...

Probably the most famous was "The Parrot."

Once, as through the streets I wandered, and o'er many a fancy pondered.
Many a fancy quaint and curious, which had filled my mind of yore;
Suddenly, my footsteps stumbled, and against a man I tumbled,
Who, beneath a sailor's jacket, something large and heavy bore,
"Beg your pardon, sir!" I muttered, as I rose up, hurt, and sore.
But the sailor only swore.

Two months after the poem's publication, in the March of 1845, an elocution book, a tome designed to be a manual for clear, precise speaking, included "The Raven" as an oral exercise.

"I knew it was an excellent poem," Poe said, "but I never dreamed its popularity would exceed 'The Gold Bug.' It appears that the bird bit the bug."

***

Overnight, Poe became a celebrity. Not only was his face instantly recognizable, but the poem had earned him the nickname "The Raven." Now the recognition and adulation he had dreamed of in Richmond and Philadelphia had finally come to be his. Everywhere he went, people wanted to meet him, get his autograph, chat with him, ask questions about his stories, and congratulate him on his success. Despite the fame, Poe made a total of $9 on "The Raven," the payment for its publication in *Godey's* women's magazine. All of the other publications, mostly newspapers, simply reprinted the poem from the *Evening Mirror* and paid him nothing. He had made ten times that amount on "The Fall of the House of Usher" and twenty times that on "The Gold Bug."

One afternoon the following May, Poe and Virginia were strolling along East 83rd Street after lunch when they approached a group of children playing in the street.

"Look," said one of the boys. "It's 'The Raven.'"

Then the playful child, with outstretched arms like wings, began to glide around Poe and Virginia again and again like a circling bird, all the while cawing and making bird-like sounds.

Instantly, the other children took up the cawing while still others launched into a chorus of "Nevermore! Nevermore! Nevermore!"

Several moments later, after they had passed the children, Virginia turned to him.

"You have achieved what you came to New York for. You are now famous."

For a moment, he studied her without answering.

"Yes," he said finally. "My name is on the lips of every New Yorker, but my purse remains empty. I'm famous, but I'm broke."

23
Magazine Owner

The following week, Griswold made Poe a proposal over lunch.

"You haven't drawn on the full potential of 'The Raven,'" he said. "You should do readings and perform the poem in front of crowds."

"What are you suggesting?"

"Imagine this," Griswold said. "You are dressed totally in black, holding only a candle like a supplicant and walking about a darkened room quoting the poem in dreary, frightening tones."

He stopped and peered at Poe.

"Do you get the picture?"

Poe stared off into space for a moment.

"Yes," he said thoughtfully. "I like the idea."

"You would scare people out of their underwear. Especially women. Every time you said the word 'nevermore,' audience members would tremble with fright. Some would scream and run."

"Do you truly believe so?"

"Yes. And it should very profitable, but we need to move rapidly while the popularity of the poem is fresh in people's minds."

"How would we do it?"

"Let us proceed with a trial performance here in New York. If it is successful, we'll do a tour."

"My parents were actors," Poe said with a laugh. "Why should I not follow in their footsteps?"

***

The following week, Griswold rented a small theatre building at 83rd Street and Second Avenue next door to Blackstone's Books. It was a small, windowless venue with gas lighting and a seating capacity for seventy-five people. It had an open layout, which meant single chairs could be arranged in groups of ten to fifteen each so Poe could walk among the audience as he performed. That night, they did a dress rehearsal. Poe, decked out in a totally black outfit and holding a single candle with both hands in front of his face like a supplicant, walked among the empty tables in the darkened room quoting the poem.

"Your voice is catching the melody of the verses," Griswold said after the first trial, "But each time you say 'nevermore,' you should lower your voice to create an ominous, sinister tone. A sense of impending darkness and doom. Can we do it again?"

Once more, Poe went through the poem, this time following Griswold's suggestions. He had a natural mastery for reading the lines with absolute precision and, this time, when he reached each "nevermore," he injected a slight pause, which heightened the dramatic effect. When Poe was finished with the new improved version, Griswold was applauding with delight.

"Great!" he said. "We're going to scare the living daylights out of them."

***

Griswold set the trial performance in New York for the night of October 9, 1844. Earlier that week, he had overseen the printing of the programs. Advertisements for the performance ran in the *Evening Mirror* and the *Tribune*. Griswold even hired a food vendor to be present so patrons could have a sandwich or a glass of wine during the performance. Finally, on the morning of the performance, Griswold was in the theater box office selling tickets. The seventy-five tickets sold out in less than two hours.

"This is going to be good," Griswold said. "Very good."

That night, once the crowd was seated and quiet, Griswold doused the house lights. For a moment, the auditorium was in total darkness, then Poe lit a candle and all that was visible was a tall, ghastly figure dressed all in black, carrying a candle like a supplicant, which cast dark, ominous shadows across his face as if he were some mysterious creature from another world.

At the sight of Poe's face, the audience tensed with frightened expectation and Poe began to move slowly among them quoting the poem.

"Once upon a midnight dreary, as I pondered weak and weary..."

Those very words, which the crowd knew only too well, caused women to draw back in fright. Men's eyes dilated with interest at the mysterious sound and ghastly sight. There were muffled gasps. Some people's faces were instantly frozen in fright.

As Poe began the third stanza, "And the silken, sad, uncertain rustling of each purple curtain, Thrilled me—filled me with fantastic terrors never felt before..." one woman, frightened beyond her capacity, screamed and ran out of the auditorium. Other audience members remained transfixed as Poe continued the fifth stanza.

"Deep into that darkness peering, long I stood there wondering, fearing, Doubting, dreaming dreams no mortal ever dared to dream before..."

Each time he emphasized the word "nevermore" in a dark, ominous tone, and looked directly into people's faces, their expression instantly screwed up in fright.

As he began the sixth stanza... "Back into the chamber turning, all my soul within me burning.. Soon again I heard a tapping somewhat louder than before...." one woman suddenly jumped out of her seat, then began tugging the arm of her husband to leave, but he was mesmerized. Seeing it was useless, the woman finally released his arm and rushed out alone.

Finally, Poe was reciting the final stanza:
And the Raven, never flitting, still is sitting, still is sitting
On the pallid bust of Pallas just above my chamber door,

And his eyes have all the seeming of a demon's that is dreaming,

And the lamp-light o'er him streaming throws his shadow on the floor;

And my soul from out that shadow that lies floating on the floor

Shall be lifted—nevermore!

Once he had quoted the final "nevermore," Poe blew out the candle, then, after a moment of total darkness, Griswold brought up the house lights and the audience gave a collective sigh of relief. With the lights up, many audience members continued to stare at Poe, then, when he did a polite bow like a theater player at a curtain call, the dream state was broken and the crowd burst into a frenzy of applause.

"Bravo!"

"Well-done!"

"Absolutely beautiful!"

Once the applause ended, members of the audience came forward to meet him.

"Oh, my God!" said a middle-aged woman in a bulky print dress. "I've never been so frightened in all my life."

"That's the most frightening poem ever written," said one well-dressed young man. "No other work comes even close."

"I thought I was receiving a visitation from the dead," said a bald-headed middle-aged man. "I thought my dear wife had come back from the grave."

***

The following morning, Poe collected $22 for his performance. Griswold explained that total proceeds amounted to $55. There was $5 for renting the hall plus $6 for printing and advertising, which left $44 for them to split equally.

"It's an enormous success," Griswold said. "We're going to have to do a tour."

"A tour?"

"People will come in droves to see your performance. I could see the sheer terror in the eyes of the women tonight.

People love to be frightened to the edge of their wit's end. We should do a month's tour with a week each in Boston, New York, Philadelphia, and Washington. With two performances a night, it would do quite well financially."

"But we need money to finance such a venture. Where would it come from?"

"I'll front the money for expenses and be your manager. Once expenses are paid, we'll split the remainder."

"How do I know I can trust you?"

"You know you can always trust me," Griswold said with a sly smile, putting his arm around Poe's shoulder. "I have been your guiding light thus far and you've done well. Why would I abandon you now?"

Poe studied him for a moment.

"We'll have to make arrangements with Nathaniel to be off work."

"I think he will agree. Publicity for you is publicity for him."

"When do you want to start?"

"On Monday, we're going to Boston. Pack your bags."

***

The Raven tour began officially on October 26, 1844. In Boston, Griswold could only rent the theatre for a total of four days, so there were only eight shows in that city, but every night, the auditorium was filled to capacity. Back in New York, Griswold rented the same venue they had used for the original trial performance and, once again, it sold out for all ten performances. During one performance, after the lights came up again, one woman in the audience had fainted in her chair.

"I fear my wife is dead!" her husband said. "Your performance has killed her."

Poe took the woman's hand. She had a pulse. He patted her hand. Suddenly, she awoke. Upon seeing Poe, she jumped out of her seat, rushed forward, and threw her arms around Poe's neck, trying to kiss him on the mouth.

"I love you! I love you!" she screamed.

Quickly, Poe, trying to escape the kisses, pulled away.

"Samantha! Samantha!" the woman's husband said. "What in God's name are you doing?"

"I shall love this man forever," the woman said as her husband started to pull her away. "Our hearts shall be forever entwined."

"I'm terribly sorry," the husband said. "My wife has some problems. You know, mental problems."

"I understand!" Poe said. "It's quite all right."

***

Then in Philadelphia, disaster struck. When the show was finished, one attendee, an older well-dressed man, collapsed as he was leaving the theater and was taken to the hospital.

"Your show frightened him to the point he had a heart attack," said the man's distraught wife. "If he dies, I plan on taking legal action against you."

"Every audience member who attends one of our performances does so at their own risk," Griswold said. "If he knowingly was at risk of a heart attack, he should not have attended the performance."

"We shall see what fate holds," the woman said.

On the train to Washington, Griswold was worried.

"If the old man dies and his family sues, it could destroy the profits for the entire tour. I hope that doesn't happen."

In Washington, there were new problems. After three nights of successful performances, a portion of the auditorium roof caved in, drenched the audience, and the theatre had to be evacuated. Recent heavy rains had caused large accumulations of water on the building's flat roof and its weight had caused the disaster. There was no damage to patrons other than wet clothes, but the remainder of the Washington stand had to be cancelled.

"Thank God no one wanted to take legal action," Griswold told Poe on the return train trip to New York. "Two lawsuits could wipe us out."

"I know that."

310

When they parted on Saturday night at the train station in New York, Griswold said they would settle the money the following Tuesday.

That night, back at the Brennan farmhouse, Poe was happy to be back home. Once he entered, Virginia and Maria rushed to embrace him. Then he plopped down in a chair and, while Virginia removed his shoes, Maria began making a fresh pot of tea. Over the next hour, Poe regaled them with the highlights of the tour. Finally, around midnight, they went to bed.

***

November 18, 1844. There are no words to describe my delight at returning to the breasts of my beloved Sissy. She is the adhesive that bonds all the separate parts on my miserable being into a single whole. She is the glory, the shining light in my soul. I did not realize her contribution to my happiness until I was away from her for so long. Without her, I am nothing more than a lowly worm without solace or purpose. Never again will I be away from her for such a long period.

***

The following week, Poe was back at the *Evening Mirror* offices carrying out his editorial duties. When he arrived at work, Griswold was at his desk poring over proofs for the current week's edition. On his desk, Poe found a huge stack of letters. Instantly, upon seeing him, Willis called him into his office.

"I'm delighted to have you back," he began. "You're the star at the *Mirror* now and I want you to continue in that role. Nothing would please me more than to have another poem of the same caliber as 'The Raven.'"

Poe studied him for a moment.

"I must tell you a poem like that appears once, maybe twice, in a lifetime. You cannot snatch such works out of the air like picking apples off a tree."

Willis laughed.

"I don't believe that. The deep well from which 'The Raven' sprang has similar works contained within. I am certain of it. You simply have to plumb the depths to discover those further works."

A pause.

"I did want to tell you the *Mirror* is running a front-page article this week about your reading tour."

"Thank you!"

"Don't thank me. Publicity for you is publicity for me."

Back at his desk, Poe began going through the letters. At the bottom of the stack, he found a letter from Henry C. Watson, publisher of the *Broadway Journal*.

December 3, 1844
Dear Edgar Poe:

I was quite impressed with your poem 'The Raven.' Further, I have read about the success of your readings tour.

I must tell you, at this very moment, you are more famous than our sitting President John Tyler.

An author such as yourself can not only raise the popularity of my publication, but boost subscribers to new levels.

I kindly request that you appear in my office this week so we can discuss new opportunities for you and your talents.

Sincerely,
Henry C. Watson

Poe looked up from the letter and turned to Griswold at the desk beside him.

"Do you know anything about the *Broadway Journal*?"

"I know they have been on the verge of bankruptcy for over a year."

"Publisher wants to talk to me about a job."

"Oh, he would love to pull you away from the *Mirror*. Before we went on tour, I heard he was trying to hire Margaret Fuller."

"Why would he want Margaret Fuller?"

"Plenty of women read the *Journal* and they want to hear about women's issues like voting rights and fair wages in the workplace."

A pause.

"If you leave the *Mirror*, will you take me with you?" Griswold asked.

"You don't like the *Mirror*?"

"They promise so much and deliver so little."

"I'll let you know."

***

Three nights later, when Poe arrived at the Brennan farmhouse from the office, Maria presented him with a letter.

"Who is it?"

"Your foster father again."

"More hatefulness?"

Maria nodded.

Poe took the letter.

November 28, 1844
Edgar Poe:

> *You miserable, despicable cur!*
>
> *You vile, ungrateful dog! I curse the very day I ever saw you.*
>
> *Your slothful, indifferent attitudes and your blaring ingratitude has proven to be the anathema of my existence.*
>
> *Nothing would please me more than to see you strung up like a dog and flailed to death.*
>
> *My hatred and malice for you knows no end.*
>
> *Rest assured, you vile creature, you will never hear from me again.*

John Allan

Poe looked up from the letter.

"Forget it!" Maria said. "Let it be!"

Poe inhaled.

313

"I know you are right. I will let it pass."

***

On Thursday of that week, Poe met with Watson. After initial small talk and mutual praise, Poe was ready to get down to business.

"So what is your proposal?" he asked.

"Let me go to the heart of the matter," Watson said. "If you'll leave the *Mirror*, I'm make you a full partner in the *Journal* and give you total editorial control of the magazine."

Poe was taken totally aback. He tried to contain his excitement at the mere suggestion of owning his own publication.

"Interesting proposal," Poe said. "What will it cost?"

"Three hundred dollars, but I must warn you the publication is heavily in debt. It has made a profit in only three of the last nine months. If you come on board, I'll be depending on you to bring up subscriptions and revenue."

"I like your offer, but I must find available cash. I am settling the money with my manager on the reading tour today. Once that is done, I will reply to your offer."

"Fair enough!" Watson said.

***

That afternoon, Poe sat down with Griswold at the *Mirror* office to do a final accounting of the tour.

"Your total share from the tour is $226," Griswold said. "Total revenue from the tour was $3,667.24. Total expenses amounted to $3,115.24. That leaves a remainder of $552, which we agreed to split."

Poe peered at him in disbelief.

"Two hundred twenty-six dollars? Is that all? Some of the readings had over a hundred attendees."

"There were expenses," Griswold replied. "Lodging, transportation, meals, and incidentals like rent for the auditoriums, newspaper ads, and printing costs. I paid for all of that out of my pocket. Also, if the woman in Philadelphia takes legal action, we will have that hanging over our heads. There will be solicitor fees and court costs."

Poe shook his head warily.

Griswold could see Poe was unhappy.

"Did you want me to book cheap hotels?" he said. "You can't be the big star and take your lodging at cheap hotels."

"No, but..."

"Didn't you want to have decent meals and comfortable transportation?"

"Yes, but..."

"Would you rather have taken a dray wagon from Philadelphia to Washington than the B&O railroad?"

Seeing Poe was still not satisfied, Griswold pulled a sheaf of papers out of his pouch.

"Here are the receipts. All in black and white. You can inspect them for yourself."

Poe looked at the stack of papers and shook his head disapprovingly.

"I'm not good with numbers. Long lists of numbers make my head hurt."

"Numbers make my head hurt too, but someone has to tally them."

Poe studied him for a moment, then took a deep breath.

"All right! All right! I acquiesce to your position. Where is my $226?"

Griswold opened his pouch, then counted out $226.

Poe took the money.

"Now can I borrow another $75?"

"What do you need that for?"

"To buy a full partnership in the *Broadway Journal.*"

"I'll let you borrow it if you'll take me with you."

"That can be arranged."

"There will be 15 percent interest."

"So shall it be."

24
Messenger of Misery

The following week, Poe and Watson were at the solicitor's office to draw up the final papers for Poe's partnership in the *Broadway Journal*.

"To be successful, the *Journal* must be more serious, more intellectual than the *Mirror* or the *Tribune*," Watson said. "This means we have a smaller audience and therefore can expect to be less successful financially. We want to emphasize literary reviews, but also feature criticism of art, theater, and music as well as poetry and articles on politics."

"Agreed," Poe said.

"Now, you must realize, before you embark on this agreement, the business is $4,465 in debt," Watson said. "At the end of each month, the first bill to be paid is the bank note."

"I'm aware of that."

"So, anything else?"

"I want to bring on a friend of mine."

"Who is that?"

"Rufus Griswold."

"That's acceptable," Watson said. "You must remember that each additional expense weighs heavily on the publication's bottom line. Every penny you spend should be considered for its worthiness to the company's overall financial health."

"Agreed."

***

That night over dinner, Poe told Virginia and Maria about the deal he had struck with Watson.

"My lifelong dream of owning my own magazine has finally come to fruition. Now I can publish what I like when I wish without having to deal with that group of hapless idiots known as editors. I can control the life of my work. No more snide, critical comments, no more fears of rejection. Hallelujah!"

"Oh, my darling," Virginia said, "I'm so happy for you. When will you begin work at the *Journal*?"

"In two weeks. I still have some matters to clear up at the *Mirror*. I told Nathaniel I would leave his employ on May 20. That is two weeks away. Tonight, I am participating in an author's salon at Knickerbocker Books."

***

In early January of 1845, Poe moved into his new offices at the *Broadway Journal*. Located in lower Manhattan at 153 Broadway, it was a two-story, red brick building between a tailor's shop and an insurance company. Once Poe's name appeared on the magazine's masthead, subscriptions shot up. Readers were coming to the office "to meet the man who wrote 'The Raven'." The *Journal*, with Poe's addition, made almost $500 in September, of which Poe received half. Poe bought a new piano; Virginia bought two new dresses and two new hats. On Friday nights, they began dining at the city's most exclusive restaurants and, with each jaunt, they received the same adulation and celebration they had received with the initial publication of "The Raven." They even attended the theater twice, seeing a performance of *My Country Cousin* and Shakespeare's *Othello*. Over the next few months, Maria accumulated two silver tea sets, one Paul Revere and one Witherspoon. It was not Philadelphia, but it was close.

***

One night, a week later, when Poe arrived at the Brennan farmhouse, Maria greeted him at the door. She was holding a letter.

"Who is it from?"

"Your foster father."
Poe shook his head, then took the letter.

January 9, 1845
Edgar Poe:

My doctors tell me my death is near, but I wanted to use these last few days to tell you what a loathsome scrap of human garbage you are.

It was your mother, not I, who wished to bring you to New Dundonald and I rue the day you first entered my door.

During the twelve years you were in my home, I never had a single moment of affection for you. And I never shall.

You low, unrepentant dog!

Rest assured you will never hear from me again.

John Allan

Poe looked up from the letter.

"Forget it!" Maria said.

"No! I feel I must go to see him one final time," Poe said. "He and I have some unfinished business."

"From the sound of his letters, he is not going to be very friendly."

"That's why I must go. Destiny demands it."

A pause.

"Do you think he will leave you anything in his will?"

Poe laughed.

"There has been no love last. On the other hand, I remember how terribly he treated me as a child."

"Forget it," she said. "It's not worth it."

"No! I must go to Richmond. I must see John Allan one more time before he leaves this earth."

***

The following morning, Poe was on the train to Richmond. Upon arrival, he collected his suitcase and took a taxi carriage from the station to New Dundonald. As the carriage rolled across the countryside, his mind was flooded with memories of his childhood days at the plantation, his days frolicking along the banks of the James River with Robert Stanard and his dog Reynolds, his poetry discussions with Jane at Moldavia, his friendship with Amos, and his ongoing skirmishes with his foster father.

When the carriage pulled up to the front entrance, Poe exited and went to knock on the front door. Moments later, Nettie appeared.

"Mr. Eddie!" she said, upon seeing him. "My! My! Now aren't you a sight for my eyes."

"Where is Dolina?"

She stopped and stared at him.

"Didn't you know? Mother went to heaven four years ago. She got the croup early one morning and was dead before sundown."

"I'm sorry to hear that."

"Why are you here?"

"I've come to visit my stepfather."

"Do you think he wants to see you?"

"You'll have to ask."

"Come with me."

As Nettie led him to the stairs, he saw a photo of a woman he did not recognize at the bottom of the stairwell.

He stopped.

"Who is that?"

"That's the master's new wife."

For a moment, he studied the portrait, then followed Nettie up the stairs to the main bedroom. At the door, they paused for a moment, then Nettie opened it.

"Mr. Allan," she said, sticking her head inside. "You have a visitor."

"Who is it?"

"Edgar Poe."

"Edgar Poe? What does that ungrateful whelp want here?"

Poe opened the door wider. Inside the room, he could see Allan sitting up in bed, looking very frail and weak.

John Allan peered at him. His face formed a snarl.

"Haven't my letters informed you that I consider you a worthless, vile, loathsome dog?"

A pause.

"Father! I didn't come to argue with you," Poe said. "I heard you were near death and I wanted to see you one final time. May I come in?"

Allan studied him for a long moment.

"Oh, all right, come on in," he said finally. "I guess a few minutes won't hurt anything."

Poe stepped inside. At the bedside, he could now see a nurse in a white uniform and the new wife, a bulky, matronly woman with a round face.

Allan looked like a dead man. His eyes were sunken and hollow, his movements were slow, his hands trembled with palsy, and his face was etched with the signs of constant pain.

"As you can see, I am very ill," he began. "My time is short, but I have had a long and prosperous life. I am one of the richest men in Richmond, I have been married twice, and have three children without the benefit of wedlock. I have done all the things I ever wanted to do in my life except one."

"What might that be?"

"Discover the lowly dog who destroyed my marriage to your foster mother."

"How do you mean?"

"I have never discovered who told your mother that the Churchill woman and I were in the shipping office in London. That incident ruined my marriage."

"Are you sure you want to know?"

"Of course, I'm sure. Do you know who it was?"

"Yes."

"Who?"

"It was I."

Allan studied him for a moment. Somehow the thought was not quite registering.

"You?"

"Yes. Nathan and I had witnessed you and the Churchill woman going in and out of the shipping office every Wednesday afternoon for several weeks. It was like clockwork.

Once I discovered your dalliance, I felt Mother should know that you were defiling your marriage vows."

"So you led her to the office?"

"That is correct."

Allan's face turned red with fiery anger.

"You ungrateful whelp of a whore!"

Then, in livid anger, he grasped a glass of water from the bedside table and attempted to fling it at Poe. As he started to bring the glass forward, his face suddenly grimaced in pain and he grabbed his chest. As he did, the glass of water fell clumsily out of his hand on the floor.

"Oh! Oh!" he cried out, holding his chest with both hands, his face wincing in pain.

The nurse and the wife rushed forward as his body writhed violently on the bed.

"Mr. Allan! Mr. Allan!" said the nurse.

"John! John!" said the wife.

For a moment, the nurse, grasping both of his arms, tried to hold his writhing body on the bed. Then suddenly, the writhing stopped, his sunken eyes peered in livid anger at Poe, and his body fell limp. The nurse, still grasping his arms, gently laid the body into the pillows. Then she checked his breathing.

"He's dead."

The new wife, stark anger in her face, turned to Poe.

"Look what you've done. You have killed him. You have killed my husband! Get out of this house. Get out! Now!"

***

The following morning, Poe was seated in the Allan family solicitor's office waiting to hear the deceased's last will and testament. The attorney, an unsmiling, middle-aged man with balding hair and glasses, was solemnly reading.

"To my beloved second wife Henrietta, I leave half of my worldly possessions, which includes New Dundonald plantation, eighty-three slaves, eight rental homes, and $185,000 in cash money.

"To my three children born without benefit of matrimony, I leave the following:

"To Sarah Alice Ferguson, my child with Betsy Elaine Ferguson, I leave $25,000 with the request that the money not be squandered by her drunken, worthless husband.

"To Catherine Rosanna Peele, my daughter with Rhoda Harrison Peele, I leave $25,000 with the request that some part of the money be spent repairing her home.

"To Alice Maria Churchill, my offspring with Rosalee Bradford Churchill, I leave $50,000 and the rental home on James River Lane, which she requested during a recent visit in America.

"For my worthless foster son Edgar Allan Poe, I leave only my contempt and utter scorn for the ungrateful manner he conducted himself while living under my care."

Suddenly, Poe burst out laughing. The other beneficiaries, annoyed, turned to peer at him. Once he saw the others were staring, he ceased his laughter.

The solicitor looked up from the document.

"All of those receiving payments should be present at my office Tuesday morning at 9 a.m. to receive bank drafts. This proceeding is now closed."

Ten minutes later, as Poe walked down the courthouse hallway to the front door, he was still laughing. Even five minutes later, as he waited to hail a cab carriage back to the railway station, he continued laughing.

***

Two days later, when Poe arrived back in New York, the new piano had been delivered to the Brennan farmhouse. After dinner that night, Maria announced that, since they had a piano again, she wanted them to "be a family again."

Ten minutes later, the three were gathered around the piano. Virginia was playing and they were singing the popular song "Somewhere I Hear a Voice Calling" when suddenly, in the middle of the song, Virginia ceased to play and began a long fit of coughing.

Poe, who was standing behind her, was concerned.

"Sissy! Are you all right?"

She coughed again, then took a handkerchief out of her pocket and spit into it.

Immediately, Poe saw the splotch of red blood in the handkerchief.

"You've ruptured a blood vessel in your mouth," he said. "How do you feel?"

"I feel fine. I'm not sure what happened."

Poe looked ominously at Maria.

"That's enough for tonight," he said. "I'll fetch the doctor tomorrow. I want him to examine you."

***

Dr. Joshua Goodnight was a tall, thin man in his late forties with a kind face, thinning gray hair, and glasses.

"I fear to say this," he said after the examination. "But I must tell you she has consumption."

"Oh, no," Maria said.

"I was afraid of that," Virginia said.

Poe shook his head sadly.

"What can we do?" he asked. "Is there medicine she can take?"

"There are some herbal remedies which seem to help. Some of my patients use dandelion tea with good results. Another patient showed improvement after taking a concoction of boiled honey and buttermilk. It relieves the symptoms, but there is no cure."

"How long does she have?"

"Difficult to say. So long as you can keep her free of worry, she could linger for several years. Mental stress weakens her body's defenses and allows the disease to take a firmer hold. Best medicine is to keep her quiet and worry-free."

They were quiet for a moment.

"What can we expect?" Poe said.

Dr. Goodnight inhaled.

"There will be a slow, steady withering away of her body. The lack of oxygen to her lungs will slowly weaken the body, so there will be loss of appetite and weight as well as long bouts of coughing. Expect night sweats, high fevers, and shortness of breath. Muscle activity will slowly diminish down to almost nothing. Most patients are bed-ridden within six months."

Poe dropped his head.

Moments later, his visit finished, Dr. Goodnight was saying good-bye.

"I'm sorry to bring such dreadful news," he said as he shook Poe's hand at the front door.

"Such is my fate."

***

Over the next week, Poe and Maria prepared for the onslaught of Virginia's disease. On Wednesday morning, Virginia was helping Maria wash dishes, when she suddenly felt faint.

"Are you all right?" Maria asked.

"I can't get my breath."

"Come on," Maria said. "Let's go to the bed so you can lie down."

Once in bed, Maria offered her a piece of fried chicken.

"I'm not hungry," she said. "I want to sleep."

For a moment, she lay quietly on the bed, then suddenly sat up and launched into a long spell of coughing. With the coughing came small clots of blood. Around noon, she went to sleep.

That night, when Poe arrived at home, she was still asleep.

***

March 3, 1845. The messenger of misery has arrived. Death has cast its dreadful shadow upon my beloved Sissy and now I must suffer the agony of watching this loathsome disease take her life inch by inch. What have I done to suffer such a fate? How have I offended the gods? Have I not been honorable and trustworthy in my work and deeds? What are the charges against me? Who have I offended to deserve sorrow of such magnitude? Now I have only anguish and grief awaiting me.

April 14, 1845. I am elated upon arriving home today and seeing the improvements in Sissy's health. She was sitting up in bed and reading Daniel Defoe's Robinson Crusoe. *She greeted me with the old smile I knew from our courtship days and she had a vigor I have not seen in some time. For almost an hour, we conversed happily and fondly remembered our days in Baltimore. Muddy said she had eaten a small steak with vegetables and a large piece of chocolate cake. Eating is always a sign of improvement. Oh, dear god, please permit a continuation of this trend for both my sake and hers.*

May 2, 1845. This wretched gloom and dark despair has enshrouded my poor soul once more. This afternoon when I entered Sissy's room, she was gasping for breath. Muddy said, throughout the day, she had had intermittent bouts of fitful sleep, then wakefulness, all the time coughing and spitting up blood. Muddy said she had not taken a single bite of food. I know now why men of medicine call the disease consumption. It slowly but surely wastes away the body of the victim. My poor Sissy weighs no more than seventy pounds. Dare I raise my hopes again for recovery?

25
A Woman Scorned

Over the next few months, to distract himself from the misery at home, Poe threw himself headlong into his job as editor-in-chief at the *Broadway Journal*. In the new role, he learned very quickly that being an editor with a staff was not the bed of roses he had imagined. Now his duties extended far beyond the mere tasks of seeing that the editor received quality, correct copy; now he was faced with a budget, staffing decisions, proofs, printing problems, delivery issues, and the dreaded 18-hour Thursdays when he had to put the paper to bed. The hours were longer, there was much more responsibility and, as the publication's front man, he was expected to display a demeanor of dignity and honor. This was frontline publishing.

During that same period, word spread quickly throughout the city's literary circles that Virginia was extremely ill. When friends asked about her condition, he explained she was ill but was expected to recover. While she had good days and bad days, every night when he arrived back at home from work, he feared what he might find.

Once she was bed-ridden, Poe began to appear alone at author events and, with it, women, both young and old, began to appear out of the woodwork. Some invited him for private teas for discussions about poetry. Other asked him to speak to their social club; still others slipped him notes outlining plans for romantic trysts.

July 11, 1845. Rufus Griswold, despite my doubts about his honesty, is a trooper in the editorial room. He is my ace in the hole. Griswold is an excellent editor, he knows how to spot a good poem, he can read proofs quickly and accurately, and he is not afraid of working long hours. He seems to be honest on the surface, but somehow, I feel I was cheated on the tour proceeds. He is too concerned about money and he has too many schemes up his sleeve to be totally trustworthy.

***

The following week, Elizabeth Lummis Ellet, decked out in a flowery Hemet full circle dress with ringlet curls dancing about her shoulders, appeared at the *Journal* offices to hawk her latest poems.

"Good morning, Edgar," she began. "Have you read the five new poems I posted to you last week?"

"I'm only interested in four. How much are you asking?"

"Ten dollars each."

"That's too much. I have a budget to meet."

"Would you pay $5 each?"

"Still too high."

"Then what is your offer?"

He studied her for a moment.

"If you will donate the four poems, I will run a free page three ad for your book *Women in the American Revolution*."

"What is the normal cost of a page three ad?"

"Twenty-five dollars."

"The ad would run across the top of page three like a spread?"

"That's correct."

"When will the advertisement appear?"

"I suggest mid-October. Weather will begin to turn colder; readers will be inside more and therefore be reading more."

"A splendid idea. Do you truly feel it will help sales?"

"A definite boon for your book. When readers open the newspaper, the first thing they will see is the ad for your book at the top of the facing page. It can't help but boost sales."

"Then we are decided. I trust you and your judgment."

"I shall notify you when the page three advertisement appears."

Poe waited for her to end the conversation. She changed the subject.

"I understand your poor wife is gravely ill."

"Yes."

"I'm sorry to hear that. She always seemed like such a sensible person. I hope she fares well over the days ahead. Is she expected to survive?"

"I certainly hope so."

"Poor child! May I pay her a visit?"

"Certainly. I think she would like that."

***

Two days later, when Ellet appeared at the Brennan farmhouse with flowers, Maria answered the door. Once Ellet announced who she was, Maria returned to Virginia.

"Elizabeth Lummis Ellet to see you. Are you feeling well enough to receive her?"

"Show her in."

Moments later, Ellet was seated at Virginia's bedside.

"Oh, I'm pleased to see you again," Ellet began. "I'm sorry to hear about your illness."

"We all have our crosses to bear."

"May I ask about the nature of your illness?"

"I have consumption."

"Oh, that's so sad," she said. "It is an incurable, horrible disease. One friend of mine who had the disease lingered several years. She would spend days coughing and spitting up blood. The final days were terrible. Has the disease interfered with your marriage?"

"I'm not sure what you mean."

"Can you still perform your wifely duties to your husband?"

"I'm not sure I wish to discuss that."

"I don't mean to be nosy," Ellet continued. "I do know your relationship with your husband has been the subject of much gossip. After all, you were a thirteen-year-old child marrying a twenty-four-year-old man."

Virginia paused.

"I'm not sure I follow you."

"It doesn't matter," Ellet said. "How do you spend your days? It must be lonely being imprisoned in this bedroom day after day."

"I occupy myself. I read. My mother is here with me. I manage to stay entertained."

"I'm sure you miss your husband while he is away. He is such a fine man. And so intelligent."

"Yes. I am very happy to have Edgar in my life."

A pause.

"How long do you think you will live?"

"You certainly ask a lot of personal questions."

"But I don't mean to be nosy. I am simply trying to make conversation."

Another awkward pause.

"So the only people you have in your life are your husband and your mother?"

"That is correct," Virginia said.

"You're quite lucky. I left my husband after he was unfaithful to me. He participated in amorous congress with our housekeeper, a black woman and former slave. I always believed he would be faithful. I must tell you men are not trustworthy."

"Edgar is totally devoted to me."

"You're quite lucky."

Another awkward pause.

Ellet stood.

"I told Edgar I would pay you a visit. Now I have done so. I hope your health improves. I know the disease is incurable, but I'm sure you will maintain a happy countenance until the end."

"I'm fighting every day."

Ellet got up to leave.

"Thank you for the flowers," Virginia said.

"Good-bye!"

Once Ellet was gone, Maria peered after her as she strode down the walkway.

"A strange woman!" Virginia said.

Despite his new editorial duties, Poe continued to make appearances at author salons and signings to sell his poetry collections. The following Saturday night, Poe was one of four authors at an author's salon at Fillmore's Books at Third Avenue and 81st Street. Seated at the table beside him was Frances Osgood.

"Looks like it's going to be a slow night," Poe said.

"Fillmore's doesn't field the same traffic as Knickerbockers. If I sell five books tonight, I will be surprised."

She looked about the room.

"Where is Elizabeth Lummis Ellet?"

"She's not here."

"Fine with me."

"You don't like her?"

"There is no love lost. She has been my neighbor for years. And I must say a poor one."

Moments later, a middle-aged couple appeared in front of Osgood's table. Instantly, she turned and went into her sales spiel. The woman examined her book of poems, then made a purchase. Once the customer was gone, Osgood turned back to Poe.

"I have a new poem I penned today," she said.

"May I see it?"

She withdrew a piece of paper from her purse.

"The title is 'The Broken Heart's Appeal'."

Poe took the poem and read it.

"Beautiful poem."

He reread the last stanza aloud to savor the words.

Take the cup and take the gem!
What have I to do with them?
Loose the garland from my hair!
Thou shouldest wind the night-shade there;
Thou who wreathest, with flattering art,
Poison-flowers to bind my heart!
Give me back the rose you stole!

Give me back my bloom of soul!

"I want to publish it," Poe said. "I'll pay you $15."

"Done! I'll bring a clean, edited copy to your office next week."

***

August 9, 1845. I can feel my heart being drawn to that of Frances Osgood. Her innocent, childlike qualities remind me of my beloved Sissy. There is a freshness in her countenance and, behind her words, I sense a deep, rich intellect. We both were born in Boston; both of us have deep poetic natures and imaginations which can reach to the furthermost realms of the universe. Behind those large grey eyes dwells a heart of magnificent beauty. At the moment, it is little more than a flirtation. Dare I make it more than that? My heart must tread carefully.

***

Four months passed. In early December of 1845, Ellet, a smile on her face and her ringlet curls dancing about her shoulders, was back in Poe's office at the *Journal*.

"Oh, Edgar, how can I repay you for the success you have brought to my book. Only three days after the new advertisement, I have sold over 100 copies at Fillmore's and over 200 at Knickerbocker. I could not be happier."

"Do you have new offerings?"

"As a matter of fact, I do."

She opened her purse and withdrew a sheaf of papers.

"There are three poems here. I want you to read 'Love is Forever' first."

Poe peered at her.

"Go ahead! Read it!"

Poe took several moments to read the poem.

"An excellent poem. Our women readers shall enjoy it."

"It was written for you...."

There was a long pause, then Ellet smiled and peered into Poe's eyes.

"You know, Edgar, I have been fond of you since the first day I met you in Richmond."

"You are aware that I'm a married man."

"I'm a married woman, but that shouldn't prevent us from bringing some spice into our lives."

"Let us just remain friends."

"But we could be so much more."

"As I said, I'm married. How much do you want for 'Love is Forever'?"

"Ten dollars."

"I can't pay that. If you will donate the poem, I shall print another page three advertisement for your book."

"Agreed. Thank you, Edgar!"

She got up to leave.

"I do wish you would consider my earlier statement."

"Which one?"

"That you and I could be so much more."

He smiled.

"I shall consider it."

"Thank you! I knew I could count on you."

Once Ellet was out the door, Griswold turned to Poe.

"She's still got her eye on you," he said. "She wants you to till her garden."

"I'm a married man. She is all yours."

"Oh no! Never again! She is a man inside a woman's body. Did she pay a visit to your wife?"

"She did."

"Rest assured it was not a visit for well-wishes. It was a scouting mission by an evil woman."

"I have no interest in her. I'm interested in another woman."

"Who might that be?"

"Read my poem 'Valentine' in the new edition. It is a riddle. I think you can figure it out. I am only stringing Ellet along so I can get her poems as cheaply as possible."

"If she discovers that, there will be hell to pay."

"Why do you say that?"

"I know her. She is vicious, vindictive, and cruel. She will go to the ends of the earth to wreak her revenge. If she fails to get revenge, she will instruct her brother George to give you a thrashing."

"In a fist fight, I would have him on the floor in a heartbeat."

"You may get your chance."

***

Over the next week, Poe received a total of six love letters from Ellet. All were delivered to his office at the *Broadway Journal*.

January 4, 1846
My Darling Edgar:
For too long now, I have yearned to know the innermost secrets of your heart. Night after night, you have been in my dreams as a friend, a confidant, and a lover.

I am quite aware that your poor wife is gravely ill and cannot perform her wifely duties.

I know full well that we would have to be discreet. Therefore, I propose we make secret plans for dinner and a romantic interlude afterwards.

I too am lonely, not having seen my husband for over two years.

Listen to my words, darling!

We must follow our most delicious fancies and allow them to fly wild and free.

I await your reply.

All my love,
Elizabeth

Poe shook his head with disapproval, then folded the letter and placed it in his desk drawer. Then he took quill in hand to write another letter to Osgood.

January 6, 1846

My Darling Frances:

All of my thoughts and passions seem now merged into one consuming desire, to make you see that for which there is no human voice, the unutterable fervor of my love for you, for too well do I know your poet-nature.

Oh Frances! Frances! I feel sure if you could but look down now into the depths of my soul with your pure spiritual eyes, you could not refuse to speak to me with the same passion and desire with which I am penning this missive.

All my love,
Edgar

***

Three days later, he received her reply.

January 9, 1846
My Darling Edgar:

My heart is too shrouded with the same fiery passion you expressed in your previous missive. When my thoughts are of you, my body trembles with both delight and trepidation.

As we sat together last week at the book signing, I could feel my heart reaching out to touch your most intimate self. Your kiss. Your caress. The all-consuming power of your passion.

That I could reach out and touch your most intimate self is my fondest wish.

Awaiting you and your touch.

All my love,
Frances.

***

Over the next ten days, Poe received a total of seven love letters from Elizabeth Lummis Ellet. The final four, which were received on successive days of the week, went unopened and Poe put them in his locked desk drawer for safekeeping.

***

By the late 1840s, Knickerbocker Books had emerged as the premier book seller in not only New York City, but the entire USA. Located at 128 Broadway, it stocked the fullest line of books, including new releases from England and Europe, of any book seller in the city. As a result, it was a magnet for authors looking to sell their books and management was well-prepared to meet the demand by having a special designated room inside the store for author salons.

Such events, organized by Griswold's Society of Extreme Literary Enthusiasts, featured authors seated at tables with their works prominently displayed in front of them. Readers could chat with authors, ask questions about their work, and, if so inclined, buy a signed copy of their latest work straight off the table. Of course, the company saw fit to create a festive air by providing warm bread, fresh butter, and plenty of hot coffee for all attendees.

On the night of February 22, 1846, due to the rainy weather, only four authors were present for the event. This included Poe, Margaret Fuller, Elizabeth Lummis Ellet, and a young, relatively unknown author named Herman Melville who was selling a book titled *Typee*. As the event unfolded, the dreary weather, which had kept most authors away, was keeping readers away as well and, from the first, most of the authors saw only a trickle of readers coming to their table to purchase books.

Meanwhile, Ellet, thanks to the recent page three ads in the *Evening Mirror*, had a steady stream of buyers for *Women in the American Revolution*. Ellet, dressed in an expensive Hemet bustle dress and her signature ringlet curls, was seated at a table at the end of the room with a huge stack of books in front of her. Sitting behind her was her brother, Lieutenant Colonel George Lummis, a commandant at Fort Gibson on nearby Ellis Island. A large man in his early forties, he wore his uniform to perfection and exuded a full-dress military bearing. Quite often, Ellet's brother accompanied her to author events; she told friends he was her "protector."

Once the event had been in progress for some thirty minutes, Griswold, his face red with livid anger, suddenly burst into the room. The moment he spotted Elizabeth Lummis Ellet, he marched straight to her table. For a moment, he stood in front of her, glaring angrily.

Ellet, who was signing a book, briefly glanced up at him, then returned to the task at hand.

Suddenly, the relative quiet of the bookstore was disrupted.

"You mad wench! You low-life, trashy, vile, petty bitch," Griswold shouted. "What are you doing sticking your nose in my marriage?"

Ellet, taken aback by the suddenness of the attack, ceased signing books.

"What's your problem?"

"My problem is that you have meddled in my divorce when you have no right or cause to do so. Have I not always been kind to you? I helped you get your poems published. Did I not help you publish your new book? Even when you rebuffed my romantic advances, I accepted you and continued to be your friend. Why are you now interfering in my divorce?"

Somehow, Ellet was at a loss for words.

"Tell me!" he shouted.

Feeling he was being ignored, Griswold was angered even further. He stepped forward and slammed his fist on the table.

"Give me an answer! Why are you interfering in my divorce?"

Suddenly, Lieutenant Colonel Lummis stood up.

"What ho!" he said, raising his voice. "Why are you speaking to my sister in such an ungodly manner?"

Then, as if he had not heard, Griswold stepped forward and grabbed Ellet's right hand as she started to sign another book.

"Stop! You're hurting my arm!"

Instantly, Lummis was on his feet.

"Unhand my sister!" he shouted, then he stood up, rushed at Griswold, and in a single motion, slammed a mighty right hand into Griswold's jaw. Instantly, Griswold went to the floor. Smaller but feisty, Griswold was quickly on his feet again, ready to fight.

For a moment, the two men danced around one another, fists raised. Suddenly, Lummis moved in on the smaller man, and with a one-two combination, sent Griswold to the floor again.

"I'll kill you for speaking to my sister in this manner," he said. Then he kicked Griswold's leg. Griswold grabbed the leg in pain.

"Do you hear me? I'll kill you!" he said, moving forward to kick Griswold again.

Poe was immediately on his feet. As Lummis prepared to deliver another kick, Poe jumped in front of him and roughly pushed the soldier aside.

"Halt! Enough! Enough!" Poe shouted.

Lummis, seeing Poe meant business, backed away.

Poe helped Griswold to his feet. Blood was trickling from Griswold's mouth and the left side of his face had bruise marks.

"You should tell your friend to watch his words," Lummis said. "I allow no man to insult my sister in such a manner."

"Tell your sister to mind her own business," Griswold said.

"You apologize to my sister," Lummis said.

"I'll do no such thing," Griswold said.

"Remove this scoundrel from my sight," Lummis said.

Poe, calmer now, turned to Griswold.

"Come with me outside."

By now, the store manager, a smallish, middle-aged man with glasses and a balding head, was on the scene.

"Out! Out! Everyone out," he shouted. "This author's salon is now at an end. You authors are like unruly schoolchildren. Fighting and arguing. Out! Out! All authors gather up your books and leave the premises. Now!"

Instantly, Fuller, Melville and Ellet, with her brother's help, began gathering up books.

"You!" he said, glaring at Griswold. "You are forever banned from coming into this store. If you appear here again, I'll call the constable."

"You miserable dog!" Griswold said.

"Out! Out! Now!" the manager shouted.

"Come on!" Poe said. "Let us go!"

Moments later, Poe and Griswold were on the street.

"Rufus! What inspired your anger to such magnitude?" Poe said.

"I'm going to kill Elizabeth Lummis Ellet," he said, wiping the blood from his lip. "I'm going to take a pistol, put it to her head, and pull the trigger. It will be such a beautiful, bloody mess."

"What did she do?" Poe said.

Griswold took a deep breath. Calmer now, he began to speak.

"As you know, I've been attempting to get a divorce from my current wife Charlotte Myers so I can marry Harriet McCrillis. I have been in a loveless marriage with Charlotte for over two years. Two days ago, Elizabeth went to Charlotte, who is one of her friends, and urged her to not agree to the divorce. She told Charlotte she would be left penniless if she divorced me and claimed that I should suffer for the mental cruelty I had subjected her to during our marriage."

"Such an act is totally indefensible," Poe said.

"That's not all. Yesterday she went to Harriet, who she does not even know, and urged her to not marry me, citing my use of alcohol and speaking poorly of me in general."

"What was Harriet's reply?"

"She said our marriage is now off. She says, if a person of Elizabeth Lummis Ellet's social standing speaks out against me, then she has no intention of being my wife."

"Why would Elizabeth do something so vile?"

"She's a vile, loathsome woman. She only lives to create trouble in the lives of others."

"What do you intend to do?"

"There is nothing I can do. Harriet says my marriage proposal is dead and she shall seek a husband elsewhere."

Poe inhaled.

"I can't believe she would commit such a vile act. If I were in your shoes, I would be equally offended."

"She's very fond of you."

"I know, but I have no romantic interest in her. If she wants to be in love with me, I shall let her. I only string her along so I can obtain her poems as cheaply as possible. As a woman, I find her loathsome."

"She's an evil, vicious woman," Griswold said. "If you cross her, she'll hunt you to the ends of the earth to have her revenge."

"Let her hunt!"

***

Two days later at the office, Poe received still another love letter from Ellet.

March 18, 1846
My Darling Edgar:
Over the previous night, your handsome visage appeared in my dreams again and again. I dreamed you were in my arms loving me, touching me, thrilling me with every ounce of your being.

I have shared my intellect with you in the most gracious and enlightening way I know. Now I wish to share my body with you.

All you must do is ask and I am yours.
Awaiting your touch!

All my love,
Elizabeth

Once he finished reading the letter, he locked it in his office desk like all of the others.

***

The following Saturday night, Poe and Griswold were present at an author's salon at Blackstone's Books on West 82nd Street. As usual, tables for the event had been scattered about to provide places where authors could sit and display their wares. There was a festive air as customers helped themselves to warm bread and butter and coffee as they stopped at tables to chat, ask questions of authors, and make book-buying decisions. In attendance were Poe, Margaret Fuller, Melville, Griswold, and Ellet. Once again, Ellet's table was receiving a steady stream of traffic.

Halfway through the event, Ellet left her table to go to the ladies' room. As she passed Poe's table, she slipped him a note.

Poe read it.

"My darling, come and receive it tonight at my sister's house at 10:30. The address is 522 East 90th Street. Awaiting your love."

Promptly at 9:50 p.m., a store employee entered the room where the salon was being held and announced the store would be closing in ten minutes. Instantly, Poe, Griswold, and the authors began to gather their books to leave.

Five minutes later, at the front door, customers were streaming out of the store. As Poe and Griswold approached the small welcoming table at the store's front entrance, they saw Ellet waiting. As Poe drew nearer, she smiled at him.

"Are you ready?"

Poe turned coldly to her.

"I'm sorry. I must forfeit our arrangements."

"Forfeit?"

"I have other plans."

She stared at him in disbelief.

"But you said…"

"Let us just remain friends. I must go now."

Quickly, he turned and started walking away.

Ellet rushed after him. She grabbed his arm.

He turned to face her again.

For a brief moment, he looked coldly into her eyes, then jerked his arm roughly from her grasp.

"I told you I have other plans."

Then he turned and strode away.

"Edgar! Edgar!" she called after him.

He failed to turn around.

"Please, Edgar! Edgar!" she called again.

Then she watched the front door close behind him.

Griswold, who had been watching the drama from the other end of the welcoming table, went to her and began mocking her.

"Please, Edgar! Edgar!" he mocked in a shrill imitation of a woman's voice. "Silly, stupid woman! He has no interest in your feminine wiles. Only in your poems. He strings you along like a dog with a bone so he can get your poems as inexpensively as possible. He has been doing that for years. He is in love with another woman."

"Another woman? That sickly little child bride of his?"

"No. Another woman."

"Who?"

"Don't ask me! Read his poem 'A Valentine' on the front page of this week's *Journal* and discover it for yourself. Her name is hidden in the first seven lines. To discover it, write down the first letter of the first line, then the second letter of the second line, and so on."

She studied him for a moment.

"I have a copy here."

She pulled a copy of the previous week's *Broadway Journal* from her purse and opened it.

"How do you know this?"

"Because he told me."

She unfolded the newspaper and began reading the lines, all the while noting the first letter of the first line, the second letter of the second line, etc. in succession.

A Valentine
For her these lines are penned, whose luminous eyes,
Brightly expressive as the twins of Lœda,
Shall find her own sweet name that, nestling, lies
Upon the page, enwrapped from every reader.
Search narrowly this rhyme, which holds a treasure
Divine — a talisman — an amulet
That must be worn at heart. Search well this measure;

She spoke aloud the letters as she noted each line.

"F-R-A-N-C-E-S."

"Now who do you think that is?" Griswold said.

"Frances? Frances Osgood? Fanny Osgood?"

"Oh, my dear, you are so very clever!"

"How long has this been occurring?"

"Longer than you wish to know."

His taunting was not ended.

"Read the lines!" Griswold said. "Savor the words. '…whose luminous eyes brightly expressive as the twins of Laeda.' Do they not ring lovely upon your ears?"

Ellet was too angry to speak.

"What's wrong?" Griswold goaded. "Can't you face the truth?"

Suddenly, Ellet brought her right hand around to slap his face, but Griswold caught it.

"The worm has turned," he said.

His sarcastic laughter echoed across the walls of the small welcoming vestibule.

In livid anger, Ellet slapped over a vase of roses sitting on the welcome table, spilling the water and roses onto the white tablecloth and sending the glass vase to the floor, where it was dashed into a hundred pieces.

"That low-down dog! How dare he print such a poem to another woman on the same page as mine?"

She shook her head in livid anger.

"Stringing me along, was he? I'll fix his little red wagon."

26
Forbidden Love

On the morning of April 9, 1846, which was a Thursday, Elizabeth Lummis Ellet appeared uninvited at the Poe home.

Maria answered the door.

"Good morning," Ellet said. "May I speak with Mrs. Poe?"

"Come right in."

In her bedroom, Virginia had just finished breakfast. When Ellet entered the room, Maria rushed to remove the dishes and the small wooden tray that sat across Virginia's lap when she took food in bed.

"Please have a seat," Virginia said, indicating a chair at her bedside.

Ellet took a seat.

Moments later, Maria returned.

"Can we speak privately?" Ellet said.

Virginia turned to her mother.

"Can you give us few minutes alone?"

"As you wish."

Maria turned and left the room.

"I have news of the gravest importance," Ellet began.

Virginia stared curiously at her.

"What might that be?"

"Please understand that I am sharing this information only because I consider you my friend and a decent woman."

"What do you have to say?"

Ellet hesitated again.

"Go ahead."

"I fear to tell you that your husband has not been faithful to the sacred vows of your marriage."

Virginia studied her for a moment.

343

"How do you know this?"

"Because I have seen letters and heard conversations that your husband and a certain woman were engaging in acts of lust behind your back."

"What are the origins of the letters? And the conversations?"

"I cannot betray my sources."

"Then why should I believe you?"

"Because I'm an honorable and trustworthy woman."

A long pause as Virginia turned from her and gazed thoughtfully out the window. Then she turned back to her visitor.

"Who is this woman?"

"A friend of yours."

"What is her name?"

"Frances Osgood. Please understand that I am informing you of this matter only because of my respect for you as a woman."

Virginia's face screwed up in a frown.

"I find your words difficult to swallow. My husband and I are very much in love."

"I must tell you that you are only aware of his actions here in this home. Now that you are confined to this bed, he has many hours of freedom out of your sight."

"Are you saying he is meeting this woman secretly and engaging in amorous congress with her?"

"That is exactly what I mean."

Virginia shook her head and looked away, still unable to grasp the thought.

"Why would Frances commit such an act?"

"The spirit of lust runs to remote, dark corners. That is its nature. Sin seeks to hide its existence."

A long pause.

"I felt you should know this," Ellet said finally.

She got up from her seat.

"I have now done my duty as a woman. I must go."

"I thank you for your visit. I shall take your words to heart."

"I feel that would be wise."

Moments later, Maria escorted Ellet out of the house, then returned to Virginia's bedside.

"What did she want?"

Virginia did not answer at first.

"Well... what did she say?"

"She said Eddie has been unfaithful."

Anger flashed across Maria's face.

"That is an absolute lie!"

"She says Eddie has been meeting Frances Osgood in clandestine places for amorous congress."

"I don't believe that. There may have been a romantic flirtation through letters. That's the way poets are, but Eddie has no carnal knowledge of her."

"Have you noticed anything about him which might indicate he is being unfaithful?"

"No. If he had, I would have noticed. What reason would he have for being unfaithful?"

"Since my illness has arrived, I have not been able to perform my wifely duties. His manly fluids have not been released for more than six months. At least not with me."

"It's a lie. I tell you it's all a lie."

Virginia was quiet for a moment.

"Before I became ill," she continued, "he always looked forward to our marital couplings."

"You're letting your imagination run wild on the words of an evil woman. You are worrying and bothering about something of no consequence. I know Eddie. He lives only for you. His heart is now and forever with yours."

"Do you really think so?"

"I know so. Now take your medicine, lie back, and rest."

"Perhaps you're right."

***

That night, it was past 10 p.m. when Poe arrived at the Brennan farmhouse. When he entered Virginia's bedroom, she was asleep. Maria prepared his dinner and sat quietly with him while he ate. Once finished, he returned to Virginia's bedroom. She was awake.

"Oh, my darling," he said. "I'm so happy to see you. How are you feeling?"

"I had a tolerable day. I am weak, but no pain. Have a seat. I want to talk to you."

Poe obediently took a seat at her bedside.

He took her hand and looked into her eyes.

"Now, my dear, ask me whatever your little heart desires."

"Since the advent of my illness, it makes over six months since we have joined our bodies in amorous congress. Do you miss our marital couplings?"

"Oh, my darling, my desire to see you well again takes precedence over the needs of my manhood. My solemn hope is that the day will arrive when your body will be well again."

"You failed to answer my question. Do you miss our amorous congresses?"

"I don't miss it. I just don't think about it. Why do you ask?"

"I was just wondering."

"Shall I read to you tonight?"

"I'm tired. I want to rest."

***

That night, in the wee hours, Maria was awakened by Virginia making sounds in her sleep. Instantly, she got up and went to her room.

"Oh no! No!" Virginia was saying in her sleep. "Not that. Anything but that. Not my beloved Eddie!"

Maria could see Virginia was feverish. Her body was tossing back and forth across the bed. Maria leaned over her.

"Virginia! Virginia! Wake up!"

The daughter suddenly sprang wide awake. She looked into her mother's eyes.

"What's wrong?" Maria said.

"Oh, Mother, I had the most terrible dream. I dreamed I entered Eddie's room and a strange woman was in his bed."

"You were having a nightmare. Calm yourself."

"Sit for a moment and talk to me."

Maria sat on the edge of the bed.

"Elizabeth Ellet has raised fearful thoughts in my mind."

"It is all a lie from the mouth of a vile, evil woman."

"But I must know the truth."

"How do you propose to do that?"

"I want you to invite Frances Osgood to pay me a visit."

***

Two mornings later, Frances arrived at the Brennan farmhouse. Once she was seated, Virginia came straight to the point.

"You're the best friend I have. I trust you and your words to the highest degree. Now I must ask a favor."

"It would please me to help you in any way possible. What would you have me do?"

"As I have been sick for some time now, I have not been able to perform my wifely duties to my husband. He needs the touch of a woman."

Virginia stopped for a long moment, unsure of how she should proceed.

"How does that concern me?"

"I want you to quench his carnal desires."

For a moment, Osgood recoiled at the words.

"You're asking me to seduce your husband?"

"Yes. For my sake."

"Why did you choose me?"

"He is very fond of you. You have a certain restraining effect on him. Remember that he gave up drinking at your suggestion."

"I am quite fond of Edgar."

"I am aware that you and your husband are estranged. I know he has a special respect for you and your work. More than anything else on this earth, I want my husband to be happy."

"That's a very bold request."

"I'm aware of that. Will you do it?"

For a long moment, Frances studied her friend.

"Let me see what I can do."

Moments later, Frances said goodbye and left the premises. Once she was gone, Maria went into the room. Virginia told her what she had asked of Osgood.

"Do you feel you have taken the rightful course of action in this matter?"

"I have no interest in right or wrong. I'm only concerned about my husband's happiness."

***

Three days later, when Poe arrived at the *Journal* office, he found a stack of mail on his desk. As he skimmed through it, he noticed a letter from Frances. He opened it.

May 3, 1846
For Edgar

"Speak - speak to me, darling!
Hide thy sweet blush in my breast,
Breathe but one dear small murmur,
Thine eyes shall tell the rest. "
Say only thou wilt be mine, love,
Whisper me one small 'Yes!'

Ah! thou art silent,- thy soul, love,
Feels not my pleading caress
Low as the sigh of a flower,
Heard in the stillness of night,
Came the fond tones of the maiden,
Trembling with fear and delight.

Upon reading the letter, Poe smiled, then picked up quill pen and put it to paper. Once the poem was finished, he posted it to Frances Osgood.

***

The following morning, when Osgood received her mail, she had a letter from Poe.

348

MAY 6, 1846
TO FRANCES
THOU wouldst be loved? Then let thy heart
From its present pathway part not!
Being everything which now thou art,
Be nothing which thou art not.
So with the world thy gentle ways,
Thy grace, thy more than beauty,
Shall be an endless theme of praise,
And love—a simple duty.

Postscript: A visit to my office tomorrow to discuss your latest poems – including the one written for me – would be appreciated.

***

The following morning, Poe had a meeting with *Journal* creditors and was late to the office. Griswold, who was already in the office, smiled broadly when Osgood arrived just before noon. With overdone politeness, he got up from his desk and approached her.

"Good morning, Mrs. Osgood. May I be of assistance?"

"I'm here to see Mr. Poe."

"He's not in yet," he said with a wanton smile. "Is this about your poems?"

"Yes."

"I'll be more than pleased to help you."

"I'll wait for Mr. Poe."

"Suit yourself."

Griswold, miffed at the rejection, returned to his desk. With that, Osgood took a seat in the office reception area. Ten minutes later, Poe arrived.

"Good morning, Frances," he said with a broad smile. "Please come into my office."

Moments later, they were in Poe's office.

"Have you had lunch?"

"I thought you wanted to discuss my poems."

"Yes, but I would rather do it over lunch."

"What did you have in mind?"

"Let us purchase beef sandwiches and ginger snaps and have a picnic at St. Paul's graveyard. It's a beautiful day."

"Excellent idea!"

***

Thirty minutes later, lunches in hand, Poe and Osgood were meandering among the winding avenues of headstones at St. Paul's graveyard on Broadway looking for a grave suitable to spread out a lunch. Finally, they seated themselves on a large, ground-level slab of marble. Its marker read: James Littleton Harker. 1781-1838.

"I don't think Mr. Harker will mind if we have lunch on his grave," Frances commented.

Poe laughed, then they spread out the food.

"You have a macabre sense of humor, which I adore."

Moments later, they were eating quietly. Some twenty feet away, a group of some ten to twelve people were scattered around a large marble family mausoleum, laughing, talking, and eating their lunch.

"I wanted to say that your new poem 'The Violet's Love' is a lovely piece of poetry. Your sense of rhythm and measure is impeccable."

She smiled.

"I appreciate your kind words."

"I absolutely love the last stanza."

For a moment, he laid aside his sandwich and withdrew a piece of paper from his breast pocket. Then he began to read.

But as she lay listening to that low lullaby,
A smile lit the tear in the timid flower's eye;
And when death had stolen her beauty and bloom,
The ray came again to play over her tomb.

He turned from the paper and peered at her.

"I could feel the beating of your heart when I read that final stanza," he said.

"It was written with you in mind."

He smiled.

"The beauty of your poems represent testimony to a beautiful soul," he said.

She blushed.

"Edgar, when you talk like that, I get ideas. As you know, I am separated from my husband."

"My observation was not necessarily an overture."

"I wish it had been," she said with a smile. "I've always been an admirer of you and your work. I find you to be a very handsome man."

Poe looked into her eyes.

"Are you truly fond of me?" Frances asked.

"Very much so."

"Do you feel we should act upon our feelings?"

He had not expected that.

"Do you mean should we plan a clandestine tryst?" Poe asked.

"I think that would be appropriate."

"Where? When?"

"At my home. On Friday night after the author salon at Fillmore's. Will you be present at the author's salon?"

"Yes."

"When the salon is finished, we could go to my home. We will have the house to ourselves."

She paused.

"We'll take separate carriages," she continued. "That way, no suspicions will be raised."

He smiled, then put his face to hers and kissed her lips.

"I've been yearning to do that for some time," she said. "Can you do it once again?"

Poe kissed her again.

"Then we are decided?" she said.

"We are decided."

***

The Osgood home, located just east of Broadway on East 83rd Street and directly across the street from Elizabeth

Lummis Ellet's home, projected an aura of wealth and status. The two-story dwelling, constructed of orangey-red Flemish bricks, featured French windows, a black metal roof complete with spires and a lush, well-manicured garden. When Poe arrived that night, he emerged from the cab carriage, opened the wrought-iron gate, then strode up the walkway to the front door.

"Hello!" Frances said when she opened the door. "Please come in."

Once inside, no words were needed. There were several feverish kisses at the door, then they went straight up the stairs. Inside the main bedroom, the only source of light was a candle flickering at the bedside. After several more kisses, Frances went to the opposite side of the bed and began to remove her clothing. First the outer garments, then the corset, and finally undergarments. Poe, on the other side of the bed, gazed at her white naked body as she pulled back the covers, then slipped under them.

"I'm waiting."

On the other side of the bed, Poe was disrobing. After several moments of nervous fumbling with his cravat, he finally managed to get it untied. Finally, his clothes and shoes removed, he turned to look at her. She was lying in bed, the bed covering partially pulled away to reveal her breasts and a portion of her thighs.

He started to blow out the candle.

"No!" she said. "I want to see you when you mount me."

He smiled, then crawled into the bed. For a moment, there was a spate of feverish kisses and furious fondling.

Suddenly, Poe stopped.

Osgood pulled back.

"What's wrong?"

Poe shook his head.

"What's wrong?" she asked again.

"No! No! I cannot do this. I must not do this."

"Why?"

"My body has the need, but my soul will not allow it. I cannot violate the trust of my darling wife."

Then, quickly, he got up from the bed and hurriedly pulled on his clothes and shoes.

"I'm sorry. I must go."

Some ten minutes later, as Poe was striding back down the walkway of the Osgood home, Elizabeth Ellet was sipping tea on the second-floor balcony of her home across the street. In the light of the gas streetlamp, she watched with interest as Poe, his clothing disheveled, hurried out to the street and hailed a cab carriage. Once he was inside, she watched with interest as the driver turned the carriage around and headed north up Broadway toward the Brennan Farmhouse on 84th Street.

Ellet smiled at the sight.

"Fresh fodder," she said to herself.

***

The following morning, a Sunday, Osgood was back at the Brennan farmhouse to report to Virginia.

"I have come to report the events of the previous night," she said.

Instantly, Virginia called for Maria.

"Mother!"

Maria appeared in the doorway.

"Come in here. I want you to hear this."

Maria was immediately at her bedside.

"My dear friend," Frances began. "You have my warmest congratulations. I must tell you that your husband's heart is irrevocably bound to yours forever and forever. During our rendezvous of last night, he turned away from me for love of you."

For a moment, Virginia waited for the thought to register.

"What were his words?"

"'My body has the need, but my soul will not allow it.'"

Suddenly, Virginia burst into tears.

"I knew it all the time," Maria said.

"Your husband is a treasure among men," Osgood said.

"We have known that for some time," Maria said.

"Then I shall depart," Osgood said. "Have you any further need of me?"

"Only to thank you for your service."

"You're quite welcome And I bid you good day."

Once Osgood was gone, Virginia turned to Maria.

"We know the truth now. Never again will you allow Elizbeth Lummis Ellet to enter this house."

"It shall be."

"One other thing," Virginia said. "You must never breathe a word of this to Eddie. Promise?"

"Promise."

"I would never want Eddie to think I doubted his love."

"My lips are sealed."

27
The Ellet Incident

That afternoon, Virginia was in bed reading the poems of Elizabeth Barrett Browning when Maria suddenly appeared in her bedroom.

"Look who's coming!"

Virginia peered out the window. It was Elizabeth Lummis Ellet.

"Oh no! That woman is not to enter this house. Dispatch her with all due speed."

Maria went to the door.

"Good morning. May I speak with Mrs. Poe? I have some news for her."

"No! We have no interest in your lies! Remove yourself from this house at once!"

"But you don't understand. I have urgent news about your daughter's husband."

"You shall not enter here! Get out!"

Suddenly, Ellet brushed past Maria and started across the living room toward Virginia's room. Instantly, Maria grabbed her arm from behind and spun her around.

"Leave this house. Now!"

Ellet, not moving, glared angrily at her.

Seeing that Ellet was resisting, Maria quickly went around a corner and grabbed a broom. Then she rushed forward to attack, wildly swinging the broom at the younger woman. Ellet dodged the first two blows, but the third caught Ellet square across the right side of her face.

"That hurt!"

"I meant for it to hurt. Leave these premises! Now!"

"You old bitch!"

"I'll show you who's the bitch."

Now, in a furious attack, Maria rushed at Ellet, swinging the broom. When Ellet tried to dodge the blows, Maria slammed the broom into the top of her head. For a moment, Ellet was dazed, then, seeing it was time to flee, she turned and ran out of the house. In the middle of the walkway, she stopped. Seeing Maria was right behind her with the broom, Ellet raced down the walkway to the gate at the picket fence. Once behind the security of the gate, Ellet stopped.

"You old bitch!" she shouted, shaking her fist. "I'm not finished with you people."

Then, in livid anger, she slapped the metal rooster weathervane sitting atop the gate post.

"Do you understand?" she shouted. "You people have not heard the last of me!"

Once she was gone, Maria was back in Virginia's bedroom.

"Edgar must never know of this," Virginia said.

"My lips are sealed," Maria said.

***

The following morning, a Thursday, Poe and Griswold were busy putting the week's paper to bed. Griswold, who had been working with the composer making corrections, was returning to his desk with a page proof when he glanced toward the front entrance. Quickly, he turned to Poe, who was sitting behind him at his own desk in the corner.

"Here comes trouble," Griswold said.

Poe looked up. Elizabeth Lummis Ellet, her face flushed with anger, was striding across the floor toward him.

Poe got up from his desk and stepped forward.

"How can I help you, Elizabeth?"

"This is a demand for the return of my love letters. Apparently, you have no interest in me, therefore I want to relinquish any hint of that interest. Where are my love letters?"

"In my desk."

"Give them to me! Now!"

Poe hesitated.

She went to the desk and started rifling through the drawers.

"Whoa! Whoa!" Poe said. "You can't come into my office and start going through my personal effects."

"I'm going to find my letters."

"They're locked up."

She stopped.

"Then give them to me."

"In due time…"

"No! I demand them now!"

Then she began throwing items out of the drawers.

Poe roughly grasped her shoulders and, with Griswold's help, they started pushing her toward the door.

"Let go of me!" she shouted. "You're hurting my arm."

"Get out of this office!" Poe shouted

Moments later, once the two men managed to get her outside, they released her.

"If you return to this office, I shall have you arrested."

"What about my love letters?"

"Your letters will be delivered at your doorstep tomorrow morning."

"You're a liar."

"I have nothing further to say," Poe said.

"If they are not, then you shall have to deal with my brother."

Then Poe, dismissing her threat with a wave of his hand, returned into the office.

***

The following morning, when Poe arrived at the office, he unlocked his desk and removed the six letters. He placed them in a bag and took a cab carriage to Ellet's home. Upon arrival, he asked the driver to wait. Then he went to the door and knocked. No answer. After he knocked three more times, still without an answer, he left the package on the doorstep, then returned to the carriage.

***

The following day, around midmorning, Poe and Griswold were inspecting the latest editions of the *Broadway Journal*. Suddenly, Poe glanced up from his work toward the front door.

"Look who we have this time," he said.

Lieutenant Colonel George Lummis, accompanied by his redheaded younger brother Thaddeus, was striding across the floor toward them.

Poe got up from his desk to meet them.

"How can I help you?" Poe said.

"I am here to demand my sister's love letters," Lummis said.

"The letters were returned yesterday morning by my own hand. They were left at her doorstep."

"You're a liar."

Poe pulled back at the words.

"A liar... am I?"

"Yes. A bald-faced, blasphemous liar," Lummis said. "And I challenge you to meet me in the street so we can settle this like gentlemen."

Poe was unshaken.

"With great pleasure," he said.

Moments later, the two men were outside in front of the office building. As they faced off, a crowd of passersby began to gather to witness the confrontation.

"Now what were you saying?" Poe said.

"Hand over my sister's love letters or I shall give you a sound thrashing."

Poe laughed.

"Are you aware that I am also capable of giving a thrashing?"

"Produce the letters!"

"I no longer have them. They were delivered to your sister's doorstep yesterday morning by my hand."

"Liar. You intend to use those letters to scandalize my sister."

"Your sister deserves to be scandalized. She is a vile, loathsome wench!"

Suddenly, Thaddeus, Lummis' redhaired younger brother, stepped forward.

"You low-life dog," he shouted, "How dare you speak of my sister with such words. I'll kill you myself."

Poe laughed, then turned back to Lummis.

"Have you sent a child to do a man's work?"

"I'm not a child," the younger Lummis shouted. "I'm seventeen years old."

"Enough! Enough!" the older Lummis shouted. "That's enough of your insults. I demand satisfaction."

"By what means?"

"A duel. I challenge you to a duel."

"Then let us proceed."

"I have a brace of pistols," said a member of the crowd, a tall, middle-aged man in a three-cornered hat.

"Bring them forth," Lummis said.

Lummis turned to Poe.

"I must warn you I am a military man and an expert with firearms."

"I too am a military man and a firearms expert."

"That shall make our duel even more interesting."

Seconds later, the man in the three-cornered hat reappeared with two dueling pistols in a case. The man turned to Poe.

"Who will be your second, sir?"

"That would be I!" said Griswold.

The man turned to Lummis.

"That would be me!" said his younger brother Thaddeus.

"Then so be it," said the man with the pistols. "Choose your weapons."

Griswold and Poe inspected the weapons.

"Choose the one with notches on the handle," Griswold whispered. "The other is an English bulldog pistol. I remember them from Bunker Hill. They shoot high and to the right."

Poe chose the pistol with the notches.

Lummis quickly took the other pistol.

Then the man in the three-cornered hat, still holding the empty gun case, stood ready to preside.

"The rules of a duel are known universally," he said. "Both of you will stand back-to-back, take ten steps forward, then turn and fire at will. Are you ready?"

"I'm ready," said Poe.

"And I," replied Lummis.

"Then let us proceed."

The man who owned the pistols arranged Poe and Lummis back-to-back with pistols pointing upward, then prepared to give the signal to begin.

Suddenly, a member of the constabulary, dressed in a blue uniform, came running up the street.

"Stop! Stop!" he shouted. "Halt this madness at once. Duels are illegal in the state of New York. After Burr killed Hamilton, duels have been outlawed. Both of you men could go to jail for engaging in a duel."

Poe and Lummis looked at one another. The man who was overseeing the duel started to take back the pistols.

"Oh no!" said the law enforcement official. "I'll take those."

"But they belong to me," said the man in the three-cornered hat.

"Not anymore. Now that dueling is illegal, they belong to the state of New York. Whatever differences you men have must be settled by some other means."

"If not pistols, then what?" Lummis said. "Fists?"

"Fists it shall be," said Poe.

Moments later, Poe and Lummis had stripped off their shirts and were circling one another with fists raised. Lummis was older than Poe by four, maybe five years and slightly shorter, but muscular and better conditioned than the poet.

Lummis charged at Poe swinging wildly, again and again. Poe, calm and ever alert, punched and counter-punched with authority. During one charge, Poe caught his opponent with a hard right hand, which knocked Lummis to the ground.

"Get up! Get up!" the crowd urged.

Lummis put his hand to his face and felt the warm blood trickling down his face. Then he glared at Poe.

"I'm a soldier. I feel no pain."

As Lummis returned to his feet, the crowd cheered. They loved a good fist fight.

"I put ten dollars on the tall one!" said one man.

"I'll take that!" said another.

"I'll make that twenty!" said still another man.

"You have a bet!" said another.

The men began to circle one another again, then Lummis charged into Poe once more with erratic, poorly aimed punches. After each charge, Lummis was bloodied further and had a new spate of cuts and bruises. This continued for another thirty minutes. By this time, the crowd could see that Lummis had been severely thrashed. His face had several deep cuts from Poe's punches and a knot on the side of his head was swelling. Finally, Lummis made one final, all-or-nothing charge into Poe. As he did, Poe caught him on the left side of head with a mighty right hand. For a moment, Lummis staggered backward and fell on the ground. When he sat up, the crowd could see that his left eyeball was hanging out of its socket onto his cheek.

For a moment, Lummis sat up on the ground and looked around helplessly. Then, on all fours, he thrashed about the ground as if he were a blind man. His younger brother Thaddeus knew immediately something was wrong. Terribly wrong. Quickly, he went to his older brother.

"George! Brother George! What's wrong?"

"I can't see! I can't see!"

Thaddeus waved his hand in front of his brother's eyes.

No response.

"Oh, my God!"

The younger brother turned to Poe.

"You've blinded my brother," he shouted.

"He got what he deserved," Poe replied.

Seeing the fight was at an end, Poe, his right eye swollen and his face bloodied from several cuts, put on his shirt.

The crowd began to disperse as young Thaddeus tried to help his brother to his feet. As Poe and Griswold started back inside, young Thaddeus stood up and shouted after them.

"You've blinded my brother," he shouted, brushing back his red hair from his eyes. "Someday, I'll make you pay for this. Do you hear? Someday, I'll have my revenge."

Poe dismissed his words with a wave of the hand then disappeared into the journal building.

***

Over the month of June, Elizabeth Lummis Ellet spread the word throughout New York's literary community that Poe and Osgood were having a torrid affair. Already the public had hints of the scandal from the sappy poems that had been printed in the major New York newspapers. Many had been published under pen names, but the writers' names were so thinly disguised that the city's literati knew exactly who each of the major players were. Once word spread that Poe had thrashed Ellet's brother in a dispute over love letters, the scandal gained new momentum. Rumors and half-truths were stacked atop outright lies. Old women whispered in back rooms that Ellet's brother had fought Poe because he secretly believed his sister was pregnant by Poe. Another rumor claimed that Poe had deserted Virginia and eloped to Europe with Osgood. Still another held that, after the fight, Poe had hired an assassin to kill Ellet and dump her body in the East River. At one point, Osgood's estranged husband Samuel became involved and publicly threatened to come to New York and put an end to Poe. Local newspapers, without using names, hinted at the scandal with headlines like "Poets, Secret Lovers, and Lies!" and "Poets in Love Triangle!"

***

In early September of 1846, Virginia, who was well-aware of the scandal, presented her husband with a poem she had written, which mentioned "the tattling of many tongues."

"This is for you, my darling," she said when she handed him the sealed letter that morning. Poe took the letter, opened it, and began reading.

For My Darling Edgar

Ever with thee I wish to roam —
Dearest my life is thine.
Give me a cottage for my home
And a rich old cypress vine,
Removed from the world with its sin and care
And the tattling of many tongues.
Love alone shall guide us when we are there —
Love shall heal my weakened lungs;
And Oh, the tranquil hours we'll spend,
Never wishing that others may see!
Perfect ease we'll enjoy, without thinking to lend
Ourselves to the world and its glee —
Ever peaceful and blissful we'll be.

Poe looked up from the poem.

"Yes, my darling. I know those tattling tongues as well as you. We are both being subjected to an avalanche of lies, rumors, and half-truths. I must tell you, however, that this too shall pass."

She smiled.

"I love you," she said.

"And I love you."

28
Born to be Broke

Over the next few months, the Ellet incident was forgotten. Poe had far more pressing matters at hand. During the first week in April, Watson called Poe into his office and handed him a court document.

"What is this?"

"A summons to appear in debtor's court. The bank is trying to close down the *Journal* for the money it owes."

"We can't let that happen," Poe said. "Owning my own publication has been my long-time dream."

"Then we're going to have to come up with some money or get an extension on the foreclosure."

"We've started to make some money over two of the last four months. Does that count not for anything? Doesn't that say we are turning the tide?"

Watson shook his head.

"We'll have to see what happens at the hearing."

***

Two weeks later at the hearing, the judge, an older, gray-haired man with a sharp nose and glasses, began the proceedings by calling Poe and Watson to face him in front of the bench.

"You realize you must show cause as to why this foreclosure action should not proceed. What do you have to present?"

"Your Honor, we have been paying the interest on the indebtedness for nine months now," Watson said, "but the business has not been able to make enough profit to make payments on the principal."

"At what point do you feel the operation can start repaying the principal?" the judge asked.

"I'm not sure, but of the last four months, we have made a small profit in two of them. This month, we expect to make a profit again. Each month, our profit grows."

"What was your profits last month?"

"A total of $425."

"That's a good start. How much do you expect to make this month?"

"Somewhere in the neighborhood of $500."

"I can see the profits are growing," the judge said.

He turned to the bank's solicitors.

"Your Honor, this is the same weak excuse the defendant has used for six months," he countered. "Nothing has been paid on the principal for almost two years. Simply paying the interest is not sufficient."

"I see your point," the judge said, "but it appears that the business is gaining ground with each new monthly profit."

"Your Honor, that may be true, but the fact remains that our bank must carry this $4,465 balance forward month after month. This is dead money. If this money were in the bank's possession, we could be lending it to businesses that were making a profit."

"Yes. I know," the judge replied. "Banks like to keep rolling their money so they can make more and more."

This brought a ripple of laughter from the courtroom audience.

"Mr. Watson," the judge said. "Can you make any sort of lump sum payment on the principal?"

"We can try. If you will grant us an extension, we will come up with one."

"In what amount?"

"Five hundred dollars."

"That not enough," the bank representative said. "To be fair, we expect at least half of the outstanding note."

"We cannot accomplish that," said Watson.

"Then, your Honor, it's only fair that you allow the foreclosure to proceed," said the bank's representative.

The judge looked from one to the other.

"The defendant's offer seems fair," the judge said. "At least the defendant is making an effort to fulfill their obligations."

The judge turned back to Watson and Poe. "Can you promise a lump sum payment of at least $500 within three months?"

"We can!" Watson said.

The judge took a deep breath, then studied the documents in front of him.

"The defendant has made a convincing case," he said. "They have shown that the newspaper operation has made a small profit during two of the past four months and, based on the current outlook, should continue to do so in the months ahead. With those considerations in mind, I hereby grant the requested three-month extension with the stipulation that a $500 payment will be made on the principal by the end of the three months."

Fifteen minutes later, Poe and Watson were elated as they walked down the courthouse hallway.

"Where are we going to get $500?"

"I'm not sure," Watson said. "We'll have to figure out something."

***

Six months passed. During that time, Poe and Watson were striving at every turn to cut costs at the newspaper to keep it afloat. Printing paper that had been held in reserve was used rather than buying new. Rather than using six street hawkers to sell papers, they decided to use only four. Further, they agreed to lay off Griswold and each of them shoulder his editorial workload.

When Griswold was told he was out of a job, he did not appear upset.

"That's fine," he said. "I have other avenues I can explore."

***

In early March of 1847, the annual International Author's Symposium was held in New York at the Algonquin Hotel. Poe, who had never attended the event, particularly wanted to meet British novelist Charles Dickens, with whom he had been corresponding over the past year.

On the morning of the event, Poe was up early, dressed, and took the horse-drawn railcar to lower Manhattan. When he arrived at the Algonquin, it was abuzz with reporters, authors, publishers, and some of the most notable authors of the day. In the morning session, attendees listened to speeches about international copyright law, the stress of being a publisher, the rising cost of printing paper, and the new, improved steam-powered printing presses. In the afternoon, there were three one-hour discussion panels where members of the audience asked questions of the authors.

That night, at the dinner banquet, Poe was seated at the table of honored guests, which included Charles Dickens, James Fenimore Cooper, Washington Irving, Nathaniel Hawthorne, Herman Melville, and a whole host of lesser-known authors. Griswold was noticeably absent from the event.

During table conversation, Melville, a twenty-three-year-old with boyish good looks and well-trimmed mustache, droned on and on to Dickens about how he admired his work.

"Your stories about young boys in London's sweat shops are some of the finest novels being written today," he said.

"Thank you," Dickens replied. "Each and every one of them was loosely based on my boyhood days in London. Oftentimes as I was writing, I would remember the horrors of those sweatshop days and break down in tears."

"*A Tale of Two Cities* continues to be my favorite," said Cooper, a tall, muscular man in his forties with the healthy look of an outdoorsman. "It brings together the separate cultures of England and France in a poignant, touching manner."

"I agree," said Irving, a smallish man in his sixties with a paunch and thick sideburns. "A beautifully constructed work. I have never attempted a work with such length. My mind does not venture into such large visions."

A pause.

"What about you, Poe?" Cooper asked. "Are you familiar with Dickens' work?"

"Oh yes. I am familiar with *The Pickwick Papers* and *Oliver Twist*, but my favorite is the *Old Curiosity Shop*. The quiet, abiding faith of Nell Trent is an inspiration to people all over the world. Watching her struggle against seemingly insurmountable odds brought tears to my eyes."

He turned to Dickens.

"Have you read any of my work?"

"Oh yes," Dickens replied. "'The Raven,' 'The Telltale Heart,' 'The Black Cat,' 'The Cask of Amontillado.' All of your work seems to be imbued with a quiet madness. Your main characters are either raving mad or on the brink thereof. Each time I sit down to read your work, I am transported into a world of half-crazed characters whose lives are swirling within a boiling cauldron of darkness, evil, and death."

Poe started to speak, then Dickens interrupted him.

"That is not to say that I dislike that swirling world of darkness and death. I find it very entertaining."

"Thank you!" Poe said.

A slight pause, then Poe spoke.

"It is true that my mind gravitates to the darker side of human existence," Poe replied. "Death and darkness have stalked me since the day of my birth. As you know, I was born in a funeral home."

"Oh, great irony of ironies," Dickens said with a big laugh. "On the other hand," he continued, "I must tell you your story 'Murders in the Rue Morgue' is probably the most important short story of this century. You have invented the detective story, an entirely new class of literature. In years ahead, thousands, perhaps even millions of books will be written about detectives just like yours solving crimes."

"It is ratiocination," Poe said. "The process of deducing conclusions from available clues with exact, thorough, logical thinking."

A pause, then Poe turned back to Dickens.

"Charles! Did you receive my letters last month asking you to help me find a publisher in England?"

"I did, but it is a useless task," Dickens said. "Why should publishers pay an author for his work when they can pirate it? There are no international copyright laws to protect an author's work outside his own country. American publishers do the same thing with my work. It's a goldmine for publishers."

Cooper turned to Poe.

"Your poem 'The Raven,'" he said. "Has it brought you financial success?"

"I made a total of $9 on the poem."

The others turned to him in surprise.

"That's all?"

"I'm afraid so. I did do a reading tour, which earned around $300, but once the expenses were paid, there was little left for me and my manager."

"Who is your manager?"

"Rufus Griswold."

Cooper quickly turned back to him.

"Rufus Wilmot Griswold?"

"That's the one."

Cooper and Irving looked knowingly at one another.

"That man is as dishonest as the day is long," Cooper said. "He defrauded me and Irving out of a large sum of money."

"How did it happen?"

"We joined his literary society and gave him copies of our books to sell at his events. When it was time to settle the money, he made up a cock and bull story about how the books were destroyed before they were sold."

"How much did he get?"

"I gave him around 1,800 copies of *Last of The Mohicans*. I estimate my profits should have been about $2,200, but I never saw a penny."

He turned to Irving.

"Washington, how much money did Rufus Griswold steal from you?"

"About $2,500. I provided him a total 2,000 books to sell for me. I never saw a penny of the proceeds."

Cooper turned to Hawthorne.

Nathaniel Hawthorne was a stocky, thick-chested bear of a man, his face encircled with a forest of thick salt and pepper hair.

"Nathaniel, do you remember Rufus Griswold?"

"Oh yes. The king of shysters. I refused to allow that Godless man to draw me into his nefarious schemes. I could see the devil in his eyes the first time I met him."

"I wish I had never trusted him," Irving said.

"I feel the same," Cooper said. "You've heard that Christ was a fisher of men. Well, Rufus Griswold is a fisher of authors. He takes the works of trusting authors, sells them, then keeps the money for himself."

"Why didn't you take legal action?" Poe said.

"Because once you pay for solicitors, spend time in and out of court, and suffer all of the aggravation… it's not worth it."

"So do you feel Rufus defrauded me?"

Cooper laughed.

"Without a doubt."

"As sure as the sun rises in the east," Irving said.

"But he had facts and figures to back up his claims," Poe said.

"HIS facts and figures. He is quite clever with a pen and a list of numbers. He always makes them turn out in his favor."

Poe shook his head sadly.

"Why do you think Rufus is not in attendance at this meeting?" said Cooper.

"Why?"

"Because he doesn't want to face Irving and myself," Cooper said. "He knows he cheated us. Also, he knows that we know he cheated us."

Poe studied him for a moment.

"I intend to speak with Rufus about this matter the next time I see him."

***

Two nights after the conference ended, Poe went to the Blue Acorn Tavern on West 73rd Street to find Griswold. He knew it was Griswold's favorite watering hole. It was where

Griswold had taken him to celebrate the signing of the contract for joining his society. When Poe entered the tavern, it was noisy and crowded, but after some searching, he found Griswold at the bar near the rear door. After greetings, Poe leveled the charges made by his fellow authors.

"Cooper and Irving are just two old fools who like to gossip and make all manner of charges against persons they don't like," Griswold said. "During my dealings with them, I have been honest to a fault."

"What about me? Have you been honest with me?"

"Edgar! How could you ask such a question? Of course, I have been honest with you every step of the way. I care too much about you as a person to defraud you. Did I not offer to be your second when Elizabeth Lummis Ellet's brother challenged you to a duel? Haven't I always been there to oversee your finances and guide your career?"

Poe inhaled and took a sip of beer.

"I wish I could believe that."

"You know it's the truth."

Suddenly, two men, their shadowy faces mostly covered with scarves, appeared behind Griswold. One tapped him on the shoulder.

"Are you Rufus Griswold?"

"That I am."

One of the men thrust himself between Poe and Griswold.

"You're going with us," said the first man.

"I'm going nowhere."

"Then I shall kill you here and now," the man said, pulling a flintlock pistol from his waistband.

"What's the meaning of this?" Griswold said.

"You're going with us," said the man with the pistol.

"I am not."

Suddenly, the man with the pistol punched Griswold hard in the midsection with the barrel of the gun.

"Oh…" Griswold said, grimacing in pain.

"What happening here?" Poe said.

"You stay out of this!" said the man with the pistol.

"But what has he done?"

The man turned the pistol on Poe.

"I told you to stay out of this."

"All right! All right!"

Then, the two men, each grasping one of Griswold's arms, started to push him toward the rear door. Moments later, the three disappeared out the back door. Strangely enough, amid the smoke, clamor, and noise of the crowded tavern, no one other than Poe saw what happened. For a moment, Poe wondered why they wanted Griswold, then, unable to contain his curiosity, he made his way through the crowd to the rear door and stepped into the dark alley. He looked both ways, first to the street then to the other end of the alleyway. Griswold and the two men were nowhere to be seen.

***

The following morning, when Poe awoke and went into the kitchen for coffee, Maria had some news.

"Your friend Rufus Griswold's home burned last night."

"How do you know?"

"I heard the fire wagons in the night and saw the smoke from down around 72nd Street this morning. When I walked to the railcar tracks, one of the drivers said the house belonged to Rufus Griswold."

"Was he in it?"

"I don't know."

"I'll going to investigate."

Moments later, Poe was outside walking down West 84th Street. When he reached Broadway, he peered southward. Somewhere around West 72nd Street, some twelve blocks away, he could see black smoke billowing into the morning sky. Several minutes later, he was on a horse-drawn railcar in route to the scene.

When he arrived, a crowd was gathered. The old house where Poe had signed the contract with Griswold was now a smoking rubble of charred timbers and ashes. All that remained of the original structure was part of what had been Griswold's office and a back porch. Inside the office, Poe could see the old oak desk where he had signed the contract, stacks of business contracts, and a ledger stacked among some books. Poe's eyes fell on the ledger.

Constable Abner McClarey, the beat policeman in the area whom Poe knew, was guarding the smoldering ruins.

Poe approached him.

"Where's Rufus?" he asked.

"His body was found by firemen after they extinguished the blaze. It appears that he was murdered, then the house was set afire to hide evidence."

"What was the motive?"

"No one knows."

Poe stepped into the smoldering ruins to the office. Then he started nosing through the books on the desk.

"Poe," the constable said. "What are you doing?"

"I want to get the ledgers. He was my business partner."

"No one is allowed to touch anything that remains."

"But he was my business partner. Now that he is gone, I need the ledger to balance my own books."

The policeman studied Poe for a moment.

"Oh, all right," he said finally. "I know you two worked together. Go ahead!"

Poe delicately waded through the smoldering ashes and charred ruins to the desk and took the ledger. Then he gingerly stepped back out of the smoking rubble to the front yard.

Nervously, he opened the ledger. Inside, he found a year-by-year running total of profits with personal comments at the end of each column. Starting at 1838, he continued flipping through the pages until he came to the year 1842. Then he started flipping through the pages for each successive year, closely examining each one.

1840: Poems of Henry Wadsworth Longfellow: profit: $2,291. Thanks, Hank, for a bountiful year!

1841: *Women in the Nineteenth Century*: profit $3,678. You be the feminist, Margaret Fuller! I'll be the banker!

1842: Collected works of Washington Irving: profit $2,180 Thank you, Mr. Irving. Your loss is my gain!

1843: *Last of the Mohicans* profit: $3,322. Thanks, James! You save the Indians, I'll take the money!

1844: The Raven tour profit - $5,422. Yes, Edgar. You got the women, but I got the money.

When he saw the last column, his heart flew into his mouth. Cooper and Irving had told the truth.

***

At the end of July of 1847, Poe and Watson had been unable to come up with the promised $500 for the bank. They had cut corners for salaries, the cost of printing paper and ink. Over the last two weeks of the month, they had personally delivered printed copies to street vendors. To raise cash, they had sold an old backup press, three office desks, an old daguerreotype processor, and a folding machine, which had been in storage for several years. In September, the operation had made a paltry $88. Watson had cleaned out his personal savings; Poe had nothing to offer. Finally, once the total was tallied, they had $384.

"There's nothing else we can do," Watson said. "Let's offer this and see if the judge will stave off the foreclosure a little longer."

***

At the hearing the following week, the judge showed no sympathy.

"The agreement was that you would have $500 to pay on the principal at the end of September. You have not done that."

"Your Honor, this business is our livelihood," Poe pleaded. "The money we are offering shows that we have acted in good faith."

"A fulfilled promise speaks louder than good faith."

"What about an extension of just one more month?" Poe said.

"No. My decision has been made. Remove your personal items from the building and vacate at once. Foreclose is granted and the creditor may proceed with an auction to liquidate immediately. Case closed."

***

August 4, 1847. The gods never intended for me to have wealth. By hook and by crook, by greed and chicanery, by outright fraud and carefully crafted half-truths, I have been denied the wealth that seems to come so easily to other men. First my riches were abruptly interrupted by Burton's sudden bankruptcy, then more wealth stolen by Griswold, and now my dream of owning my own magazine has been snatched away by creditors. As I approach my thirty-eighth year, my most influential works are behind me and I have nothing substantial to reply upon. So be it. I will go to my grave with empty pockets and a prayer on my lips, knowing I have been denied that which I so richly deserved. But I shall not be crushed by this unhappy happenstance, I shall accept my fate without fretful grief or ill-conceived illusions, I shall go to my grave a pauper. I was born to be broke.

29
Annabel Lee

Eight months passed. During that time, the Poe family was living hand to mouth again, subsisting on funds he borrowed from friends and the occasional bank draft Poe received for old short stories and poems.

On the morning of April 3, 1848, Virginia woke up coughing violently and spitting up blood. Instantly, Maria and Poe were at her bedside.

"She's taken a turn for the worse," Maria said. "You better get the doctor."

An hour later, Poe returned with Dr. Goodnight, the physician who made the original diagnosis.

"Has she been experiencing unusual worrying of late?" he asked.

"Yes," Poe said. "There has been quite a bit of malicious gossip in our lives. It has not been a pleasant experience."

After a pause, Dr. Goodnight cleared his throat.

"Worry, especially of extreme magnitude, weakens her body's defenses against the disease. Nothing harms her condition more than mental stress."

"Is there anything you can do?"

"I can give her laudanum for pain. There are some herbal remedies that can help her breathing, but there is little I can do to halt the ravages of the disease. Most of all, she needs a quiet, peaceful locale where there is little stress and worry. Also, she's going to need a trained nurse."

"You think a move to the countryside would improve her health?"

"Absolutely. Clean air. Bed rest. Quiet surroundings… all of those will improve her condition."

"How long does she have?"

"Hard to say. Two, maybe three months. It will vary with the mental stress she is under."

After the doctor left, Poe pulled Maria aside.

"I intend to get out of the city," he said. "The toll of worry and stress on Sissy over the past few months has been unbearable. There are too many wagging tongues and ill temperament from my enemies to remain here. The air in the city is foul and so is the majority of the people. Sissy's health is my first concern."

***

That afternoon, Poe scoured the latest edition of the *Evening Mirror* for advertisements relating to available housing in the city. He found two rentals of interest, one near West 99th Street and Ninth Avenue in an area known at the time as Elmwood on the Upper West Side. When Poe spoke to the first landlord, the man explained that the four-room farmhouse had a leaky roof, which he would provide the pitch for, but Poe would be responsible for doing the work. After Poe explained that he knew nothing of roof repair, he turned to the second option, a small, four-room cottage surrounded by cherry trees on a hillside in Fordham Village, a small hamlet of some 600 persons located fourteen miles north of lower Manhattan. It was home to the recently founded St. John's College, a Jesuit school, which would later become Fordham University.

When Poe met the cottage's landlord, he was a medium-height, dark-haired man in his early forties who smoked a pipe. His name was John Valentine.

"It's small," Valentine said. "But it has a good roof, a clean well, and is warm in the winter. The rent is $100 a year."

"I'll take it," Poe said.

***

Over the next two days, Poe and two helpers, using a hired dray wagon, moved the family's belongings from the Brennan farmhouse to the cottage at Fordham. He sold the piano for

$50; an ornament table, a large clothes cabinet, the bust of Pallas, and the collected works of Cicero were also sold for a total of $18. He was going to lighten his load, he told himself. Also, he would need the money to pay for a nurse.

In the 1840s, Fordham Village was considered quite rural and only recently had been connected to the city by horse-drawn rail cars. While moving in, Poe had witnessed a plowing competition in a large, fallow field on the east side. To the west and north, the home was surrounded by open pasture with roaming herds of dairy cattle and calves grazing quietly. The new digs were smaller and less commodious than anything they had lived in previously. On the first floor was a sitting room and a kitchen; its unheated second floor had a small bedroom and Poe's study. When Poe announced to Maria that the new home was "small, very small," Maria promised they would find a way to fit their lives into it.

***

The following morning, Poe began canvassing the village for a nurse. When he spoke to the owner of the village apothecary, the man said he should speak with a young woman who was well-known in the village as a nurse. Her name was Marie Louise Shew.

"She's young and well-qualified," the man said. "Both her father and her late husband were physicians."

Marie Louise Shew was a smallish woman, aged 25, neatly dressed with dark hair, chestnut-brown eyes, and a quick smile. Poe explained his situation with Virginia and, after some haggling about the cost of her services, she was hired.

When the nurse arrived at the cottage the following morning, she undertook to make wholesale changes. When she found the only covering for Virginia's bed was an old military cloak, a remnant of Poe's army days, she left, went to her home, and returned with a large green comforter and several bottles of wine. Also, she picked flowers from the nearby fields for Virginia's bedside table and suggested that Maria brighten up the room with some colorful curtains.

Over the next few weeks, with the arrival of the nurse, Virginia's condition improved. In the mornings, after breakfast, the nurse would give her a small glass of wine. Virginia took it smiling, even when it was difficult to get down. In the afternoons, Miss Shew would read poetry, especially the works of Robert Herrick and Elizabeth Barrett Browning, to keep her entertained. Some mornings, Miss Shew would pick cherries from the trees in the yard, remove the pits, then grind them up into a fine powder. This would then be mixed with warm water and served to Virginia as medicine. She always breathed easier after ingesting the concoction. For pain, if needed, Miss Shew would give her laudanum provided by Dr. Goodnight.

On Sundays, Miss Shew and Maria would wash Virginia's bed linen. To accomplish this, Poe would carry Virginia from her bed to the sitting room downstairs. There he would entertain her with a captured bobolink he had been training. Poe would demonstrate how the bird would not pass through a divider in its cage simply because food, in this case, chickpeas, was available on the other side. However, with a stimulus, like the ringing of a bell, the creature readily hopped through the divider to the chickpeas. Each time Poe performed the demonstration, Virginia would giggle with schoolgirl delight.

"Oh, Eddie, you're so clever."

Poe smiled.

"I'm so happy to see you feeling better," he said. "I believe the disease has subsided since we moved to the countryside."

"Oh yes. The nurse has made a large contribution to my improvement. My air is coming easier and I am eating more. Quite a bit more."

"That makes me very happy," he said.

***

Seven months passed and, during that time, Virginia's health continued to stabilize. Poe, Maria, and the nurse worked out a schedule which provided 24-hour supervised care. In the daylight hours, Miss Shew was present to monitor her condition and provide needed services while Maria attended to

379

the household chores of cooking and cleaning. Once the nurse left, Maria would take up the watch and, if she needed time to perform household duties, Poe would sit at her bedside. Virginia was no longer awakening in the middle of the night gasping for breath and spitting up blood. She needed the laudanum only occasionally and she was eating more. She even gained a little weight.

Some mornings, with Poe's help, she would slowly creep down the stairs to the breakfast table. Other days, she would spend mornings with Poe on the front porch as he entertained her with more songbirds he had captured. He had trained one, a jaybird, to sing for its food and still another, a red robin, to course through a long wooden box to find food.

Meanwhile, inside his mind, Poe was fighting for his sanity. At all times of day and night, Poe, wearing a heavy, billowing cloak, would take long, contemplative walks from the cottage across the "High Bridge" to the Manhattan side of the Harlem River. The river was an eight-mile tidal strait which wound southward across the Upper West Side and connected the Hudson and the East rivers. In the spring of 1842, the "High Bridge" was built across the river to serve first as a pedestrian bridge between the Bronx and Manhattan, and secondly, to support the Croton Aqueduct, a huge water line into New York City which provided fresh water for households and to fight fires.

Many nights, broke, depressed, and drinking too much, Poe would make the trek to escape the despair at the cottage. For the past few months, he seemed paralyzed to do any real literary work. His attempts to regain his earlier prosperity as a writer and editor were meeting with failure after failure. He would have an idea for a poem or a story, then, when he sat down to record it, the words would not come to flesh out the images. Finally frustrated, he would get up from his writing desk and go walking. Many times, he would walk the entire two-and-one half miles, pacing the solitary pathways for hours without meeting a single human being.

November 3, 1848. My soul and my work have become afflicted with this terrible contagion. This illness—this constant horrible oscillation between hope and despair—can only be cured with Sissy's death. This illness I suffer nobly as a man, but it is the thought of not knowing how much longer she will live that is driving me to the total loss of my reason. While I dread the moment of her death, I know it shall be a relief.

At Thanksgiving, 1848, there was no money for a celebratory meal. In early November, Poe had received $25 for a short story titled "Imp of the Perverse" from *Godey's Magazine,* but it was used to buy firewood, pay Miss Shew, and buy necessities, such as flour, coffee, beans, and lard. Four days before the holiday, a kind neighbor who had recently killed three hogs brought over a slab of ham hock. Their Thanksgiving meal consisted of ham hock sandwiches, boiled cabbage, and cornbread.

Christmas was little different. On Christmas eve, Poe went to the pawn shop in Fordham Village and asked the broker to give him $5 for an old gold ring he had won in a card game while in the army. The broker, who immediately recognized Poe, examined the piece.

"It's not worth more than $2," he said. "But if you will provide me with a signed copy of your poem 'The Raven,' I will give you the $5. After all, it is Christmas!"

"You're so very kind," Poe replied. "Merry Christmas!"

Once Poe had the money in hand, he instructed Maria to go into the village and buy for the holiday meal. On Christmas day, the family dined on fried chicken, boiled potatoes, black beans, and biscuits. For dessert, Maria made a cherry pie from cherries she had picked and canned the previous fall.

***

The morning of January 18, 1849 was a bitterly cold winter day. When the mail arrived that morning, Maria thumbed through several letters. There were bills, a letter from a solicitor, an advertising pamphlet, and a strange-looking letter without a return address. It was addressed to Virginia. As always, Maria left the letters addressed to Poe on his writing desk, then took the single anonymous letter to her daughter. Virginia took it and opened it.

Dear Mrs. Poe:

I am only writing this letter out of concern for your well-being.

By now, I am quite certain you know Fanny Osgood fled New York for Boston to escape the scandal of her lusty interlude with your husband.

Three days ago, I learned that she has delivered a baby boy to her estranged husband Samuel Osgood. I am being told by friends in Boston that the child looks remarkably like your husband with his dark hair and already it is being whispered in New York that your husband is the father of the child.

One such whisperer related to me, in strictest confidence, of course, that her husband plans to take legal action against the Poe family for support of the child. Your husband's sins have found him out.

Please understand this letter is being sent only to warn you of what sorrowful tidings fate may bring to your doorstep in the future.

All the best,
Anonymous

Virginia looked up from the letter then burst into tears. When Miss Shew entered the room a few minutes later, she could see Virginia had been crying.

"What the matter?"

"I have received a letter," she said, pointing to it on the bedside table.

"May I read it?"

"Sure."

Miss Shew read the letter.

"Is there any truth to this?"

"It is only the hatred of a vile woman."

Miss Shew left the room, went downstairs, and showed the letter to Maria.

"That damn Elizabeth Lummis Ellet," Maria said. "I should take a gun and go to her home and kill her."

"So you know who sent this letter?"

"Yes. An evil, loathsome woman."

"This is anathema for your daughter's condition. In the future, you must not show her any new letters with this handwriting."

"Your words will be heeded."

"Has Edgar seen this letter?" Maria asked.

"No."

"Then I shall have it," Maria said, taking the letter. "And you must never mention it."

"I will heed your words," said Miss Shew.

"Let sleeping dogs lie."

***

That night, in the wee hours, Maria was awakened by the sound of loud coughing coming from Virginia's room. Instantly, Maria was at her bedside.

"Oh, Mother," Virginia said, looking up helplessly. "The old ghosts have returned."

Her head hung on her chest, her shoulders drooped forward, and the front of her nightgown was red with small spots of blood.

"Let me get you cleaned up," Maria said.

Moments later, Maria had a damp cloth and was cleaning the blood from around Virginia's mouth and the front of her nightgown.

"Do you want to change the nightgown tonight?"

"No. Let us wait until tomorrow. I'm too weak at the moment."

"Sit up!" the mother said.

Virginia sat up in bed so Maria could plump her pillows.

"Now lie back and rest. Try to get some sleep," Maria said, pulling the covers up to her daughter's chin.

"Elizabeth Lummis Ellet is putting me in my grave," Virginia said.

Maria looked away.

"Try to stay calm and get some rest."

***

The following morning, Poe penned a letter to his old friend Nathaniel Parker Willis, publisher of the *Evening Mirror*.

February 2, 1849

My Dear Nathaniel:

Throughout my association with you, I have regarded you as a kind and sympathetic friend. Your words not only inspired me to the writing of "The Raven," but your publication brought it to the world's attention.

Now I must ask a favor of you.

My dear wife Virginia is at death's door with consumption. My concerns for her health have rendered me helpless to perform gainful employment the past few months and the hand of fate weighs heavily upon our financial fortunes.

With these considerations in mind, I am requesting that you lend me $50 to make it through this trying time. I promise you that it will be repaid at some point in the future. As you know, I am an honorable man and I hope you will believe me when I say these words.

Trusting that you are in good spirits and good health.

Your devoted friend,
Edgar Allan Poe

Two days later, Poe received a bank draft in the mail for the requested amount.

***

Three days later, on February 7, 1849, an announcement appeared on the front page of the *Evening Mirror*.

384

Illness of Virginia Poe, wife of Edgar A. Poe. – We regret to learn that Mr. Poe's wife Virginia is dangerously ill with the consumption, and that the hand of misfortune lies heavily on their temporal affairs. We are sorry to mention the fact that they are so far reduced as to be barely able to obtain the necessaries of life. That is, indeed, a hard lot, and we do hope that the friends and admirers of Mr. Poe will come promptly to his assistance with donations in his direst hour of need.

This public announcement launched a stream of visitors, friends, curiosity seekers, and old acquaintances to the Poe cottage. Some brought food, others brought money, and all brought condolences. One of these was a woman named Mary Starr, a fellow boarder when the Poe family was living on Greenwich Street. As the visit was nearing an end, Virginia called Poe to her bedside and pressed Starr's hand into his.

"Mary, please try to be a friend to Eddie and do not forsake him."

"I shall do so," the woman replied.

Upon seeing Virginia, another old friend, a Mrs. Ruth Willingham, wrote to a friend: "She looked so young. Far too young to be dying. She had large dark eyes and a pearly whiteness of complexion which was a perfect pallor. Her pale face, her brilliant eyes, and her raven hair gave her an ethereal, unearthly look. One felt that she was like a disrobed spirit, and when she coughed, the observer knew for certain that she was rapidly passing away."

February 10, 1849. I have accepted that my beloved Sissy's death is near. This morning, she was too weak to go to the breakfast table, so I picked her up in my arms and carried her down the stairs. On so many occasions in the past, I have carried her and I know only too well her healthy weight. She weighs less than 50 pounds. Now I know why men of medicine call her disease consumption. It slowly wastes away the body until nothing remains. In the face of her illness, I feel so helpless. I only wish there was something I could do to thwart death, to dull its sting, to keep her memory alive in spite of this dreadful contagion, but I know it is only a hopeful dream in my tortured mind.

***

February 12, 1849. A poem! Poets write poems! How vacuous of me to not have realized that earlier! What better way could a poet immortalize his love? I will compose a poem commemorating our love. An anthem to the glory of our happiness together. A monument to our eternal devotion. A symbolic ballad which retells the story of our love and will survive long after Sissy and I and Muddy and all the others have slipped off into the great darkness. In this poem, I will render our love immortal. It shall be a victory over death.

An hour later, he was at her bedside.

"I plan to write a poem to commemorate our love."

"Oh, my darling, that's wonderful, but you must be hasty. My time is not long."

***

An hour later, Poe, quill pen in hand, was in his writing parlor. It was a story of two lovers who lived by the sea and they "loved with a love that was more than love." Once he had painted a portrait of their great love for one another, it was time to narrate her death. At the thought of the heroine's death, Poe stopped. He could go no further. He got up from the writing desk and went downstairs.

"Dear, why are you not writing?"

"I was forced to stop."

"Why?"

"Oh, my darling, I came to the moment in the narrative when I must write of your death, but I could not do so. The realization, even if imagined, was too horrible to face."

She laughed then reached out for his hand. He took it.

"My darling Eddie, you must write of my demise. My impending death is just as much a part of our love story as all the rest. The kiss under the chinaberry tree, planting of the daffodils, and our engaging…"

She stopped. A broad smile spread across her face at the memory.

"… Engaging in amorous congress in the most unlikely places. It's all part of our story."

Poe also smiled at the memory.

"I know you're right."

"But you must hurry. With each fleeting moment, my time is becoming shorter and shorter. I am fighting to live until the moment you finish the poem."

"Tomorrow, my darling. I promise!"

***

That night, he worked feverishly to complete the poem. The poem's concept was full in his mind; all he had to do was record it. Once he sat down and started writing, without even realizing it, his poetic nature suddenly returned in full measure. The words were flowing again with delicious swiftness; the rhythm, the meter and the rhyme poured freely out of him. He had only needed inspiration sufficient to bring forth the words. Around midnight, he had a first draft. Next, he edited, parsed, rephrased, and omitted lines until he felt it was perfect. Then he read it aloud to see how it played on the ear. Finally, around 2 a.m., tired and beaten, he fell asleep on a small cot in the writing parlor.

***

February 14, 1949
Dear Miss Shew:

My kindest, dearest friend, my poor Virginia still lives, although failing fast and now suffering much pain.

May God grant her life until she sees you to thank you once again!

Her bosom is full to overflowing, like my own, with a boundless, inexpressible gratitude to you.

Lest she may never see you again—she bids me to say that she sends her sweetest kiss of love and will die blessing you.

But come, oh please come tomorrow to remain for the night.

Yes, I will be calm and perform everything you so nobly wished to see of me.

My mother sends you, also, her "warmest love and thanks."

She begs me to ask you, if possible, to make arrangements at your home so that you may stay with us throughout tomorrow night.

I feel that will be the hour of our final farewells.

May heaven bless you!

Edgar A Poe

***

Most of the daylight hours of February 15, 1849, Virginia spent sleeping. In the late afternoon, she awoke and called Miss Shew to her bedside.

"I want to express my gratitude for your kindly services. You have added immeasurably to my life these past few months."

Then she raised herself up one elbow, reached under her pillow, and withdrew a picture of Poe. For a moment, she gazed at the portrait, then she kissed it and gave it to the nurse.

"I want you to have this. A token of my gratitude."

"My many thanks!" the nurse said.

"Will you hand me my work box?"

The nurse reached under the bed and retrieved Virginia's box of personal belongings. Once she took the box, she withdrew a small wooden case.

"This is a little jewelry case my father gave me when I was a little girl."

Miss Shew examined the oblong box.

"Do you see the inscription?" Virginia said.

"Yes. It says 'I love you, Jenny!'"

"Jenny," Virginia repeated the word wistfully. "That's what my father called me. Don't you think it's a nice name?"

"Oh, yes."

"The box is yours now. I have no further need of it. Now I have one final request."

"What might that be?"

"Will you marry Eddie after I'm gone? You have been so good to me. I know you will take good care of him and make him happy."

The nurse peered curiously at Poe.

He gave her a furtive wink.

"Eddie's the kind of man who needs a woman to love and care for him," Virginia continued. "He hates being alone."

"I will consider it," the nurse said.

"Thank you!"

Then she turned to Maria.

"Oh, my darling mother, I love you, but I must go to meet my death."

"Oh, my baby! I know. We shall always love you."

Then Virginia turned to Poe.

"Eddie? Is the poem ready?"

"Yes."

"I want to hear it. For the past few days, I have been fighting to live until I can hear your poem. Now read it."

Poe turned to the poem.

"The title is 'Annabel Lee'."

Poe cleared his throat and began reading.

"It was many and many a year ago,
In a kingdom by the sea,
That a maiden there lived whom you may know
By the name of Annabel Lee;
And this maiden she lived with no other thought
Than to love and be loved by me.

"I was a child and she was a child,
In this kingdom by the sea,
But we loved with a love that was more than love—
I and my Annabel Lee—

With a love that the winged seraphs of Heaven
Coveted her and me."

He stopped, tears in his eyes, and looked at her.
"I love it," she said. "Please continue."

"And this was the reason that, long ago,
In this kingdom by the sea,
A wind blew out of a cloud, chilling and killing
My beautiful Annabel Lee;
So that her highborn kinsmen came
 nd bore her away from me,
And shut her up in a sepulcher
In this kingdom by the sea."

Then, overcome by tears again, he stopped to wipe his eyes.

"But our love it was stronger by far than the love
Of those who were older than we—
Of many far wiser than we—
And neither the angels in Heaven above
Nor the demons down under the sea
Can ever dissever my soul from the soul
Of the beautiful Annabel Lee;

For the moon never beams, without bringing me dreams
Of the beautiful Annabel Lee;
And the stars never rise, but I feel the bright eyes
Of the beautiful Annabel Lee;
And so, all the night-tide, I lie down by the side
Of my darling—my darling—my life and my bride,
In her sepulchre there by the sea—
In her tomb by the sounding sea."

He stopped.
Virginia turned to him.
"Oh, Eddie. I love it. I could not have asked for more. May
I see it?"
Poe handed her the poem.

She took the poem and reread the refrain:

"For the moon never beams without bringing me dreams
Of the beautiful Annabel Lee;
And the stars never rise, but I feel the bright eyes
Of the beautiful Annabel Lee;
And so, all the night-tide, I lie down by the side
Of my darling—my darling—my life and my bride,
In her sepulchre there by the sea—
In her tomb by the sounding sea."

She stopped.

"Those are the most beautiful lines of poetry I've ever read."

She turned to her mother.

"My darling mother, when I leave this earth, will you console and take care of my poor Eddie? Promise me you will never, never leave him?"

"I promise, dear."

"He needs someone."

"I know, dear. I know."

Then she turned to face her husband one final time.

"I love you, my darling, but I must leave this world and go to the next one. The poem of my life is fast approaching its final line."

"May heaven receive you with the greatest kindness," Poe said.

"Oh, Eddie, I love you with all my heart."

"Oh, my darling. And I love you."

Then, holding the poem in one hand and Poe's hand in the other, her body heaved violently as she tried to draw more air into her lungs, but new breath wouldn't come. Then, staring straight into her husband's eyes, the color in her face slowly began to take on a dark-bluish tinge, her eyes closed, her head dropped to one side, then her hand fell lifeless over the bedside.

"She's gone," Poe said.

"The Lord giveth and the Lord taketh away," Maria said.

For a long moment, Poe peered down at his wife's body. Then he stepped forward and removed the daffodil necklace from around her neck. He bent over her and kissed her on the lips. Her lips were still warm.

Moments later, Miss Shew stepped forward, removed the poem from her hand, crossed her arms in prayer, and pulled the bed covering over the lifeless body.

For a long moment, Maria peered sadly into Poe's eyes. Then she rushed into his arms and together they began to sob uncontrollably.

30
Madman

The first few weeks following Virginia's death were the most difficult days of Poe's life. The very foundation of his existence had been shorn away. That which he had worshipped with such unrelentingly ferocity for so many years had now disappeared into the vastness of the universe. His grounding point was gone; he was a rudderless ship flailing about helplessly in an unknown sea. At odd hours, sometimes in the dead of night, he would leave the cottage and go sit by her grave, drink brandy, and, shivering and cold, pretend to talk to her. During waking hours, he would pick flowers in the nearby fields and place them on her grave, all the while muttering over and over about how much he missed her. Sometimes, late at night, Maria would hear him in his writing parlor sobbing uncontrollably. Drink was his only solace. When he went to bed, he put a bottle of brandy under the pillow; the moment he woke up, he reached for the bottle.

"You've got to come out of this," Maria said. "Your life must go on."

"I don't want to go on. I do not care whether I live an hour, a day, a week, or a year. She was my heart, my life, my soul."

***

At the end of the first week, Maria went to his room one morning and found him on the floor unconscious. He had not eaten in two days.

"Eddie! Eddie!" she said, bending over and shaking him.

For a moment, he tried to raise himself to one elbow, then suddenly, he collapsed back on the floor. His face was drawn and horror-stricken; he was sweaty, unshaven, and his hands were trembling. He peered up at Maria through helpless, bloodshot eyes.

"Leave me alone! I want to die."

"No. There'll be no such talk. If Virginia were still here, she would want you to live."

"Go away! Leave me to die!"

"Get up! Let me help you into bed. You have poisoned your body with alcohol."

"Go away! Get away from me!"

Then, Maria, with all her strength, took his arms and dragged him across the floor. After some struggling, lifting one end at a time, she finally managed to get him into bed. Then, as she wiped his face with a wet washcloth, he mumbled incoherently. It was something about John Valentine, "the little house across the river" and his childhood dog Reynolds. Finally, he drifted off to sleep. Over the next thirty minutes, Maria went through the house searching for alcohol. She found three separate bottles in various stages of emptiness. Outside, she smashed each of them on the stone well housing.

That afternoon, when Poe awoke, the first thing he asked for was a drink.

"There is no more. I gathered all the bottles and smashed them."

"Damn you!"

"I've got some vegetable soup."

"No! I want a bottle!"

Again, he peered up at Maria with helpless, bleary eyes, then collapsed back on the bed again sound asleep. Over the next two days, he remained in bed alternating between delirium and lucidity. He would suddenly awaken from deep sleep, then ramble aimlessly about some "idiot editor" or "the flowers on Virginia's grave," then drift off to sleep again. An hour later, he would awaken and launch into a long diatribe about the moral teachings of Tacitus, then about Amos, the slave that was his childhood friend. Finally, he was asleep again.

That night, Maria was awakened by loud screams. When Maria went into the room, he was sitting up in bed, his face horror-stricken, staring fearfully at the floor.

"Rats!! Rats! There are rats all over the floor! Get them out!! Do you hear me? Get them out!"

"There are no rats," Maria said calmly.

"I saw them! There were hundreds of them!"

"They're gone now! Just lie back and sleep."

Maria took his shoulders and gently pushed him back to the bed. As she looked into his eyes, she could see the madness in his face. For several moments, he stared wide-eyed up at the ceiling.

"Are the rats still here?"

"They're all gone now!"

"Are you sure?"

"I'm sure!"

"Promise?"

"I promise! Now just lie back and rest."

In a few moments, he was sound asleep again.

***

On the afternoon of the third day, Poe was lucid when he awoke. A wild-eyed expression on his face, he looked around the room to see Maria sitting in a chair beside his bed reading the Bible.

"How long have I been in this bed?"

"This is the fourth day. Are you hungry?"

"I could eat a horse."

Fifteen minutes later, he was eating fried chicken, green beans, and corn bread. It was the first full meal he had had in over a week. After finishing the chicken, he started eating a bowl of vegetable soup. The color had returned to his face. His hands were no longer trembling. The sweating had ended, and Maria could see the whites of his eyes again. After finishing the soup, he handed her the empty bowl then peered out the window.

"Looks like it going to be a beautiful day."

An hour later, he was out of bed, bathed, shaved for the first time in two weeks, and put on fresh clothes.

"Where are you going?"

"Walking."

Over the next two hours, he took a long, contemplative walk across "High Bridge." It was a cold night and the north wind blew mightily down the Harlem River, billowing his heavy cloak behind him. He was evaluating his life, having a talk with himself, considering what had gone before and what could be waiting in the future. Once he reached the Manhattan side of the bridge, he stopped and, for a long moment, peered eastward down the river. *Muddy is right*, he told himself. *Sissy would want me to continue living. I must go on.*

When he returned to the cottage, Maria was seated in the living room peeling potatoes. She looked up when he closed the door.

"I have reviewed my life," he said. "I'm ready to live again."

"Thank God!"

***

The next morning, Poe dressed himself, had breakfast, and took the horse-drawn railcar into lower Manhattan to the offices of George P. Putnam, his old friend and original owner of the famous publishing house. A stocky, gray-haired man in his early forties, Putnam had a hawk-like nose and wore glasses. He was surprised to see Poe.

"Edgar! How are you?" he said, offering his hand. "Did you bring me your latest poems?"

"I haven't been writing lately, but I intend to begin again soon."

"So what is the reason for your visit?"

"Two matters. I'm seeking work. Do you have a review assignment?"

"I can find one. Four new books came across my desk last week. One, a historical romance, looks particularly interesting."

For a moment, he scavenged across his cluttered desk and pulled out a newly published book.

"Take this and review it!"

"Thanks!"

A long pause.

"What's the second matter?"

"Will you loan me $25? I'm in the most desperate of straits."

Putnam studied him for a moment.

"Only on one condition," he said finally. "That you promise to bring your next major work to me."

"Done!"

An hour later, upon his return to the cottage, he gave the money to Maria.

"I want you to use this to bring the household back to order. I plan to start writing again in the next few days."

***

June 4, 1849. The death of my beloved Sissy has made me profoundly more cognizant of my own mortality. The termination of my life is nearer than the beginning and I am haunted by the belief that I still have not fulfilled my potential as a creative artist. Forsooth, my name is forever enshrined in the halls of American literature, but the sparkling pinnacle of intellectual achievement I have secretly kept hidden away all these years remains to be realized. Forthwith, I desire some project which will place my name above the highest mountain.

***

The following morning before breakfast, Maria sent him to the village square to buy eggs, baking flour, and lard. In route, he stopped at a curiosity shop when his eye caught a triangular piece of glass in the window which had been positioned so the morning sun would shine through it and produce the colors of the spectrum on a white background. Poe was mesmerized.

"It's called a prism, an invention from Sir Isaac Newton," the clerk said. "It demonstrates that white light is made up of the different colors of the solar spectrum. It's a new science called spectroscopy."

"Do you have a book on the subject?"

"As a matter of fact, I do."

Then clerk reached up to the shelf and took down a volume entitled *Our Physical Universe.*

Thirty minutes later, prism and book in hand, Poe was back at the cottage. Once he had delivered the food items to Maria, he started to the writing parlor.

"Don't disturb me. I want to read this book."

"Breakfast will be ready in fifteen minutes."

"I'll eat later."

The book was a layman's summary of the latest scientific knowledge of the day, including astronomy, chemistry, mechanics, electromagnetism, the nature of matter, heat transfer, and optics. This last subject was the one Poe delved into first and he read the entire chapter in less than thirty minutes. He was fascinated with the concept of how light changes speed as it moves from one medium to another. After reading the optics chapter, he took the prism outside and toyed with it, first displaying the lights of the color spectrum on the side of the house, then on a book, and finally, on the well housing. Back in the cottage, he pored over the chapters on the planets, their gravitational attraction for one another, the makeup of matter as a collection of smaller particles, and scientific theories about gravitational attraction and energy transformation.

That night, he was unable to sleep. His mind was a mighty torrent, shifting ideas about light, the nature of the physical universe, and the earth's gravitational attraction for the planets. All the time he had been reading, he was jotting down notes about his observations and thoughts on each and every concept. He was up all night. The next morning at sunrise, he ventured outside to watch the sun rise. As he watched the rosy fingers of dawn reach across the eastern horizon, he had a vision which, to him, was of earth-shattering proportions. Instantly, he went to his desk and began writing.

Thirty minutes later, when Maria knocked on the parlor door for him to come to breakfast, he said he couldn't be disturbed. Finally, two hours later, he went to the breakfast table.

"I have been visited by a great vision. The physical structure of the world, as well as the relationship between God and man, has been revealed to me. I have been chosen to understand the unity of the cosmos."

***

Early the following morning, he was back at Putnam's office.

"What brings you to my office so early?"

"I am working on my magnum opus," Poe said excitedly. "Over the years ahead, this work will be remembered while my poems, including 'The Raven' and 'Annabel Lee,' will vanish into obscurity. I shall be remembered as a man of science rather than letters, and learned men of the future will look upon this work and rejoice with gladness at the depth, the detail, and the scientific prognostications contained therein."

"Sounds interesting. What's the subject?"

"The universe."

Putnam's face screwed up in a quizzical frown.

"The universe?"

"This work will explain the beginning and end of the universe as we know it. It will change the essential basis of human thought. Scientists, artists, politicians, philosophers… men from all walks of life shall embrace the concepts in this work with unrelenting enthusiasm."

"Will it sell?"

"Of course. The first printing must necessarily be no fewer than 50,000 copies."

"That's a bit ambitious. What's the title?"

"*Eureka: An essay on the material and spiritual universe.*"

"Eureka? Isn't that the term gold miners use when they have discovered a major vein of treasure?"

"It is also the word Archimedes used when he raced naked through the streets of Athens after discovering his famous principle."

"I know that story."

A long pause.

"Will you publish it?"

"Yes. When will it be finished?"

"Two, maybe three weeks."

***

Over the next few weeks, Poe was in the writing parlor fifteen to sixteen hours a day working feverishly. Only food could bring his labor to a halt. Sometimes he would work twelve hours straight, then, tired and hungry, he would stumble into the kitchen to eat. One afternoon, after he had worked more than twenty hours straight, he told Maria he wanted to take a nap.

"Let me sleep for two hours. Then awaken me."

After two hours, Maria, seeing he was still sleeping soundly and knowing how hard he had been working, would let him sleep for another two hours.

Finally, when she awakened him, he would be angry that she let him sleep the extra hours.

"Muddy, I told you to awaken me after only two hours. Now two hours have been wasted. I could have written another twenty pages during those two hours."

***

Finally, after twenty-three days, the work was finished. At 146 pages, it represented a rag-tag compilation of Poe's personal theories about the nature of the material universe, complete with hand-drawn diagrams and sketches designed to explain them. Once finished, Poe spent an additional two days editing, rewriting, and polishing the work, then he took it to Putnam.

"Here it is!" Poe said, handing over the manuscript. "I am now leaving the crown jewel of my creative life with you."

Putnam pushed his glasses up on his nose, peered at the volume, and thumbed through it.

"I shall peruse this tonight. Can you return to my office tomorrow so we can discuss it?"

"I shall be here."

***

The following morning, when Poe entered Putnam's office, he was anxious to hear the verdict.

"So what are your thoughts?"

"I don't know what to make of this," Putnam said. "I've never seen anything like this. It is not a poem; it is not a novel. It's not even an essay. On face value, it appears to be little more than a mish-mash of assorted scientific treatises."

"It's a prose poem. One must have a basic understanding of the machinations of the universe to appreciate a work like this."

Putnam shook his head.

"I'll print 500 copies as a first run to see how the public receives it. If you ask me, at this point, there is not a market and never has been a market for a work such as this."

"Five hundred copies? The work deserves ten times that. I'm telling you this work shall change the course of human thought."

"That's the best I can do."

"Can you pay me an advance?"

"You already owe me $25. Let me get it published and we'll see what the reading public thinks."

"You don't have a personal appreciation of the material."

"I appreciate what sells," Putnam said. "I have serious doubts that this will sell a single copy."

***

During the first week after publication, a total of twenty-three copies were sold and newspaper reviews began to trickle in.

The *New York Tribune* said of the work:

"Poe's latest work is a strange, eruptive, delirious book: a cosmological treatise on the origin, expansion, and collapse of the material universe that takes the form at various points of a prose poem, a polemic, a scientific report, and a malicious joke. That the 'machinery of the universe' could be, as Poe memorably put it, *guessed*—disclosed 'through mere dint of intuition'— is as dubious a suggestion as the thought that pigs can fly."

The *Evening Mirror* reviewer commented:

"*Eureka* is a wagonload of pure unabashed humbug. For me, my sincere sentiments are that Poe should affix his talents to writing verse. As a scientist, he not only fails to have the qualifying credentials, but has presented himself as a laughable failure. *Eureka* is a slipshod compilation of current scientific thought, physics, mathematics, phrenology, astronomy, optics, and a healthy dollop of Poe's own inimitable imagination."

"Blithering fools," Poe said after reading the reviews. "They have no understanding of deep intellectuality. A combination of poetry and scientific theories is lost on these muscle-headed, brainless idiots."

***

Over the following weeks, Poe would deliver impromptu lectures on his theories to anyone who would listen. At Jeremiah's Pub, the main watering hole in Fordham Village, he held up a copy of *Eureka* and told his fellow barroom patrons:

"Herein lies the truth of the beginning and the end of our world. This little book explains the machinations and mechanisms of our cosmogony."

"Cosmogony?" said another patron standing next to him. "What is cosmogony?"

"It is the collective concept of our universe. It is the total world that we know and live in each and every day."

"Never heard that word before," the patron said, shaking his head doubtfully. "You better let me buy you another drink. Sounds like you need it."

This brought another round of laughter from the other patrons.

***

Two days later, he stopped at a fruit vendor's stand in the Fordham town square. After buying an apple, he lingered to lecture an old man who was inspecting the pears.

"My dear sir, are you aware that our visual senses are nothing more than windows? Windows stacked atop other windows. Someday, these windows will take over the world. There will be little boxes that sit on desks and display images of heads that can talk to you. They will deliver the news, sell you products, educate you, and present entertainment."

For a moment, the man stared at Poe as if he were a madman, then, without buying anything, he quickly turned and disappeared down the street.

***

On the night of August 9, 1849, the following advertisement appeared in the events section of the *Evening Mirror*.

"Esteemed poet Edger Allan Poe will deliver a lecture on his new prose poem 'Eureka: The Nature of the Material and Spiritual Universe' tonight at 7 in the lecture hall at the Fordham Civic Building. Admission is 50 cents. Copies of the work will be available for sale at the door."

***

When Poe arrived at the lecture hall that night, a crowd of some forty to fifty people were waiting to hear him. To his infinite surprise, one of the attendees was his old friend Thomas Pickering Jones. Now in his mid-forties, Jones had the same boyish good looks, the same impish smile, and the same unruly shock of hay-colored hair.

"Tommy," Poe said, offering his hand. "What brings you to Fordham?"

"I was visiting friends when I saw the announcement about your lecture in the *Mirror*. I thought I'd see what you're doing these days."

"I'm delighted to see you. Have a seat. The lecture begins in five minutes."

The lecture room was a windowless, high-ceilinged affair with a lectern on a raised dais at the front. Adjacent to the lectern stood a grade-school blackboard and chalk, and in front of the lectern was a table containing pamphlets about Poe, his career as a poet, and the writing of *Eureka*. Seated at the door was Miss Margaret Simpson, Putnam's assistant and a frumpy, unattractive matron, whose job was to collect admissions and sell copies of "Eureka."

Once the crowd was seated, Poe introduced himself, thanked the crowd for their patronage, explained he would deliver his theories over the first hour, then there would be a question and answer session.

"Some of these concepts may seem overly complex, but with some gentle reasoning, I feel everyone here can grasp them."

With that, over the next twenty minutes, he launched into a prolonged discourse about the nature of matter.

"Let me begin by saying our universe is finite. It came about with the 'radiation' of atoms out from a single 'primordial Particle.' What Newton called gravity is nothing more than that the attraction of every atom to every other atom with which it shares a common identity. These countervailing forces of repulsion and attraction are what holds matter together."

At this point, some fifteen minutes into the lecture, audience members were beginning to fidget uncomfortably. Their faces took on expressions of confusion and uncertainty. Several members of the audience got up to leave.

Next, Poe turned to the subject of optics.

"From a luminous center, light emanates by irradiation and the quantities of light received upon an object on any given plane will vary with the distance between the source and the object upon which the light falls. Thus, the number of light particles received upon the shifting plane will be inversely proportional with the distances of the plane."

By now, some thirty minutes into the lecture, more audience members, confused and restless, were shaking their heads and leaving.

Once finished with optics, Poe attempted to define the nature of God.

"God is an author. Each of us are nothing more than characters in a drama written directly by His hand. The lives that we live every day are nothing more than figments of God's imagination."

By now, more than half of the audience had abandoned the lecture and Poe sensed that he should take action to salvage the event.

"In conclusion, let me say that, over the next 200 years, these principles shall enable humankind to achieve scientific discoveries which exceeds all bounds of current imagination. Particularly with regards to electricity. Lightning, the bright streaks of light which flash across the sky during a rainstorm, are essentially tiny particles of electricity which humankind will learn to capture, isolate, and harness for his own purposes.

"He will codify, arrange, rearrange, and assign values to each little electronic particle and create a machine which will solve the most complex mathematical problem in the twinkling of an eye. The face of these machines will be tiny squares of light the size of a tobacco pouch, into which human beings will view, communicate, and conduct their business with one another. Using this machine, any human being on Earth will be able to view and communicate with any other human being at any time and from any place. Life will no longer be lived; it will be observed through these little windows."

Again, he stopped to take a sip of water, then continued.

"These same concepts will enable humankind to create flying machines, which will take him to the moon. Scientists will discover that diseases are caused by little bugs too small to see. Men will create weapons of war so mighty they could kill every living thing on Earth. There will be machines that swim under the water like a fish. All in all, the advancements I'm describing will change the lives of future generations for years to come."

He stopped and took a drink of water.

"That concludes the lecture portion of this event. Now I will take your questions."

For a moment, a bewildered hush fell upon the crowd. Less than a third of the original audience remained. Finally, a short-statured, older man in a three-cornered hat stood up.

"You say man will go to the moon. How will he accomplish that? Sprout wings?"

"He will create a flying machine which will take him there."

Suddenly, the room erupted in boisterous laughter.

"To the moon?" shouted an older man in a top hat who was shaking with laughter. "How's he going to get back?"

"The same flying machine will return him to Earth."

Another round of belly-slapping laughter.

Poe raised his hands for order.

"Gentlemen! Gentlemen! Please!"

Finally, the crowd was quiet again.

"You say scientists will discover medicines which will cure all diseases. How so?"

"They will discover that diseases are caused by little bugs too small to see. They will develop medicines to kill the little bugs and therefore cure the disease."

With that, the entire room erupted in more derisive laughter.

"Diseases are caused by little bugs you can't see?" one attendee sneered. "Bah! Humbug! I've had enough of this hogwash."

He arose from his seat and stalked out.

"I'm trying to tell you the truth," Poe said. "This is the future of our world."

Now only five attendees remained. When another started to leave, Poe called out, "Why are you leaving?"

"Sir, you are neither a man of science nor mathematical expertise. Your vocation is that of a poet, a novelist, a man of letters. How can you pretend to present yourself as an expert in fields of knowledge for which you have no training?"

"Training of any sort is little more than an adjunct to natural thinking…"

Poe stopped. The man walked out before he could finish.

The last two audience members arose to leave.

"Gentlemen, why are you leaving?"

One of the men, an older gentleman in a top hat, turned to face Poe.

"You're a madman, Poe. Each and every one of the subjects you have put forth here is centered on mathematics. You have no credibility to forebear yourself as knowledgeable in this field. This is the field of Newton, Copernicus, and Galileo."

"Must one be a watchmaker to tell time? Some concepts stand on their own logical merits and remain as such despite every form of calculations and mathematical malingering one may apply. I tell you these matters can be intuited… divined."

"Bah! Humbug," said the man in the top hat.

"Fools!! Fools! All of you are blithering fools. Your imaginations are unable to extend themselves beyond the here and the now. I am telling you the truths of the future and you are laughing."

Now the hall was empty save for Poe, Jones, and Putnam's secretary.

Miss Simpson stepped forward.

"We didn't sell any books, Mr. Poe," she said.

"It's just as well. The world is not ready for the truth."

"Here!" said Jones. "I'll buy one."

Then he reached down to take a copy from the stack Miss Simpson was holding.

"That will be one dollar!" she said.

Jones fished a dollar out of his pocket.

"Now you didn't come away completely empty-handed."

Poe shook his head sadly.

"My world is crumbling around me."

"Enough of this tomfoolery," Jones said. "Let's go down to the saloon on the square and knock back a few."

***

Over the next two hours, Poe and Jones drank ale and regaled one another with stories from the past. Jones talked about his wife, his two children, and his rise to lieutenant colonel in the U.S. Army. Poe recalled his marriage, his days in Philadelphia, his early career in New York, and the loss of Virginia.

"So what are your plans?" Jones asked.

"Last week, I sent out seven letters seeking employment to Boston, Philadelphia, Washington, and Richmond. Four to magazines and three to newspapers."

"Are you leaving New York?"

"Absolutely. Too many wagging tongues, too many sidelong glances, and too many evil people who want to vilify me. I've got my heart set on Boston, the city of my birth, but I would not be disappointed to return to Philadelphia or Richmond."

"Sounds like you're ready to enter the fray once again."

"Oh, yes. I'm ready to live again."

Thirty minutes later, Poe said his good-byes to Jones with a promise to write him in care of Fort Moultrie.

***

September 22, 1849. There will be no buckling this time. Never again will I allow another misfortune to drag me to the depths of despair I suffered at Sissy's death. Never again! Perhaps my adventure into scientific postulation was ill-advised, but I had to attempt it. I certainly have no regrets. While today's world is unable to fathom my thinking, I feel in my heart that someday, forward-thinking men will read "Eureka" and realize the truthfulness of it. They may disparage me, ridicule me, and call me names, but I stand by the truth of my offerings. As for my rightful place in this world, I remain undefeated. At age forty, soon to be forty-one, I still have quite a large measure of powder left in my keg. I am not going anywhere. At least, not anytime soon.

31
Nevermore

Two weeks passed. On the morning of October 5, 1849, Maria was in the cottage sitting room darning socks when Poe, looking very tired and haggard, entered carrying a suitcase. A cab carriage was waiting at the street.

"Oh, my dear Eddie," she said. "I have never seen you so forlorn."

"My poor heart has been torn asunder. Not many fragments remain to be preserved."

"I know, dear. You must be strong and continue with your life. Where are you off to?"

"I'll be in Richmond for two days. I am going to the *Messenger* to talk to Oliver Highsmith about an assistant editor's position. Remember Oliver? He's the publisher now."

"He helped you and Virginia get a marriage license."

"Yes. If he makes me a favorable offer, do you want to move back to Richmond?"

"If I have no choice. The Lord said we must accept that which he provides."

"I'll talk to Oliver on Friday. If he hires me, I will let you know."

A pause.

"Before I go, I have a favor to ask."

"What's that?"

"Do you remember the treasure Mother gave me on her deathbed?"

"The book of Lord Byron's poems?"

"Yes."

"I want you to take them."

"Why? It was your mother's most precious gift."

He produced the ragged book of Byron's poem his brother Henry had tried to destroy thirty-seven years earlier. Maria took it.

"Is that all?"

"Two more items."

Then he produced the silver daffodil pendant and the green medicine bottle with the lock of Jane Stanard's hair.

Maria took them.

"What would you have me do with these?"

"I feel my days are short. I know not when or where my death shall find me, only that it is certain. When the ungrateful day appears, bury these treasures with me so they shall be forever in my possession."

"I shall do as you wish, Eddie."

"Thank you!"

He turned to go, then suddenly, he stopped, reached into his pocket, and withdrew a piece of paper.

"Read this after I'm gone," he said.

"What is it?"

"Something I wrote for you."

She smiled and took the piece of paper.

Poe hugged her, then turned and started down the walkway to the waiting carriage.

"I love you!" she called.

"I love you too!"

Once the carriage had disappeared down the street, she unfolded the piece of paper.

To My Mother

Because I feel that, in the Heavens above.
The angels, whispering to one another,
Can find, among their burning terms of love,
None so devotional as that of "Mother,"
Therefore by that dear name I long have called you—
You who are more than mother unto me,
And fill my heart of hearts, where Death installed you.
In setting my Virginia's spirit free.
My mother—my own mother, who died early,

Was but the mother of myself; but you
Are mother to the one I loved so dearly,
And thus are dearer than the mother I knew
By that infinity with which my wife
Was dearer to me than was my life.

***

An hour later, Poe was at the B&O Railroad station in lower Manhattan waiting in line to buy a ticket. The clerk was a fiftyish man with gray hair and glasses.

"Destination?"

"Richmond."

"We have departures at 1, 4 and 7 today. I must tell you there is an overnight lay-over in Baltimore. You will arrive in Baltimore at 6:34 tonight and leave again tomorrow at 1."

"I shall take what I can get."

***

The trip to Baltimore was uncomfortable. A crowd of unruly soldiers were on board and the middle-aged woman and her daughter in Poe's compartment chattered endlessly about their dogs. For dinner, he had corned beef and cabbage. As always, train food disagreed with him and he had to buy tablets from the conductor to relieve it. That night, he arrived in Baltimore and took a room in a small hotel near the station.

October 6, 1849. My poor heart clings to the memory of my beloved Sissy with such ferocious tenacity. Since I am in such close proximity to the old home, I shall take a walk down memory lane tomorrow before I continue my journey. I yearn to see the old house, the garden with the weeping willows, and the white swing where Sissy and I planted the daffodils. I long to see the evidence of our lives and our love.

***

The following morning, after breakfast, Poe checked out of the inn and took a cab carriage to the ancestral Poe home on Amity Street. Upon arrival, he exited the carriage and stood in front of the white picket fence. The white swing was still there, the daffodils were in bloom, and the weathervane with the old witch was still spinning about in the wind. For a long moment, he lingered, his mind filled with glorious thoughts of his days with Sissy. He remembered their breakfasts in the garden. At the middle, upper-story window, where his writing parlor was located, the curtains had been changed. Finally, his heart was satisfied with precious memories.

Then, suitcase in hand, he started walking north of Amity Street. He knew he still had more than three hours to kill before he was due to board the train for Richmond. Finally, he decided to go to Ryan's Tavern at Amity and Hartwell Streets. It had been fourteen years since the last time he was there. He wondered if his old friend Sophia was still there.

When he entered the tavern, few patrons were about, mostly a lunch crowd more interested in food than drink. Immediately, he saw Sophia waiting tables. He waited until her eyes fell on him, then she came rushing over. She was in her late thirties now, the lines around her eyes and lips had started to deepen, her eyes looked a little sadder, but she remained an attractive woman.

"Eddie!" she said. "Aren't you a sight for sore eyes! What are you doing in town?"

"My dear, I came to see you!"

"Oh, you naughty devil! Sit down and tell me all about your life."

Poe took a seat at the bar.

"What are you drinking?"

"Mint julip."

Over the next twenty minutes, they chatted about their lives.

"Since the last time I saw you, I have been married and divorced," Sophia said. "A decent bloke, he was a sailor and he had a good heart. Then one day, after an argument, he disappeared. Last time I heard, he had gone to California to dig for gold."

As they chatted, two men came in and seated themselves at a nearby table. One of the men, a tall, early twenties man with red hair, caught sight of Poe. Once he did, he continued to stare. Finally, he got up from the table and went to the bar to face Poe.

"Isn't your name Poe? Edgar Poe?"

"That's me. Who might you be?"

"I am Thaddeus Lummis, George Lummis's younger brother. Do you remember?"

"Oh, yes. You were the younger brother of the unfortunate gentleman I thrashed with my fists some years ago in New York."

"Your thrashing, if you recall, left my brother permanently blind, which led to his death a year later."

"The low-life scoundrel deserved what he received."

"And do you remember that I promised to take revenge?"

"I recall you spewing out some idle threats."

"They were not idle."

"Ha!!! You should watch your tongue or you shall receive the same treatment as your dead brother."

"This I wish to see."

Suddenly, he reached out and slapped Poe across the face.

Instantly, Poe stood up and roughly pushed the younger man in the chest.

The other bar patrons stood back as the two men, fists raised, circled one another. Suddenly, Lummis rushed at Poe and threw a haymaker. As he did, Poe stepped aside and delivered a savage right hook to the younger man's jaw, which sent him to the floor. Lummis touched his face with his hand and saw the hot, red blood. Quickly, he arose from the floor

"You're finished, Poe!"

He reached inside his back pocket and withdrew a black metal baton.

"A truncheon!" Poe said. "I need only these two fists."

Again, the two men circled one another.

Suddenly, Lummis rushed in. Poe, seeing another haymaker coming, sidestepped the blow. As he did, Lummis struck a savage blow on the left side of Poe's head with the truncheon. For a moment, Poe was addled, then, seconds later, upon regaining his senses, he rushed forward, grasped the truncheon, then using all his might, swung the younger man around. As he did, Poe slammed him full in the face with a hard right hand. Young Lummis collapsed on the floor.

Instantly, several bar patrons loomed over him. He was not moving.

"I think he's dead," said one patron.

"Police! Someone go and get the constable!" shouted the man who had entered the bar with Lummis.

"The man in the black coat is the murderer," said another patron, pointing to Poe.

Quickly, Sophia stepped forward.

"Eddie!" she said. "Come with me!"

Moments later, Sophia was hustling Poe down the back alley, then up a flight of stairs to the small room where she lived.

Inside, Poe sat on the bed while Sophia examined him.

"That's a loathsome knot on the side of your head," she said. "It's getting bigger."

Poe put his hand to his head. He could feel the swelling.

"You need to change clothes so the police will not recognize you," she said.

Instantly, she turned and began pulling men's clothes out of the closet and throwing them on the bed.

"Whose clothes are those?"

"My former husband's."

He hesitated. He seemed preoccupied.

"Move!" Sophia said. "Get these on! The police will be here shortly!"

Quickly, Poe donned the clothes she had laid out.

She inspected him.

"They won't recognize you in these clothes," she said.

Then she studied the knot.

"The knot is growing larger."

"I know. I can feel it. Where's the back way?"

"Go down the stairs, turn right, and go up the alley. You'll see Amity Street."

"Thanks!"

"Good luck!"

Moments later, Poe was running down the back alley. When he reached Amity Street, he started walking casually up the sidewalk. After walking half a block, he collapsed in the gutter.

Several passersby slowed to stare at him, then skirted around him. Finally, a young couple stopped to examine him.

"Is that Edgar Poe, the Raven?" the woman said.

"I believe it is," said her husband. "For the love of God, what's he doing lying in the gutter?'

Another passerby, a man, stopped.

"It IS Edgar Poe. He is a friend of Dr. Moran's. His office is up the street. I shall notify him of Mr. Poe's catastrophe."

Ten minutes later, Dr. Moran arrived.

A crowd had gathered. A policeman was there.

"He's drunk!" the policeman said. "I've a good mind to run him in."

"No need for that," Dr. Moran said. "He has been injured. Severely injured. We must make all haste to get him to the hospital."

***

An hour later, at the Washington Medical College Hospital, Poe was delirious, coming in and out of consciousness. The knot on his head was as large as a small lemon. He opened his eyes and looked around.

"Dr. Moran?"

"I'm here."

"What has happened to me?"

"You took a blow to the head, which ruptured a major blood vessel. Your brain cavity is slowly filling with blood."

"Is there anything you can do? The pain in my head is unbearable."

Dr. Moran reached into his black bag and withdrew a partial bottle of peach brandy. There was enough for half a glass. The physician took a small glass from the bedside table and poured the contents.

"This will help."

Poe took the glass and drank its contents in a single swig.

"Can you give me some laudanum? It would make my passage into the next world much more comfortable."

Dr. Moran peered at the swelling on the side of his head, then reached into his bag and withdrew a bottle and a spoon. Then he poured a small amount of white liquid into the spoon.

"Sit up!" he said.

Poe slowly raised himself; the doctor put the spoon to his lips and Poe drank down the liquid.

"Thank you. You know I can't sleep until I've had some laudanum."

Poe was quiet for several moments. He started off into space for a moment, then his eyes began to take on a glassy look. The opium was taking effect. He turned to Dr. Moran as if he were a great orator.

"This fever that men call life is but a dream within a dream. My life of mistresses, poetry, and stimulants were but a brief spot in time, awash with turmoil, pain, and a multitude of tears. The only victor is the conqueror worm."

He was quiet for a moment. He smiled. He was remembering something that made him happy.

"Reynolds! Here, boy! Oh, so fondly I remember those days we tromped across the fields and rivers in Southern Virginia. Playing in the creeks, chasing the rabbits, and hooting back at the whippoorwills."

"Edgar, who is Reynolds?" Dr. Moran said.

Poe did not hear.

He turned, still holding the empty glass, and peered out the hospital window.

"Look! Look!" he said. "My darling Sissy is coming down the road."

"What?"

"Look out the window!"

Moran craned his neck to look out the hospital window. He saw nothing.

"She is coming to take me with her. Oh, my darling, I'll be so happy to see you again."

He stopped for a moment. Then he took one final deep breath.

"I must go now. My darling Sissy is waiting to receive me... May God have mercy on my soul."

For a moment, he stared straight into Dr. Moran's face, then his hand fell, the empty glass crashed on the floor, and Edgar Allan Poe drifted off down that shadowy river that flows forever to the unknown sea.

Dr. Moran stood up, closed Poe's eyes, and pulled a sheet over him.

***

Three days later, Maria was sitting in the parlor of the Poe family home hemming an old dress when there was a knock on the door. Quickly, she set aside her sewing and went to the door. It was her landlady and neighbor Mrs. Valentine.

"Good morning, Mrs. Clemm," the woman said.

"Morning!"

"I have something I think you should see."

The neighbor handed her a recent newspaper clipping from the obituary section of the *Baltimore Sun*. Maria took it and read it.

Edgar Allan Poe, aged 40 and reportedly a New York resident, died October 7 of unknown causes at the Washington Medical College Hospital. As no family members came forward to claim the body, the remains were interred at county expense in the Potters' Field burying ground.

Maria looked up from the letter.

"Mrs. Valentine, may I ask a personal favor?"

"What's that?"

"May I borrow $20 to go to Baltimore?"

Mrs. Valentine studied her for a moment.

"In this case, yes."

"I promise to pay you back."

That afternoon, Maria was on the train to Baltimore.

***

Upon arrival in Baltimore, Maria exited the train and began looking for a cab carriage. It was a windy day and, as she stepped off the train, she had to hold her hat to prevent it being blown off. Nearby, at the station door, a member of the constabulary was watching her.

"Where are you going?" the officer asked.

"To Potter's Field."

"Any particular grave?"

"Yes."

"You should talk to Demetrius," he said. "He takes the bodies to the Potter's Field for the county."

The policeman turned and called to the driver of one of the cab carriages waiting in line at the street.

"Demetrius!"

A black man, who was seated in one of the cab carriages, turned at the sound of his name. The officer waved him over. Moments later, the man and his carriage appeared.

"This lady is going to Potter's Field."

"What's the name?" Demetrius said.

"Poe. Edgar Allan Poe."

"Oh, yes. I remember him. It was only a few days ago. He was a poet. Wrote a poem titled 'The Raven'."

"That's the one."

"Get in! I will take you to his grave."

Moments later, the carriage was rumbling along the dirt and gravel street to the public burying ground.

"I heard him read 'The Raven' one time when I was in New York," Demetrius said. "Those white people would not let me into the lecture room to have a seat, so I had to stand out in the hallway. Hearing him read that poem scared the living daylights out of me."

They rode quietly for a moment.

"Are you a relative?"

"I'm his mother-in-law. Why aren't you on a plantation?"

"I'm a free man. I bought my freedom three years ago."

Long pause.

They rode quietly for another moment, then the driver pulled the carriage around a wide curve and suddenly stopped in front of a white oak tree.

"Well, look at that!" Demetrius said.

"What is it?"

"See that oak tree over there," he said, pointing some fifty yards away.

"I see it."

"That's where he's buried. Look at all those ravens sitting in those limbs over his grave. There must be twenty oak trees in that graveyard and every one of those ravens are sitting on the one over his grave."

A pause.

Then he turned to Maria.

"Go over there! You'll see a fresh grave over there under that oak tree," Demetrius said. "You can't miss it. They put two pine boards for a marker."

Moments later, Maria was out of the carriage and standing in front of the grave. For a moment, she peered at the two pine boards: E.A. Poe: 1809-1849, then suddenly she broke down in uncontrollable sobs. Finally, she stood up and took the medicine bottle and the daffodil pendant out of her pocket. Then she knelt by the grave, burrowed her hand into the fresh soil, and buried the two items.

Then she stood up and, still holding her hat firmly to her head, started back to the carriage. Halfway back to the carriage, she suddenly felt her pocket and remembered the book of poems. Instantly, she turned and started back to the grave.

As she approached the grave, she withdrew the book of poems, but as she did, she stumbled and fell. Then, as she watched, the mighty gusting wind blew the pages out of the book apart and scattered them in a thousand different directions across the moss-covered tombstones, the black wrought-iron fence surrounding the cemetery, and the leafless oak trees.

"Oh Lord, is there no peace in this world," Maria said to herself.

After a minute, she regained herself and returned to the carriage.

"Let's go!" she said.

Demetrius took another look at the ravens, then slapped the reins and the carriage started out of the cemetery. At the gate, he stopped one last time to look back at the oak tree.

"Look at that! All those ravens are still sitting in that oak tree over his grave. It's like they know where their home is."

The black man suddenly trembled as if a sharp chill had passed down his spine.

"Even in death, this Edgar Allan Poe is still scaring people. Too spooky for me."

He slapped the reins.

"Git up there, horse!" he said. "Let's get out of here!"

32
Afterword

After Poe died, Maria was left without income and, over the first two years, she survived largely from the generosity of Poe's friends and admirers, especially Henry W. Longfellow and Charles Dickens. Over the next fourteen years, she lived in a succession of private homes in Milford, Connecticut, Alexandria, Virginia, and Putnam, Ohio. In the spring of 1863, she returned to Baltimore where she had hoped to be admitted to the state's widows' home. After she was unable to obtain the $150 fee, she instead became a resident of the Episcopal Church Home for the indigent in East Baltimore. When she died on February 16, 1871, she was buried in the cemetery behind the church.

***

Frances "Fanny" Osgood, upon returning to Boston in the fall of 1846, reconciled with her husband Samuel, a professional portrait painter. Over the next four years, the couple lived happily together as a family with the two daughters fathered by her husband and a young son, paternity unknown. In the late fall of 1849, Osgood contracted consumption and, during the last two months of her life, was unable to speak. When she died on May 5, 1850, her final word was "angel," which she had written on a slate to her husband. She was buried in the Osgood family's plot at Mount Auburn Cemetery in Cambridge, Massachusetts.

***

In the late spring of 1851, Elizabeth Lummis Ellet interfered in the divorce of another for the last time. Her long-time friend, Catherine P. Cowdall, was seeking a divorce from her husband Horace, a successful New York banker. In the proceeding, the husband was contesting the divorce on the grounds that the requested monthly payments of $100 were excessive, claiming that, by paying such a huge amount, he would not have sufficient monies to support himself. At the hearing, Elizabeth Ellet testified that the wife deserved the $100 a month as repayment for the vile manner in which her husband had treated her over the course of the marriage. The judge agreed and granted both the divorce and the large payments. When the hearing ended, Ellet left the courthouse and was about to enter a carriage on the street when Mr. Cowdall suddenly rushed up and shot her point-blank in the chest. When it became apparent Ellet was only wounded, he stepped forward with a large knife and plunged it straight into her heart. Giant streams of red-hot blood gushed forth from her breast, and moments later, as she lay dying, her expensive blue calico dress was bathed in a great river of red liquid. Cowdall then withdrew a second pistol and took his own life.

***

In 1875, twenty-six years after his death, Poe's friends and admirers in Baltimore launched a charity drive to raise enough money to provide him a more respectable resting place. After all, they said, Baltimore's most famous poet should not be left to spend eternity in the city's public cemetery. In total, the group raised $3,485, enough to pay for a plot at Baltimore's respectable Westminster Hall and Burying Ground, a marble monument with a bronze medallion of his likeness and a reburial crew, which would be responsible for removing Poe's remains from the Potter's Field to the new location. With much fanfare, the task was completed on October 1, 1875. When the head of the reburial crew was asked how he knew the remains were Poe's, he replied, "The moment I opened the coffin I knew we had the correct one. Instantly, I recognized his most distinguishing characteristic, a broad, slightly-mounded forehead." So, without further ado, Poe was reburied once more in the new, more respectable plot and the marble monument was placed, dedicated, and appropriately memorialized.

***

In the fall of 1877, the same group of civic-minded citizens who had financed Poe's reburial decided it would now be appropriate to move Maria's remains to the same plot. Many local Baltimore residents remembered Maria's often-repeated wish to lie in death beside her beloved Eddie. As a result, again with much fanfare, Maria's remains were disinterred from the rear of the old Episcopal Church, then reburied across town at the Westminster site alongside Poe.

***

In March of 1875, the Valentine family cemetery at Fordham was about to be destroyed to make way for a new railroad. Since there were no kin to claim Virginia's remains, William Gill, an early Poe biographer, gathered her bones and stored them in a box he hid under his bed. Several years later, when the Baltimore group learned Gill had the remains, they voted to reunite Virginia with her husband and her mother. As a result, Virginia's remains were reburied alongside her husband's on January 19, 1885, the 76th anniversary of his birthday and nearly ten years after the monument was erected. With that single act, the trio who had struggled so mightily in life were reunited in death for all eternity.

***

When the reburial crew went to the Potter's Field in Baltimore to remove Poe's remains, they had been instructed to search carefully through the grave's fill soil for two objects: a silver pendant shaped like a daffodil and a lock of hair in a green medicine bottle. The workmen, diligent to a fault, spent more than four hours sifting through the fresh earth, digging through small stones, the remains of old tree branches, rotting leaves, and molded plants of various kinds in search of the two objects. Despite their most meticulous efforts, the pendant and the lock of hair were never found.

The End

Author's Note

This novel is a dramatization of the life of Edgar Allan Poe. As such, I have taken some liberties with not only dialog and situations and the addition of some made-up characters, but also with certain events and/or the dates they occurred.

Most noteworthy are:

(1) When Poe's aunt, Maria Poe Clemm, first enters his life.

(2) The date Virginia Clemm Poe died.

(3) The date and circumstances under which Rufus Wilmot Griswold died.

(4) Some dates when Poe's works were actually published.

Other than those four mentions, all other major dates in the story line are closely aligned with the dates of the real-time events in Poe's life. Additionally, Poe's actual cause of death has always been a mystery and the events I have outlined are purely conjecture on my part.

Other books by John Isaac Jones

A Sagebrush Soul: A Biographical Novel of Mark Twain

The Bird of Time: A Story of Friendship

The Hand of God

Alabama Stories

The Duck Springs Affair

Thanks, PG!: Memoirs of a Tabloid Reporter

Thirteen Stories

The Angel Years

For Love of Daniel

Tembo Makaburi

Going Home

The Last Cowboy

The Agreement

Other books may be viewed at:
https://www.amazon.com/stores/John-Isaac-Jones/author/B008PR3DQ8?

Editing and Formatting by BZHercules.com

Cover design by MiblArt

Made in the USA
Las Vegas, NV
25 November 2023